# FANTASY

# FANTASY

## A SHORT HISTORY

*Adam Roberts*

BLOOMSBURY ACADEMIC
LONDON • NEW YORK • OXFORD • NEW DELHI • SYDNEY

BLOOMSBURY ACADEMIC
Bloomsbury Publishing Plc
50 Bedford Square, London, WC1B 3DP, UK
1385 Broadway, New York, NY 10018, USA
29 Earlsfort Terrace, Dublin 2, Ireland

BLOOMSBURY, BLOOMSBURY ACADEMIC and the Diana logo are
trademarks of Bloomsbury Publishing Plc

First published in Great Britain 2025

Cover design: Matt Thame
Cover image © grandfailure/Adobe Stock

A catalogue record for this book is available from the British Library.

A catalog record for this book is available from the Library of Congress.

ISBN:  HB:    978-1-3504-0783-1
       PB:    978-1-3504-0782-4
       ePDF:  978-1-3504-0784-8
       eBook: 978-1-3504-0785-5

Typeset by Integra Software Services Pvt. Ltd.
Printed and bound in Great Britain

To find out more about our authors and books visit www.bloomsbury.com
and sign up for our newsletters.

# CONTENTS

# Contents

# PREFACE

A history of fantasy could be a history of almost everything, for fantasy, in the sense of stories with magical, supernatural, marvellous and monstrous content, in-story elements that are not features of the actual world in which we live, is the default mode of human storytelling. Mimetic, or more narrowly realist, fiction is a recent and, in this larger context, still relatively small-scale cultural development. For most of human history stories have included gods and magic, heroes and monsters, talking animals and enchanted locations, fantastical extrapolations of imaginative expansion beyond the confines of the merely real. But to begin with the *Epic of Gilgamesh* and Homer and proceed through *Beowulf* and medieval romances, through *A Midsummer Night's Dream* and *Paradise Lost*, Arabian Nights and Tolkien to Harry Potter and *Spirited Away* – and everything in between – would produce an unmanageably gigantic book. The focus of the present study is more modest. It aims to trace the pre-history, the florescence and the ongoing development of genre fantasy: the Tolkienian and Lewisian type of story, of Sword and Sorcery, of neo-Gothic and Grimdark: of fantasy as it is recognized by fans today, as shelved under this rubric in bookshops.

The account offered here is of a twentieth-century form, with its roots in the nineteenth-, that has developed, expanded and diversified into the twenty-first. This mode does not exist sealed away and separate from the larger context mentioned above. On the contrary, it draws extensively upon it, apprehends and develops it: classical epic, medieval romance, Arthurian legends, *Beowulf* and Norse myth, Bunyan, Walter Scott all have a place in the developing mode of fantasy. Two things that draw on these discourses, and which both have a key role in fantasy's history, are Tolkien's two novels – *The Hobbit* (1937), *Lord of the Rings* (1954–5) – and Ballantine's Adult Fantasy List (1965–74). As Jamie Williamson argues, what we think of today as fantasy is really the creation of the Ballantine list.[1] Ballantine published their fantasy series to tap into the success of *Lord of the Rings* by reprinting it and other books in a similar manner and style, some recently published or original titles, rather more reprints of work published as far back as the 1890s and early 1900s: books by William Morris, Lord Dunsany, Eddison, Hope Mirrlees and others. This reflects the fact that there was a burst of fantasy writing in the 1920s, reacting to, and in many cases written by individuals who had fought in, the First World War. Fantasy, which is often militarist, both in the sense that it often posits specific military engagements and in the sense that it construes the world of its stories as a war between 'good' and 'evil', is in one sense a response to this particular, terrible, traumatizing war: a reaction by which the grim mechanized impersonality of

---

[1]Williamson, *The Evolution of Modern Fantasy: From Antiquarianism to the Ballantine Adult Fantasy Series.*

the slaughter, the cynicism of the realpolitik underlying it, the horrific modernity of it, is reversed, and an idealized chivalric nobility of medieval battle restored (although, very often, modern dehumanizing total war seeps through into edges of the vision: in *Lord of the Rings* Pelennor Fields and Helm's Deep are sites of medieval battle and siege respectively, but Mordor resembles the blasted horror of the Western Front). An intriguing question, to which I am not sure I have an answer, is why there was a half-century lag in the impact of these works. I can see why fantasy novels would be written in reaction to the horrors of industrialization and mechanized warfare; I am not sure I can see why it took so many decades for those novels, and the form they iterated, to break through into a wider and eventually global mainstream.

That breakthrough, and the latter-day global reach and popularity of fantasy, follows the (for a novel published 1954–5, belated) bestseller status of Tolkien's *Lord of the Rings* in the 1960s, and the Ballantine list's subsequent expansion of the canon. The initial slate of titles, with original publication dates and Ballantyne release dates added, was:

1. *The Hobbit*, J. R. R. Tolkien ([1937] August 1965)

2. *The Fellowship of the Ring*, J. R. R. Tolkien ([1954] October 1965)

3. *The Two Towers*, J. R. R. Tolkien ([1954] October 1965)

4. *The Return of the King*, J. R. R. Tolkien ([1955] December 1965)

5. *The Tolkien Reader* (September 1966)

6. *The Worm Ouroboros*, E. R. Eddison ([1922] April 1967)

7. *Mistress of Mistresses*, E. R. Eddison ([1935] August 1967)

8. *A Fish Dinner in Memison*, E. R. Eddison ([1941] February 1968)

9. *The Road Goes Ever On*, J. R. R. Tolkien and Donald Swann ([1967) October 1968)

10. *Titus Groan*, Mervyn Peake ([1946] October 1968)

11. *Gormenghast*, Mervyn Peake ([1950] October 1968)

12. *Titus Alone*, Mervyn Peake ([1959] October 1968)

13. *A Voyage to Arcturus*, David Lindsay ([1920) November 1968)

14. *The Last Unicorn*, Peter S. Beagle ([1968] February 1969)

15. *A Fine and Private Place*, Peter S. Beagle ([1960] February 1969)

16. *Smith of Wootton Major* and *Farmer Giles of Ham*, J. R. R. Tolkien ([1960, 1949] March 1969)

17. *Tolkien: A Look behind 'The Lord of the Rings'*, Lin Carter (March 1969)

18. *The Mezentian Gate*, E. R. Eddison ([1958] April 1969)

This is the first iteration of the list. Under the editorship of Lin Carter it went on to add another sixty-five titles. That the first four items, there, are Tolkien and that he fills another four slots (almost half of the whole) is testimony to his importance to the lineaments of fantasy as its canon is constructed. The present history considers all these books, and most of the rest of the Ballantine list, amongst many others.

Williamson argues that Carter did for the fantasy canon what Robert Maynard Hutchins and Mortimer Adler had done with their 'Great Books of the Western World' series (published by *Encyclopædia Britannica* in fifty-four volumes, 1952), effectively codifying a list of canonical 'great' works that ended up homogenizing what we think of as fantasy: 'a sort of timeless Platonic Form, involving magic and invented preindustrial worlds' is how Williamson puts it.[2] One consequence of this, Williamson suggests, is a tendency today to misread earlier works, a misreading that proceeds from 'viewing pre-genre fantasy through a postgenre lens'. These earlier examples, Williamson argues, actually drew on the traditions of *Romantic antiquarianism*. The antiquarian movement of the eighteenth and early nineteenth centuries included actual scholars and antiquarians but also pseudo-antiquarians like James Macpherson (the forger of 'Ossian'): Thomas Percy's *Reliques of Ancient English Poetry* (1765), Francis Grose's *The Antiquities of England and Wales* (six vols 1773–87), Walter Scott's *Minstrelsy of the Scottish Border* (1801–3) and his many novels. In effect these authors invented a new way of writing stories: an elegiac, archaic style, the discovery of the past in the present, ballads and other things embedded in the main body of the work as expressive revenants of a notionally older culture, lots of footnotes and appended essays on context. Williamson argues that these were adopted as methods to enhance verisimilitude by what he calls 'literary fantasists' such as Morris and Tolkien, although he also argues that more recent fantasy has turned its back on this older tradition, 'in retreat from the revolutionary intentions of many of the Romantics'. This, though, is an overstatement: major examples of twenty-first-century fantasy employ it, perhaps most notably Susanna Clarke's great fantasy novel *Jonathan Strange & Mr Norrell* (2004).

This brief history construes three phases. First, it considers the roots of what would become, via Tolkien, Lewis and Lin Carter's editorial choices, genre fantasy as we understand it today. Those roots are [1] the allegorical fantasyland of Bunyan's *Pilgrim's Progress*, hugely popular in the nineteenth century and consistently generative and influential, not least on [2] Victorian children's literature; and [3] nineteenth-century medievalism – the novels of Walter Scott, nineteenth-century Arthuriana, Wagnerian opera. That's the first phase, which leads, through the late prose romances of William Morris, and a number of 1920s and 1930s works (Dunsany, Hope Mirrlees, Eddison and others) through into the Middle Earth and Narnia books, and so, as the success and influence of those works played out, into the great delta of fantasy writing that has become so prominent a feature of cultural production over the last half-century. This is the genealogy of the mode in a nutshell.[3]

---

[2]Williamson takes a more extremist genre-definitional line than I do, namely, that 'in 1960 there was no commercial fantasy genre' at all: 'when the term was used to designate a literary type, it did not usually connote the kind of material that came to typify the genre when it coalesced' [12].

[3]Nuts are hard, sometimes indigestible, and this book's nutshell is liable to be shattered – cloven in two, as the axe-wielding fairy-feller is about to chop his nutshell in Richard Dadd's great Fantasy painting 'The Fairy Feller's Master Stroke' (1855–64) – by counter-arguments and alternate genealogies. That is to be expected and indeed welcomed. The brevity of the present volume imposes the rather oversimplified summary of this paragraph upon me, for reasons of clarity. 'Turn'd and troop'd the goblin men … One began to weave a crown/ Of rough nuts brown/(Men sell not such in any town)' [Christina Rosseti, *Goblin Market* (1862)].

The present study comprises three sections. The first is an attempt to define fantasy via an account of the influences that fed through into it, and leans more theoretical and analytic than chronological. The second is a more linear narrative account of fantasy, via its most important titles, through the twentieth century. The final section is an account of twenty-first-century fantasy. Proximity to and, in the later stages immersion in, this later material makes critical objectivity and distance harder to maintain, but the vitality and global spread of the mode are remarkable and essential to any account such as this one. Fantasy has spread from novels to a position of dominance in cinema and TV; it is a major element in video games; it has accrued populous fandoms that consume, reflect upon and engage with key fantasy texts: fan conventions, cosplay, adaptation and fan-writing. This renders a habitus of fantasy, an as-it-were 'classic' version of the mode: a narrative of adventure (quest, travel, a war of good versus evil, an apparently humble character rising to a position of prominence) set in a pre-industrial quasi-European world that operates by means of magic (wizards and witches) rather than science; a distribution of in-effect racialized populations of men, elves, dwarfs, goblins and monsters: dragons, wraiths, ghosts, trolls. To write about a pre-modern world from a modern perspective is, inevitably, to do history, and though the chronicles of fantasy texts are fictional, imaginary, and although they include things that cannot be part of actual history (magic, monsters, prophecy), fantasy construes history in significant ways.

The imaginative excessions of these retellings are also expressive: a Eurocentric, racially configured version of history as a war of good against evil is not, after all, an ideologically neutral undertaking; and folding the imperialism, militarism, racism and violence of that history away into a 'magical' container of chivalric nobility and magical glamour is a political action. Two developments in twentieth-century fantasy address this. One is 'Grimdark', fantasy novels that make manifest, and indeed explicit, the violence of that operation, repudiation of the elevating idealization of classic fantasy. The other is that, as fantasy has become globally popular, writers from different provenances have replaced the European template for fantasy worldbuilding with historical cultures and histories from around the world: novels set in African-derived, South American, Asian and East-Asian coded worlds have diversified the nature of fantasy as such. It is true that many of these new books are also extremely violent. Each volume of American author N K Jemisin's *Broken Earth* trilogy (2015–17) won a Hugo Award, an unprecedented achievement that marks a climacteric in fantasy's whiteness. As Jemisin herself says, jauntily but with point: 'y'know, maybe erasing all the brown people from your fantasy continent, or making them allegorical orcs, is a bad idea'. Matthew Sangster notes the ongoing transformation in 'how fantasies have been written and valued':

Jemisin's sequence of Hugo Award wins for the *Broken Earth* trilogy has been taken as a key sign of change, but her works are part of a larger groundswell seeking to broaden Fantasy out from its white medievalist defaults. Writers such as G L Clark, Aliette de Bodard, Naseem Jamina, Fonda Lee, Rebecca Roanhorse, Tasha Suri and Kai Ashante Wilson (along with many others) have brought culture and forms of experience into Fantasy that have made it vastly richer.[4]

Fantasy generally returns to a pre-Industrial world to tell its stories. Some of the facilities provided by later industrial and technological development may be provided by 'magic' in these worlds, but the trajectory from modern to pre-modern is crucial, and very often is included specifically in the text. That is to say, many fantasy novels tell of modern characters who move into the pre-modern world of magic and peril and adventure, for example, individuals from 'our' world who pass through a portal into a medievalized Fantasyland, as do the Pevensie children in Lewis's *Narnia* books, or else people like Tolkien's bourgeois eighteenth-century (or thereabouts) hobbits, who leave the rural comforts of the Shire (well-made houses, tea and crumpets, tobacco pipes, waistcoats) to venture across a marvellous, perilous pre-modern world, the quasi-medieval Gondor, the Anglo-Saxon Rohan. The transition is key.

As it is, in a larger sense, a historical motility, so, and for related reasons, fantasy is often a movement from adulthood to childhood. Some children's literature is mimetic (though it is arguable whether any is realist in the sense of *le naturalisme*) but most children's literature is a confluence of fantastical writing, stories of magic and marvel, of monsters and imaginary lands – books for and about children by Lewis Carroll, Frank L Baum, Tove Jansson. These are books in which the border between adulthood and childhood is mixed. Tolkien's hobbits are child-sized, Lewis's characters grow to adulthood and ungrow back again. The land of faerie, though ancient, is youth. Relatedly, talking animals figure very largely across a range of fantasy works: the actants of nursery stories and Aesopian fables magnified and centred as a means of connecting the deracinated modern to the enchanted and mythic bestial authenticity. Nonsense and its epigone Surrealism have their place in the narrative, although my inclusion of the latter in a history of fantasy may strike some as counterintuitive. Nonetheless, surrealism, or perhaps it would be better to say a surrealist cultural logic is an important element in even the most generic of genre fantasy works: the juxtaposition of diaparities, modernity and antiquity superposed, a faun walking through a forest carrying an umbrella, a wizard smoking pipe tobacco.

There is a crucial mytheme here, and it is crucial to what fantasy does: a return, a fort-da back-again-ness. Fantasy retrogresses Max Weber's disenchanted modernity, returning us imaginatively to pre-modern, still-enchanted versions of the world (I say more about this below). This coextends, on a social level, the individual: undoing Wordsworth's grown-up lament that there hath past away a glory from the earth, and returning us to the child for whom 'meadow, grove, and stream, the earth, and every common sight' are 'apparelled in celestial light, the glory and the freshness of a dream'. There is a transcendent dimension to this; courses of transport, enchantment,

---

[4]Sangster, *Introduction to Fantasy*, 425–6.

through which flow what Carl Schmidt calls 'liquidated theological concepts'.[5] Key fantasy authors – Tolkien, Lewis, Wolfe, Rowling, Clarke – write out of religious faith, working allegories of enchantment that dramatize Christian incarnation, sacrifice and resurrection. Other writers, not themselves motivated by specific faith, work patterns derived from these types, and for related reasons. The fantasy novel is, in its core form, an escape into an older, more primary world, a more magical world, a better place. Escapism is sometimes denigrated, as deplorable or evasive, but the heart of fantasy validates it. 'I have claimed', Tolkien wrote,

> that Escape is one of the main functions of fairy-stories, and since I do not disapprove of them, it is plain that I do not accept the tone of scorn or pity with which 'Escape' is now so often used: a tone for which the uses of the word outside literary criticism give no warrant at all. Why should a man be scorned if, finding himself in prison, he tries to get out and go home?[6]

Childhood, history, religion and myth: the reversion is a cleansing vision. The opening to William Morris's epic assemblage of verse romances and fantasies, *The Earthly Paradise* (1868–70), invites us to

> Forget six counties overhung with smoke,
> Forget the snorting steam and piston stroke,
> Forget the spreading of the hideous town;
> Think rather of the pack-horse on the down,
> And dream of London, small, and white, and clean,
> The clear Thames bordered by its gardens green.

This location of the poem is not actual London, but a fantastical variant of it:

> A nameless city in a distant sea,
> White as the changing walls of faërie,
> Thronged with much people clad in ancient guise.

This city is also an important figure in fantasy: Bunyan's Zion, Oz, Gormenghast, Viriconium. The pre-industrial city in beautiful countryside with an enchantment upon it.

> They reached the great Bay of Fairyland (as we call it) beyond the Magic Isles; and saw far off in the last West the Mountains of Elvenhome and the light of Faery upon the waves. Roverandom thought he caught a glimpse of the city of the Elves on the green hill beneath the Mountains, a glint of white far away. [Tolkien, *Roverandom* (1925), 73–4]

---

[5]Schmitt, *Political Theology*, 36.
[6]J R R Tolkien, 'On Fairy Stories', *Tree and Leaf*, 55.

'Elfland is what Lord Dunsany called the place', says Ursula Le Guin. 'It is also known as Middle Earth, and Prydain, and the Forest of Broceliande, and Once Upon a Time; and by many other names'. Le Guin's conceit is that these are all versions of the same place, what this study thumbnails 'Fantasyland': 'a vast and beautiful place where a person goes alone on foot to get in touch with reality in a special, private, profound place'. Le Guin said this in 1973, responding to the then recent explosion in fantasy writing, and she said it to deplore the commercialization and instrumentalization she saw in many of the works of the new boom. Fantasland for Le Guin is 'like a great national park'.

> A great many people want to go there, without knowing what it is they're really looking for, driven by a vague hunger for something real. With the intention of under the pretence of obliging them, certain writers of fantasy are building six-lane highways and trailer parks with drive-in movies, so that the tourist can feel at home, just as if they were back in Poughkeepsie.[7]

The particular magic of Fantasyland depends upon it *not* being home, although the through-line of much fantasy is precisely the return home, the re-encounter home which is, in Eliot's phrase, 'to arrive where we started/And know the place for the first time'. Estrangement is the medium, and estrangement is as Le Guin notes harmed by the over-familiarity of over-production, when fantasy becomes a set of easily recognized conventions, characters, figures and storylines, as much of it is today. Enchantment wilts under the commodified productivity by which the forms are mass-produced. And though the work, as Tolkien styles it, is one of 'recovery, escape and consolation', the entry to Fantasyland cannot be too facile. Re-enchantment is always also an index of what has been lost. Keats, moved by the song of the nightingale, opens a window onto Le Guin's Elfland as enchantment that is, crucially, also loss.

> The same that oft-times hath
> Charm'd magic casements, opening on the foam
> Of perilous seas, in faery lands forlorn.

'Forlorn! the very word is like a bell', the poem continues, 'to toll me back from thee to my sole self!'

I note that this history is, designedly, short, which is another way of indicating what this history is not. It is not absolutely comprehensive, even within the narrowed parameters I have set myself. It would not be possible to mention every single work of fantasy published over the last 150 years, and selecting for 'importance' (notable commercial success, markworthy influence) will certainly mean omitting specific works that some readers may hold dear, or consider worthy of inclusion. It is not, therefore,

---

[7]Le Guin, 'From Elfland to Poughkeepsie', *The Language of the Night: Essays on Fantasy and Science Fiction*, 70.

a mere itinerary of titles considered under the rubric of fantasy: I undertake critical engagement, including value judgment, and aim to develop a thesis with which the reader is at liberty (of course) to disagree: the three main channels of nineteenth-century proto-fantasy that fed through into a new kind of post-Morris writing in the 1920s and a flourish of important fantasy children's writing in the 1930s–40s, from which – drawing on medievalism, Gothic, Victorian children's literature, surrealism, the beast fable and what Cambridge University calls ASNAC (i.e. Anglo-Saxon Norse and Celtic) sources – became what we now think of as fantasy in the 1950s and 1960s, growing in popularity, engaging in reaction, globalizing and renewing itself through the subsequent decades. The works discussed herein are not necessarily my personal favourites; indeed, I have omitted many personal favourite titles, because they did not seem to me to meet the necessary criteria of inclusion: widespread popularity and manifest influence, contemporary or belated.

Related to this is the question of critical objectivity. Jenny Davidson opens her 2017 monograph on Jane Austen with a personal note.

> I first read a battered yard-sale copy of *Pride and Prejudice* at the age of eight or nine. I am slightly ashamed to say that over the thirty-five years since then, I have probably read the novel as many as fifty times … I love most of the authors I write about regularly, but I don't turn to any of them especially for comfort or consolation. I love Austen in a different way than I love Swift or Burke, which invites the question of whether or not love and associated states like identification and immersion are at odds with the goals and values of criticism, which include objectivity and analytic traction.[8]

This question is apropos. Across the years of working on the present volume I have read many new-to-me works of fantasy, some of which I have found to be good, much bad. I have also re-read a good deal of fantasy I already knew, and re-engaged with texts I read from an early age, and have continued read throughout my adult life, works I love in a different, more deep-rooted and personal way than those other books: Carroll, Le Guin and, especially, Tolkien. 'The topic of how we respond to books we love', Davidson notes, 'as well as how that affects the critical discourse about them, has become a legitimate object of study in its own right'. Fans engage with the texts they love. There is a jungle of fannish reaction to fantasy, and writing about fantasy, online. Indeed, for much of the stuff covered in this *History*, that's all there is, in the sense that few literary critics have addressed or analysed many of these works. But fannish writing is not the same as literary criticism: it makes no pretension to disinterestedness; often it is gush, articulations of passionate approbation, or disapprobation, indices of excitement. It tends to focus on things like characters, treated as if they were real people, to love or hate. It is interested in in-text consistency, of worldbuilding or characterization. I have

---

[8]Davidson, *Reading Jane Austen*, ix–x.

here written a literary-critical account of fantasy as a mode, and seek to avoid those approaches. But I am also a fan. And I find what Davidson says about navigating her own fannish and critical sides, with respect to her beloved author, illuminating:

> I strongly believe that rather than canceling each other out, a productive tension exists between the different modes involved in loving books and in reading them to understand how they work, what they mean and why they matter, not least because both orientations depend heavily on the practice of repeated rereading, even or perhaps especially in the case of books we already know very well.

This repetition is one of the topics to which this *History* returns. For most of my life I have reread the *Lord of the Rings* every year. The experience of a text repeatedly reread is different to one read only once (interestingly, fannish discourse is much exercised by the question of 'spoilers' in reviews, or disseminated online, although of course a spoiler can only spoil a first reading). The repetition of reception is a vital part of fannish textual engagement: reading your favourite book over and over again. It is also, manifestly, part of the textual production of fantasy: it is not enough to write one book of *The Wheel of Time*, or make one *Star Wars* movie; these individual texts must be extended, written again, basically the same story reproduced, reinstated, again and again. Fantasy is particularly prone to this: the first *Dragonlance* novel is repeated literally hundreds of times, rewritten and reissued under different titles with various minimal variations of character and detail, but basically the same tale, the same world. A single book is not enough; there must be a trilogy, or a trilogy of trilogies. Fandom not only rereads and rereads its beloved texts, it *rewrites* them, repeats them, remakes them, over and over: as discussed below, J. K. Rowling, having made seven Harry Potter novels, has been hugely overtaken by fannish textual production: nearly half a million distinct *Harry Potter* texts have been uploaded to AO3; the internet is awash in Potter memes and reworkings and engagements. Over and over they go. It relates particularly to fantasy, I think, because these faux-historical pasts, these enchanted histories of medieval or dark age or ancient worlds, are in themselves a form of reversion. We do not love to turn to these texts, these worlds, so much as we love to *re*turn to them. In this the various elements of the argument of the present volume come together: our yearning towards re-enchantment, rehearsing history, recuperating childhood, the subconscious promptings of surrealism, the sense of nonsense. There is, as Adam Phillips says, no future in repetition, and fantasy is the literature that reverts from futurity to an idealized, enchanted, juvenility of pastness. At the same time, and by exactly this logic, fantasy is not about the past, but about the present from which it flees.

# PART 1
## THE ROOTS OF MODERN FANTASY

# CHAPTER 1
# ORIGINS

To the proposition that fantasy as a genre is broadly 'of the past' and Science Fiction 'of the future' we might add this equally dubious claim: Science Fiction is a relatively recent cultural growth, going back no further than the late nineteenth century, whereas fantasy has deep roots. The former claim in the previous sentence touches on the popular belief that SF 'begins' somewhere between Shelley's *Frankenstein* (1818) and the later century scientific romances of Jules Verne and H. G. Wells, in contradistinction with a sense that 'Fantasy' goes back a long further – to the medieval Romances, allegories, to *Beowulf* and the Norse Sagas (studied as they were and taken as influences as they manifestly have been by Tolkien, Lewis and their imitators), and perhaps even further back to Apuleius, the *Odyssey* and the *Epic of Gilgamesh*.[1]

These claims seem reasonable enough. After all, these texts, *The Odyssey* as much as *Lord of the Rings*, *Gilgamesh* as much as *Conan*, are stories of strong magic, of heroes and monsters, of magical kingdoms and marvellous adventures. They are, that is to say, fables of enchantment. And it is a major premise of this study that the success of contemporary fantasy lies in its attempt, as fiction and fable, to instaurate 'enchantment' in a disenchanted modernity.[2] It seems common-sense to position 'Fantasy' as a way of addressing the discontents associated with disenchantment. Viewers of Disney's *Sleeping Beauty* (1959), players of *Skyrim* (2011), readers of *The Sword in the Stone* (1938) or *A Wizard of Earthsea* (1968) love these texts because they remedy, even if only in fictional, imaginative ways, the sense of industrialized deracination that defines an uglier, unmagical, bureaucratized present-day existence. SF (the argument suggests) goes the other way, pushing-through the complicated nexus of love-hate we feel for our socially definitional technology into an imagined future in which the Sublime, under

---

[1]'How', asks Lucie Armitt, 'can texts as diverse as the biblical Book of Genesis, Tennyson's "Lady of Shalott", Orwell's *Animal Farm*, J M Barrie's *Peter Pan* and Bunyan's allegory *The Pilgrim's Progress* all shelter under the same literary umbrella, fantasy?' [Armitt, *Fantasy Fiction*, 8]. She provides a twofold answer: one, they all 'deal in the unknowableness of life' and two, they all 'threaten infinity', conveying 'a world not necessarily known through the senses or lived experience'. The present study takes a different line to Armitt's.

[2]Max Weber, *The Protestant Ethic and the Spirit of Capitalism*; Charles Taylor, *A Secular Age*. See also Michael Warner, Jonathan VanAntwerpen and Craig Calhoun (eds), *Varieties of Secularism in a Secular Age*. One analysis particularly relevant to the present study is Andrea Erizi's, who re-reads Weber's 'disenchantment' in order to crystallize what 'secularization' means and set it alongside a related but occluded concept, 'subrogation': 'compared to secularization, subrogation conveys the substitution of a religious figure with a secular one which, albeit independent as to its origin, is able to reproduce, at least to some extent, the functions of the former' [Andrea Erizi, 'Different Origin, (Almost the) Same Function: The Concept of Subrogation in Max Weber's Work', 233].

the rubric of a 'Sense of Wonder', blasts to futuristic marvels of immensity, far-reaching travel in space and time, all the thrills of boldly going.

But this is wrong. In fact I would argue that things are the other way around. Fantasy is not 'of the past' but in important and specific ways of the present, shaped in reaction to and therefore by mechanized, industrialized, bourgeois modernity – it is, specifically, a literature 'of' the First World War and its aftermath. SF is not 'of the future' but, counter-intuitively, of the past ('a long time ago', as the cinematic opening screenshot to *Star Wars* so famously declared, 'in a galaxy far, far away'). We can argue that it is SF that 'goes back a long way', foundationally tangled, in complex ways, in the Protestant Reformation.[3] Fantasy is the more recent phenomenon. Recency defines High fantasy – either gleam-lit like Tolkien himself, or grimdark like George R. R. Martin – as well as the sword-and-sorcery tradition with its emphasis on warrior strength and barbarian vitality (Howard's Conan, Burroughs's Tarzan), as well as a comic fantasy tradition that reaches a particular summit of popularity in the Discworld novels of Terry Pratchett. Recency also births the Lovecraftian Weird and its many imitators, as it does Gothic forms of fantasy, like Peake's *Gormenghast* trilogy (1946–59) or Rowling's fantastical *Harry Potter* sequence (1997–2007), although Rowling imports elements of the Tolkienian tradition (wizards, dragons, dwarfs) into the rather different tradition of the English Public School story from Hughes's *Tom Brown's Schooldays* (1857) and Farrar's *Eric* (1858).

This is to generate a critical narrative in dialogue with other critical accounts of fantasy. Richard Matthews' *Fantasy: The Liberation of Imagination* opens with a catch-up chapter 'From Antiquity to Infinity: the Development of Modern Fantasy' before getting to the meat of its argument: his second chapter reads Morris's *Well at the World's End* on the understanding that 'Tolkien documented that Morris was, for him, a pleasure and an inspiration' [86] in order for him to move on to the main attraction: 'Shaping Modern Fantasy: Cosmic Light and Dark, J R R Tolkien's *The Lord of the Rings*'. Edward James and Farah Mendlesohn's more capacious *The Cambridge Companion to Fantasy Literature* has room for rather more works, chronologically speaking but also in terms of work by women and writers of colour. Nevertheless, this study still concedes that Middle Earth and Narnia, between them, are foundational for the broader popularity of the mode was concerned: the relevant chapter, by James, is called 'Tolkien, Lewis and the Explosion of Genre Fantasy'. Ria Cheyne notes that James 'traces the current popularity of fantasy fiction to the cult status Tolkien's works achieved in the 1960s', adding the position of Brian Attebery's *Strategies of Fantasy*, which 'positions *The Lord of the Rings* as the prototypical text around which the genre clusters. Such texts do not constitute the entirety of contemporary fantasy fiction, but they are the predominant popular form'.[4]

Fantasy is about re-enchantment, and its expansive, continuing popularity speaks to an appetite for re-enchantment, although in some cases in quite complicated ways. Here I draw on Alan Jacobs's argument about fantasy as a mode, itself an engagement

---

[3]This is the argument of my *History of Science Fiction*.

[4]Cheyne, 'Fantasy: Affirmation and Enchantment', in *Disability, Literature, Genre: Representation and Affect in Contemporary Fiction*, 109.

with Charles Taylor's *A Secular Age*.[5] Taylor makes the distinction between porous and buffered sensibilities:

> Almost everyone can agree that one of the big differences between us and our ancestors of five hundred years ago is that they lived in an 'enchanted' world, and we do not; at the very least, we live in a much less 'enchanted' world. We might think of this as our having 'lost' a number of beliefs and the practices which they made possible. But more, the enchanted world was one in which these forces could cross a porous boundary and shape our lives, psychic and physical. One of the big differences between us and them is that we live with a much firmer sense of the boundary between self and other. We are 'buffered' selves. We have changed.

Jacobs glosses:

> To put that shift in simple terms, a person accepts a buffered condition as a means of being protected from the demonic or otherwise ominous forces that in pre-modern times generated a quavering network of terrors. To be a pre-modern person, in Taylor's account, is to be constantly in danger of being invaded or overcome by demons or fairies or nameless terrors of the dark – of being possessed and transformed, or spirited away and never returned to home and family. It is easy, then, to imagine why a person – or a whole culture – might, if it could, exchange this model of a self with highly permeable boundaries for one in which the self feels better protected, defended – impermeable, or nearly so. The problem with this apparently straightforward transaction is that the porous self is open to the divine as well as to the demonic, while the buffered self is closed to both alike. Those who must guard against capture by fairies are necessarily and by the same token receptive to mystical experiences. … Safety is purchased at the high price of isolation.

For Jacobs, a yearning back to porosity, and its attendant enchantments, is behind the great contemporary vogue for fantasy:

> Might it not be possible to experience the benefits, while avoiding the costs, of both the porous and the buffered self? I want to argue here that it is precisely this desire that accounts for the rise to cultural prominence, in late modernity, of the artistic genre of fantasy. Fantasy is an instrument by which the late modern self strives to avail itself of the unpredictable excitements of the porous self while retaining its protective buffers. Fantasy, in most of its recent forms, may best be understood as a technologically enabled, and therefore safe, simulacrum of the pre-modern porous self.

---

[5] Alan Jacobs, 'Fantasy and the Buffered Self', 4–5.

The relative newness of fantasy, in other words, is an iteration of the disenchantment of, precisely, modernity. And this yearning for re-enchantment is not only prompted by the disenchantments of modernity, but *determined* by them. Modern fantasy, in presenting its various pre-modern imagined worlds, is shaped by the forces that excavated the enchantment in the first place: Protestantism, the rise of the bourgeoisie, rationalism, mechanism and technology. In what follows I discuss Adorno's reading of Wagner's works as intensely bourgeois (think of Tolkien's burghers, burglars, hobbits)[6] and how far he went, despite all his grand mythic posturing, to accommodate the middlebrow respectable tastes of his audience.

What disenchants the older enchantment? Protestantism does. Which is to say: science does, materialism does, capitalism does, but all do so as iterations of this earlier breach: Weber's famous book is, after all, called *The Protestant Ethic and the Spirit of Capitalism*. Charles Taylor's *A Secular Age* also sees the Protestant Reformation as 'central to the abolition of the enchanted cosmos and the eventual creation of a humanist alternative to faith'.[7] What this means is that the project of 're-enchantment' is inevitably tangled-up with the, to Protestant modernity, dangerous allure of the Catholic past. Walter Scott, a foundational figure in the writing of the kind of novelistic romance that shaped the logic of later fantasy fiction, is profoundly about this.

One implication of this account is that, genealogically speaking, there's something going on in fantasy, though often in subterranean ways, to do with Christianity. This remains true even as fantasy is produced, increasingly, by non-Christian writers, written out of Jewish, Islamic, animist, Buddhist, Confucian, atheist and other cultural and spiritual traditions. Lewis was steeped in medieval allegory, and in his Narnia books articulated Christian allegory (like Bunyan before him). Lewis was also perhaps the most influential Christian apologist of the twentieth century. Like *Beowulf* before it, Tolkien's novel is an emulsion of pagan and Christian, but the thing that fascinated Tolkien (and which is picked up, consciously or otherwise, in myriad Tolkien-derivative fantasy novels) is not allegory but incarnation. And Tolkien claimed that his novel was 'a fundamentally religious and Catholic work'. This, he said, was why 'I have not put in, or have cut out, practically all references to anything like "religion", to cults or practices, in the imaginary world. For the religious element is absorbed into the story and the symbolism'.[8]

So: Bunyan, nineteenth-century medievalized Arthurian literature and Wagner. Of the three, Bunyan is probably the most influential. Though only moderately successful on initial publication in 1678, and largely neglected during the eighteenth century,

---

[6]Tom Shippey's *The Road to Middle Earth* notes that Bilbo is

> a *bourgeois*. That is why Gandalf turns him into a Burglar. Both words come from the same root (*burh* = "town" or "stockaded house") and while they are eternal opposites they are opposites on the same level. By the end of *The Hobbit*, though, Bilbo as burglar has progressed so far as to rub shoulders with heroes, even to be (just) considerable as one himself.
>
> [Shippey, 67]

[7]Taylor, *A Secular Age*, 77.

[8]Tolkien, letter to Robert Murray, S.J. [2 December 1953]; *Letters*, 172.

*The Pilgrim's Progress* was rediscovered by the Romantics and became immensely popular through the nineteenth century, reprinted in the millions, widely read, shipped out from Britain across the world as a missionary text.[9] For many in Britain Bunyan was second only to the Bible in their reading; and for many key Victorian writers and thinkers *Pilgrim's Progress* had a shaping effect upon them. It was more than the religious content of this book that gave it such centrality: '[I]t is Macaulay who, in the well-known and widely influential review of Southey's 1830 edition of *The Pilgrim's Progress*, defined for the Victorians the "highest miracle of genius" that he found Bunyan to possess: "that things which are not should be as though they were, that the imaginations of one mind should become the personal".[10] Bunyan's great novel worked, in other words, as fantasy, and as a profound influence on the way fantasy, in the sense in which the present study is interested, came to be written.[11] This points up the question of allegory and fantasy, historically and presently, which I look to unpack a little below. But I do so to move my larger argument in two other directions: the nineteenth-century vogue for neo-medievalist art and its iteration in Victorian Arthurian fantasy – since so much contemporary fantasy is either explicitly Arthurian or else refashions Arthurian knights, quests, swords, wizards and so on – together with the later century impact of Wagner, who left his own mark upon the direction fantasy then took.

---

[9]See Isabel Hofmeyr, 'How Bunyan Became English: Missionaries, Translation, and the Discipline of English'. Hofmeyr opens with this anecdote, illustrative of a great many of its kind: '[O]n 31 October 1847 the *John Williams*, a ship of the London Missionary Society, left Gravesend for the Pacific Islands. Its cargo included five thousand Bibles and four thousand copies of *The Pilgrim's Progress* in Tahitian.'
[10]Quoted in C. Stephen Finley, 'Bunyan Among the Victorians: Macaulay, Froude, Ruskin', 78. See also Isabel Hofmeyr, *The Portable Bunyan: A Transnational History of the Pilgrim's Progress*.
[11]Farah Mendlesohn rightly calls *The Pilgrim's Progress* a 'taproot text for modern fantasy', a work of extensive shaping influence and continuing presence [Mendlesohn, *A Short History of Fantasy*, 3].

# CHAPTER 2
# ROMANTICISM

Fantasy emerges, not coincidentally, at the time when the novel, and its subset the realist novel, was enjoying its greatest popularity and cultural penetration. The high water mark of Realism also saw a return to the storytelling traditions of the Romance, in, as the physicists say, equality and opposition. Gillian Beer's definition, from *The Romance* (1970), identifies

> themes of love and adventure, a certain withdrawal from their own society on the part of both reader and romance hero, profuse sensuous detail, simplified characters (often with a suggestions of allegorical significance), a serene intermingling of the unexpected and the everyday, a complex and prolonged succession of incidents usually without a single climax, a happy ending, amplitude of proportions, a strongly enforced code of conduct to which all the characters must comply.[1]

These are aspects that feed-through into the way fantasy fiction in the twentieth century is written, and they stand oppositionally to the textual strategies of the 'realist' novel.[2] Three elements from Beer's definition are worth drawing out: withdrawal, 'simplified characters' and 'allegorical significance'. Rather than talking of withdrawing from our own society into fantasy-romance, we might, as this study does, talk of the re-enchantment *of* society, from a magical, or mythic past or alterity. This is a way of talking about the way fantasy and romance engage a mode of historicity. The question of character is also complex. British writer Brian Aldiss spoke of his dislike of Tolkien's *Lord of the Rings*, since, he insisted, it contained no characters at all, as he understood the term, with one exception: Gollum.[3] But this is to betray a characteristically post-Romantic bias, for what characterizes (in this sense) Gollum is his divided nature, the dialogue of his mind with itself, his mixed motives. This speaks to a preference for complexity that

---

[1]Beer, *The Romance*, 10.

[2]Amanda Hodgson compares the opening of Morris's *The Wood between The World* (1894) with that of George Moore's *Esther Waters*, a realist novel from the same year. Both books, as she says, concentrate on physical details, but Moore's details are of the ordinary life of 1890s England, where Morris designs to 'take us as far as possible from the world we know'. Moore writes 'an unadorned style' and attempts 'fidelity to the dialect of working people'; Morris's descriptions are of a 'fairy-tale setting: a wood in which a young hero has to evade the machinations of a witch and an evil dwarf. ... The characters are idealized, closer to the types of legend than the complex reality of people as we perceive them ... the language is one that no one ever spoke, highly archaic in syntax and vocabulary. The total effect is of elaborate artifice. Our response must be to the book's strangeness, the distance between our everyday experience and that offered by the work of art' [Hodgson, *The Romances of William Morris*, 3].

[3]I was conducting a public interview with him for the Cheltenham Literary Festival, 2003.

misses the actuality of human subjectivity, which is not in itself defined by streaming consciousness, blizzards of specific detail. The real salient here is not 'complexity' as such, but interiority as opposed to exteriority. Characters in a novel by Henry James or Virginia Woolf are figured with richer interior than exterior lives. Characters in romance and fantasy are construed exclusively in exteriorized terms. Aldiss preferred Gollum because, alone of all the characters in Tolkien's novel, he approximates the former state; but even he dramatizes his divided nature as an exteriorization, referring to himself in the third-person; Peter Jackson's movie adaptations captured this well, staging the relevant scenes by having two versions of Gollum on screen at the same time talking to one another. This is not a marginal aspect of fantasy as it has developed; it also construes the pre-Romantic historical dynamic: individual psychologicization supplanting exterior socialization; guilt succeeding shame; contract supplanting status; industrialized and alienated modernity versus the enchanted, pre-industrial feudal world. Matthew Arnold lamented in 1853 that with *Hamlet* and Goethe's *Faust* 'the dialogue of the mind with itself' had commenced in Western culture, and that a new, morbid and self-destructive mode of sensibility itself had entered art. Morris's romances are not just pre-modern in prose-style and story-construction; they embody a world that refuses this morbid mind-dialogue.

The change happens with Romanticism, *c*. 1780–1830.[4] In M H Abrams's thumbnail phrase, we move from mimesis to illumination: *The Mirror and the Lamp*: pre-Romantic aesthetics saw the business of art as reflective, the artist holding in Polonius's phrase, as 'twere, the mirror up to nature. Art was to be judged by its fidelity to the exterior world. Romanticism conceived of art and the artist differently, with a premium on the individual artist's imagination as not a mirror but a lamp that illuminated the world. As a consequence Romantic art is very often about the mind and imagination of the artist: Blake's mythological epics are primarily about Blake; Wordsworth reconfigures epic away from nationalist adventure and quest and towards the self – *The Prelude* a great epic of, precisely, Wordsworth, the growth of a poet's mind. This is the context into which fantasy, as this study understands the term, comes into being; in reaction, although dialectically so, such that many of the masterpieces of fantasy are informed by the very Romantic and post-Romantic aesthetic premises that the mode is seeking to pre-configure. Blake's mythological art and poetry are fantasy, although of a flavour very different to Tolkien. Or it might be better to say, Tolkien's personal 'mythology', his idiosyncratic reimagining of Anglo-Saxon, Norse, Arthurian, medievalized, Shakespearian and Scottian source material into Middle Earth's legendarium, marks, in its difference to Blake, the benchmark of fantasy as a modern mode as such. Blake's are works of radical originality and potency, but they are mythographic rather than fantastical. The myth is of a primal spiritual man, Albion, comprising four 'zoas', anthropomorphic figures called Urthona, Urizen, Luvah and Tharmas – representing energetic creativity, law, passionate love and

---

[4]See William Gray's *Fantasy Myth and the Measure of Truth* for a detailed account of the ways Romanticism pays forward into the Fantasy of George Macdonald, C. S. Lewis, Tolkien and Philip Pullman.

sensation respectively – each with their 'emanation' or female partner, Enitharmon, Ahania, Vala, Enion. The myth is of a fall from original unity into this material world of suffering and constraint, and of the tensions and contrarieties of the struggle to recover the bliss of eternity. His short epics are visionary embodiments of great power, all self-published. A string of early works recast contemporary events in the lineaments of Blake's mythological dramatis personae: the American and French revolutions, the continental war: *The Marriage of Heaven and Hell* (written 1790–3), *Visions of the Daughters of Albion* (1793) and *America a Prophecy* (1793). Later, longer works elaborate the mythic patterns of Blake's imagined world, and are mostly unfinished: *The First Book of Urizen* (1794–1818), *Milton* (written 1804–10) and *Jerusalem: The Emanation of the Giant Albion* (1804–20 with various additions up to 1832). There is little narrative in these works. Blake does not build magical worlds and populate them with characters, and his worlds do not invite the reader in. And, indeed, readers stayed away. In the words of Herbert Tucker, 'William Blake was the first among [Romantic] poets in every respect save that which a public can pay – since as an epoist he had no public to speak of'.[5] Nor was this a problem for him. It was the creation itself that mattered to Blake, not the reception. Los – the fallen form of Urthona, the blazing principle of artistic productivity – declares:

I must Create a System, or be enslav'd by another Man's;
I will not Reason and Compare: my business is to Create. [*Jerusalem*, ch 1]

Blake is radically committed to freedom, to escape: his is an art of spiritual liberation. To 'fit' his imagination into another's conceptual or visionary system (to the systems of conventional Christianity, to the imagined world of Milton's *Paradise Lost*, to the philosophies of Locke or the scientific systems of Newton) would be, disastrously, to become enslaved. He creates his own, engaging dialectically with these various things in creative opposition. And by implication he is saying: we should do the same. The title page of *Milton* carries this epigraph, from Numbers 11:29: 'would [to] God that all the Lord's people were prophets'. Blake does not want us to inhabit *his* system, but to generate our own spiritual visions and prophesies, to be our own epoists. This is necessarily fantastical, since to create mimetic or realist art would be only to fit our imaginations to the prison-house of the mundane world.

---

[5]Tucker, *Epic: Britain's Heroic Muse*, 62.

# CHAPTER 3
## VICTORIAN MEDIEVALISM

The frame for what follows would be the fundamentally historicizing claim that, very broadly, the nineteenth century represented a congeries of disenchantments, in the Weberian and Taylorian sense of the word: the Industrial Revolution and its attendant social upheavals and reconfigurations; urbanization; increasingly pervasive materialist ideologies of revolution – American, French, other European, the coming of Marxist and socialism; advances in scientific knowledge; and what J Hillis Miller called 'the disappearance of God', up to and including Nietzsche's 1880s *Gott ist tot*. We might suggest that as every action provokes an equal and opposite reaction, as the world broadly proceeded into increasing disenchantment, culture retreated into a fantasy vision of notional pasts, mythic and magical, re-enchanting the world. This might be a practical project, as with Thomas Carlyle's very influential *Past and Present* (1843), a work which presents the reader with a straightforward contrast, a valorized medieval past as against a grim vision of modern disaffection. From the former Carlyle concentrates upon the community formed by a monastery, retelling the story of Samson of Tottington, a twelfth-century monk who eventually became Abbot of Bury St. Edmunds. Carlyle does not pretend the medieval past was a utopia, nor even that the monks he describes were ideal or even admirable (he repeatedly calls them 'blockheads' on account of their superstition and lack of education) but he does insist that, because they lived and worked in a community premised on mutual respect, an orderly and harmonious hierarchy, and worked spiritual as well as physical labour, theirs was genuine, authentic living. This he contrasts with nineteenth-century workers, deracinated and exploited, bound not by ties of duty and respect and community but only by the 'cash-nexus', by contracts and legal expropriation, a flattened and machinic sort of existence.

Two decades later English jurist Henry Sumner Maine, deeply influenced by Carlyle's writing, published *Ancient Law; Its Connection to the Early History of Society, and Its Relation to Modern Ideas* (1861). His thesis is that society had shifted from human identity and being-in-the-world as defined by one's status – one's place in the social hierarchy, the great chain of being – to our social being and interactions as governed by contracts. In some ways, since contracts (unlike status) can be engaged voluntarily, Sumner sees this as an improvement. But there are losses too, and those losses are what *Past and Present* is about. Carlyle argues less like a lawyer and more like an artist, and he is certain that what has been lost is *reverence*, something no contract can bestow: 'at public hustings, in private drawing-rooms, in church, in market, and wherever else have true reverence, and what indeed is inseparable therefrom, reverence *the right man,* all is well; have sham-reverence, and what also follows, greet with it the wrong man, then all is ill, and there is nothing'. The contrast Carlyle draws between industrialized irreverential contemporaneity and the vivid life of his imagined medieval world establishes precisely the contrast that the Tolkienian and Lewisian mode of fantasy would later valorize:

> Behold therefore, this England of the Year 1200 was no chimerical vacuity or dreamland, peopled with mere vaporous Fantasms, Rymer's Foedera, and Doctrines of the Constitution, but a green solid place, that grew corn and several other things. The Sun shone on it; the vicissitude of seasons and human fortunes. Cloth was woven and worn; ditches were dug, furrowfields ploughed, and houses built. Day by day all men and cattle rose to labour, and night by night returned home weary to their several lairs. In wondrous Dualism, then as now, lived nations of breathing men; alternating, in all ways, between Light and Dark; between joy and sorrow, between rest and toil, between hope, hope reaching high as Heaven, and fear deep as very Hell.[1]

It is a key feature of the Victorian fascination with medievalized fantasy worlds that it takes the imaginary realm as being, in an important sense, *more* real than present-day actuality. Its solidity, brightness and vivid colours are, as it were, pledges to its ideal actuality. In his Narnia books Lewis rationalizes this via Plato, such that the 'real' world in which we, his readers, live is mere cave-wall shadowplay compared to the bright sunshine of Narnia, and the blazing glory of the ultimate reality, revealed at the end of *The Last Battle*, of which even Narnia is but a copy.[2] But most fantasy worlds don't feel the need to provide superstructural justifications via philosophy: for them the sheer fact that these worlds are enchanted – Carlyle's 'reverence' – and our world is not, is justification enough.

It is hard to overstate the impact of Carlyle's *Past and Present* on nineteenth-century thought and culture, feeding as it did through into the Victorian vogue of neo-medievalism that manifested especially in a revival in interest in Arthurian legend, especially in poetry: Matthew Arnold's *Tristram and Iseult* (1852), Tennyson's *Idylls of the King* (published between 1859 and 1873), William Morris's *Defence of Guinevere* (1858), Wagner's *Tristan und Isolde* (1865) and Swinburne's *Tristram of Lyonesse* (1882) are all proto-fantasy, marvellous and wondrous recreations of a pre-industrial world, chivalry and adventure, magic and peril, quests and noblesse. We can also mention the Pre-Raphaelite Brotherhood, whose many medievalized, colourful canvases provided

---

[1]Carlyle, *Past and Present*, 2:1.
[2]In the last chapter of *The Last Battle*, as the protagonists move 'further up and further in', Digory Kirke exclaims: 'it's all in Plato, all in Plato: Bless me, what do they teach them at these schools?' See James Bryson '"It's all in Plato": Platonism, Cambridge Platonism, and C. S. Lewis' for a fuller discussion of this.

the visual prototype for much twentieth- and twenty-first-century fantasy illustration and art.[3] More so even than Scott's bestselling medieval-set novels – *Ivanhoe* (1820), *Quentin Durward* (1823) *The Betrothed* (1825), *The Talisman* (1825) – important though those novels were – and more so than Augustus Pugin's 1836 celebration of medieval architecture as a model for contemporary building *Contrasts* (it is to Pugin that we owe the neo-Gothic Houses of Parliament in London) – and much more so than the late-eighteenth-century vogue for often medievalized 'Gothic' novels, Carlyle presents his fantasy world not merely as nostalgic past but as idealized possibility. William Morris, who took a great deal from Carlyle, rendered this in his future-set, thoroughly pastoral and medievalized utopia *News from Nowhere* (1890), in which Carlyle's past becomes England's future. This same *Past and Present* gesture underlies Morris's meta-epic collection of epics *Earthly Paradise* (1868–70) which begins, as we have seen, with an exhortation to abandon the smoky-spectral industrial present and travel instead to a more substantial fantasia of England. Critics have, rightly, made much of the influence of Morris's late career prose romances upon the development of twentieth-century fantasy, but these books are also Carlylean exercises in quasi-Arthurian writing.

Then there is the question of that dominant medieval mode of literature, allegory. Fantasy is not 'allegorical' in the simple, roman-a-clef sense in which medieval allegory often is: simple in the sense that once the 'meanings' of the in-text characters have been decoded, the work exhausts its interpretive generosity. Fantasy allegory is complex, not necessarily in the sense of being intricate (although sometimes it is that) but in terms of being folded into textual-topographical baroquenesses. It is not that the in-text characters gesture towards an out-text explanation or solution, but rather that the text itself, iterating versions of mundanity, also enfolds enchantments, wonders, terrors and splendours. Allegory is a parallel track for the development of fantasy, as something both in itself medievalized – for allegorical romance is a central mode of medieval literature – and something distinctively nineteenth century. C. S. Lewis's first work of scholarship, 1936's *The Allegory of Love: A Study in Medieval Tradition*, is a fruitful gloss on Lewis's own Narnian Fantasies. But the nineteenth-century tradition of allegorical fantasy is at once less schematic and more imaginatively fantastical than most medieval romances. To return to Bunyan: *The Pilgrim's Progress* (1678), its Fantasyland a combination of early-modern mercantilism and medieval romance, knights in armour battling giants and monsters, spoke to the whole Victorian world.[4]

---

[3]On the prodigious influence of Carlyle's book on Victorian medievalism, see Alice Chandler, *A Dream of Order: The Medieval Ideal in Nineteenth-Century English Literature* and Joanne Parker and Corinna Wagner (eds) *The Oxford Handbook of Victorian Medievalism*. Robin Gilmour argues that Carlyle's real significance was in the way he turned Victorian medievalism 'away from Anglo-Catholic and Tory-mythmaking' [Gilmour, *The Victorian Period* (Routledge 1993) 49] represented by, for instance, Scott's novels and Disraeli's 'Young England'.

[4]James Forrest and Richard Greaves, *John Bunyan: A Reference Guide*, vii. On Bunyan's vast reach into Victorian culture, see Emma Mason's 'The Victorians and Bunyan's Legacy', in Anne Dunan-Page (ed) *The Cambridge Companion to Bunyan* and Michael Davies and W R Owens' *Oxford Handbook of John Bunyan*.

*Pilgrim's Progress* was often given to children to read, and the development of 'children's literature' as such, distinct from the limited, largely didactic-moralistic works for younger readers of previous centuries, very largely shows its influence.[5] Some nineteenth-century children's novels are, broadly, mimetic in approach, as with the quasi-realist school story tradition that began with Hughes's *Tom Brown's Schooldays* (1857) and Farrar's *Eric* (1857); but a more significant, and more enduring, style of children's fiction presented either far-flung adventure narratives or fantasy novels. The former style is represented by such popular successes as R M Ballantyne's *Coral Island* (1858) or Stevenson's *Treasure Island* (1883) – 'Late Imperial Romance' as this genre is sometimes called; not strictly fantastical but colourful and exotic, and in some cases bleeding into the fantastic (e.g. Rider Haggard's *She*, 1887). But more important by far is the strong tradition of major fantasy novels for children in the second-half of the nineteenth century: John Ruskin's *The King of the Golden River* (1851); George MacDonald's *Phantastes* (1858); Charles Kingsley's *The Water-Babies, A Fairy Tale for a Land Baby* (1863), Lewis Carroll's *Alice in Wonderland* (1865) and *Through the Looking-Glass* (1871). Each of these texts had a palpable influence on the development of fantasy as a twentieth-century mode – C. S. Lewis, who read *Phantastes* as a teenager, later spoke of it as 'baptizing his imagination'.[6] Ruskin's 'fairy tale' draws on the Germanic traditions that came to cultural prominence with the publication and translation of the Grimms' tales (the *Kinder- und Hausmärchen* collection, first published 1812, was repeatedly expanded, reissued and translated: the seventh edition in 1857, it had 210 unique fairy tales), and the allegorical *Phantastes*, in which the hero 'Anodos' travels across a magical 'Fairy Land' in search of a beautiful lady, quickened from an alabaster statue, touches on Arthurian legend (a major episode in the story sees Anodos encounter Sir Percivale, in rusted armour and upon a red horse).

Farah Mendlesohn's structuralist study *Rhetorics of Fantasy* distinguishes between what she calls 'immersive fantasies' and 'portal quest fantasies': the former being those types of world that exist in and of themselves, like Tolkien's Middle Earth, the latter those Fantasylands that are accessible from 'our' world via some kind of portal or

---

[5]Children's literature is a large matter, and cannot be easily summarized. Broadly: Romanticism, following the influence of Jean-Jacques Rousseau's *Émile* (1762) generated a new and valorized sense of childhood as a worthwhile, even holy, status ('the child is father to the man' in Wordsworth's phrase). Books written for children to enjoy on their own terms, rather than, or in addition to, for reasons of instrumental didacticism, come to be a feature literary culture by the mid-nineteenth century, and constitute a major mode of writing in their own right by the end of the century. See Kimberley Reynolds, *Children's Literature: A Very Short Introduction*; Shelby Wolf, *Handbook of Research in Children's and Young Adult Literature* and Jack Zipes, *The Oxford Encyclopaedia of Children's Literature*.

[6]'I had no not the faintest notion what I had let myself in for by buying *Phantastes*' [C. S. Lewis, *Surprised by Joy*, 139]. 'I have never concealed the fact that I regarded [MacDonald] as my master; indeed I fancy I have never written a book in which I did not quote from him. It must be thirty years ago that I ought … the Everyman edition of *Phantastes*. A few hours later I knew I had crossed a great frontier' [Lewis (ed), *George Macdonald: An Anthology*, xxxvii].

access-point, like the Wardrobe in Lewis's *The Lion, The Witch and The Wardrobe*.[7] In *Phantastes* the portal is Anodos's bedroom:

> I saw that the branches and leaves designed upon the curtains of my bed were slightly in motion. Not knowing what change might follow next, I thought it high time to get up; and, springing from the bed, my bare feet alighted upon a cool green sward; and although I dressed in all haste, I found myself completing my toilet under the boughs of a great tree, whose top waved in the golden stream of the sunrise with many interchanging lights, and with shadows of leaf and branch gliding over leaf and branch, as the cool morning wind swung it to and fro, like a sinking sea-wave. [MacDonald, *Phantastes* ch. 2]

Escape into re-enchantment sets in train an episodic series of beautified adventures until 'faith' is encountered, and 'I rose, loving the white lady as I had never loved her before'. When the story re-enters our world, it is through 'the Door of Dismay':

> Then I walked up to the door of Dismay, and opened it, and went out. And lo! I came forth upon a crowded street, where men and women went to and fro in multitudes. I knew it well; and, turning to one hand, walked sadly along the pavement. [MacDonald, *Phantastes* ch. 19]

This to-and-fro, between enchanted Fantasyland and the dreary mundanity of real life, is often replicated in later fantasy writing. In Kingsley's *Water-Babies*, the 'portal' is death itself: Tom, the young chimney-sweep protagonist, abused and exploited by his wicked master Grimes, unbaptized and ignorant, is cleaning the chimneys of a country house when he stumbles into the bedroom of a white-skinned, white-clad girl called Ellie. Scared that he is in trouble he runs away, falls down a slope and drowns in a nearby river. But although Tom is mourned and buried in the 'real' world, in the story he is transformed into a 'water baby', a type of axolotl, beginning a new life in the river. From here, Kingsley's formally macaronic tale, archly humorous, restlessly inventive, peripatetic (and often racist), figures as a Bunyanesque 'progress', passing through magical realms, meeting all manner of amazing and monstrous creatures. As he quests Tom must learn the moral and spiritual lessons he did not learn as a human boy, and variously encounters actual fauna and allegorical figures, as for example the two fairies, twin embodiments of the ethical 'golden rule', 'Mrs. Doasyouwouldbedoneby' and 'Mrs. Bedonebyasyoudid'. In *Pilgrim's Progress* the pilgrim, Christian, must drown in the river of death in order to reach 'Zion' (i.e. heaven) at the end of his journey – an ultimate, extreme baptism.

---

[7]Mendlesohn, *Rhetorics of Fantasy*. The book also distinguishes 'intrusive' and 'liminal' types of fantasy, although 'immersive' and 'portal/quest' types constitute the lion's share of her analysis (indeed, 'intrusive' fantasies are portal/quest stories in which the fantasy world invades 'our' world, rather than the other way around).

Kingsley's water progress moves Tom down river to the sea, and then out into the great ocean, and finally to (and beyond) the north pole, with some splendid icescapes to a kind of purgatorial castle in which Grimes, himself now dead in the 'real' world, is trapped. By freeing him Tom earns reincarnation: 'and he is now', Kingsley concludes, 'a great man of science, and can plan railroads, and steam-engines, and electric telegraphs, and rifled guns, and so forth; and knows everything about everything, except why a hen's egg don't turn into a crocodile, and two or three other little things which no one will know till the coming of the Cocqcigrues' [Kingsley, *Water-Babies*, ch.8]. It would not be correct to say that the allegory here is 'looser', although it is less directly schematic, less a straightforward grid mapping in-text element to extratextual key. But allegory is the book's mode nevertheless. There is tremendous centripetal energy in the telling, and Darwinist Kingsley draws on a series of quite specifically Rabelaisian textual strategies as correlatives for the bustling, glorious fecundity of the natural world, something he finds both beautiful and profoundly Godly; and it is this last aspect of the universe that informs Kingsley's textual strategies in a novel like this. For him, as for Browning, this world of ours is not blank or blot, it *means* intensely and means good.

The title of MacDonald's *Phantastes* comes from Phineas Fletcher's Renaissance allegorical poem *The Purple Island* (1633), but the more direct influence is later. The protagonist's name, Anodos, records the Greek word ἄνοδος, which means 'a path', and more specifically, an upward path – that is, 'a progress', a name MacDonald chooses because his character travels, like Bunyan's pilgrim, through an allegorical landscape of increasing self-knowledge and wisdom. Anodos entering fairyland searches for the White Lady, whom he several times discovers and loses. At one point he travels underground where various dwarf-creatures mock him for his failure to apprehend her.

> Crowding about me like bees, they shouted an insect-swarm of exasperating speeches up into my face, among which the most frequently recurring were – 'You shan't have her; you shan't have her; *he! he! he!* She's for a better man; how he'll kiss her! how he'll kiss her!' The galvanic torrent of this battery of malevolence stung to life within me a spark of nobleness, and I said aloud, 'Well, if he is a better man, let him have her'. [*Phantastes*, ch. 17]

Returning to the above-ground, Anodos finally discovers the White Lady, living on an island and happily married to this 'better man'. At first he cannot accept this, and his resentment causes the destruction of the island; but after further adventures, heroic deeds, his own knighthood, he comes so see that the better man is his master and deserves the White Lady. He goes so far as to sacrifice his life for the couple, dying in fairyland to reawaken in our world, back in his own home. He has spent many years on his adventures, but his sisters tell him that he has been missing for only twenty-one days. The different speeds at which time passes in 'our' world and in fairyland were taken up by C. S. Lewis in his Narnia books; but Macdonald himself took it from Bunyan, whose Pilgrim lives an entire life in the real world, but passes much more rapidly (a reasonable estimate is: a year) through the allegorical land of the novel.

Edwin Honig finds in Coleridge the 'principal source of the modern opposition to the concept of allegory', via the Coleridgean distinction of allegory from symbol, and the association of the former with 'the mechanical, the self-conscious, and the fanciful', as opposed to the more organic imaginative esemplasy of greater art.[8] The difference is behind Coleridge's important distinction between mere 'fancy' and 'the imagination' deployed or inhabited by great artists; although Honig argues that Coleridge's imagination engages with 'the medieval belief' in 'the formal and functional truth of objective reality', reformulating this 'with a different emphasis, giving, as it were, a centripetal instead of a centrifugal direction'. Honig repudiates Coleridge's negative criticism of allegory, arguing that allegory does not always, and does not necessarily, instantiate a preconceived and mechanistic set of mapping devices, but can instead be rich and complex, fluid and developmental, expressive of what Honig calls 'the irrational' but which I am here appropriating (via the subconscious) to the transcendent and re-enchanted. 'Allegory', says Honig, 'has offered the rational consciousness a way of regulating imaginative materials that otherwise appear confounded by contradictions and bristling with destructive implications'. In terms of nineteenth-century writing for children it is clear enough that occasions when writers essayed the former of these two approaches – as with, say, Christina Rossetti's Bunyanesque-titled narrative poem *The Prince's Progress* (1866) – they achieved less than when they essayed the latter – as Rossetti did in her vastly superior, fantastical-allegorical verse-tale *Goblin Market* (1862). Of Carroll's two Alice books, the second more obviously resembles allegory in the traditional sense, and might indeed be read as a commentary upon, perhaps even a satirical deconstruction of, older allegorical models. Alice passes through a portal (the looking glass) into a vibrant, varied and surreal fantastical realm, where she has a series of episodic adventures. But every step she takes in 'Looking Glass World' corresponds, via a key included at the beginning of the book, to a move in a chess game. *Alice in Wonderland* has no such external schema, but flows through the fluidities of dream-logic, to greater imaginative resonance and power.

Scott's immense popularity was grounded in idealized and simplified historical actualities, although his version of novelistic romance flirts, especially in its medievalized mode, with fantasy. In his novels, what seems at first blush supernatural or magical is explained away, as in *Woodstock* (1826) or *Anne of Geierstein* (1829). Yet the fantastical is not thereby banished from Scott's romantic, influential storytelling. It continues to haunt it. Scott's *Count Robert of Paris* (1831) is historical fiction, set in the eleventh century, and concerning the titular Frankish Count's (historical) journey through the Byzantine empire on his way to the Holy Land and crusade. The scheming Byzantine

---

[8] Edwin Honig, *Dark Conceit: The Making of Allegory*, 44. The two quotations that follow are from pages 49 to 53. Of the distinction between 'traditional' allegory (medieval Romance, Spenser, Bunyan and the like) and more recent, less rigid allegory, Honig says: 'it is as though the typical formula for the Christian hero, which Dante set up and Bunyan renewed, had been adapted by Kafka with all the old terms intact save the consolation of a supernatural grace. Kafka's incomplete adaptations of the formula suggest those picture puzzles appearing in the old Sunday supplements under the caption, *What's Wrong with This Picture?*' [76].

emperor Alexius, and his courtiers, plots to detain and kill Robert, but his warrior strength and true heart win through. Scott extracts an idealized romantic adventure from this baseline historical material, and in this novel – as in some others – goes a little beyond even this simplified factual matter. The novel's account of Constantinople, a place Scott himself never actually visited, is sketchy: a few streets, a gatehouse, a bit of coast, a church here, an arena there. The exception is the imperial palace, which is described in wonderful, Gormenghastly detail: a vast pile containing labyrinths of levels and corridors, trapdoors and cells and halls and secret chambers, filled with wild tigers and trained Orang Utans, prisoners in oubliettes whose beards have grown down to their feet, giant mechanical lion-automata working as robot guardians (Count Robert, imprisoned in the palace, smashes one of these in his escape) and various other tasty details. And if there is something Gothic, or orientalist-Gothic, in Scott's version of this great castle, then there is something, contrastingly, spacious and wonderful in the open-air and cleanly chivalric ambition of Count Robert himself, an aspect of the novel that looks forward to the modes of Pre-Raphaelite and Tolkienian visionary medievalism. *Count Robert* gives its reader tantalizing glimpses of a novel in which Robert, and his beautiful warrior wife the Countess Brenhilda, have a series of exciting 'Fantasy' adventures, even if this is not the novel Scott ends up actually writing. Arriving in the vicinity of Constantinople by boat, Robert 'looks among the scattered trees which fringed the shores, down almost to the tide-mark, to see if he could discern any by-path which might carry them more circuitously, but more pleasantly, to the city, and afford them at the same time, what was their principal object in the East, strange sights, or adventures of chivalry'. One such is there:

> A broad and beaten path seemed to promise them all the enjoyment which shade could give in a warm climate. The ground through which it wound its way was beautifully broken by the appearance of temples, churches, and kiosks, and here and there a fountain distributed its silver produce, like a benevolent individual, who, self-denying to himself, is liberal to all others who are in necessity. [Scott, *Robert of Paris*, ch 10]

They disembark and immediately encounter some Orc-like Scythians –

> a party of heathen Scythians, presenting the deformed features of the demons they were said to worship, flat noses with expanded nostrils, which seemed to admit the sight to their very brain; faces which extended rather in breadth than length, with strange unintellectual eyes placed in the extremity; figures short and dwarfish, yet garnished with legs and arms of astonishing sinewy strength, disproportioned to their bodies.

Robert and Brenhilda defeat these monstrous foe battle. They have entered faerie, or something very like it. Nearby is 'the rich island of Zulichium', somewhere off the Byzantine coast 'amid storms and whirlpools, rocks which, changing their character, appear to precipitate themselves against each other'. The island contains one 'stately, but ruinous castle' inside which a beautiful princess sleeps, the victim of a curse laid upon her by a wizard, 'one of the Magi who followed the tenets of Zoroaster'. A Frankish knight had previously attempted to rescue this dormant beauty: 'never seemed there a fairer opportunity for that awakening to take place than when the proud step of Artavan de Hautlieu was placed upon those enchanted courts'.

> He passed on to a little ivory door, which, after a moment's pause, as if in maidenly hesitation, gave way like the rest, and yielded access to the sleeping apartment of the Princess herself. A soft light, resembling that of evening, penetrated into a chamber where every thing seemed contrived to exalt the luxury of slumber. The heaps of cushions, which formed a stately bed, seemed rather to be touched than impressed by the form of a nymph of fifteen, the renowned Princess of Zulichium.

The knight kisses the princess upon the lips. Things don't go the Perrault-fairy-tale way one might expect, however:

> Never had so innocent an action an effect more horrible! The delightful light of a summer evening was instantly changed into a strange lurid hue, which, infected with sulphur, seemed to breathe suffocation through the apartment. The rich hangings, and splendid furniture of the chamber, the very walls themselves, were changed into huge stones tossed together at random, like the inside of a wild beast's den, nor was the den without an inhabitant. The beautiful and innocent lips to which Artavan de Hautlieu had approached his own, were now changed into the hideous and bizarre form, and bestial aspect of a fiery dragon. A moment she hovered upon the wing, and it is said, had Sir Artavan found courage to repeat his salute [*that is, his kiss*] three times, he would then have remained master of all the wealth, and of the disenchanted princess. But the opportunity was lost, and the dragon, or the creature who seemed such, sailed out at a side window upon its broad pennons, uttering loud wails of disappointment.

But this is only an aside, an inset story: Robert and Brenhilda don't ever visit this island, or follow up its cursed princess, instead pressing on to Byzantium, court politics, the crusades and historical actuality. It leaves the reader wishing Scott had made it, and similar, the main point of his story.

# CHAPTER 4
# FOLK AND FAIRY TALES

These overlapping magisteria – the medievalism of resuscitated Arthurian chivalric art and Bunyanesque allegory as a vehicle for linking reality with a fantastical territory of re-enchanted wonder – in turn overlap with a third tradition: the recuperation into general culture of Germanic, or (less narrowly) northern-European Germanic, Scandinavian and British cultural idioms. Before the nineteenth century, cultural prestige derived from two traditions more removed from northern Europe: the classical heritage of ancient Greece and Rome, and the shaping religious idiom of Hebraic Judo-Christianism out of the eastern Mediterranean. The nineteenth century did not exactly see a shift away from 'Hebrew and Hellene' as shaping cultural forces, for, of course, both traditions continued to represent a powerful force on the cultural production of the day.[1] But aboriginal cultural heritages of the north came out of the shadows of cultural dismissal or embarrassment – as rude, uncultivated, peasant-ish, compared to the polish and refinement of the classics – to occupy an increasingly important position, as a reservoir of genuineness, authentic social identity, Völkish truth and therefore as a portal back to a form of 'enchanted' original being-in-the-world.

A large mover in this regard was the success of the Grimm brothers collecting and curating (and in some cases inventing) 'authentic' völkisch folk tales in their collection. There was a good deal of interest in 'folk art', especially popular oral ballads, in the eighteenth century, and Perrault's collection of 'contes du fée', *Histoires ou contes du temps passé, avec des moralités* (1697), sometimes known as *Contes de ma mère l'Oye*, 'Mother Goose Tales', was popular throughout the 1700s. These are polished, courtly, mannered tales, more often than not rewarding the persistence of hero or heroine with a royal marriage, and sidelining 'fantastical' elements – the booted, talking feline of 'Le Chat Botté', Puss in Boots, the Cinderella magical transformations of 'Cendrillon ou la petite pantoufle de verre' – in favour of these elaborated fables of courtship and social elevation. The tales in the Grimms' collection have a different, more proletarian emphasis: peasants and blacksmiths, old women in cottages and farmers with smallholdings, and above all, in place of Perrault's polished marble palace floors and ballrooms, the wide, dark, mysterious Germanic woodlands. The huge impact of the Grimms' *Kinder- und Hausmärchen* ('Childrens' and Household Tales', 1812) was a function of two main cultural forces. One was a new interest in the child as such.[2] The other was a Europe-wide

---

[1]See David DeLaura, *Hebrew and Hellene in Victorian England: Newman, Arnold, and Pater*.
[2]See Ann Wierda Rowland, *Romanticism and Childhood*; Peter Coveney, *The Image of Childhood: the Individual and Society: a Study of the Theme in English Literature*; Martina Domines Veliki and Cian Duffy (eds) *Romanticism and the Cultures of Infancy*.

surge of interest in land, history and folk-art, in turn a function of nascent nationalism. In the early 1800s the multitudinous German statelets were starting the long process of political coalescence, and an engagement with the roots of specifically German folk-ness was a major driver of this.[3] Something similar happened across the continent, but its particular social acuity in Germany is one reason why it is the German versions of these (often) universal stories that have become treated as the default versions.[4] Another important aspect of the German-ness of these *Märchen* is the way 'the Germanic' played in a wider Romantic context. Marilyn Butler describes the fundamentally ideological division in the writing of English writing Romanticism between a 'right-wing' reactionary Germanic-influenced tradition and a 'left-wing' liberal classical emphasis on the Mediterranean. She is discussing De Staël's *De l'Allemagne* (1810), which praised German culture 'as a rallying-point for opposition to Napoleon':

> Europe had two dominant cultural traditions: the classical, Mediterranean inheritance, perfectly expressed in comedy, and culminating in a predominantly French modern classicism; and the Northern or Germanic alternative'. The German races did not organise themselves into large states. Man was isolated in very small communities, effectively on his own and dwarfed among the vast, oppressive, unmastered phenomena of Nature. He was obliged to look inward for inspiration, or upward to the mountains or to God. The literature of the North accordingly became introspective, pessimistic and essentially religious. Its religion was not social but individual, an intense unfulfilled aspiration which was perfectly expressed in Gothic architecture, or in the passionate irregularity of Shakespearian tragedy. The Northern or Romantic tradition (which as Madame de Staël makes plain is the unified culture of the Germans and the English, Napoleon's leading enemies) has become the most vital and imaginative intellectual force of the present day.[5]

Butler slightly overstates her ideological perspective by way of explaining why the younger, liberal or radical writers – Byron, Shelley and Keats – gravitated so enthusiastically towards classical Greek and Roman literature. But she identifies something important about the way the Grimms' Tales 'worked', certainly for the first few generations of readers through the nineteenth century, and so into the twentieth and twenty-first centuries too. A great deal of that fantasy draws on northern European history, legend and myth, either first-hand (as Tolkien took names and story elements from the *Völsungasaga* the *Poetic Edda* and *Beowulf*). More usually this has found its way into modern fantasy at second or even third hand, as writers copy writers who copy writers inspired by this.

---

[3] Jakob Norberg, *The Brothers Grimm and the Making of German Nationalism*.
[4] Peter Watson, *The German Genius: Europe's Third Renaissance, the Second Scientific Revolution and the Twentieth Century*.
[5] Marilyn Butler, *Romantics, Rebels and Reactionaries*, 120.

Wagner worked these sources into *Gesamtkunstwerke* fantasy texts of superb grandeur and resonance, that fed through into the fantasy writing of the twentieth century: *Tristran und Isolde* (1865) and *Parsifal* (1882) as adaptions of Arthurian legend, and *Der Ring des Nibelungen* (1869–76). The *Ring* is, in Franco Moretti's phrase, a 'world text', 'rebelling against the slow decline of the sacred, and seeking to restore lost transcendence'.[6] The impact of Wagner's opera on culture in the late nineteenth and early twentieth centuries was very significant.

Framed in part by this mix of actual and faux antiquarianism the nineteenth century crucibled emerging nationalities. The Grimms' project was more than just assembling an anthology of folk stories. It was advancing a new model of German national identity, rooted in, precisely, the *volk*, as a repository of ancient, authentic value, community, strength, worth and cohesion. This Herderian version of national identity as rooted in a deep past, as völkisch (as, among other things, racial) and as expressed via a shared aboriginal culture, stands at odds with eighteenth-century contractual 'rights of man'-style theories of nationhood. It informed German unification. Finnish independence and national identity coalesced around Lönnrot's work (the *Kalevela* still has a central place in Finnishness today). Scott's novels in effect 'created' modern Scotland – in practical terms, as a tourist destination, not least – as Wordsworth 'created' the Lake District. In this situation a fictional or fantastical world, by being rooted in this sense of heritage, can become superposed upon the world as such. Dickens's London is in a sense a topography of urban fantastika, a melange of Gothic, melodrama and naturalism, that, although it doesn't adumbrate specifically magical or fantastical elements, feeds through into some of the most significant fantasy of the twentieth century: Peake's Gormenghast most notably. But though Dickens's novels are, obviously, fictional, an enduring culture of Dickens tourism emerged early on. William Hughes's *A Weeks Tramp in Dickens-land* (1891) traces a series of pilgrimages through the imaginary land of its title through the actual topography of London, Kent and the Midlands.[7] Fantasy interpenetrates reality. In a 2008 poll Hogwarts School was voted one of the best schools in Scotland, outranking many actual schools.[8] Middle Earth plays a substantial role in the budgeting of the New Zealand tourist board. Reality and fantasy interpellate one another.

---

[6]Franco Moretti, *The Modern Epic*, 109.
[7]See Juliet John, *Dickens and Mass Culture*.
[8]'Harry Potter's school outranks Loretto', *The Scotsman* [31 March 2008].

# CHAPTER 5
## NINETEENTH-CENTURY BUNYAN

This takes us back to Bunyan. *The Pilgrim's Progress* superposes two ways of understanding reality: a chronological lived-experience 'real world' way and an allegorical spiritual fantastical way. Various things happen in the story of *The Pilgrim's Progress*, people are encountered, places are visited, and all of these are allegorical representations of various things that are happening in another story, which we can intuit from what we read but which is not specifically told: the story of a person trying to live a life true to their Christian faith in 'our' world. In a sense the book is about this precisely balance, or tension, between the allegorical and the real. This doubled story entails a man, called Christian, who previously went by the name Graceless, travelling through a richly varied Fantasyland on a quest to locate a beautiful city. He begins in a different city, the City of Destruction, which is our world. Resolving to go on pilgrimage, he abandons his wife and four sons and soon meets a man called Evangelist, 'walking out in the fields', who directs him to the 'Wicket Gate' through which he must pass, and so begin his trek to the 'Cœlestial City' of Zion, which is heaven. On the way to this gate Christian falls into the Slough of Despond, a boggy mire that is the sink of all the sins of his city's inhabitants, but he is pulled out by Help, and he gets to the Wicket Gate and through it onto the road of Salvation. We understand that this is not the account of a life as such, but specifically an account of a *spiritual* journey. The man called Christian in this spiritual realm is presumably called something quite different in our material realm. It perhaps looks odd that Christian simply abandons his wife and four children to go on his pilgrimage, never to return (scripturally, of course, Christ enjoins his faithful to abandon their earthly duties and follow him, to 'let the dead bury their dead' Luke 9:60). But we must presume that this abandonment only happens, as it were, in the spiritual realm, and that in the material realm he continues living with his family, materially supporting them as was his duty. Bunyan's story is allegorizing the spiritual separation that must grow between a husband who has been born again and a wife who hasn't, even if they're still living in the same house. Indeed, we must assume that this peripatetic narrative describes the actual life of a man who himself has most likely never travelled anywhere – who stays all his life in the same town or village where he was born, as almost everybody did in seventeenth-century England.

The allegory is complex. Figures and places in Bunyan's story represent spiritual embodiments or externalization of key qualities in our 'real' world. But some of the things in Bunyan's allegorical land are actual things from our land. For example, in *Pilgrim's Progress Part 2* (1684) Christian's wife Christiana, belatedly embarked upon her own pilgrimage, visits the House Beautiful and is shown various allegorical things, and even actually given a golden anchor representing the steadfastness and hopefulness of her faith.

But she is *also* shown the actual artefacts by which Abraham so nearly sacrificed his son Isaac – not an allegorical representation of those things, but the real things themselves, 'the altar, the wood, the fire, and the knife, for they remain to be seen to this very day'. Some of the characters in this novel have names like Envy, Superstition, Mr Dare-not-ly and Mr Worldly-Wiseman, but some of them have names like James, Matthew, Gaius and Mnason, and some have names (such as Mercy or indeed Christian) that are both nominative and denotative. At one point Great-Heart greets a fellow on the road that he recognizes:

> Greath: *Well, now we are so happily met, pray let me crave your Name, and the name of the Place you came from.*
> Hon: My Name I cannot, but I came from the Town of *Stupidity*: it lieth about four Degrees beyond the city of *Destruction.*
> Greath: Oh, *Are you that countryman? Then I deem I have half a guess of you: your name is Old* Honesty, *is it not?* So the old gentleman blushed, and said, Not Honesty in the *Abstract*, but *Honest* is my name; and I wish that my nature may agree to what I am called. [Bunyan, 194]

*I wish that my nature may agree to what I am called.* Edinburgh is four degrees of latitude north of London, so Bunyan is styling Honest as a Scot (of his hometown he says 'we lie more off from the sun, and so are more cold and senseless'), a coded reference to the Scots Covenanters, nonconformists and former allies with the English Parliamentarian army in which Bunyan had served, and implacable opponents of the established Church of Scotland and its bishops. But what's significant here is how his character, Honest, is *so* honest that he cannot simply nod-past the notion that these actors only exist on an abstracted or allegorical level.

Or consider Little-faith, who is robbed on his pilgrimage by 'three sturdy rogues, and their names were Faint-heart, Mistrust, and Guilt, three brothers' [Bunyan, 97]. The allegory here is that an insufficiency of faith leaves a Christian prey to these debilitating qualities; and indeed Guilt strikes Little-faith on the head with a huge club 'and with that blow felled him flat to the ground, where he lay bleeding as one that would bleed to death'. But though the thieves take his money, they don't take his 'jewels', which allegorically represent his remaining possibility of salvation. So 'those he kept still', but he 'was much afflicted for his loss, for the thieves got most of his spending-money'. So, Bunyan's imaginary world includes some valuables that function as currency and exchange within the in-text economic logic of this land, and also valuables that function as allegorical representations of purely spiritual truths, outwith the logic of fiduciary exchange. In other words, it's not that Bunyanland is a place inside which everything stands for something else, it's that it is *both* real *and* allegorical at the same time. Sometimes wealth allegorically represents purely spiritual riches, and sometimes, as with Demas's silver mine, or the energetic moneymaking of Vanity Fair, it represents only itself. Metaphor and semiotic identity tangle with one another.

This is not a flaw in the novel. On the contrary, it is at the heart of what gives Bunyan's text its richness and multidimensionality, elevating it beyond one-dimensional religious polemic – and in doing so, paying the book's imaginative vision forward into fantasy writing. The novel works because the directness of Bunyan's gorgeously idiomatic and expressive prose evokes a world of lived experience, and prevents the whole from sliding into theological abstractions; but it also works because on the level of worldbuilding it is able to hold its actual and its spiritual worlds in a close and productive tension. One small example, from Christian's encounter with Apollyon.

> So he went on, and *Apollyon* met him; now the monster was hidious to behold, he was cloathed with scales like a Fish, (and they are his pride) he had Wings like a Dragon, and out of his belly came Fire and Smoak, and his mouth was as the mouth of a Lion. [Bunyan, 46]

That parenthetical 'and they are his pride' functions on both levels of the novel at once, meaning both 'these monstrous and conspicuous scales *allegorically represent* his sinful pride' and that he is proud of his shiny fish-scales: – that he preens himself over them as he goes about, which says something about his character as well as his appearance. There are a great many moments in the work that generate real heft and power out of the folding an allegorical spiritual numinousness out of the precisely observed and vividly evoked quiddities of actual life.

At the other end are the counter-intuitive topographies of Bunyan's allegory on its largest scale. Consider Vanity Fair. On the one hand, according to the cartography of Christian's journey this place is one city among many, alongside such places as the City of Destruction, the Town of Carnal-Policy, the Town of Stupidity and others. But in another sense, Vanity Fair is not a town *in* the world, but rather the *world itself* inside which all towns are contained: as old as the world (Bunyan specifies 5000 years) and containing within it every material thing, 'all such *Merchandize* sold, As Houses, Lands, Trades, Places, Honours, Preferments, Titles, Countries, Kingdoms, Lusts, Pleasures, and Delights of all sorts, as Whores, Bawds, Wives, Husbands, Children, Masters, Servants, Lives, Blood, Bodies, Souls, Silver, Gold, Pearls, precious Stones, and what not' [Bunyan, 70]. Within Vanity Fair are all the world's countries. something Bunyan parenthetically indicates in case we miss his allegorical point:

> So here likewise, you have the proper Places, Rows, Streets, (*viz.* Countreys and Kingdoms), where the Wares of this Fair are soonest to be found. Here is the *Brittain* Row, the *French* Row, the *Italian* Row, the *Spanish* Row, the *German* Row, where several sorts of Vanities are to be sold. But, as in other *fairs*, some one Commodity is as the chief of all the *fair*, so the Ware of *Rome* and her Merchandize is greatly promoted in *this fair*; only our *English* nation, with some others, have taken a dislike threat. [Bunyan, 70]

That a small section of Bunyan's imaginary topography can, in one sense, contain the whole landscape of which it is a part only appears paradoxical; because, in a spiritual sense, the whole vast material cosmos is an insignificant portion of the spiritual infinitude of the divine. The way reality is folded into fantasy, universality folded into location and specificity, the infinite into the finite – a Deleuzian-baroque formal logic – is important for fantasy, and is something to which I return below.

One thing for which Bunyan does not get enough credit is the depth and nuance of his characterization. Christian is a very impressively rounded creation: not an Everyman, or blank allegorical signifier onto which the reader can project themselves, but a distinct individual. This comes into particularly sharp focus when a reader turns to Part 2, and not only notes that the frequently uncertain, stumbling and doubtful Christian is now remembered as 'a lion-like man', a peerless warrior and straight-arrow – and so are invited to reflect upon the difference between this report and the rather more flawed character we had actually encountered in Part 1 – but also to see how very different Christiana is to her husband. Though her husband's epigone in terms of spiritual awakening, Christiana is by far the more sensible and grounded human being: practical, determined and immune to the more volatile and psychologically melodramatic moods that govern Christian. Her distinguishing feature is that she has visions, where Christian's distinguishing feature (and, really, this is so central to Bunyan's characterization in *Pilgrim's Progress* it's remarkable critics don't discuss it) is his depression.

In all sorts of situations Christian reverts to his signature move: he despairs. The book starts with him depressed at home ('when the morning was come, they would know how he did; he told them worse and worse') and before he even gets to the wicket gate, Christian falls into the allegorical swamp of despond ('he wallowed for a time, being grievously bedaubed with the dirt … but could not get out, because of the burden that was upon his back'). As at the beginning, so at the end: at the culmination of his pilgrimage, with his eternal celestial reward directly in front of him, what does Christian do? He despairs.

> They then addressed themselves to the Water; and entring, *Christian* began to sink, and crying out to his good Friend *Hopeful*, he said, I sink in deep waters, the Billows go over my head, all his Waves go over me! *Selah*.
>
> Then said the other, Be of good chear, my Brother, I feel the bottom, and it is good. Then said *Christian*, Ah my friend, the sorrows of death hath compassed me about; I shall not see the Land that flows with Milk and Honey; and with that a great darkness and horror fell upon *Christian*, so that he could not see before him; also here he in great measure lost his senses, so that he could neither remember nor orderly talk of any of those sweet refreshments that he had met with in the way of his Pilgrimage. [Bunyan, 121]

This final act in Christian's life recalls us to the main events of his pilgrimage, and two major ones in particular: falling into the Slough of Despond, becoming imprisoned by Giant Despair. In both cases he manages to drag another into despair/despond with him, as is often the way with this malign pathology. At most of his setbacks, despair nips at Christian's metaphorical heels: when fighting with Apollyon Bunyan says '*Christian* began to despair of life'. Variants of the phrase 'the Pilgrims then, especially Christian, began to despond in their minds' appear and reappear during Christian's journey, though there's nothing like them in Christiana's. Early in the pilgrimage the Interpreter shows Christian a man in a cage ('he sat with his eyes looking down to the ground, his hands folded together, and he sighed as if he would break his heart') who tells him 'I was once a fair and flourishing Professor' (Bunyan means: a professor faith, a Christian) 'I am *now* a Man of Despair, and am shut up in it, as in this Iron Cage. I cannot get out. Oh, *now* I cannot!' [Bunyan, 30]. Bunyan has theological reasons for seeing despair as a terrible sin, and we can believe he had personal experience when it came to clinical depression; but it's the psychological acuity of this that is so impressive. Take the episode of Christian in Giant Despair's castle. Christian leads his companion, Hopeful, from the proper road because the side-path looks more attractive, but soon enough they're lost and in the ground of Doubting Castle. It strikes me as the sort of insight a depressed person can offer about depression. You might think depression is hard to endure, and so it is; but falling into depression is lamentably easy to do, and getting out of it extremely hard. *Facilis descensus dejecto.*

In *The Origin of German Tragic Drama* Walter Benjamin seeks to distinguish tragedy in the Classical sense from the dramatization of sorrow or mourning (*Trauer*) that happens in the work of a group of minor sixteenth- and seventeenth-century German playwrights who wrote the *Trauerspiele* that give the book its title (in German: *Ursprung des deutschen Trauerspiels*). This kind of grief, Benjamin says, is the mood inherent to a particular, seventeenth-century metaphysical structure, and needs to be distinguished from the elevated or dignified suffering of classical tragedy. According to Benjamin, it is the 'comprehensive secularization of the historical' that leads to a situation in which 'History merges into the setting' to become natural history, whose affective correlative is a 'melancholic contemplation of things which derives enigmatic satisfaction from its very recognition of their transience and emptiness':

> For all the wisdom of the melancholic is subject to the nether world ... it is secured
> by immersion in the life of creaturely things, and it hears nothing of the voice of
> revelation. Everything saturnine points down into the depths of the earth.[1]

For Benjamin this particular melancholy awareness of the distance from sad earth to transcendent heaven is unlocked by allegory as form, or more specifically the way allegory developed in the seventeenth century (in other words at the time of Bunyan's intuitive deployment of the mode). He is dismissive of the later Romantic tendency to elevate the 'aestheticized symbol' at the expense of degrading the concept of allegory. *Origins of Tragic German Drama* is in large measure an attempt to recover what Benjamin thinks of as the core theological concept of the symbol that underpins authentic allegory: 'a profound but paradoxical religious unity of material and transcendental'. To read

---

[1]Benjamin, *The Origin of German Tragic Drama*, 139.

Bunyan under this aegis is not only to treat *Pilgrim's Progress* as fantasy – that is, a journey through a luminously transcendent, though still perilous, land – so much as it is to insist, as Bunyan himself repeatedly does, that the text be redirected back to the real world, to compel a particular sort of hard-labour upon its reader: awareness of death and sin, mortality and despair. 'This Book will make a Travailer of thee', Bunyan declares in his dedicatory poem, 'If by its counsel thou wilt ruled be'. *Travailer* hangs nicely between traveller and labourer/worker: somebody setting out hopefully, yes; but also somebody under Adam's curse, eating their textual bread in the sweat of their face. Bunyan's novel presents itself not as a diversion but as something to be experienced, as lived-through, and to that end it recruits allegory in just the way Benjamin thinks of the mode:

> In Benjamin's analysis, allegory is pre-eminently a kind of experience. A paraphrase of his exposition might begin by stating that allegory arises from an apprehension of the world as no longer permanent, as passing out of being: a sense of its transitoriness, an intimation of mortality, or a conviction, as in Dickinson, that 'this world is not conclusion'. Allegory is more than an outward form of expression; it is also the intuition, the inner experience itself. The form such an experience of the world takes is fragmentary and enigmatic; in it the world ceases to be purely physical and becomes an aggregation of signs … Transforming things into signs is both what allegory does – its technique – and what it is about – its content. Nor is this transformation exclusively an intellectual one: the signs perceived strike notes at the depths of one's being, regardless of whether they point to heaven, to an irretrievable past, or to the grave.[2]

On the level of didacticism, Bunyan's allegory carries a particular content but on the level of form it is doing something rather more theologically complex and ambitious, Benjaminianly fusing material and transcendental elements to ironize the 'relationship between appearance and essence', and working a nuanced and potent version of characterization as evolution, as *progress*, in such a way that it rubs sparks of sadness from the unyielding, carceral model of character as a static, Godly given. Bunyan's allegory is powerful sad stuff. And that sadness emerges in unexpected but unignorable ways in fantasy, a disaffection in which Protestantism and Bourgeois sensibility rub up against the cosmic. The Keatsian casement opens on fairylands that are wondrous, enchanted, beautiful; but they are also forlorn. From an early age I realized that the saddest line in literature I knew was the very end of *Return of the King*:

> But Sam turned to Bywater, and so came back up the Hill, as day was ending once more. And he went on, and there was yellow light, and fire within; and the evening meal was ready, and he was expected. And Rose drew him in, and set him in his chair, and put little Elanor upon his lap. He drew a deep breath. 'Well, I'm back', he said.

---

[2]Cowan, 'Walter Benjamin's Theory of Allegory', 110.

I'm not sure teenage me could have explained to you why he found this so heartbreaking. Indeed, I'm not sure sixty-year-old me is entirely sure why it continues to move him. It has something to do with the way Sam, having gone through all he has gone through, having suffered and endured and, he thought, triumphed not returns from losing all his closest friends. It has something to do with the way grand drama and enchantment devolves, inevitably, into the quotidian. It's a pathos rather than a tragedy in any Aristotelian sense, and yet it encapsulates Benjamin's notion that tragedy in its broader iteration happens when history 'loses the eschatological certainty of its redemptive conclusion and becomes secularized into a mere natural setting for the profane struggle over political power'.[3]

To return to the Victorian period. The nineteenth century saw a great vogue for 'fairy paintings', illustrations of folk tales or *A Midsummer Night's Dream*, or else images conjured out of the artists' imaginations, and engagements with a non-localized but vibrant fantasy.[4] But the great masterpiece of this mode, Richard Dadd's *The Fairy Feller's Master-Stroke*, though as energetically inventive and busy as any fairy painting, is imbued with profundities of sadness too. It took Dadd nine years to paint (1855–64) whilst he was detained in the Lunatic Asylum of Bethlem Royal Hospital – Bedlam – after murdering his father with a knife. The canvas is crowded with fantasy life, miniature fairy figures bustling in amongst gigantic blades of grass, and at the heart of the image is the 'feller', his axe aloft ready to fall on an acorn, to cleave it in two with a single stroke. A white-bearded patriarch has his right hand up, ready to cue the feller to action. All around fairy figures, soldiers, peasants, a giant dragonfly (or normal-sized dragonfly, since the other creatures are all fairy tiny) plays a trumpet. Oberon and Titania watch from the side of the canvas. It is a bustling composition, obsessively worked in immense, miniature detail, *horror vacui* and almost fractal in the way it draws the eye in. Yet it is also an intensely sad picture: the colour-palette a series of melancholic browns and tans, scrabbled over with distracting grass stems and twigs like a proto-Jackson Pollock, and as redolent as Pollock of tanglement and blockage. Near the top, Dadd's murdered father looks mournfully out of the canvas at the viewer, holding a pestle over a large stone mortar (Robert Dadd was, by profession, a chemist), whilst a young boy – presumably Richard as a child – reaches out towards his coat. What might be blood pours from the boy's fingers. The magician-like patriarch, ready to initiate the axe-blow wears a golden papal crown (Dadd saw the Pope during a visit to Rome in 1843 and had to be restrained, overwhelmed by a violent impulse to attack him). The axe held high, ready to fall, soldiers, the expectant crowd: it resembles, in a way, the execution of Charles the First, a popular topic for Victorian historical painters. The axeman is beheading – a Freudian would say, castrating – the pater patriae. It's hard to avoid the sense that this

---

[3]Peter Osborne and Charles, Matthew. 'Walter Benjamin' *Stanford Encyclopaedia of Philosophy*.
[4]See Jeremy Maas, *Victorian Fairy Painting*.

image, ostensibly about cleaving a nut to make a fairy-queen's carriage, is actually about killing the father. The painting is a complex allegory of parricide, filled with penile extrusions and its forest floor littered with acorns and horse-chestnuts, like severed heads, or symbolic testicles. The image's sorrow is comprehensible: Dadd refracting his own crime it through fairy-fantasy, miniaturizing it as if to rob it of its awful forces of guilt and regret.

# CHAPTER 6
## ARTHURIANA AND THE FANTASY TRILOGY

Arthuriana has greatly informed modern genre fantasy. Both the mood and the specific narrative shapes of the Arthurian legendarium are present in a thousand genre fantasy novels – a hidden prince who reveals himself, the battle to unify and define the kingdom, warrior-heroes abiding by a chivalric code, quests, monsters, adventures, a wizardly Merlin-figure who guides or advises the hero, complications of a love plot, the 'last battle' and, most of all, a once and future king, the Tolkienian kingly *return* – all inflected via a pseudo-medievalized worldbuilding. There are many contemporary fantasy novels that are straightforward retellings of Arthurian legend: from T H White's *The Once and Future King* (1958) – together with its spin-offs, the *Camelot* musical (1960 music Frederick Loewe, lyrics Alan Jay Lerner) and the Disney *Sword in the Stone* (1963), directed by Wolfgang Reitherman) – to Rosemary Sutcliff's *Sword at Sunset* (1963) and Marion Zimmer Bradley's *Mists of Avalon* (1983) through to many hundreds of Arthurian novelizations and film-adaptations produced in the twenty-first century so far. Beyond that, fantasy novels not specifically Arthurian in address do, in very many cases, draw on Arthurian prototypes. John Teehan identifies five elements which he argues have been ported from Arthurian myth into contemporary fantasy writing more generally: the commoner who is really a king; the wizard who guides the hero; an enchanted sword or other magic artefact; the Quest and what Teehan calls 'diverse companions', a 'round table' or fellowship.[1]

There are many medieval Romances about Arthur, in English, French and Latin, and he figures largely in those Norse medieval chivalric sagas known as the *riddararsögur*. But in the seventeenth and eighteenth centuries stories about Arthur went out of fashion. Milton contemplated writing an Arthurian epic, but decided instead to versify the Hebrew Bible in *Paradise Lost*. The 'neoclassical' era drew on ancient Greece and Rome, alongside biblical sources, for its art. But, as is noted above, Arthur came back into popularity in the nineteenth century in a major way, with a great many significant works. This second flourishing of Arthuriana is, inarguably, a significant cultural phenomenon in its own right, as well as something that pays forward in significant ways into the next century's big boom in fantasy.[2] There is, in these works, a focus on Arthur as an English rather than a Continental king. In the medieval Arthurian romances Arthur conquers the whole continent, and his knights are as much French chivalric ideals (as the surname of Lancelot du Lac indicates) as anything else. More recent versions of the story are no

---

[1] John Teehan's *Complete Guide to Writing Fantasy*.
[2] This is discussed in my *Silk and Potatoes: Contemporary Arthurian Fantasy*.

longer interested in that. Nineteenth-century Arthur and most of his twentieth-century epigones are pointedly English, defending England against incursion from pagan Saxons.

In this larger two-step history, the medieval florescence of Arthurian storytelling, its hiatus and its nineteenth- and twentieth-century reflorescence – Spenser's enormous, unfinished, Arthurian epic *The Faerie Queene* (1590–6) has an important place: the last major work in the first phase, and a direct influence on the Romantic and Victorian medievalist recrudescence in Arthurian fantasies. *Faerie Queene* is a major work of Arthurian storytelling, a major allegory and a major work of proto-fantasy. A number of knights in fellowship quest and adventure across a magical, wondrous, perilous Fantasyland, battling monsters, combatting sorcerers and dangers, rescuing maidens, in service of the 'fairy queen' herself, a version of Spenser's own monarch, Queen Elizabeth 1st. In Book One, the Redcrosse Knight, who represents holiness, travels with his lady Una, fighting the monster Errour. The two are separated when the evil wizard Archimago tricks Redcrosse into believing Una has been unchaste. Redcrosse is deceived by the false Duessa and imprisoned by the giant Orgoglio; Una overcomes various perils, encounters Arthur and is able to rescue Redcrosse. In later books, other knights – Sir Guyon, representing temperance, the lady knight Britomart who represents chastity, Sir Artegall who is justice and Sir Calidore who represents courtesy – have various adventures. Prince Arthur recurs, pursuing his infatuated love for the fairy queen herself. Spenser's verse is spacious, vivid, marvellous, and the replicated, reiterated folding-together of episodes of knight-errantry and questing, of peril overcome and magic encountered, actualize a world in which the reader can lose herself in transport.

Frank Kermode argues that readers often misunderstand the allegory of *Faerie Queene* by failing to grasp how, for Spenser and his audience, myth, history and religion braid together. Specifically, Spenser's poem expresses a distinctly *English* Protestantism, one where Una is 'the True Church', Prince Arthur the secular true knight and Redcrosse the true knight of faith. For Kermode the important thing is the breadth, as it were, of Una's signification, premised on 'the claim that English Christianity was older than the Roman church'. Renaissance Anglicans considered this claim – that Anglicanism predated Catholicism, and was the true and aboriginal version of Christianity as such – to be historically as well as theologically true. 'All the apologists of the Settlement made the appeal to history as a matter of course':

> Whoever agreed that the English was the true catholic church had to think of her history as beginning not with the convulsions of Henry VIII's reign, but … with the arrival in England of Joseph of Arimathea. For Christianity came here not from Rome, but from the East; and Una is descended from kings and queens whose 'scepters stretcht from East to Westerne shore' [*Fairie Queene*, 1.5] … but 'this catholic unity did not long continue' says Foxe — thanks of course, to the papacy. And Foxe enables us to recognise in Spenser's text the features of certain especially guilty popes who were the progenitors of Duessa.[3]

---

[3]Frank Kermode, *Shakespeare, Spenser, Donne,* 17–18.

This is the context in which Spenser's fantasy worldbuilding and allegorical signifying are best understood: 'Rome has divided the world and exiled the Catholic church. Who will restore and re-establish it?'

> The right and duty of restoring the Church to her pre-Hildebrandine purity (Canterbury independent of Rome, the sacrament administered in both kinds to the laity, no transubstantiation, proper respect for Romans 13) belonged to the heiress of Empire, to Elizabeth, whom Spenser in the dedication of his poem calls 'most high, mightie and magnificent Empresse'.

This comes centrally to inform important aspects of modern fantasy. It is, in other words, one of the things at stake in a commitment to English Arthurianism: the direct line of Christ's 'true' church from Jerusalem to Glastonbury, via Joseph of Arimathea: Eden relocated to Avalon, Christian transcendence specified as an English topographic intensity. This in turn speaks to the Anglocentrism of modern fantasy as it first emerges. Lewis and Tolkien, as Britons, understandably work versions of Englishness into their fantasy realms, but writers from other nationalities and traditions feel the pull of this too. American Ursula Le Guin talked of the effect of this on her own fantasy writing: 'Britishness of tone, setting, language, mood, everything', she wrote in 1971; 'I personally like it and prefer it vastly to the Instant American style and locale used by some writers'.[4] Not all fantasy assumes an, as it were, British default, of course; and increasingly the larger narrative of fantasy as a mode is a diversification of national and ethnic grounding, a move away from medieval Europe to global cultures. But the intense Englishness of *Faerie Queene* is, as it were, in the DNA of fantasy as it develops.

Joachim of Fiore (1135–1202) is important this larger story. Many from medieval thinkers to seventeenth-century radicals were taken by the Joachimite position that the first two of the three ages ordained by God (a 'Father' age, a 'Son' age and a 'Holy Spirit' age) had been completed, and the time for the *tertium status* was at hand. Various critics have stressed how important Joachim's cyclical historiography and 'eternal evangel' theology have been to the later development of Western society – Erich Vögelin forcefully asserts that 'Joachim created the aggregate of symbols which govern the self-interpretation of modern political society to this day'.[5] The four symbols Vögelin specifically identifies are: (1) a 'third age', which Vögelin reads into the third positive status of Auguste Comte and the Third Reich of the Nazis; (2) a leader, a king or 'Fuhrer', who shows people the way into the third age; (3) an inspired Gnostic prophet who assists the leader; and (4) a new order of a spiritual community. Nor was this some kind of niche fascination. Marjorie Reeves and Warwick Gould discuss, at length, Joachimite presences in the work of Hegel, Lessing, Schelling, Michelet, Quinet, Pierre Leroux, George Sand, George Eliot – whose *Romola* (1862–3) is, amongst other things, a fictional engagement with Joachimite ideas – Renan, Matthew Arnold, Huysmans, Yeats, D H Lawrence and James

---

[4] Le Guin, *The Language of the Night*, 29.
[5] Erich Vögelin, *The New Science of Politics*, 112.

Joyce.[6] A who's-who of nineteenth- and early-twentieth-century thought and literature: all of whom saw the broader logic of history as essentially trinitarian and looked forward in varying ways, to a 'third age', a *tertius status*, a global utopian spiritual (in some cases, literally Holy Spiritual) community to be governed by a *rex futurus*, heralded by a wizard-evangelist gnostic prophet. As Reeves and Gould note, this is at once an iteration of a wider tendency to see 'threes' as significant in some fundamental or cosmic sense – they quote Joseph de Maistre to the effect that '"thinking in threes" is a universal human style'[7] – and something more specifically Joachimite, a fantasy in the religious and indeed psychoanalytic sense that, I am suggesting, informs fantasy in a generic sense.

The connection with Fascism can't be ignored. Hitler's dream of a 'Third Reich' filtered Joachim via a specific German intellectual tradition, and the fascistic political logic of much commercial fantasy certainly shouldn't be brushed under the carpet: the valorization of the warrior-king, the conflation of politics and magic, the emphatic racialization of the built world. Norman Cohn explores in detail the throughline connecting Joachimites to 'modern Nietzschean primitivists and their elite of amoral supermen' and so on to the Nazi revival of a medievalist chiliast known as the Revolutionary of the Upper Rhine.[8] Kermode quotes Ruth Kestenberg-Gladstein's theory that 'Third Reich' was a translation of Joachim's *tertius status*. Lenin and Hitler both, according to Cohn, knowingly 'secularized and revived' traditions of apocalyptic fanaticism to serve their own political ends. 'There are aspects of Nazism and Communism alike', he notes, 'that are incomprehensible, barely conceivable even, to those whose political assumptions and norms are provided by liberal society.'[9] This is a very important truth, and one that can be restated, in more watery form, by saying: Fantasy, and its idioms of magic and myth, because they are not rational, can never really be liberal, and are structurally (i.e. ideologically) compatible with fascism.

We're at that dangerous intersection where history blurs into – or is deliberately confused with – myth. As Kermode puts it:

> Arthur is not merely a Tudor ancestor, not merely a mirror of that chivalry which preserves the virtues in a troubled time, but also a Tudor version of that ancient eschatological dream, the Emperor of the Last Days.[10]

The eschatological emphasis is particularly notable. Wagner's *Ring* is, straightforwardly, about the end of the world; *Lord of the Rings* is set at the end of the Third Age, as the world of magic and wonder the novel construes is dying, and its main storyline is an

---

[6]Marjorie Reeves and Warwick Gould, *Joachim of Fiore and the Myth of the Eternal Evangel in the Nineteenth Century*.

[7]'Ce nombre [trois] en effet se montre de tous côtés, dans le monde physique comme dans le moral, et dans les choses divines' [de Maistre, *Soirées*, quoted in Reeves and Gould, 59].

[8]Norman Cohn, *The Pursuit of the Millennium: Revolutionary Millenarians and Mystical Anarchists of the Middle Ages*.

[9]Cohn, *The Pursuit of the Millennium*, 288.

[10]Kermode, *Shakespeare, Spenser*, 21.

apocalyptic war to end wars ('I am glad you are here with me', Frodo tells Sam, as Mount Doom spews its cataclysmic lava. 'Here at the end of all things.') In George R. R. Martin's Westeros the dead have declared war on the living, and a terminal winter impends. There is an end-of-the-world valence in the fantasy mode. The wrinkle is that Tolkien adds-in a new terminus to his *Götterdämmerung* prototype: the eucatastrophe, the unexpected final happy-ending (I discuss eucatastrophe below). And there's one other element which is important here. The religio-political discourse that frames Spenser's epic is one deeply suspicious of the Papacy for political as well as theological reasons:

> The most insistent of all [Protestant] complaints against the papal antichrist is, probably, that which concerns the usurpation. Thus Foxe, like Luther, is always on the emperor's side against the pope, and, like John Jewel, holds that the emperor has the power to call General Councils and the right to exact temporal obedience from the Bishop of Rome; an argument of great importance to the English.[11]

Tolkien was of course a Catholic; but he also self-identified as English (indeed: as intensely English) and there are certainly ways in which the broader cultural assumptions of English politico-theology feed into his legendarium, and so through him into late-twentieth- and twenty-first-century commercial fantasy more generally. Spenser builds his allegorical fantasy around two knights, Arthur and Redcrosse, because he believes the secular knight and the knight of faith are both equally needful in the battle against the antichrist. Tolkien divides his anti-Sauron labour between his *quondam-et-futurus* king Aragorn on the one hand, and Gandalf, an Istar (a kind of angel) on the other, for related reasons. The Tolkienian eucatastrophe is a theological device rather than a plot-trick to toy with our emotions. It is a way of saying that our individual mortality – our human deaths, as functions of our human sinfulness – can be brilliantly if unexpectedly redeemed in Christ, such that although it looks like we are doomed and continues looking like we are doomed until the very last moment, in that lastness lies the possibility for doom to be miraculously averted. As for the individual, so for the whole: the gloom of Pagan dying, and the severity of the Old Testament version of the Law, is unexpectedly transformed into mercy by the coming of Christ. Tolkien certainly took the Trinity seriously. The manifest trinitarianism of design of *The Lord of the Rings* is not a case of him playing games with this divine pattern, but rather of him expressing something he believed true of the universe in a deep sense, and working that truth into his subcreation. And that trinitarian pattern is both prominent in the novel – perhaps its very obviousness has meant that critics have tended not to discuss it – and, through Tolkien's influence, has become a mainstay of genre fantasy more broadly.

We could put the question this way: why is the trilogy so predominant a form for publishing contemporary fantasy? It goes back to Tolkien, although the decision to issue *Lord of the Rings* as three separate volumes was originally publisher George Allen &

---

[11]Kermode, *Shakespeare, Spenser,* 17.

Unwin's rather than Tolkien's – he hoped to publish *The Lord of the Rings* as a single volume divided internally into six component 'books', but was persuaded to publish the work as three separate volumes to spread the financial risk. We might, in other words, think of the 'trilogy' form as something merely adventitious that became 'baked-in' to the structure of fantasy (and other) publishing because of the extreme success of Tolkien's book. But this would be a mistake. That Tolkien sometimes spoke of his major work as, variously, a trilogy and as a unity, does not adduce contradiction, since it is entirely the nature of the Christian trinity to be both three and one at the same time. Tolkien was aware of the nineteenth- and twentieth-century tradition of neo-Joachimite thought in which not just history but the universe itself divide into a 'father', a 'son' and a 'holy spirit' logic. *The Lord of the Rings* takes place in a 'Third Age', after the First Age in which God the Father creates the world and the 'Second Age' in which Sauron rises and falls and the world is remade from a flat plate into a globe.

The question of why this peculiarly English religio-mythology has migrated so far out of specifically English contexts to become a strand of world culture – fantasy now being a globally popular literature – is larger than Tolkien. It's there in *The Faerie Queene*, hidden in plain sight behind the allegorical mode of the poem, where (to quote Mary Thomas Crane) 'allegory repeatedly breaks down into more complex and confusing figures like metaphor'. It's because this is a function of the poem's worldbuilding, and so says something about fantasy as a whole: 'throughout the *Fairie Queene* Spenser presents us with a world – landscape and characters – which, he repeatedly tells us, ought to be intelligible but rarely is'.[12] We could say something similar about Middle Earth, Narnia, Westeros. It is integral to the mode.

Tolkien's insistence that his fantasy is *not* an allegory, his cordial dislike of the mode, expresses itself, in fact, at that moment in the preface to his big novel at which he reports that people had assumed *The Lord of the Rings* was an allegory of the Second World War, a reading Tolkien denied, although – interestingly – his was a denial offered not on grounds of applicability as such but rather of specific inappositeness:

> The real war does not resemble the legendary war in its process or its conclusion. If it had inspired or directed the development of the legend, then certainly the Ring would have been seized and used against Sauron; he would not have been annihilated but enslaved, and Barad-Dûr would not have been destroyed but occupied. Saruman, failing to get possession of the Ring, would in the confusion and treacheries of the time have found in Mordor the missing links in his own researches into Ring-lore, and before long he would have made a Great Ring of his own with which to challenge the self-styled Ruler of Middle-earth. In that conflict both sides would have held hobbits in hatred and contempt: they would not long have survived even as slaves.

---

[12]Crane, *Losing Touch with Nature*, 101–02.

Tolkien's point is not that *The Lord of the Rings* exists in some hermeneutically sealed-away bubble within which it signifies only itself, but rather that its broader relevance works according to the right sorts of decoding. The issue is not allegory as such but of a too narrow conception of how allegory works. 'Of course my story is not an allegory of Atomic power', he wrote to a friend in the later 1950s, 'but of Power (exerted for domination)'.[13] Tolkien's fantasy means, in extra-textual and complex ways, because he believed the world as such had been created to mean, in extramundial and complex ways. Kermode distinguishes between the trivial or obvious allegories of *Fairie Queene* and the more involved, opaque and complex allegories, and there's something similar at work in *Lord of the Rings*.

This is to elaborate a more straightforward, or less contentious, point: that the way fantasy as a mode re-enchants is always already compromised by a dangerous elision of the numinous into the political realm. To quote John Millbank:

> The tension therefore between priest and king is still more complex than theology has always allowed, and more genuine to the entire nature of Christianity than is usually recognised. The Christological conundrum of kingship means that the king is, for here and now, insofar as he is concerned with natural matters, 'above' the priestly function. But as regards matters pertaining to the ultimate welfare of our soul, the king is subordinate to the priest. Yet in a third sense the latter's role is penultimate, not ultimate. As regards human 'spirit', the whole person and the ultimate resurrection of the whole person, soul and body, the king and the concerns of kingship are symbolically more ultimate, since they are a remote foreshadowing of the eschaton. If Christ is to return, then so too is Arthur, so also Charlemagne, Frederick II and King Sebastian of Portugal (lost in battle against the Moors and one day to return to shore from the sea, where he is rumoured to wander over the waves).[14]

The *rexque futurus* element is clearly important, both to (political) myth and to fantasy. Its connection to the Holy Grail, which is to say, to the rebus that it encodes – England as the aboriginal Christian land, Protestantism the aboriginal Christian faith, and Roman Catholicism a kind of aberration from that ancient truth – is not adventitious. It is no coincidence that Tolkien takes the 'quest motif' that derives, ultimately, from the *Sangraal* legend and *inverts* it, so that the point is to destroy, not recover, the grail. And indeed his quote-unquote 'grail' has a big hole in it, such that we call it a ring.

Contemporary fantasy authors, most of whom start out of fans, internalize the tropes and conventions of their chosen genre such that even those writers seeking to reverse their polarity tend to do so in terms of moral valence or socio-economic sophistication rather than any more fundamental or formal dissolution. These are simply the props and settings and assumptions of the mode, and we have forgotten, if we ever knew, why we have them.

---

[13]*Letters of J.R.R. Tolkien*, 246.
[14]Milbank, *Beyond Secular Order*, 250.

# CHAPTER 7
## WAGNER AND TOLKIEN

Wagner's staging of the love-story of Tristram and Iseult emphasized the intensity of the doomed connection: the richness and magnificence of the musical language of the piece, the haunting 'love-chord' and the chromatic expressivism, serve the drama. The Arthurian setting and the magical appurtenances frame the notion of love's intensity as enchantment, at once a fulfilment and a lostness. Love is also part of the tapestry of *Der Ring des Nibelungen* (1869–76), although in this, Wagner's masterpiece, the scope is greater. Across four lengthy operas [*Das Rheingold* (1869); *Die Walküre* (1870); *Siegfried* (1876); *Götterdämmerung* (1876)] Wagner tells a story of gods and mortals, mighty warriors and Valkyries (female psychopomps from Norse mythology who guide the souls of the dead to the afterlife in Odin's hall Valhalla), wicked dwarfs and terrifying dragons, flying horses and magic helmets, of battles, quests and ultimately the coming of Ragnarok, the apocalypse of the gods and the end of the world. It is designed as a *Gesamtkunstwerk*, a 'complete work of art', blending stage drama, poetry, orchestral music and visual art into a whole. It is a fantasy text of immense grandeur and influence. It is also a statement of German national identity, and was appropriated by the Nazis as an assertion of Germanic supremacy: Adolf Hitler often attended performances at Bayreuth, and in a 1922 speech praised Wagner's works for 'glorifying the heroic Teutonic nature … greatness lies in the heroic'.[1] Wagner last great opera *Parsifal* (1882) returns to Arthurian myth, telling the story of the titular Sir Percival for the Holy Grail. It is a work of superb musical beauty that is at the same time marinated in anti-Semitism – Parsifal, an Aryan knight of truth, overcoming the Jewish-coded sorcerer Klingsor.

The relationship between these Fantasies and twentieth-century fantasy writing is a rich one. The *Ring* opera tells the story of a magical ring that grants its owner great power, and of a heroic warrior who overcomes a dragon, with the help of a talking bird – we might think of *The Hobbit* – and of a mighty quest and of the ending of an age of the world, as is the case in *Lord of the Rings*. Tolkien would not have thanked us for the comparison. His story is not the same as the *Ring* cycle, his ring, he insisted crossly, not

---

[1]Spotts, *Bayreuth: A History of the Wagner Festival*, 140.

the same as Alberich's ring.[2] But we can be honest: much of the heft and force of *Lord of the Rings* derive from the way Tolkien draws on the same broader cultural, mythic, northern-European heritage as Wagner. What saves *Lord of the Rings* is that it is not about Germany, or about England; or to be more precise, that it is about England and Germany only secondarily, in an eloquently oblique manner. Tolkien found a way of articulating the same deep-rooted cultural concerns in a way that avoids being poisoned by the cultural specificity of European Fascism. This doesn't entirely absolve Tolkien, as far as racial and ideological content goes. The point here is not a value judgement of his fiction, so much as an explanation for why *Lord of the Rings* has done so extraordinarily well – resonated so powerfully with so many people – in the post-war period. It supplied the gap that more culturally specific art had supplied before that kind of art was discredited by the 1940s. There was nothing inevitable about Tolkien's fame and influence. It might have fallen to a different writer. But the particular kind of writer Tolkien was, and the specific ways in which his (often very idiosyncratic) versions of magical quasi-historical fantasy manifested, have had large-scale consequences for the mode as it now exists.

Theodor Adorno argues that Wagner's appeal to a timeless, mythic, fantasy realm of gods and heroes is not something separate from his bourgeois German respectability, but precisely an iteration of it. 'The power of the bourgeoisie over Wagner is so absolute that as a bourgeois he finds himself unable to satisfy the requirements of bourgeois respectability.'[3] He embodies 'an early example of the changing function of the bourgeois category of the individual':

> In his hopeless struggle with the power of society, the individual seeks to avert his own destruction by identifying with that power and then rationalizing the change of direction as authentic individual fulfilment … the focal points of decay in the bourgeois character, in terms of its own morality, are the prototypes of its subsequent transformation in the age of totalitarianism.

---

[2]'Nettled, Tolkien retorted "both rings were round, and there the resemblance ceases"' [*Letters* 306]. His biographer Humphrey Carpenter uses this example to support his claim that 'comparison of his Ring with the Nibelungenlied and Wagner always annoyed Tolkien'; Carpenter also alludes to Tolkien, while still a schoolboy, making 'a passing jibe at Wagner whose interpretation of the myths he held in contempt'. Some subsequent commentaries have taken this at face value; Giddings, for example, sees any Wagnerian associations with Tolkien as a 'taint' derived from his mixing 'with the rabid Wagnerite C.S. Lewis'. The shift towards a more objective and informed appraisal begins with Tom Shippey, who points out that Tolkien had an intense dislike for people noticing superficial resemblances between his works and others, especially when this tended to obscure what really mattered about them. Shippey is the first to directly challenge Tolkien's dismissal of any Wagnerian connection: 'the motifs of the riddle-contest, the cleansing fire, the broken weapon preserved for an heir, all occur in both works, as of course does the theme of "the lord of the Ring as the slave of the Ring", *des Ringes Herr als des Ringes Knecht*' [Shippey, *The Road to Middle-earth*, 343–4]. Moreover, Shippey implies a reason why Tolkien might have responded to Wagner, albeit negatively: he was 'one of several authors [including Shakespeare] with whom Tolkien had a relationship of intimate dislike' and who he believed 'had got something very important not quite right' [Jamie McGregor, 'Two Rings to Rule Them All: a Comparative study of Tolkien and Wagner', 133].

[3]Adorno, *In Search of Wagner*, 7.

This interrelation between the bourgeois and the mythic-legendary is the structure of the portal fantasy: the twentieth-century Pevensie children passing through the wardrobe into the Fantasyland of Narnia. But the distinction is almost always enacted in immersive fantasies as well, as respectable burghers Bilbo, and later Frodo, step out into the enchanted, perilous wider world of Middle Earth. Middle Earth is geographically divided between the bourgeois hobbits of the north west and medieval city-states, and even older, the and the feudal horselords, of the South. Beorn may spend half his time as a bear, but he keeps as tidy a little bourgeois house, with all the creature comforts, as any hobbit, and bourgeois possessiveness for material objects is shown, through Gollum's longevity and through the fundamental, stubborn *toughness* of his Being-in-the-World, to be superior to Boromir's feudal puissance in terms of holding out against the Ring. Tom Shippey's observations on the etymological connections – the sort of connections that particularly appealed to Tolkien – between the word *burglar*, Bilbo's dwarf-assisting career, and *bourgeois*, Bilbo's social identity – have been previously mentioned.

One of the threads of particular interest in tracing the Tolkien and C. S. Lewis pedigree of fantasy from the 1950s into the twenty-first century is the fact that two Christian writers, writing tacitly (or in Lewis's cases allegorically-explicitly) Christian fantasy, came to influence a whole tradition not specifically Christian, or drawing on quite other religious traditions. For many fans, perhaps, the Christian element in Middle Earth or Narnia is something they simply ignore. But the fact that these two were Christian and wrote Christian works is pertinent. We could frame it as the *Beowulf* problem, since that's a poem that parses pre-Christian, pagan and monstrous-magical story material through a notionally Christian frame. Considering how important *Beowulf* was to Tolkien's own imaginative development, and with the merest glance at the great mass of commercial fantasy, we can see the tension between the pagan-mythic and the Christian-allegorical in fantasy in terms of this more strictly social-historical, ideological tension. The *Ring* is all Germanic legend and no Christianity, but Wagner not only wanted to express his grandiose mythic pagan-Nativism, he also wanted to pay the bills. 'There was one particular remark which cut Nietzsche to the quick', Adorno notes:

> The conversation had turned to the poor attendance of the Bayreuth Festival. Nietzsche's sister reports that Wagner had once observed angrily. 'The Germans no longer wished to have anything to do with heathen Gods and heroes; what they wanted was something Christian.'[4]

So much for *Gott ist tod*. *Parsifal* swiftly followed, to supply this market need: not only the most explicitly Christian of Wagner's operas, but also the most nakedly anti-Semitic. Modern fantasy emerges out of an emulsion of Pagan and Christian. It is the bourgeois Christianity of Bunyan, of *Idylls of the King* and Wagner's final compromise with his

---

[4]Adorno, *In Search of Wagner*, 12.

audience, through Tolkien and Lewis, that feeds the river that becomes the delta of the modern genre.

This of course has to do with magic, that necessary component of fantasy worldbuilding, which we can understand in terms not only of the spiritually transcendent, the numinous, but in the reified logic of magical systems, spells, wizards with which fantasy is so liberally supplied:

> A contradiction of all autonomous art is the concealment of the labour that went into it, but in high capitalism, with the complete hegemony of exchange-value and with the contradictions arising out of that hegemony, autonomous art becomes both problematic and programmatic at the same time. This is the objective explanation for what is generally thought of in psychological terms as Wagner's mendacity. To make works of art into magical objects means that men worship their own labour because they are unable to recognize it as such. … The work of art endorses the sentiment normally denied by ideology: work is degrading.[5]

This is why fantasy is filled with aristocrats and warriors, or at the least of hobbits of independent means: with travellers and questers (which is to say: with holidaymakers) – as, also, with rascals, thieves, rogues and the like. The point is that fantasy cannot be written in the John Berger, or even the Zola mode: not because of the generic mismatch of fantasy as *le naturalisme*, or not only for that reason, but because fantasy is a realm where work as such is always transmuted magically *into magic*. There's also the prominence given to swords in this mode. Not usually to rapiers or xiphoi; but to *Excaliburs* and *Glamdrings* and *Terminus Ests* – that is, big swords, mighty swords, claymores and broadswords, to say nothing of all those axes, those hammers, all those battles, all that bashing and crashing. It's a way of externalizing the genre's rationale of force, the emblematic articulation of forcefulness as such:

> Wagner not only took up the bourgeois profession of conductor, he was also the first composer to write conductor's music in the grand style. This is not said with the intention of echoing the threadbare reproaches of unoriginality, of with the design of unduly emphasising mere orchestral skill – something that pales by the side of Wagner's overwhelming art of instrumentation. What it alludes to is the fact that his music is conceived in terms of the gesture of striking a blow and that the whole idea of beating is fundamental to it.[6]

Adorno doesn't specifically mention, although presumably he has in mind, the music that famously accompanies the descent to Nibelheim in *Das Rheingold*, scored for not one but *eighteen* hammers-and-anvils (tuned to F, three octaves apart). A related point has to do with the sheer size of many of our fantasy texts.

---

[5] Adorno, *In Search of Wagner*, 72.
[6] Adorno, *In Search of Wagner*, 20.

Compared to Viennese classicism, Wagner's music reckons with people who listen to it from a great distance, much as Impressionist paintings require to be viewed from a greater distance than earlier paintings. To listen from a greater distance also means listening less attentively. The audience of these giant works lasting many hours is thought of an unable to concentrate – something not unconnected with the fatigue of the citizen in his leisure time. [Adorno, 22]

Something similar may be true of the manifest textual bloat of modern fantasy: not only the shelf-sagging bulk, but its *stasis*, the narrative *inertia* of Robert Jordan, George R. R. Martin and their ilk. This is literature not written to be consumed on the level of individual, marvellous sentences, but by the metric tonne. Aficionado may feel such bulk only appropriate to the epic heft and scope of their favourite stories, but I wonder if the point is not heft, for which one needs *density* – contemporary fantasy novels may spread over thousands of pages, but many have the texture of expanded polystyrene – so much as a kind of defocusing, an attempt at blurring the focus on the specificities of the whole. Fantasy plays with history, as with myth, as it plays with an ethos simultaneously bourgeois and feudal. Too close an attentiveness to these contradictions is to be discouraged.

Wagner showed himself to be bourgeois through and through in his conviction that poetic depth is synonymous with the omission of historical specificity. His image of the universally human requires the dismantling of what he supposes to be relative and contingent in favour of the idea of an unvarying human nature. What is actually substantial appears to him as a residue. He therefore finds himself reduced to a stratum of subject-matter that acknowledges neither history nor the supernatural nor even the natural, but which lies beyond all such categories. Essence is drawn into an omnisignificant immanence; the immanent is held in thrall by symbol. This stratum, where all is undifferentiated, is that of myth. Its sign is ambiguity; its twilight is a standing invitation to merge irreconcilables – the positivistic with the metaphysical – because it firmly rejects both the transcendental and the factual. [Adorno, 104]

With this, I think, we approach something really key about the post-Tolkienian fantasy tradition. The 'universally human' becomes, in these kinds of books, pseudo-ethicized, narratively situated in a Cosmic drama of Good versus Evil. Actual moral choice, and the more destabilizing moral complexity of actual life, is not the currency of these sorts of tales. And it's surely the case that Commercial fantasy does indeed reject both the transcendental and the factual. In the case of Tolkien the absence of gods (except, in the deep background of the text, and Silmarillionic exegesis) and the absence of 'actual' England, Germany, 'Northern Europe' and so on, are revealed as versions of one another. I suppose the problem with this as a reading of Wagner is precisely the problem of the actual political – which is to say, historical – uses to which the Nazis put his art (uses to which Tolkien really can't be recruited). Adorno's 'authentic historical conflict' actually only describes one kind of pseudo-historical, or Scottian, mode; where history-as-ideology is immanent throughout Wagner.

> If in the *Ring* mythic violence and legal contract are confounded, this not only confirms an intuition about the origins of legality, it also articulates the experience of the lawlessness of a society dominated in the name of law by contract and property.[7]

If the lawlessness and violence of 'Grimdark' fantasy are part of its popular appeal (as an imaginative release for those times when Civilisation and its Discontents chafe against our senses of self: 'in such a place I can kill who I like … ') then that very lawlessness is, as Adorno suggests here, *grounded* in a minutely and even pettifogging sense of contract law as such: the precise nature of the bloodline of the individual 'rightfully' king, the minute particulars of the magical prophesy that must be proved true. Indeed I wonder if we can go further, and say that the copresence of Might-is-Right mythic violence with a universe magically structured by bourgeois contract law (e.g. the way the witches' prophesies in *Macbeth* are precisely honoured in their deal with Macbeth, or the contract-lawyer 'I am no man' gloating of Eowyn discovering a loophole in the Nazgul's magic charm) is foundational for the genre as such. Nor is this an arbitrary feature of the genre. It's how fantasy links itself back to life:

> The opacity and omnipotence of the social process is then celebrated as a metaphysical mystery by the individual who becomes conscious of it and yet ranges himself on the side of its dominant forces. Wagner has devised the ritual of permanent catastrophe. [Adorno, 108]

Earlier I mentioned, briefly, the Weberian notion of 'subrogation' as (in Andrea Erizi's reading) a necessary parallel to secularization. For Erizi, a key example of that in modernity is history – history, we might say, as such, as conceptualized, as underpinning Whiggish and Marxist worldviews both. 'A proper surrogate of a religious world view', is how Erizi puts it, 'is the philosophy of history'.[8] It might be a stretch to dignify contemporary fantasy's obsession with its own pan-generational chronologies a *philosophy* of History. When Tolkien adds lengthy annalistic appendices to *Lord of the Rings* spelling out in exhausting (though, as later publications make clear, not exhaustive) detail he does not philosophize his historicism. He simply presents it, as an unleavened lump, alongside the more carefully worked bourgeois-novelistic narrative of *The Lord of the Rings* itself.

---

[7]Adorno, *In Search of Wagner,* 108.

[8]'Philosophy of history and Christian religion share a common framework which sets the need for redemption at the core of the way they look at the world. … "Their [the disprivileged] particular need is for release from suffering. They do not always experience this need for salvation in a religious form, as shown by the example of the modern proletariat. Furthermore, their need for religious salvation, where it exists, may assume diverse forms"' [Weber quoted in Erizi, 237].

In all this is the question of how conservative, with a small as well as a large 'C', fantasy is. Jürgen Habermas, writing in 1990, identified 're-enchantment' as core to twentieth-century Conservatism for whom 'a disenchanted modernity has to be satisfied by a process of re-enchantment'. For Habermas, Conservatism adopts 'an affirmative stance towards social modernity, and the devaluation of cultural modernity' requiring 'the legacy of tradition be preserved in as static a form as possible'.[9] Conservatives embrace processes of modernization in terms of the economy and administration, but reject them in cultural and religious realms, where they require 'the legacy of tradition ... be preserved in as static a form as possible'. Where stasis and preservation are insufficient to counter modernity, instauration, even 'nostalgic invention of traditions' may be required. Key fantasy works undertake precisely this.

---

[9]Habermas, *The New Conservatism*, 201.

# CHAPTER 8
## CHILDREN'S FANTASY

The 1860s saw the publication of a number of wide-reaching and influential fantasy novels for children. Two have been previously mentioned, Kingsley's *The Water-Babies* (1863) and Carroll's two *Alice* books (1865, 1871). One of these remains influential to this day, and has indeed exercised a shaping force upon modern fantasy – Carroll's. Kingsley's book has fallen out of currency, partly because its aggressively didactic and proselytizing religiousness jars for modern readers, partly because it contains undigested chunks of racist and eugenicist exhortation. But for half a century and more *Water-Babies* was one of the most-read children's books in the world, and its particular mode of fantasia, a fable of instauration, has important implications for what comes after. Still, it is Alice that has endured. In the words of Juliet Dusinberre, 'by the time of Carroll's death in 1898 *Alice* had supplanted *The Pilgrim's Progress* in the popular imagination'.[1] And there are parallels between *Alice* and Bunyan, but the differences are more momentous for fantasy as a developing mode.

The *Water-Babies* concerns Tom, a chimney sweep boy who 'could not read nor write, and did not care to do either; and he never washed himself, for there was no water up the court where he lived. He had never been taught to say his prayers. He never had heard of God, or of Christ.' He is, that is to say, Kingsley's version of unaccommodated man, the thing itself: a mashing together of the categories of 'innocence' and 'ignorance'. Because of this Tom's story is one of spiritual redemption, inflected via Kingsley's muscular Anglicanism, and not least of the muscularity of it is the way it burleys straight through centuries-old church debates. So, Tom, accidentally drowning, has died and also not died; in the water he transforms into a 'water baby', a tiny riverine creature with external gills, something like an axolotl. He lives in the river for a while, admiring carefully described dragonflies – another symbol of the rebirth of the dazzling soul from the chaff of the earthly body. Eventually he washes down to the sea, and has adventures there, encountering many talking sea-creatures and other magical entities. *Water-Babies* is, for all its copiousness, a Bunyanesque progress from sin to Protestant redemption. Bunyan's Christian carries his sin as a great pack on his back, which drops off at the foot of the cross. Kingsley's Tom carries his sin externally: blackened by his life up chimneys, like Blake's 'Little Black Boy' his soul is white; and washed clean by the river this becomes apparent.

Alice's progress is unencumbered by sin. She is something more than Tom, and her fantastical idiom is more fully Nonsense – a long tradition which received a boost in the nineteenth century with Edward's Lear's nonsense limericks and poems – 'The Owl and

---

[1]Juliet Dusinberre, *Alice to the Lighthouse: Children's Books and Radical Experiments in Art*, 1.

the Pussycat' (1870) is a fantasy quest with talking animals in ballad form – and Carroll's fiction. Nonsense involves the juxtaposition of recognizable elements in unusual, unexpected or irrational ways, subverting linguistic and representational conventions in ways that ludically challenge logical reasoning. Nonsense is fun, and its departures from simple mimesis – its talking animals and monsters, its abrupt transitions and strange landscapes – overlap it with fantasy. It is worth dwelling on this point for a moment, since there is a version of fantasy that sees internally consistent worldbuilding and rigorously worked-through magic systems as at the heart of the mode, and would repudiate the claim that there is anything absurdist or nonsensical involved. This, though, would be to miss a power-source of fantasy. After all, too rationalist and internally consistent an approach to writing the mode leads to the least effective, the dullest fantasy novels. Tolkien spent a long time rendering his Middle Earth internally consistent, and mapping out its history; yet it remains a novel in which trees walk and talk, Tom Bombadil pops up singing nonsense rhymes and then disappears, in which a child-sized modern individual has adventures underground, passes through wonderland into a sort of mirror-dimension, finds a ring, loses a ring and returns home for tea.

The story of the Alice books is simple, and well-known: Alice, a young English girl who, drowsing in the Oxfordshire sun one summer's day, sees a white rabbit run past wearing a waistcoat and consulting a pocket-watch. A bourgeois rabbit, anxious about timekeeping. Following, she falls down a rabbit hole into a huge and various underground realm in which she encounters many more talking animals, whilst shrinking and expanding her own bodily size repeatedly, eventually working her way into a royal court based upon playing cards. After a climactic courtroom scene she wakes to discover it was all a dream. The sequel *Looking-Glass* is set in the autumn rather than the summer, and starts with Alice indoors; passing through the mirror in her room she finds a world modelled on a game of chess, passing from square to square (each one a field bounded by a little brook) as a pawn, meeting knights and queens, until she reaches the final square and becomes a queen herself. These two peripatetic and episodic adventure narratives are crammed with fantastical inventive detail, as well as numerous, hilarious parodies of children's tales and didactic verse. Carroll was a mathematician, an academic specialist in formal logic. Where Kingsley's outspreading inventiveness is constrained by his theological impulse, Carroll's equally freewheeling creation imagination is informed and impelled by his fascination with rules, logic, paradox, his fondness for games and energies.

Nonsense has a long pedigree. Indeed, in oral form ('Hey Diddle Diddle') its history vanishes into the backward and abysm of time. Its printed mode dates to the Elizabethan and Jacobean eras.[2] By the time of Carroll and Lear we encounter two quite different modes of English nonsense, represented by the two. To quote David Langford:

> Carroll's Alice books offer a kind of intellectual nonsense based on perverse 'Read-the-Small-Print' interpretations of logic and idiom, while Lear exploits

---

[2]See Noel Malcolm, *The Origins of English Nonsense.*

disconcerting whimsies, non sequiturs and unexplained nonce-words like 'runcible'. G K Chesterton, argued in 'A Defence of Nonsense' [in *The Defendant* (1901)] that this made Lear the superior fabulist, a view not universally shared.[3]

Earlier I quoted Juliet Dusinberre to the effect that Carroll supplanted Bunyan in the popular imaginary around the turn of the century: a significant shift. Allegory (as in Lewis's *Narnia* novels) continues through fantasy; nonsense is, as it were, allegory without the deictic specifiers. If Bunyan's characters and places were not given the sign-posting names they have, we would read his story as a fairy-tale adventure, unburdened by the real-world applicability, and in many ways as nonsensical. The *Alice* books are, we could say, Bunyanesque allegory shorn of those markers, or set free from them. There have been attempts by critics to reinstate, or say rather to impose, pseudo-allegorical indices into the text – for instance, to read the stories after the manner by which Freudians 'read' dreams, such that all the jumbled oddnesses and potent strangeness become merely the manifest content that relates to a series of latent subconscious meanings, to do with desire, anxiety and sexuality. But this is in an important sense to miss the point of nonsense as a mode – and of fantasy, too. To mill the process of interpretation too finely is to miss the point of what the *Alice* books are doing.

In Peter Ackroyd's autobiographical novel *English Music* (1992), the protagonist Timothy Harcombe recalls his upbringing, home-educated by his eccentric, widowed father Clement, a faith-healer. Clement reads his son, blending together *Pilgrim's Progress* and Carroll's *Alice* books:

> But on the top shelf were what my father called the 'special' books, by which he meant the books which he was reading to me at the time. I cannot now remember all of them, but I do recall how on these particular winter nights he had begun *The Pilgrim's Progress* and *Alice in Wonderland*, reading them alternately in case I became too bored with the adventures of Alice or too fearful over the hazards of Pilgrim.[4]

Young Timothy is struck more by the illustrations, which he sees, peering past his father as he reads to him: Carroll's grim-faced Duchess with her baby ('I always assumed that the baby was about to be boiled and eaten, and that the expression on the Duchess's face was one of hunger') and Bunyan's Christian, with his huge pack weighing him down, 'an expression of horror on his face', which Timothy considers, even from his adult vantage, 'a true image of life'.

The similarities between the two books are easy enough to notate, and are numerous enough to tempt a person into thinking that Carroll is specifically rewriting *Pilgrim's Progress* with a Victorian child, rather than a seventeenth-century adult, at its heart.

---

[3]Langford, 'Nonsense', in Clute and Grant (eds) *The Encyclopaedia of Fantasy*, 691.
[4]Ackroyd, *English Music*, 23.

'As I walked through the wilderness of this world,' Bunyan's narrator begins, ' … I laid me down in that place to sleep: and, as I slept, I dreamed a dream. I dreamed'. So too Alice, in the Oxfordshire countryside (perhaps not exactly a wilderness) lies down and dreams a dream. Bunyan's dream is of a man, anxious, weighed down with the weight of a huge pack on his back; Alice's is of an anxious rabbit, running by. Bunyan's Christian falls into the Slough of Despond; Alice falls into a pool of tears. Bunyan yearns to pass through the narrow wicket gate that will set him on the path to paradise; Alice finds a narrow doorway through which she glimpses an Edenic garden, and yearns to go there. What prevents Christian from passing through the narrow gate is his huge sin-pack; what stops Alice is her too-large size. Christian sheds his pack by grace of Christ; Alice adjusts her size by the – quasi-eucharistic, as several critics have suggested – eating and drinking of materials laid out for her.

But where Bunyan's book is a didactic allegory, Carroll's book is a ludic anti-allegory. It's not that Carroll disrespected *Pilgrim's Progress*. On the contrary, he loved it: he read it over and over as a child, and was still reading it as an adult: in the summer of 1862 – two years before drafting the first version of Alice – assisting his Christ Church contemporary William Ranken at the latter's church services, Carroll incorporated readings from *The Pilgrim's Progress* [Carroll, *Diaries*, 4: 74]. But the *Pilgrim's Progress* is a thoroughly didactic work, designed, constructed and sent in the work to teach people to be better Christians, to lead more moral and religious lives. The Alice books are fundamentally *ludic* works, written to entertain by – amongst other things – imaginatively upending and parodying the traditions of didactic children's writing that had gone before. Issac Watts writes ''Tis the Voice of the Sluggard' to urge kids to be industrious rather than lazy; Carroll writes ''Tis The Voice of the Lobster' because it delights him, and he knows it will delight us to read its surrealist nonsense. Bunyan's Christian *progresses*: he learns, improves, works towards his final destination – heaven – finally arriving there. Most of Alice's questions go unanswered (why *is* a raven like a writing desk?) and she ends up back where she started. Bunyan's book is linear, in shape and in interpretive logic. Carroll's is a gorgeous curlicue. Gillian Beer talks of the Alice books' 'resilience' as being bound-up with precisely 'the work's resistance to allegory'.

This is more laconically, brilliantly, captured in Lewis's *The Hunting of the Snark* (1871), a balladic poem in eight sections, which with conscious archaism Carroll calls 'fitts', that tells of an eminently English-bourgeois of exploration voyage across the sea to a perilous realm of crags, chasms and monsters. The crew, identified by their occupations, all of which, nonsensically coincidentally, begin with the letter 'B' (Butcher, Baker, Banker, Barrister, Bonnet-maker, Broker, Billiard-marker and a talking Beaver) are led by a Bellman, who tolls them across a featureless ocean to the land where they can find, and capture, a Snark. This monster is a congeries of features: feathered, or whiskered, biting or scratching, somniferous (a Snark's 'habit of getting up late' means that it 'breakfasts at five-o'clock tea/And dines on the following day'), humourless, fire-breathing, fond of bathing machines – another 'B'-word – to the point of actually carrying these massive objects around with it (so, Snarks are evidently very large). Though the expedition is searching Snarks, they must be careful, for some Snarks are a mysterious variant known as 'boojums', and to encounter of one those is to 'softly and suddenly vanish away, and never be met with again'. If the Snark is a type of fantasy dragon, the Boojum is something more: annihilation, kenosis, a mortal transcendence. Carroll wrote the poem because he woke one day from a dream with the poem's final line in his head: 'For the Snark *was* a Boojum, you see'. From this is narrative arc is determinable: after various adventures, encounters with dangerous bandersnatches and other perils, the Baker foolishly rushes at a Snark.

> They hunted till darkness came on, but they found
> Not a button, or feather, or mark,
> By which they could tell that they stood on the ground
> Where the Baker had met with the Snark.
> In the midst of the word he was trying to say,
> In the midst of his laughter and glee,
> He had softly and suddenly vanished away –
> For the Snark was a Boojum, you see.

The fantasy here is dreamlike: a manifest apprehension of enchantment and peril, that articulates a latent narrative of imperialism and colonialism, as much fantasy, forged in the Imperial century, does. Carroll was repeatedly quizzed on the meaning of his poem, and of its terminology, and always replied that he did not know and could not explain. But the dreamwork expresses itself. 'Snark' is an Old English word (cognate with *snore* and *snort*) for snoring whilst asleep. 'Boojum' portmanteaus the onomatopoeic ejaculation of fright, 'boo!', with a word that came into English via Urdu as part of the British annexation of India: *jum* or *jhum*: 'to rain heavily', 'to glitter, sparkle, shine', 'splendour refulgence, the clash or clatter or metallic substance'.[5] This dreadful sublimity of destruction, glittering in the dark, is the caustical truth of fantasy as such. That Carroll's poem is funny, quirky, fantastical does not interfere or denature this profound existential encounter. Rather the work uses its nonsensical comedy to construe profundity: the existential cul-de-sac of imperial conquest, the dark transcendence of de-buffering modernity's consciousness into fantasy's decanted religion. *The Hunting of the Snark* is a major fantasy work because of, not despite, its rendering into nonsense, comedy and poetics.

Another key fantasy poem is Rossetti's *Goblin Market* (1864), in which the bourgeois life of two sisters, Lizzie and Laura, is invaded by the grotesque parade of goblin men who sell addictive fruit to Laura, and then disappear. As her afrugivorious sister is wasting away, even unto death, Lizzie bravely seeks out the phantasmagoric goblin creatures, and buys some more of their fruit to take back to Laura. The goblins insist she eat it there and then; when they refuse they assault her.

---

[5]Joseph T. Thompson, *A Dictionary in Oordoo and English: Compiled from the Best Authorities* (1838), 199.

Their looks were evil.
Lashing their tails
They trod and hustled her,
Elbowed and jostled her,
Clawed with their nails,
Barking, mewing, hissing, mocking,
Tore her gown and soiled her stocking,
Twitched her hair out by the roots,
Stamped upon her tender feet,
Held her hands and squeezed their fruits
Against her mouth to make her eat. [Rossetti, *Goblin Market*, 397–407]

She holds firm, and rushes home to Laura, covered in these magical, calling out to her sister:

'Did you miss me?
Come and kiss me.
Never mind my bruises,
Hug me, kiss me, suck my juices
Squeezed from goblin fruits for you,
Goblin pulp and goblin dew.
Eat me, drink me, love me'.

Laura does so, and, in a scene if remarkable sensual intensity (she 'clung about her sister,/ Kissed and kissed and kissed her:/She kissed and kissed her with a hungry mouth/ Writhing as one possessed') is cured. The two then live happily ever after, marrying and having children but never forgetting the moral of the piece, embodied in its last line: *there is no love like a sister.* Contemporary critics tend to be most interested in the buried, or not-so-buried, eroticism of this poem. Sandra Gilbert and Susan Gubar consider it a feminist work: 'there are no human men in the poem; even when the sisters becomes wives and mothers at the poem's end no husbands are described', they note. 'Rossetti does, then, seem to be dreamily positing an effectively matrilineal and matriarchal world, perhaps even, considering the strikingly sexual redemption scene between the sisters, a covertly (if ambivalently) lesbian world.'[6] Rossetti was herself deeply religious, and almost certainly died a virgin; her own beloved sister Maria was a nun. Other critics repudiate the sexuality of the poem, and see Laura's fall, through eating fruit, as an allegory of Eve's in Eden, and Lizzie eucharistically offering her own flesh to redeem her sister as an allegory of the Church. For Stephen Prickett, the poem is powerfully divided between these two interpretations, such that its power derives from this division. He concedes that 'much of the imagery is unmistakably and openly sexual', but adds:

---

[6]Gilbert and Gubar, *The Madwoman in the Attic*, 567.

This leaves many of the problems of detail unanswered. If Laura's 'fall', with its luscious pleasures and bitter aftertaste can be well enough understood in sexual terms, Lizzie's 'sacrifice', although it is couched in much the same kind of language, is much less clear. What can she bring back that will save her sister and yet leave her unsullied? The allegorical answer to this 'hair-of-the-dog' cure is, of course, love. The poem is a contrast between unreal and real, selfish and selfless loves. Laura desired sensual pleasure, Lizzie wanted to save her sister ... The poem itself gains much of its power from its resistance to simple allegory, and its hints of deeper more complex relationships. Like so many fantasies of the period, it is not difficult to find in *The Goblin Market* [sic] an image of a divided mind, and a divided society.[7]

The interesting thing, we might say, is that this balance of bourgeois religious respectability and atavistic passion and release finds its expression, precisely, in fantasy.

---

[7]Stephen Prickett, *Victorian Fantasy*, 109.

# CHAPTER 9
# WILLIAM MORRIS

James Gifford discerns 'a nineteenth-century shift from the model of Romance to something new based on the secondary world', for which 'it is reasonable to look to William Morris as a starting point'.[1] From his early life Moris was fascinated by the middle ages, and was moved to recreate and remake medieval art and crafts. After time as an architectural pupil of George Edmund Street as a young man – there remains something architectural in terms of solidity and structural heft, in all his later writing – in 1861 he established the firm of Morris & Co and spent the rest of his life realizing his medievalizing vision into material life. Some of this was about design and the visual arts. Some was literary. The poetry of *The Defence of Guinevere* (1858) is richly, sensually Arthurian and medievalized, Guinevere justifying her affair with Lancelot in terms of the sheer somatic and aesthetic beauty of their mutual desire: an erotic enchantment, or re-enchantment of magical intensity. Morris wrote a great quantity of poetry, hundreds and sometimes thousands of lines a day – he liked to compose verse on railway journeys, where the rhythm of the rolling carriage settled him into a suitable prosodic-propulsive mindset. The Greek-mythic *The Life and Death of Jason* (1867), his translation of the *Völsung Saga* (1870) and his epic *The Story of Sigurd the Volsung and the Fall of the Niblungs* (1876) are all very long. Morris considered this last title his greatest poem, and it is certainly a monumental, sinewy plenitude, a reclaiming of the fantastical heritage of Norse mythology: over 10,000 lines long, rhymed hexameter couplets written in a deliberately archaised diction and vocabulary.

> So strode he to the Branstock nor greeted any lord,
> But forth from his cloudy raiment he drew a gleaming sword,
> And smote it deep in the tree-bole, and the wild hawks overhead
> Laughed 'neath the naked heaven as at last he spake and said:
> 'Earls of the Goths, and Volsungs, abiders on the earth,
> Lo there amid the Branstock a blade of plenteous worth!
> The folk of the war-wand's forgers wrought never better steel
> Since first the burg of heaven uprose for man-folk's weal.'

C. S. Lewis praised the poem's fullness, its epic there-ness, calling it a work 'as windy, as tangible, as resonant and three dimensional as that of Scott and Homer'.[2] But it is a work forgotten today, unread and undiscussed. The comparison with Wagner's still

---

[1]Gifford, *A Modernist Fantasy: Modernism, Anarchism and the Radical Fantasti*, 14, 7.
[2]Lewis, *Rehabilitations*, 40.

living operatic version of the Sigurd story is instructive. Conscious of the likelihood of comparison and charges of invidiousness, Morris hesitated to write his work at all, but he decided to do so because he believed Wagner had gone about things wrongly. In 1873 he wrote to Harry Buxton Forman:

> I look upon it as nothing short of desecration to bring such a tremendous and world-wide subject under the gas-lights of an opera; the most degraded and rococo of all forms of art – the idea of a sandy-haired German tenor tweedledeeing over the unspeakable woes of Sigurd, which even the simplest words are not typical enough to express![3]

This is touchily written, over-defensive, and posterity has adjudicated the two works according to different criteria. Degraded tweedledeeing hardly describe Wagner's epic *Gesamtkunstwerk* ambitions, after all. But Morris is saying something important about fantasy here: not that it cannot be artificial, for Morris employed artifice in manifold ways, but that it must apprehend sincerity in order to work – that without the currency of authenticity it decays into whimsy and triviality. At its heart this is a religious differential: which is to say, a matter of pre-modern faith and modern secularity. Robert Harbison thinks the dispute between the two men was not about their respective treatments of the Nibelung source-material, but is 'seen best in their relations to religion in the more primitive forms it assumes in the legends'.

> Though Morris's interest in religion only began to detoxify itself into an interest in the churches' qualities as architecture, he saw the sagas as offering a chance to escape from enthrallment to the supernatural into the purely human, like release from a weight. Wagner, a non-believer, constructed of old stories a new oppression, embodied in a flood of sound which asked submission, whose seamlessness gave one the illusion of having no time to reflect, the simpler religion converted to sensations of power with minimal statable content fatally tied to non-individual sources of strength, like race.[4]

Longest of all Morris's poems is *The Earthly Paradise* (1868–70): a mammoth compilation of twenty-four works, each one book-length. The poem is set in 'a nameless city in a distant sea', founded many years before by a race of Greek voyagers who have maintained their language and culture. A group of medieval northern European travellers, fleeing the Black death, arrive and are welcomed. Every month the two groups get together to feast and tell one another stories from their respective cultures: the poem is divided into months, each including one verse retelling of a Greek mythological story, and one from

---

[3]Norman Kelvin (ed), *William Morris Collected Letters*, 1:205.

[4]Robert Harbison, *Deliberate Regression*, 108. Harbison considers *Sigurd* Morris's 'most vigorous rendition of the premedieval world', an 'escape from the complications of [bourgeois] morality to a place where power and virtue are not quite joined because virtue in our sense cannot exist, but where inhuman strength gives leisure for the first stirrings of conscience'.

Norse legend. The stories, all traditional or adapted from literary sources, are well-told, but the audience for long narrative poems was shrinking.

In the last decades of his life Morris's turned from poetry to prose, writing and publishing via his own Kelmscott press a series of quasi-novelistic romances. Insofar as twentieth-century fantasy has so largely inhabited the idiom of prose, it is these works rather than his earlier verse romances that have proved influential. Some of these stories are set in unnamed lands that we may assume are locations in 'our' world; others are set in named imaginary lands, subcreations. The style is archaic, as are the mores, and yet there is throughout a dialectic engagement with modernity. In all his prose fantasias, Morris was motivated by what Amanda Hodgson calls an 'acceptance of the organic unity between past and present' as well as a 'renewed belief in the force of heroic action'.[5] *A Tale of the House of the Wolfings and All the Kindreds of the Mark* (1888) concerns a tribe of first-century Goths fighting the Roman army in the foothills of the Alps. After a fierce battle the Romans are defeated, though at great cost: Wolfing Hall is only saved from destruction by the self-sacrifice of the tribal leader Thiodolf. 'It is a story', Morris wrote to Thomas Wise, 'of the life of the Gothic tribes on their way through Middle Europe, and their first meeting with the Romans in war. It is meant to illustrate the melting of the individual into the society of the tribes.'[6] For a socialist like Morris this makes it a political tale, although the historical tension – for the 'bourgeois' social logic of the Romans, as Morris construes them, must eventually triumph – is articulated via a fantastical conceit: Thiodolf is in a relationship with a Valkyrie called Wood-Sun, who has herself been expelled from 'the Godhome' for falling in love with a mortal. Wood-Sun can see the future, and, fearful that Thiodolf will die in the upcoming battle, gifts him a magic hauberk to guarantee his life. But Thiodolf realizes this magical protection must come at the cost of his tribe losing the fight; the prophylaxis 'is for the ransom of a man and the ruin of a folk'. Thiodolf understands that he must sacrifice himself for the good of his people, and does so. At the end of the tale his daughter Hall-Sun buries him, glad that he has chosen the collective good over his individual life.

In *The Glittering Plain* (1894), Hallblithe of the House of the Raven, 'a young man of free kindred: fair, strong, and not untried in battle' quests for his betrothed, who has been kidnapped by 'sea rovers' – Vikings, though they are never so-called in the novel. Hallblithe goes from England to Iceland and then to the 'Land of the Glittering Plain', also known as the Acre of the Undying, where men and women grow young again and never die.

> Then said the Sea-eagle: 'Look forth, shipmate, and tell me of the land.'
> And Hallblithe looked and said: 'The yellow beach is sandy and shell-strewn, as I deem, and there is no great space of it betwixt the sea and the flowery grass; and a bowshot from the strand I see a little wood amidst which are fair trees blossoming.'

---

[5]Hodgson, *The Romances of William Morris*, 122.
[6]Morris to T. J. Wise 17 November 1888; *Letters* 302.

'Seest thou any folk on the shore?' said the old man. 'Yea,' said Hallblithe, 'four; and by seeming three are women, for their long gowns flutter in the wind. And one of these is clad in saffron colour, and another in white, and another in watchet; but the carle is clad in dark red; and their raiment is all glistening as with gold and gems; and by seeming they are looking at our ship as though they expected somewhat.' [*Glittering Plain*, ch 9]

Though the court of the Undying King of the Glittering Plain is full of rejuvenated beautiful youths, a place where, love is forever kindling between men and women, Hallblithe is only interested in his betrothed, and so when he discovers she is not in this place either he demands to be allowed to leave. But he may not: 'so long as thou abidest on the Glittering Plain; and I see not how thou mayst ever escape thence'. After many adventures and hardships, he does manage to escape, and eventually recovers his beloved. The fantasy here is a dynamic between an archaic 'authenticity' that tends deathward and a modern fluidity, an adaptability, an ironic orientation to reality that leads through to life. It connects the stylized ornateness of Morris's art (his visual art and design, but also his prosaic art), its mannerism that, whilst it avoids stiltedness, fixes. All those flower and leaf patterns of Morris's visual art, so gorgeously medievalized-baroque, never quite come alive. They are not in process or flow, not unfolding into anything vivid. It is not a criticism to say so, for the designs are very beautiful and have proved enduring and influential. But the beauty is in the stylistic reversion, the repudiation of 'realism', and this is also the logic of fantasy as such. The 'glitter' of this novel's imagined world is bright but hard, cold, its promise of eternal youth a mode of tyranny, a dead-end far from 'our' world of Cleveland, beyond even the half-imaginary Icelandic 'Isle of Ransom'. Morris's text traces the way out of this existential cul-de-sac, a there and back again structure that finds revitalization in an acceptance of death. It's not coincidental that this is also a story that balances the present – for Morris, a present replete with the (he believed) inevitable parturition of communist social justice – and the past.

The archaic style in which these fantasy novels are written reflects Morris's antiquarian fondness for the way language used to work, back in the era he idolized. More importantly it defamiliarizes, bounces the reader out of her contemporary complacency and generates the estrangement crucial to the fantasy vibe. Or, at least, it attempts to do so. It is significant that, among Morris's many epigones, none followed him in this stylistic fundamentalism. Most writers of fantasy deploy a prose of undistinguished and sometimes comically anachronistic modernity.

*The Wood Beyond The World* (1894) imitates the form and style of Malory's *Morte D'Arthur*. It's tale of a traveller from 'our' world who passes into a magical kingdom, rescuing a maiden from imprisonment in an enchantress's castle, travelling through various adventures, fighting monsters and eventually achieving a throne in the kingdom of Stark-Wall, provides a link between Arthurian medievalism and twentieth- and twenty-first-century fantasy fiction. Lin Carter recognized the importance of this novel on later fantasy by including it in the second tranche of the Ballantine Adult Fantasy Series. Reviewing this reissue, James Blish praised Morris for recapturing the style of Sir

Thomas Malory, 'all the way down to the marginal glosses and the nonstop compound sentences hitched together with scores of semicolons. Morris also recaptured much of the poetry; and if the reader will make the small effort necessary to accommodate himself to the rhythm of the style, he will find both it and the story rewarding.'[7] Morris's *The Well at the World's End* (1896) continues the Maloryian pastiche in style and form, although *The Water of the Wondrous Isles* (1897) – its witch-haunted wood of Evilshaw from which the book's naked heroine, Birdalone, escapes in a magic boat, travelling to a succession of strange and wonderful islands – draws more specifically on the traditions of allegory. Morris's last, posthumously published fantasy novel, *The Sundering Flood* (1897), is less Arthurian-medieval than it is Norse-mythic in flavour. The story here concerns the hero Osberne Wulfgrimsson and heroine Elfhild, lovers who live on opposite sides of the titular river. Elfhild is abducted by Red Skinners, a river-Viking, and Osberne, picking up his magical sword Boardcleaver, quests to retrieve her. The key thing here is the degree to which Morris's late novels iterate a mode of antiquarianism – itself an important element in the traditions of twentieth- and twenty-first-century fantasy – as well as generating an intensity of medievalized affect.

*The Well at the World's End* (1896) is Morris's best romance. Prince Ralph is the youngest of the four sons of King Peter of Upmeads. His three elder brothers obtain royal leave to ride off: Hugh going north, Gregory west and Blaise eastward. But Ralph is ordered to stay home, so that the king has at least one heir should disaster strike the adventurers. Ralph, however, chafes at this restriction and sneaks away, riding south. He passes through the 'Wood Perilous' where he fights and kills two men who were 'leading a woman by a rope tied about her neck … as though bringing a cow to market'. The rescued woman, Ursula, tells him 'I am going to seek the Well at the World's End, and to find it and live, or to find it not, and die'. They journey together to this goal, and much of the story concerns the different social systems they encounter on this quest. Ralph comes first to Higham-on-the-Way, ruled by an abbot from the town's monastery, who commands a troop of 'men-at-arms in bright armour' by which he imposes his will on the cowed population. This tyrannical state of affairs is deplorable. Ralph travels to the next town, the Burg of the Four Fifths, the prosperity of which is founded upon slave-labour. The further Ralph travels, searching for the well, the worse are the societies he encounters. At a town called Goldburg he discovers a combination of anarchy and slavery, and further on he comes to Utterbol, a place its inhabitants call Hell, where a savage tyrant rules by violence and terror, and where Ralph is threatened with castration, no less. Passing through the mountains, Ralph and Ursula encounter an idyllic pastoral society, the 'Innocent Folk'. Here they are married, and directed towards the well, which will confer magical power upon Ralph, but only if he is worthy. He demonstrates his worth by promising to return home, 'to the little land of Upmeads, to see my father and my mother, and to guard its meadows from waste and its houses from fire-raising: to hold war aloof and walk the free fields, and see my children growing up about me, and

---

[7]Blish, *Magazine of Fantasy and Science Fiction* (February 1970), 45.

lie at last beside my fathers in the choir of St Laurence'. Barbara J. Bono calls this novel Morris's 'masterwork' in the 'allegorical mode': in this romance, she says, 'the incidents occurring along the cycle of outgoing and return have the visual intensity and symbolic suggestiveness of carefully stylized, symmetrically arranged moral exempla, devoted simultaneously to illustrating the growth of the central figure and to stimulating the education of the reader'.[8] The education is as much political as moral, and the fantasy refracts medievalized magic and enchantment through nineteenth-century practical politics.

In an address to the Society for the Protection of Ancient Building in 1889, Morris defended fantasy as a mode of historical and political engagement: 'what romance means is the capacity for a true conception of history, a power of making the past part of the present'.[9] Morris creates his mode of fantasy as a way not just of engaging history, but of recuperating it into the present, of re-enchanting the deracinated sterility of modern capitalism. 'These are tales', as E P Thomson notes,

> not of desire unsatisfied, but of desire fulfilled. The water of the well at the world's end, which Ralph and Ursula drink, is not of immortality but of more abundant life. In each tale, hero and heroine start from a secure hearth and home in a society pictured with realistic detail, pass through adventures, trials and magic experience, but return in the end once again to their homes.[10]

Creating an idiom that was to be widely copied in the twentieth century by new generations of writers of fantasy: not the stylistic archaism, but the sense of a journey from modernity into faerie that can return us to ourselves, re-enchanted.

[8]Barbara J. Bono, 'The Prose Fictions of William Morris: A Study in the Literary Aesthetic of a Victorian Social Reformer', 52.
[9]In May Morris (ed), *William Morris: Artist, Writer, Socialist*, 2:146.
[10]E. P. Thompson, *William Morris: Romantic to Revolutionary*, 646.

# PART 2
## FANTASY IN THE TWENTIETH CENTURY

# CHAPTER 10
## 1900–14

H. G. Wells, who endures for his science fiction, rarely wrote fantasy: his imagination tended to range into the future, repudiating the past as oppressive and outmoded.[1] And yet in his 1906 short story 'The Door in the Wall' he iterates a key icon of the fantasy mode with exemplary force and eloquence. Lionel Wallace, an orphaned and unhappy child, chances upon a green door in a nondescript London wall. Stepping through he finds himself in a beautiful garden: gorgeous flowers, tame panthers, friendly people, a place where he feels intense happiness. A dark woman shows the young boy the book of his own life, which he reads. When he gets to the point in this narrative at which he had entered the garden Wallace finds himself suddenly back on the dreary London street, the door nowhere to be seen. His life goes on. Later, still a child, Wallace sees the door in the wall again, but does not go through it because he is anxious about being late for school. At various points in his adult life he sees the door again: once aged seventeen, again as an Oxford undergraduate, then as an adult MP, but each time there is some reason why he does not open it and go through. Now an old man, he regrets this deeply, and despairs of ever seeing the door again. At the end of the story the narrator reports that Wallace's body has been found. In the process of extending London's underground railway a deep excavation had been opened and a doorway 'cut for the convenience of the workmen'; Wallace had walked through this and fallen to his death. The narrator concludes the tale:

> Was there, after all, ever any green door in the wall at all? I do not know. I have told his story as he told it to me. There are times when I believe that Wallace was no more than the victim of the coincidence between a rare but not unprecedented type of hallucination and a careless trap, but that indeed is not my profoundest belief. You may think me superstitious, if you will, and foolish; but, indeed, I am more than half convinced that he had, in truth, an abnormal gift, and a sense, something – I know not what – that in the guise of wall and door offered him an outlet, a secret and peculiar passage of escape into another and altogether more beautiful world. At any rate, you will say, it betrayed him in the end. But did it betray him? There you touch the inmost mystery of these dreamers, these men of vision and the imagination. We see our world fair and common, the hoarding and the pit. By our daylight standard he walked out of security into darkness, danger, and death. But did he see like that?

---

[1]Exceptions to this statement include his early novel *The Wonderful Visit* (1895) about an angel arriving in an English village, *The Sea Lady* (1902), a mermaid story that satirically reworks *Undine*, and the late novella *The Croquet Player* (1936), an atavistic fantasia.

This is not entirely the first version of the fantasy portal in literature – we have already discussed Anodos's bedroom and his secretary in *Phantastes*, Alice Liddell's rabbit hole and looking glass, and indeed the trope is older than that: King Arthur's Siege Perilous, or the magical turtle in the Japanese fairy tale *Urashima Tarō*. But Wells's brief account of it remains one of the most potent, and its influence and resonance spread through the twentieth century. It is, on one level, a story about the past: about memory, individual and historical. Wallace looking back over his life, recalling a transcendent moment of happiness followed by many regrets. Neurologist Oliver Sacks relates the case of one of his patients, 'Mrs. O'C.': born in Ireland she lost both parents before she was five and had been moved to America to be raised by her aunt. As an adult she had lost all her memories of her original homeland. In her eighties an infarction in her brain resulted in her experiencing hallucinations: vivid dreams accompanied by the Irish songs she had heard in her earliest years, the songs continuing after she awoke, sometimes loud enough in her ears to drown out other external noise. Under treatment, Mrs. O'C told him: 'I know you're there Dr Sacks. I know I'm an old woman with a stroke in an old people's home, but I feel I'm a child in Ireland again – I feel my mother's arms, I see her, I hear her voice singing.'[2] When treatment reduced her thrombosis such that the hallucinations stopped, Mrs O'C missed them. 'It was like being given back my childhood again … like the opening of a door – a door which had been stubbornly closed all my life.' At this, Sacks showed her Wells's story, and she replied, 'That's it. That captures the mood, the feeling, entirely. But my door was real. My door leads to the lost and forgotten past.' The doors of fantasy – C. S. Lewis's Narnian wardrobe, Cherryh's gates of Ivrel, Mr Benn's changing room, Gene Wolfe's *There Are Doors* – are fantasy itself, the self-reflexive embodiment of the process of reading, of entering into the lost magical past. The book we read is the portal.

There are terrors as well as delights in the world beyond the door. It is a reversion to an enchanted childhood, but it is also the place out of which we are projecting ourselves back: in the case of Mrs O'C, a woman in her ninth-decade and failing health. It is, that is, death, something Wells's story understands with its final confusion, in which Wallace entered the door that ended his life. Conceivably this wasn't a mistake. Fantasy portals do not open onto simple wish-fulfilment. The wardrobe door that admits the Pevensie children to Narnia also alters time such that, from the point of view of mundanity, they age with great rapidity. Across the seven Narnia novels a whole world is created, develops, grows, decays and dies in the space of a few of our mundane years. Narnia is more wonderful than our world, but also more mortal: intensely so, such that the hurtle towards death is the ground of its wonder.

William Hope Hodgson's *The House on the Borderland* (1908) exists as just such a portal. On the Irish coast is a strange domicile, circular with ornamentation suggestive of leaping flames. It has an evil reputation with the locals, and one inhabitant records in his diary that his study opened, via strange lights, to reveal a vast empty plain under a red

---

[2] Sacks, *The Man Who Mistook His Wife for a Hat*, 130.

sun. containing a life-size copy of the house constructed from green jade. This realm is one of horror: a place of Beast-gods, violent 'Swine-things' and a nameless horrors. Later in the story these beings burst into our world from this other dimension. The narrator experiences strange temporal distortions, in which his own body crumbles to dust and the whole cosmos dies, every star extinguishing except for a gigantic green stellar body, 'a great clot of fire; beneath which, the world lay bathed in a blaze of emerald green light'. He finds himself again in his study, to discover that the Swine-creatures have attacked his pet dog, leaving a 'horrid wound' in which a 'whitish, fungoid' substance is growing. This disease, whatever it is, spreads to the narrator – 'it has covered all my right arm and side, and is beginning to creep up my neck. Tomorrow, it will eat into my face. I shall become a terrible mass of living corruption' – and his account ends. *The Night Land* (1912) evokes similar atmospheres, at much greater length (over 200,000 words): a seventeenth-century nobleman, mourning his lost love and looking forward to a time when he might be reunited with her, has a vision of a far future world, a dark and terrible vista in which human life clings to existence inside a 'last redoubt', a huge pyramidical city under a sunless sky. Mysterious 'watchers' wait until thus city's protective shield, powered by 'earth current', fails, as it must inevitably do, whereupon humanity will succumb to the darkness. It is a striking piece of work, written without dialogue and entirely rendered into a pastiche seventeenth-century English which generates some striking local effects, although it palls at the egregious length to which Hope Hodgson extends it.

> And about this time, there came a fresh matter of trouble to our minds; for one of the Monstruwacans made report that the instruments were recording an influence abroad in the night; so that we had knowledge that one of the Evil Forces was Out. And to me there came an awaredness that a strange unquiet stole over the Land; yet I knew it not with mine ears; but my spirit heard, and it was as though trouble and an expectation of horror did swarm about me. [Hope Hodgson, *Night Land*, ch 4]

The connectivity between reality and fantasy, the portal or porosity, defines the oeuvre of Edith Nesbit, but here the boundary is also that between childhood and adulthood. Nesbit's children's fiction is divided between mimetic stories that style reality in quasi-fantastical forms – in her most famous work *The Railway Children* (1906) three middle-class children, Roberta (nicknamed 'Bobbie'), Peter and Phyllis, forced to move to the countryside by their father's disgrace, find delight in the rural railway near their new house. Their imaginations convert their drear surroundings into Fantasyland.

> A train had rushed out of the tunnel with a shriek and a snort, and had slid noisily past them. They felt the rush of its passing, and the pebbles on the line jumped and rattled under it as it went by.

> 'Oh!' said Roberta, drawing a long breath; 'it was like a great dragon tearing by. Did you feel it fan us with its hot wings?'

'I suppose a dragon's lair might look very like that tunnel from the outside', said Phyllis [Nesbit, *Railway Children* ch. 2]

Nesbit also wrote in the fully fantastical idiom, most successfully in her Psammead series (*Five Children and It* 1902; *The Phoenix and the Carpet* 1904; *The Story of the Amulet* 1906). The 'Psammead' is a kind of wish-granting fairy, living under the sand of an English beach (Ancient Greek ψάμμος, *psámmos*, 'sand'). It is a bizarre-looking, goblinoid and grumpy creature, but fundamentally good-natured, and it grants the wishes of the five children who discover it largely in order to teach them lessons about greed, improvidence, unconsideration and recklessness. The novels are varied and deliciously entertaining small-scale fantasias, but they leave their protagonists exactly where they were before the adventures started. The lack of development is, in fact, the point; as with Alice and Barrie's Peter Pan, a repudiation of growing up and all it entailed. It is not exactly a criticism of Nesbit to say so, though it limits what she is able to do with fantasy as a mode. As Gore Vidal notes:

> As an adult, writing of her own childhood, Nesbit noted, 'When I was a little child I used to pray fervently, tearfully, that when I should be grown up I might never forget what I thought and felt and suffered then.' With extraordinary perceptiveness, she realized that each grown-up must kill the child he was before he himself can live. Nesbit's vow to survive somehow in the enemy's consciousness became, finally, her art – when this you see remember me – and the child within continued to the end of the adult's life.[3]

The Psammead is a bizarre combination of friendly-cuddly – he grants wishes, he is covered in soft fur – and hideous-repellent: his eyes are on stalks like a snail, his body is compared to a giant spider, he has arms like a monkey, he is irascible and abject. In bridging this jarring juxtaposition of qualities Nesbit's externalizes the writerly imagination, and the playful engagement of the world by uncontaminated childhood, as the reality to which fantasy makes reference. At one point the Psammead, waxing Kantian, an unusual move for a children's book, announces 'Time and space are only forms of thought' [*Story of the Amulet*, ch 3]. Nesbit's books open the portal between the confinement of adult reality and the richness of childhood fantasy.

The portal that links our world and American writer L. Frank Baum's fantasyland of Oz is various. In *The Wonderful Wizard of Oz* (1900), Dorothy Gale, a young girl living on a farm in Kansas, is carried through the sky by a tornado and deposited in the fantasyland of Oz. Dorothy experiences a series of adventures thereupon, making friends with a talking lion, an ur-robotic tin man and a living scarecrow as she processes towards the titular wizard, who she believes can magic her back home to Kansas. Her antagonist is a wicked witch, whose sister Dorothy has inadvertently killed. The titular

---

[3]Gore Vidal, *Reflections Upon a Sinking Ship*, 73.

wizard turns out not to possess magical powers, and is in fact a con-man from Nebraska masquerading as a mighty sorcerer in order to rule over Oz. Dorothy does eventually get home, but in subsequent novels she returns to Oz and settles there permanently.

This novel was vastly successful, and Baum wrote many sequels, the whole series becoming one of the most influential fantasy megatexts of the American century. *The Marvelous Land of Oz* (1904) and *Ozma of Oz* (1907) introduce Princess Ozma, the ruler who succeeds the Wizard. In *Dorothy and the Wizard in Oz* (1908) Dorothy, shaken out of her mundane world by an earthquake, passes through an underground adventure and is rescued by Ozma via a magic emerald belt that teleports her and her companions to Oz. *The Road to Oz* (1909) sees Dorothy yet again travelling from our world to Oz, this time along a magic road that passes through a dimension of talking animals, rainbow beings, Scoodlers (who fight by pulling off their own heads and throwing them at others) and other wondrous things. Passage from here into Oz requires crossing the 'Deadly Desert', which in this novel is effected by a 'sand-boat'. At the end of the next volume, *The Emerald City of Oz* (1910) the portal is, in effect, shut down. An army of 'Nomes' attempts to invade Oz, and though they are repelled a magic spell is cast to prevent any future invasion, making Oz unreachable to everyone except those within the land itself. 'We must not hesitate to separate ourselves forever from all the rest of the world', declares the good witch Glinda. The spell she casts 'won't affect us at all' but 'those who fly through the air over our country will look down and see nothing at all. Those who come to the edge of the desert, or try to cross it, will catch no glimpse of Oz, or know in what direction it lies'. The novel's last chapter includes a 'note' from Dorothy Gale, 'written on a broad, white feather from a stork's wing':

YOU WILL NEVER HEAR ANYTHING MORE ABOUT OZ, BECAUSE WE ARE NOW CUT OFF FOREVER FROM ALL THE REST OF THE WORLD. BUT TOTO AND I WILL ALWAYS LOVE YOU AND ALL THE OTHER CHILDREN WHO LOVE US. DOROTHY GALE. [Baum, *Emerald City of Oz*, ch 30]

Baum, by this point tired of writing Oz books and wanting to concentrate on other things, planned to make *Emerald City* the last; but popular demand and financial exigency soon brought him back to the series. *The Patchwork Girl of Oz* (1913) opens with a prologue in which Baum explains how he was able to write the story despite Oz's magical isolation: wireless telegraphy (the novel, Baum says in a prologue, 'would not have been possible had not some clever man invented the "wireless" and an equally clever child suggested the idea of reaching the mysterious Land of Oz by its means'). The story itself is set entirely within Oz, although what was, in 1913, high-tech replicates the original portal: rapid passage through the air, now of radio waves rather than storm-tossed houses and balloons. Baum wrote seven further novels: *Tik-Tok of Oz* (1914), *The Scarecrow of Oz* (1915), *Rinkitink in Oz* (1916), *The Lost Princess of Oz* (1917), *The Tin Woodman of Oz* (1918), *The Magic of Oz* (1919) and *Glinda of Oz* (1920). A great many more have been added by other writers working with the approval of the Baum literary estate. In some of these the 'portal', as it were, reopens: for instance, in *Scarecrow of Oz* the Scarecrow travels from Oz to help two Californians who have gotten themselves in trouble, and in *The Magic of Oz* two characters are able to slip past Glinda's magic embargo by transforming themselves into animals, the implication being that Oz is forbidden only to human beings. The colour, movement and unceasing flow of invention kept the main Oz books from ever being boring.

Lewis Carroll was a manifest influence upon Baum's imagination, and in many ways the Oz books are Nonsense. In terms of in-story logic, Oz is so named its ruler, princess Ozma, an immortal fairy who will forever remain a beautiful fourteen-year-old and so will always rule Oz: 'born of a long line of Fairy Queens, as nearly perfect as any fairy may be' [*The Scarecrow of Oz* (1915), ch 21]. The real powers of Oz are women: queens and witches, similar to the red and white queens of Looking-Glass Land, or the Queen of Hearts in Wonderland. There's certainly a good deal of 'off with his/her/their heads!' in the Oz books: the villainous Princess Langwidere in Ozma of Oz keeps a collection of thirty heads in a gem-studded golden dressing room, and regularly swaps her own with any of these exchangeable crania. All are very beautiful ('no two formed alike but all being of exceeding loveliness … golden hair, brown hair, rich auburn hair and black hair; but none with gray hair. The heads had eyes of blue, of gray, of hazel, of brown and of black; but there were no red eyes among them, and all were bright and handsome') and the Princess controls her wardrobe with 'a curious key carved from a single blood-red ruby'. Jack Pumpkinhead, a main character in the novels, is a sentient pumpkin fixed on a wooden body who lives in a giant pumpkin house where he grows new pumpkins to replace his head every time it 'spoils'. He buries the rotten heads in a graveyard beyond his garden, and seems unconcerned by the ship-of-Theseus dilemma of this circumstance:

'I've a new head, and this is the fourth one I've owned since Ozma first made me and brought me to life by sprinkling me with the Magic Powder.'

'What became of the other heads, Jack?' [asked Dorothy]

'They spoiled and I buried them, for they were not even fit for pies. Each time Ozma has carved me a new head just like the old one, and as my body is by far the largest part of me I am still Jack Pumpkinhead, no matter how often I change my upper end. Once we had a dreadful time to find another pumpkin, as they were out of season, and so I was obliged to wear my old head a little longer than was strictly healthy. But after this sad experience I resolved to raise pumpkins myself, so as never to be caught again without one handy; and now I have this fine field that you see before you.' [*Road to Oz*, ch 16]

Then there are the aforementioned Scoodlers, who hurl their own heads at their enemies. There are other examples too, although these various Freudian-Oedipal decapitations are only one aspect of the novels' repeating figures of (playful) dismemberment, bodily disintegration and reintegration.

William Empson considers the *Alice* books to be pastoral, according to his particular understanding of 'the pastoral process' – 'putting the complex into the simple' – and their articulation of a unifying social force.[4] We could say something similar of Baum's magical Fantasyland. Gore Vidal, writing about his childhood obsession with the Oz books, thinks they 'revive in Baum's own terms the original Arcadian dream of America'; and that he was 'very much aware of the tension between technology and pastoralism' as one of the things the Oz books are about.

> In Oz Baum presents the pastoral dream of Jefferson (the slaves have been replaced by magic and good will); and into this Eden he introduces forbidden knowledge in the form of black magic (the machine) which good magic (the values of pastoral society) must overwhelm.[5]

It is a mythic logic we find in later fantasy: Tolkien's Shire threatened by the black magic, and actual machinery, of Saruman, and redeemed – and in later fantasy as well. Baum, writing through the opening decades of the twentieth century, was articulating it as mechanized global war swept through, an event of huge moment for the development of fantasy as a mode.

---

[4] William Empson, *Some Types of Pastoral*, 23.
[5] Gore Vidal, *Pink Triangle and Yellow Star*, 75.

# CHAPTER 11
# FIRST WORLD WAR

The period 1914–18 saw Europe, and much of the rest of the world, convulsed in catastrophic war. This conflict is of particular importance to the development of twentieth-century fantasy, not least because several of the key writers of the mode fought in it, transmuting their experience into fiction that in turn went on to shape and inform much of the work written in the late-century boom in the mode. For example, Tolkien's time on the Western Front fed directly into his account of the 'war of the ring'. In one sense we can consider *Lord of the Rings* as much an example of the First World War literature as Wilfred Owen's poems or Erich Maria Remarque's *Im Westen nichts Neues* ('All Quiet on the Western Front' 1928), although the conflict itself is refracted into fantasy rather than being mimetically replicated. The Narnia books cathect, though perhaps to a lesser degree, Lewis's war experience: he was a Second Lieutenant in the Somerset Light Infantry and fought on the Somme 1917–18. The great battle at the end of *The Lion The Witch and the Wardrobe*, between the forces of Aslan and the monstrous army of the White Witch, is elegantly styled on an idealized medieval martiality, a refuge from the industrialized horrors of modern war's actuality.

Other important works of fantasy, published in the 1920s, were similar reversions of personal experience of the war. Anglo-Irish writer Lord Dunsany fought on the Western Front as captain with the 5th Inniskilling Fusiliers. His beautiful, influential fairy fantasia *The King of Elfland's Daughter* (1924) is a love-story and quest adventure rather than a war-story, but it is striated by his experiences in the trenches. E R Eddison's stylized archaic romance *The Worm Ouroboros* (1922) takes a romanticized, heroized view of the war its two conflicting races fight across its fantasy realm, with battle as a glorious chivalric game – although the conceit of this novel, by which the war once won is refought after a sorceress turns back time, the last sentence of the novel feeding back to the beginning of its first chapter (hence the titular reference, the worm devouring its own tail) also styles war as an endless stalemate, and so touches back, in some sense, upon the reality of the Western Front. David Lindsay, who served (though in the Royal Army Pay Corps rather than at the front line) worked a vision of grotesque conflict as the underlying ontological fabric of his eccentric novel *A Voyage to Arcturus* (1920), more philosophical science fiction than fantasy, but potent and notable. Lindsay's protagonist, travelling by space-ship to a planet orbiting Arcturus, interacts with various more-or-less humanoid alien life-forms before acquiring a potent vision of the underlying nature of reality:

> a gigantic, self-luminous sphere … composed entirely of two kinds of active beings. There were a myriad of tiny green corpuscles, varying in size from the very

small to the almost indiscernible. ... And, surrounding these atoms of life and light, were far larger whirls of white light that gyrated hither and thither, carrying the green corpuscles with them wherever they desired ... the green atoms were not only being danced about against their will but were suffering excruciating shame and degradation in consequence.

This sphere of endless dolorous struggle, with two swarms distinguished by the colour of their livery, reads as a ghastly refraction of competing armies fighting across Europe.

War has no place in Hope Mirrlees' wonderful *Lud-in-the-Mist* (1926), yet that work is about the way the uncanny, unsettling and sometimes violent logic of 'fairyland' disturbs the stolid, respectable, bourgeois kingdom of Dorimare. It is, in one sense, a home-front war novel, transmuted into something magical, and its ending – the commercial triumph of Dorimare over Elfland, and its incipient trading empire, reflects the outcome of the war. American writer James Branch Cabell did not serve in the army. His two dozen fantasy novels follow the adventures of Dom Manuel, High Count of 'Poictesme', a fantasy version of medieval Poitiers – of particular note are *Jurgen: A Comedy of Justice* (1919), *The High Place* (1923) and *The Silver Stallion* (1926). They comprise witty, whimsical, sometimes ribald comedies. Yet the war runs through these novels too. There is a complex bivalve action in these books, one that we could almost describe as dialectical, in which the sunlit beauty and fineness of fantasy-medieval 'France' represent a retrenchment, a retreat into escapist enchantment away from the horrors of industrialized warfare and slaughter; and yet which, at the same time, draws the heft of its realization with a sense, translated into 'magic', of the incipient immanence *of* these destructive powers. On the one hand, Cabell describes his Poictesme as 'an epoch and society and even a geography whose comeliness had escaped the wear-and-tear of actually existing' [Cabell, *The Cream of the Jest* (1917)] – how charmingly *en point* is 'comeliness' as a description of the idealized fantasy past, precisely that which disenchanted industrialized modernity lacks. On the other, Cabell's fantasy is full of knowing ironies and sharpness, in-jokes and deliberate anachronisms, together with a propensity for sexual double-entendre so pronounced that *Jurgen* was, in 1920, prosecuted by the New York Society for the Suppression of Vice on the ground of 'lewd, lascivious, indecent, obscene and disgusting' content (the case was eventually dismissed in 1922). Cabell's 'comeliness' stands alongside the motto of Poictesme, *mundus vult decipi*, 'the world desires to be deceived'. He is playful, misleading, arch and often cynical. Dom Manuel, Count of Poictesme, seduces and betrays a string of women, and no sooner has he met the one true love of his life, Niafer ('Niafer permitted Manuel to kiss her again, and young Manuel said, for the twenty-second time, "There is nowhere any happiness like my happiness, nor any love like my love"' [Cabell, *Figures of Earth* (1921), ch 5]) that he betrays her, handing her over to Death, whom they encounter riding a great white horse, to save his own life. This is no Orwellian 'do it to Julia!' moment, but a briskly common-sense conclusion: 'I love Niafer better than I love any other person', Manuel declares, 'but I do not value Niafer's life more highly than I value my own life, and it would be nonsense to say so. No; my life is very necessary to me'. Cabell's illustrators – actually his aunt and uncle – based their visualizations on Tunbridge Wells, where they happened to live. Richard Cobb notes that Cabell had

> managed to convince himself that Tunbridge Wells, which he had never visited, would provide a suitable setting for a whimsical, mock-medieval never-never land, Poictesme, in which acts of chivalry were everyday occurrences in the whole area covered by the green Maidstone & District buses and in which slender feminine white arms holding shining swords projected themselves from the middle of deep black lakes.[1]

The heroic-archaic realms and bourgeois-mundane suburbia superpose. Cabell's *The Music from Behind the Moon* (1926) is a medieval quest and love-story in which heroic Madoc searches for the lovely Ettarre, who by an unbreakable magic prophecy has been imprisoned in 'the Waste Beyond the Moon' for 725 years. Madoc frees her by inserting that most un-medieval of markers, a decimal point, after the '7'. In all this there is inventive and ludic pleasure to be had, although the irony and lewdness destabilize and dissolve the enchantment.

A contrast to Cabell is Leslie Barringer who did serve in an ambulance unit during the war and was wounded in action. In the war's aftermath he stepped away from the conventional historical fiction for which he was known to write his Neustrian trilogy [*Gerfalcon* (1927), *Joris of the Rock* (1928) and *Shy Leopardess* (1948)], books set like Cabell's in an alternate medieval France, though to very un-Cabellian effect. The books concern peripatetic adventure encompassing war, quests, love and magic: finely written, expertly detailed, evocative and exciting, it is a surprise they are not better known, or were not more influential. The trilogy is also ingenuously heroic and chivalric.

With all this there are some obvious points to make. It is not merely adventitious that the generation of writers who lived through, and in many cases fought in, the First World War, chose thereafter to write Fantasies of pre-Modernity, often ones set explicitly or more obliquely in France, or a version of France, in which war becomes a chivalric and heroic escapade rather than the muddy stalemate and industrial-scale slaughter. Fantasy here might provide a simple refusal of modernity, a psychic retreat from the actuality of modern warfare to an idealized, inspiring past version, bolstered with magic and flavoured with wonder and charm. Or it might, more significantly, provide a platform by which to reconsider in metaphorical and imaginatively extrapolated form the intrusion of something monstrous *into* reality. Fantasy addresses Weberian 'disenchantment' of modernity in order to access again, in decontaminated mode, a complex of pre-modern unbuffered wonder *and* terror. Against this we must set the experiential intensity of the new form of warfare itself: to go from public school to the trenches was to undergo a forced un-buffering of sensibility, a stripping away of the bulwarks of familiarity,

---

[1]Cobb, Richard, *Something to Hold Onto*, 110.

civilization and comfort to confront violence and bloody death, an unpredictable and exhausting environment in which not only is man wolf to man, but is subject to the impersonal destructive forces of modern ordnance screaming out of the sky. What we now call PTSD, a legacy of this particular war (it is not recorded in any earlier conflicts) is perhaps better described by its contemporary term: 'shell-shock'. The scale and impersonality of high-explosive munitions shredded human subjectivity, shocked individual sensoria of the buffering of their 'shells'. The writing and reading of fantasy become a repersonalization of war, in some cases turning a simple flight into a more comforting vision of the pre-industrial past, in others a more complex and interesting inscription in metaphoric modes of recent experience.

The metaphoric strategy of this kind of fantasy is crucial. Attempts to translate contemporary experience more directly into fantastical fiction proved a dead end. British occultist Aleister Crowley's *Moonchild* (1917), in which 'white' and 'black' wizards and witches battle one another across early-twentieth-century Europe, is a roman-a-clef – for Crowley, though he cultivated an image of diabolic infamy, was gullibly ingenuous in his belief that magic actually existed, and wrote himself and his associates into the novel under pseudonyms. The novel begins before the war, but ends by incorporating its outbreak into the story (the 'white' wizards support the Allies, the 'black' the Axis powers), and the military hostilities are styled as merely one material manifestation of this immanent supernatural conflict. The novel lands flat, however, and not merely because Crowley's apprehension of 'magic' is so jejune, so egoist and power-fixated. Nor did Crowley serve in the war.

The case of Tolkien is much more significant for the history of fantasy. Indeed, the primacy of his wartime experiences to his fantasy writing has become part of the popular mythology of this author. The 2019 British-American biographical film *Tolkien* (directed by Dome Karukoski; written by David Gleeson and Stephen Beresford) dramatizes this: young Tolkien as a soldier, wandering the Western Front half-delirious with grief and illness, hallucinating flame-throwers as dragons and enemy troops as orcs. More considered is John Garth's *Tolkien and the Great War: The Threshold of Middle-earth* (2003) which argues the case for the influence of the war on Tolkien's writing by focusing on a particular nexus of comradeship occasioned by those years: Tolkien, G B Smith, Rob Gilson and Christopher Wiseman, all of whom were at King Edward's Grammar School together, and who called themselves the 'TCBS' (Tea Club, Barrovian Society). Gilson and Smith both died on the Somme. Tolkien was invalided home with trench fever. Garth makes a compelling case for lasting importance of the TCBS for Tolkien's writing, and he finds in this bond, rather than any more facile translation of real-world warmaking into pseudo-medieval magical conflict, the crucial carry-over from the Somme to Sauron, from the Western Front to Westernesse. The foci of the *Lord of the Rings* as a war-novel are much more fellowship, bravery and determination than large-scale set-piece battles or military hardware.

It's true that some of Tolkien's earlier fantastical re-imaginations engaged with the specifically mechanized-industrial aspect of the First World War. This, from the 1920s, is one of Tolkien's early attempts at transmuting his experience of war to fantasy, a draft of 'the Fall of Gondolin' material in which Melkor attacks the city with mechanical dragons, some made iron, some of bronze:

> Melko assembled all his most cunning smiths and sorcerers, and of iron and flame they wrought a host of monsters such as have only at that time been seen and shall not again be till the Great End. Some were all of iron so cunningly linked that they might flow like slow rivers of metal or coil themselves around and above all obstacles before them, and these were filled in their innermost depths with the grimmest of the Orcs with scimitars and spears. [Tolkien, *The Fall of Gondolin*, 69]

But these sorts of (as we might now say) steampunk accoutrements are purged from Tolkien's later, published stories, and the mythological reimagining of war retreats that much further from industrial modernity to an intricately stylized medieval world. Unlike much of the commercial fantasy that followed in *Lord of the Rings*'s wake, it's not the *materiel* of war that fascinates Tolkien so much as its spirit. And in many ways the spirit of the War of the Ring is a photographic negative of the actual war. Helm's Deep aside, Tolkien's war is very mobile, where the actual First World War was trench-bound and static. Tolkien's war is waged between separate species, where the war between England and Germany can be thought of as a battle between two wings of the same tribe (the German and British royal families are the same family; Tolkien himself was an Englishman of German familial extraction). Like a heavyweight boxer with a glass jaw, Sauron's attack is large-scale but comically vulnerable; once the one ring is destroyed it entirely unravels. I'm not sure any national military has ever been unknitted so simply in actual war. This 'photographic negative' logic specifically, and we can say dialectically, engages the actual war in order to deconstruct it. Robert Eaglestone cites Fussell's *Great War and Modern Memory* (1975) to discuss the ways Tolkien stressed both the heroism and the horror of war, when war-poets like Owen, Sassoon and Graves tended only to stress the latter. Fussell explores the way the discourse of war as such was subject to a specific kind of heroising elevation:

> A friend is a *comrade*
> Friendship is *comradeship*, or *fellowship*
> The enemy is *the foe*, or *the host*
> Danger is *peril*
> The battlefield dead are *the fallen*
> The front is *the field*
> One's chest is one's *breast*
> Dead bodies constitute *ashes* or *dust* [Fussell, 20–1]

Eaglestone explores how this 'inflationary' rhetoric is only one of several in Tolkien's novel; these sorts of 'conscious heroic archaisms' are intermixed in the novel with a different, more deflationary idiom, and as well a third, more laconic or practical one. Eaglestone locates 'one of Tolkien's greatest strength as a novelist' in the way he 'mixes and plays' these 'usually very separate rhetorics'.[2] The blend of registers tracks the mixture in cross-hatching of representational translation. History cycles through: as Tolkien worked his experiences of industrialized warfare into the idiom of heroic fantasy in the 1920s, so in the 2020s a war substantially similar to the First World War rages in eastern and southern Ukraine, whose army talks explicitly of the Russian invaders as 'orcs' and Vladimir Putin as 'Sauron'.

Three notable writers of fantasy happened, in the summer of 1916, to be on the same bit of the Western Front at the same time. Robert Graves was wounded in the fighting at Mametz Wood in July 1916. David Jones, a private in the same battalion in which Graves was an officer (the Royal Welch Fusiliers), also fought in this engagement – Mametz Wood is an important location in Jones's great fantasy poem *In Parenthesis* (1937). Tolkien, though in a different battalion, the Lancashire Fusiliers, was on the same line at the same time, only a little way north of Graves and Jones. Each of these people went on to adapt their war experience into new mythologies: in Tolkien's case as the War of the Ring, in Jones's case as the strange and beautiful fusion of Arthurian legend and modernity than informs *In Parenthesis* (1937), and in the case of Graves as *The White Goddess* (1948), his prose 'historical grammar of poetic myth', and a great many attendant poems. In each of these cases the mythography involved a radical reconfiguring of the actual experience:transforming modern reality into an alternate realm of magic cod-medievalism in the case of Tolkien, adding a superposition of English/Welsh myths to modern life for Jones, and for Graves swapping prosaic masculine reality for poetic female myth.

*The White Goddess* elaborates Graves's historical-mythic speculations that Europe had once been ruled by a matriarchal society dedicated to the worship of the triple goddess, maiden-mother-crone, which was in turn conquered by a patriarchal warrior caste who suppressed this religion, silenced women and instituted their God-the-Father deity. This thesis has the disadvantage of not being true. But it doesn't matter that it isn't, because Graves isn't writing history, or anthropology or seriously researching religious studies. In *The White Goddess* Graves confects a powerful, individual mythic story to give meaning and depth to the things (poems) that mattered most to him. Tolkien was doing the same thing at around the same time, providing himself with an imaginative mythopoeic frame for the things that mattered to him (languages, certain types of story, Englishness), and nobody confuses what he was doing with 'history'. Tolkien met Graves in 1964, describing him as 'a remarkable creature, entertaining, likeable, odd, bonnet full of wild bees, half-German, half-Irish, very tall, must have looked like Siegfried/Sigurd in his youth', adding 'but … an ass!'[3] Graves's fabulations, untethered from actual historiography or philology, were too fanciful for Tolkien's more rigorous fantastical imagination. And although part of David Jones's greatness as a poet was his willingness experimentally to meld prose and poetry (and although Tolkien embroidered the edges of his prose fantasy epics with

---

[2] Robert Eaglestone, *Reading* The Lord of the Rings: *New Writings on Tolkien's Classic*, 12.
[3] *Letters of J R R Tolkien*, 353.

inserts of verse) Graves was the only one of the three fully to commit to poetry as poetry, not just formally but in terms of an entire Being-in-the-World. In the 1949 Preface to *The White Goddess* he described poetry as his 'ruling passion': 'I have never intentionally undertaken any task or formed any relationship that seemed inconsistent with poetic principles; which has sometimes won me the reputation of an eccentric'. In 'To Juan at the Winter Solstice' (1944) Graves asserts

> There is one story and one story only
> That will prove worth your telling

That single Gravesian story entails the rejection of twentieth-century civilization and submission to the capricious demands of the Muse Goddess: 'a lovely, slender woman with a hooked nose, deathly pale face, lips red as rowan-berries, startlingly blue eyes and long fair hair; she will suddenly transform herself into snow, mare, bitch, vixen, she-ass, weasel, serpent, owl, she-wolf, tigress, mermaid or loathsome hag. Her names and titles are innumerable'. All true poems are invocations of this volatile 'Mother of All-Living', and their effect is immediate on readers – 'the hair stands on end, the eyes water, the throat is constricted, the skin crawls and a shiver runs down the spine'.[4] Graves literally believed in this muse-deity who sometimes, if rarely, granted acolyte-poets the idiom of reality truly apprehended. That reality was at once terrifying and thrilling; erotically mysterious and overwhelming. This encounter was his sensibility de-buffered, and his account of it, in prose and poetry, enjoys a long afterlife in fantasy as a mode.

Of the three writers mentioned here, David Jones was the one with the least influence on fantasy writing more broadly conceived. This is, in one sense, surprising, for his masterpiece *In Parenthesis* (1937) is an extraordinarily accomplished work, a fusion of poetry and prose, of Modernist formal experimentation and traditional modes of narrative and lyric, and above all a work of mythography of immense potency. It does not distort the book to call it a fantasy masterwork, even as it is rooted in the precisely observed *récit* of Jones's own soldierly experiences. *In Parenthesis* centres on the assault on Mametz Wood in which Jones took part, although this actual war coalesces in the telling with elements derived from Welsh and Arthurian legend as well as various battles of Late Antiquity and the Middle Ages, from the Roman invasion of Britain through to the death of Roland. One way of putting it would be to say that *In Parenthesis* considers time both in the modernist, clock-time/ timetable sense – a relatively new manner of chronological thinking, bedded-in by the exigencies of the war machine – and in the mythic sense: Chronos *and* Kairos, the time of mimetic fiction and the out-of-time glamour of fantasy.[5] Myth and reportage fuse, machinic ordnance is rendered back into chivalric language. Shrapnel cuts through the wood, 'blocks' of 'hard-edged clobber' that shred the flesh of the advancing men. It

---

[4]Graves, *The White Goddess*, 24.
[5]For the role played by the First World War in the new modes of timekeeping, see Stephen Kern, *The Culture of Time and Space 1880–1918* and David Landes, *Revolution in Time: Clocks and the Making of the Modern World*.

rides the air
as broom-stick horrors fly –
clout you suddenly, come-on you softly, search to the liver,
like Garlon's truncheon that struck invisible [Jones, *In Parenthesis* (1937), 180]

'Truncheon' is being used in its archaic rather than its modern sense ('a fragment or piece broken off from something, especially a broken-off piece of a spear or lance') although the modern sense is there too, haunting the meaning with police-style punitive force. Sir Garlon is King Pellam's treacherous brother in Book Two of *Le Morte D'Arthur*, who 'rideth alwy invisible', killing with impunity. Jones, a little over-fussily, appends a footnote to explain the allusion. But explanatory specificity is not the force of this great poem – rather it is in the larger attempt to unfix time and reimagine the quotidian in terms of the myth.

There are obvious dangers in a too hydraulic model of cause and effect when it comes to apprehending the art produced after the war. For example: it might be argued that the rise through these years of Surrealism, itself a mode of fantasy, was the direct product of a world made strange, deformed, abridged and strangely juxtaposed by new kinds of war. The catalogue of the Tate Modern exhibition 'Aftermath' (2018), exploring the act of the immediate post-war period, claims as much:

> The surrealists set out to destabilise conventional gender roles and social order. In the 1920s George Grosz and Edward Burra depicted figures that combined flesh and machine parts. These echoed the use of prosthetic limbs by war veterans and evoked anxieties about the fragility of the male body. War damage inflicted on bodies and particularly minds also shaped surrealist art and writing.

Dada and surrealist artworks interpellate their viewers into fantasy worlds, dreamlike or nightmarish depending, and of course drew on various wartime specifics. But the significant thing is not so Pavlovian as this account suggests. The war only accelerated the process of deracinating older certitudes, and projected the logic of modernity's disenchantment onto the art. But reaction came in diverse directions. The formal fragmentation of surrealism and literary Modernism cathected these changes one way; High fantasy, and its later offshoots (sword and sorcery, and after that Grimdark) in another. If Dada was automatic writing, or automatic art, prizing the scrappy immediacy a blasted-apart cosmos, then fantasy, working through richer, more subterranean idioms of memory and nostalgia, took longer to make its way through into the mainstream. Walter Benjamin, writing contemporaneously, compared Surrealism to a river: a small stream at its origin 'in France in 1919' that becomes a mighty river, capable of 'driving turbines down in the valley' in the 1920s and 1930s in Germany and elsewhere across Europe. A later iteration, of global popularity, is Monty Python, who drew as much from the traditions of English nonsense writing (Lear and Carroll, the Goons, John Lennon), turning their juxtapositions to comic ends. The Python team also produced traditional fantasy: the movie *Monty Python and the Holy Grail* (1975, directed by Terry Jones and

Terry Gilliam), a masterpiece that combines a carefully rendered mythic medievalism with modern touches and sensibilities in a way that is both hilarious and magical. Benjamin understands that Surrealism as a movement was more than a post-war flash, and more than a set of records of the provocations of dreams, or 'hashish'. He quotes from André Breton's surrealist picture-novel *Nadja* (1928):

> 'It so happens', the author recalls, in connection with an episode when sitting in a café with *Nadja*, he has a page of pictures thrust into his hand by an elderly beggar, depicting scenes from the reigns of Louis VI and Louis VII, 'that I have recently been thinking about this period because it was the age of "courtly love" and trying hard to imagine how people saw life in those days'. ... Medieval, Provençal *amour cortois* takes us surprisingly close to the Surrealist conception. 'All poets of the *stil nuovo*', we read in Erich Auerbach's splendid *Dante: the Poet of the Secular World* 'possessed a mystical beloved; the gifts which Love bestowed on them had more to do with illumination than with sensual pleasure'.[6]

Benjamin glosses: 'any kind of ecstasy in one world is shameful sobriety in the complementary world. What else is courtly love about than that chastity, too, is reverie? A being carried off into a world that lies next not only to Sacred Heart crypts and Lady altars but also to the morning before battle or after victory'. This is to say, in effect (though Benjamin does not specifically argue this), that main textual strategy of surrealism, the juxtaposing or manipulation of elements and concepts that would not otherwise be thought of as fitting together, is also the structural logic of fantasy as a mode: an enchanted past refigured combined with a version of modernity, the two realms juxtaposed, as the bourgeois modern hobbit roams through the grand and marvellous world of pre-modernity, or contemporary children stumble through a wardrobe into a magical pseudo-medieval Narnia. I am stretching 'surrealism' beyond the point where most critics of the mode would be comfortable, but it is meaningful to talk of the world of medieval and Renaissance romance, with its bizarre and striking hippogriffs and blatant beasts, its magicians and multicoloured landscapes, as surrealistic, and fruitful to talk about the ways these things generate fantasy. It is about love, and it is about memory.

---

[6]Walter Benjamin, 'Surrealism' [1929], in *One Way Street and Other Writings*, 147.

# CHAPTER 12
## 1920s: ANIMALS AND FAIRYLANDS

Surrealist art returned repeatedly to animal-human hybrids, the juxtaposition of bestial and personable, to monstrous and sometimes erotic forms. Max Ernst created a bird-person combination called 'Loplop' (as in his 1930 canvas 'Loplop Introduces Loplop'), an alter-ego that reflected Ernst's own childhood confusion of birds and people. René Magritte combines men (in suits and bowler hats) with birds, fish and lions. Picasso's minotaurs, 'the frequently recurring birds, insects, horses, dogs, cats, giraffes, elephants, lions, and cows, among others, represented in Surrealist poetry, painting, and film'. Kirsten Strom, quoted here, argues that Surrealists portrayed such animals and animal-human hybrids as 'literal embodiments of Surrealist themes such as the marvellous and the uncanny'.[1] Modernity, which has, via Darwin, crashed human exceptionalism back into the merely animal, refracts upon antiquity, where the mythic, wondrous animal divinities, Ovidian metamorphoses and monstrous hybridities – satyrs, centaurs, bull-men, swan-Zeus, jackal-headed Anubis – connect buffered sensibilities with a transcendent authenticity, a denuding re-enchantment. Surrealism as an offshoot of Nonsense returns to the marvellous, unsettling human-animal hybrids in Carroll's novels, so vividly illustrated by Tenniel – the gigantic caterpillar holding a hookah-pipe in his human arms in *Wonderland*, frog footmen, fish footmen and a baby that transforms from squalling boy to grunting pig.

Where the beast is the more 'authentic', atavistic pre-modernity and unbuffered intensity of existence, the human the buffered figure constrained in modernity. David Garnett's *Lady into Fox* (1922) is a suburban-pastoral version of Franz Kafka's rather better-known *Die Verwandlung* ('Metamorphosis' 1915) – though it's not likely Garnett was aware of Kafka's insectile fable, which wasn't translated into English until 1933. Sylvia Tebrick (née Fox), the 24-year-old wife of Richard Tebrick, suddenly turns into a fox while they are out walking in the woods, Mr Tebrick's uxoriousness is not affected by this alteration and the marriage continues. In an attempt to keep Sylvia's new nature a secret Richard dismisses his servants and, rather brutally, shoots the couples' two dogs. But as time goes on Sylvia becomes more fox-like, wild and uncontrollable, and eventually runs from the family home to live in the wilderness. The tale ends tragically, when Sylvia is killed by the hounds of the local hunt. Like Kafka's tale, it is a story about alienation, about estrangement, although the comparison brings out how sexless the beetle story is: Gregor Samsa, stuck in his room, is at first accommodated and then neglected by his family. Garnett's story is about, in one sense, sexual jealousy, although it is significant

---

[1]Kirsten Strom, *The Animal Surreal*.

that the wife is first transformed and only then, after a time, does the husband become jealous. The solitary and isolated situation of Kafka's man-turned-beetle is the point of *Die Verwandlung*; whereas Garnett was more interested in the transcendent possibilities of the 'thinking animal'.

That beasts might speak in stories is an idea as old as Aesop, and many fairy-tale and fantasy stories are premised on talking animals. Garnett is interested in beast-being as a whole world.[2] We see this not just in the doomed love affair of *Lady into Fox*, but in his later novel *A Man in the Zoo* (1924) – a man who requests to be exhibited in a cage with other simians at the zoo and, on display, reverts, or perhaps ascends, to a bestial transcendence – and *The Grasshoppers Come* (1931), in which an airman, whose plane has crashed in the Mongolian desert, communes with the insects which swarm there. One of the points of the latter novel is that human flight, so laboriously and mechanically achieved, is as nothing compared with the effortless command of the sky of insects.

As for Kafka: his reputation burgeoned only in the years after his death in 1924, largely on the strength of two posthumously published novels: *Der Prozess* ('The Trial' 1925) and *Das Schloss* ('The Castle' 1926). These two enduringly unnerving fantasias construe what John Clute calls 'polders', 'enclaves of toughened reality, demarcated from the surrounding world'. The legal kingdom of the first novel interpenetrates the 'real' world of Josef K.; in the latter a mysterious 'Castle' superintends upon reality. That both polders are nightmarishly oppressive, intricately labyrinthine iterations of the bureaucratization and Nazification of the world does not diminish their importance as Fantasies. Gabriel Josipovici argues that 'the fact that this was a reputation based largely on the two novels did not really help Kafka. The novels had been edited by [Kafka's friend, Max Brod] according to his views of what Kafka was up to, and were prefaced by Brod's interpretations … more or less to see Kafka as a modern Bunyan.' The importance of Bunyan to these works, and the complicated ways in which straight allegory mutates into the allography of the twentieth century, is entirely on point.

> Like all interpretations of Kafka, this Bunyanesque one has a good deal of truth in it. One cannot read a page of Kafka without feeling that there is a strong religious sensibility at work, allied to the kind of violent honesty of which no more than a handful of writers are capable in any generation.[3]

*The Trial* adapts and hollows-out the vision by of Dickens's *Bleak House*, in which legal protocols and lawsuits constitute the whole world; a monstrous impersonal and indecipherable system in which the individual is snared. *The Castle* figures a huge, Gothic redoubt, a deracinating and bewildering building-as-world, that anticipates and influences the work of Mervyn Peake and others. But both works render allegorical their deictic real-world specificities.

---

[2] A detailed account of Garnett's beast fantasies is found in Derek Ryan's *Bloomsbury, Beasts and British Modernist Literature*.
[3] Gabriel Josipovici, 'A Human Kafka', 9.

Rather more spacious, though just as horrifying, is the fantasy writing of H P Lovecraft. The 'Lovecraftian mythos' appears in tessellation, from hints and glimpses and vibes scattered across several dozen short stories: 'The Call of Cthulhu' (1928), 'The Colour Out Of Space', 'At the Mountains of Madness' and 'The Shadow over Innsmouth' (all written 1927, published 1931). In a typical Lovecraft story, ordinary human life is interpenetrated, to hideous, terrifying, mind-collapsing effect, by 'the old ones', elder gods from Lovecraft's invented cosmography, or kakagraphy: supreme amongst them a vast entity called Cthulhu, muscular-bodied, tentacle-headed, never exactly seen or fully described yet an immanent horror from the beyond of time and space. Despite his seemingly chthonic name, Cthulhu dwells not underground but at the bottom of the ocean somewhere in the South Seas – except that he actually dwells in men's dreams, haunting them to madness. What haunts Lovecraft's fantasias, ultimately, is history itself – history as nightmare (from which Joyce's Stephen Daedalus declared himself trying to awake). He pre-war juvenilia is conventional stuff, literary pastiche and unremarkable, and, from 1911, attempts at writing science fiction. Only after his mother, and more significantly after the war itself, did he begin writing in his mature style: his first major story, 'Dagon', was written in July 1917 and published in November 1919. Though the war did not directly affect him, Lovecraft felt it deeply: his Anglophilia (he used English spellings throughout his life) led to him to identify strongly with the allies. War, monstrous, insanifying, tentacle-cephalic, transmuted into horror-fantasy, informs his writing.

There is a critical tradition that traces Lovecraft through a set of literary influences that include the late Gothic of Edgar Allan Poe and the horror of Arthur Machen, as well as Lord Dunsany's first book *The Gods of Pegāna* (1905) which features a cosmology of invented deities,[4] although Timothy H. Evans makes a convincing case that Cthulhu draws more, especially in the 1920s (when the bulk of Lovecraft's most influential work was written) from 'folklorists and antiquarians, those who sought out authentic American traditions' such as Charles Skinner, Henry Shoemaker and others.

> Lovecraft shared with all of these men the idea that tradition was a moral system in conflict with its time, a bastion of beauty and community, an endangered resource that needed documentation and protection in the face of rapid change.[5]

One of Lovecraft's most potent, and influential, inventions is his *Necronomicon* (in 'The History of the *Necronomicon*', written 1927, published 1938): a thoroughly antiquarian conceit, an old book or grimoire, a demonic text that can destroy those who possess it. Lovecraft presents the story as a piece of pseudobiblia, describing in bibliographic detail the provenance of this codex, out of Arabia into Greece and so to its present, only-surviving Latin translation, adding to the spooky effectiveness of the whole.

---

[4]See S T Joshi, *A Subtler Magick: The Writings and Philosophy of H. P. Lovecraft*.
[5]Evans, 'A Last Defense against the Dark: Folklore, Horror, and the Uses of Tradition in the Works of H. P. Lovecraft', 99.

Lovecraft's influence has proved vastly greater than was his contemporary success, which was meagre. Through later horror writers and especially into the genre of 'New Weird', Lovecraftian elements and flavours are omnipresent. Not that everyone is persuaded by his dark gods, hinted-at terrors or ghastly dread. In 1945 American critic Edmund Wilson insisted that stories need to do more than scatter words like 'eerie', 'unhallowed', 'blasphemous', 'infernal', 'hellish' and 'unholy' to be scary – especially when, Wilson mocked, these words all refer to an 'invisible whistling octopus'. Michael Moorcock (who claimed he 'could never enjoy a Lovecraft story') is more accepting of the affect Lovecraft generates, although he considers it fundamentally immature:

An aggressive, neurotic personality, Lovecraft came under the influence of Poe, Dunsany and the imaginative writers of the Munsey pulp magazines and produced some of the most powerful infantile pathological imagery and some of the most astonishingly awful prose ever to gain popularity.[6]

It may be that Lovecraft's archly cod-genteel prose, as with his antiquarian conceits, were engaged as pseudo-adultisms, attempts at compensation for what he perhaps understood was indeed fundamentally infantile horror figurations. Then again, to describe horror as *infantile* is hardly dispraise. The ability to reach beneath the carapace maturity has created around our primal, childish terrors and unleash them is the most potent thing a writer of dark fantasy can do. Moorcock prefers Lovecraft's earlier stories, written more directly under the influence of Dunsany's cannier, more ironic work: these early works 'lighter in touch and almost completely lacking in the morbid imagery of his more successful horror stories in which death, idealism, lust and terror of sexual intercourse are constantly associated in prose which becomes increasingly confused as the author's embattled psyche received wound after wound and he regressed into an attitude of permanent defensiveness'. Still, permanent defensiveness describes the most successful military strategy of the First World War, and the reaching-back into trauma involves both the psychodynamic of the little-to-big individual human and the process of history as such.

A different relationship to history is established in Eric Rücker Eddison's *The Worm Ouroboros* (1922). Eddison's fiction drew on his deep interest in Icelandic sagas, Norse myth and medieval and Renaissance heroic literature, which he transmuted into idiosyncratic fantasy. *The Worm Ouroboros* concerns a war fought between heroic 'Demons' and wicked 'Witches' in a land called 'Mercury' – the planet, towards which a 1920s Englishman called Lessingham flies on the back of a Hippogriff in the book's opening chapter. Arriving, we discover that this is not in any material sense the actual Mercury. Instead Lessingham, landing, walks 'between shadowy ranks of Irish yews' and feels 'no touch of the ground beneath his feet, and when he stretched out his hand to touch a tree his hand passed through branch and leaves as though they were unsubstantial as a

---

[6]Moorcock, *Wizardry and Wild Romance*, 74–5.

moonbeam'. The novel then drops Lessingham – he's simply not mentioned after the first chapter – and instead immerses us in its medievalized fantasy kingdom. The whole is written in a synthetic Elizabethan or Jacobean English, more stilted and mannered even than William Morris's stylistic strategies:

> Folk now began to be astir in the castle, and there came a score of serving men into the presence chamber with brooms and brushes, cloths and leathers, to sweep and garnish it, and burnish the gold and jewels of the chamber. Lissome they were and sprightly of gait, of fresh complexion and fair-haired. Horns grew on their heads. [Eddison, *Worm Ouroboros*, ch.1]

The horns identify them as 'demons', but they are not diabolic in the usual meaning of the word: Eddison styles this race as noble, aristocratic, heroic, essentially human, although we might insist that, at the least, this horns mark them as human animal hybridities. Enchanted beasts, and the logic of the beast fable, is an important part of Eddison's work.

As the Demon court assembles, a dwarfish ambassador arrives to insist the Demons pay obeisance to the Witch monarch Gorice. Refusing so insulting a demand ("'I like not the dirty face of the Ambassador," said Lord Zigg. "If's upper lip bespeak him not a rare spouter of rank fustian, perdition catch me"') the matter is settled by a wrestling match between Gorice and the Demon champion, Goldry Bluszco. The account of this wrestle displays Eddison's weakness as a writer of action, fonder as he is of static tableaux. He is excellent at detailing clothing, faces and forms, fixtures and fittings, landscapes. When something actually has to happen, we get not dynamism but a stasis:

> The two champions advanced and clasped one another with their strong arms, each with his right arm below and left arm above the other's shoulder, until the flesh shrank beneath the might of their arms that were as brazen bands. They swayed a little this way and that, as great trees swaying in a storm, their legs planted firmly so that they seemed to grow out of the ground like the trunks of oak trees. Nor did either yield ground to other, nor might either win a master hold upon his enemy. So swayed they back and forth for a long time, breathing heavily. [ch.2]

Eventually King Gorice is killed. His successor is the sorcerer Gorice XII who uses dark magic, obtained from the untrustworthy Goblin Lord Gro, to imprison Goldry in an enchanted mountain prison. The lords of Demonland attack, are defeated and themselves imprisoned. They are rescued, and embark upon a series of quests, adventures, as well as fighting many more battles. The battle-writing, though, is vitiated by the same static conceptualizing as the wrestling match episode:

> The Demons' battle-line most gloriously maintained their array unbroken, though the outland allies broke and fled. … In which struggle befell the most bloody fighting that was yet seen that day, and the stour of battle so asper and so mortal that it was hard to see how any man should come out from it with life, since not a

man of either side would budge an inch but die there in his steps if he might not rather slay the foe before him. So the armies swayed for an hour like wrastlers locked. [ch 31]

We could, perhaps, make the case that this static quality figures as a commentary upon the stalemate in the trenches 1914–18, although Eddison's treats war as a glorious game, heroes in lovingly detailed chivalric armour hewing and smiting:

In one short while had my Lord Brandoch Daha three times a horse slain stark dead under him, yet gat never a wound himself, which was a marvel. For without care he rode through and about, smiting down their champions. I mind me of him once, with's horse ripped and killed under him, and one of those Witchland lords that tilted at him on the ground as he leaped to's feet again; how a caught the spear with's two hands and by main strength yerked his enemy out o' the saddle. His highness swapt him such a swipe o' the neck-bone as he pitched to earth, the head of him flew i' the air like a tennis ball.

*Yerked* is a lively sort of word, but 'swapt him such a swipe' is lame, and the tennis ball analogy, though licensed by Shakespeare's *Henry V*, is misjudged.

Nonetheless *The Worm Ouroboros*'s five hundred pages are readable, generously supplied with wonders, monsters, magical artefacts, challenges, hippogriff eggs – and full-grown hippogriffs, with rainbow coloured wings – crystal balls, dangers and glories. Heroes fight monsters, villains plot and scheme. Eddison also takes his world and his idiom very seriously. He commits to it, absolutely, and in doing so he generates a genuine *verfremdungseffekt*, a mannered nobility of otherness.

What the book does not have is a consistently worked-through worldbuilding. Just as Lessingham is dropped from the story and never recalled, so the specifics of the world apply with only localized coherence. Then there is the business of the names. Tolkien, though he admired and in some respects imitated this novel, wrote sternly in 1957: 'I thought his nomenclature slipshod and often inept.' Characters are called things like La Fireez, Fax Fay Faz, 'Volle and Vizz and Zigg', Gaslark Dekalajus, 'Maxtlin of Azumel'; Ojedian; Prezmyra. Eddison began composing the stories in his imaginary world as a child, and retained many details out of a loyalty to his infant imagination that ought, perhaps, have given way to the exigencies of convincing fantasy writing.

The titular worm is not a monster that appears in the story, so much as a description *of* the story. After initial setbacks in their war against the Witches, and various adventures and quests, the heroic Demon princes rally and finally defeat their foe in a great final battle. Many die in the process, although when victory is finally achieved and the Witches utterly destroyed, the Demons are not happy. 'And Lord Juss spake and said, "Now that our great enemies are dead and gone, we that were lords of all the world must turn shepherds and hunters, lest we become mere mountebanks and fops … stingless drones, with no action to sharpen our appetite."' The magical, immortal Queen Sophonisba takes pity on their plight and turns back time, with the novel ending at the place it began: 'the serving man returned with startled countenance, and, bowing before Lord Juss, said, "Lord, it is an Ambassador from Witchland and his train. He craveth present audience."' The great Worm of time bites its own tail. An appendix gives us a calendar from which we learn that 'the action of the story covers exactly four years: from the 22nd April 399 to 22nd April 403 a.c.c.', where 'A.C.C.' stands for Anno Carces Conditae, a play on the Roman dating convention Ab Urbe Condita (i.e. 'from the founding of the City'). Eddison's Latin, by pluralizing 'condita', tells us that Carcë has been founded not once but multiple times. Round and round we go, from Spring to Spring, an eternal recurrence of fantastical war. In this sense, *The Worm Ouroboros* represents a wholesale retreat from modernity. History is simply repudiated, progression denied, modernity and its discontents magically blocked from coming into being. In its style, content and ouroborian form, this novel arrests its mode.

The two most important fantasy novels from the 1920s engage history more dialectically. Both Dunsany's *The King of Elfland's Daughter* (1924) and Hope Mirrlees' *Lud-in-the-Mist* (1926) juxtapose the bourgeois realm of men with the glamour and danger of fairyland – as a 'portal fantasy' must – though with important differences too which in themselves feed through to later fantasy writing.

Edward John Moreton Drax Plunkett, 18th Baron Dunsany, Irish peer and prolific author, published many books before the war, fiction and non-fiction, often drawing on Irish mythology. *The King of Elfland's Daughter* is his masterpiece, although it was a title mostly ignored until rediscovered by its republication in the Ballantyne series in the 1970s. 'Dunsany was forty-six when he wrote *The King of Elfland's Daughter*, which is not exactly young', Darrell Schweitzer notes. 'The war was between him and that first, exuberantly imaginative phase of his career. His enchanted dreams were slipping away, but, brilliantly, rather than write weaker and weaker stories he turned this very loss into his subject matter.'[7] The parliament of the kingdom of Erl petitions its king: having been ruled by ordinary men for seven hundred years, and though they have been ruled well, they now wish for a change; for 'the generations stream away, and there is no new thing'. Accordingly they ask for 'a magic lord' to rule them. The King of Erl agrees and sends his son Alveric off to Elfland to recruit one such. In Elfland Alveric immediately falls in love with Princess Lirazel, the King of Elfland's daughter, and she with him, though her father disapproves. He loves her for her beauty and glamour, although the glamour actually runs both ways, for Lirazel is enchanted by how strange is the *un*strangeness of our world: 'she sighed for a moment for those fields, for she had heard how life beautifully passes there, and how there are always in those fields young generations, and she thought of the changing seasons and children and age, of which elfin minstrels had sung when they told of Earth' [ch 3].

Alveric and Lirazel run off together back to our world, where, in 'Thomas the Rhymer' fashion, Alveric discovers many years have passed and that his father is dead. The pair marry and have a son, Orion, and for a while Alveric rules the human kingdom of Erl.

---

[7]Darrell Schweitzer, 'The Novels of Lord Dunsany', 39–40.

But out of Elfland the king sends a troll, bearing a magic rune written on parchment, to summon his daughter home. Compelled, she goes, and though Alveric follows to fetch her back the boundaries of Elfland have retreated from where they were before, the King using 'some age-old incantation' to 'call Elfland away, drawing it further from Earth'. Alveric's search is fruitless, although his half-elfish son Orion can hear the horns of elfland blowing in the evening.

Orion grows to manhood and becomes, as his name suggests, a mighty hunter. Much of the novel is given over to him chasing, on horse and hounds a magnificent unicorn. Alveric spends decades on his quest for his lost love. When he approaches Elfland, the Elf-king (who can sense the approach of Alveric's magic sword) withdraws the boundary, but when Alveric is off in the wrong direction he relaxes his magic:

> But when Alveric with his sword was far to the North the Elf King loosened the grip with which he had withdrawn Elfland, as the Moon that withdraws the tide lets it flow back again, and Elfland came racing back as the tide over flat sands. With a long ribbon of twilight at its edge it floated back over the waste of rocks; with old songs it came, with old dreams, and with old voices … And here the unicorns fed along the border as it was their custom to do, feeding sometimes in Elfland, which is the home of all fabulous things, cropping lilies below the slopes of the Elfin Mountains, and sometimes slipping through the border of twilight at evening when all our fields are still, to feed upon earthly grass. [ch 18]

In Elfland Lirazel sits on her father's knee, on his throne of ice and mist, as years pass in the human realm. But she pines for the transient world she has left behind, and for her husband above all. Finally the King yields to her daughter's desire and, in order to bring the two lovers together, he uses the last of his three mighty runes to roll the borders of Elfland completely over the kingdom of Erl.

> And now from upper windows of the houses the folk began to see that glittering line which was no earthly twilight: they saw it flash at them with its starry gleam and then flow on towards them. Slowly it came as though it rippled with difficulty over Earth's rugged bulk, though moving lately over the rightful lands of the Elf King it had outspeeded the comet. And hardly had they wondered at its strangeness, when they found themselves amongst most familiar things, for the old memories that floated before it, as a wind before the thunder, beat in a sudden gust on their hearts and their houses, and lo! they were living once more amongst things long past and lost. And as that line of no earthly light came nearer there rustled before it a sound as of rain on leaves, old sighs, breathed over again, old lovers' whispers repeated … Then Elfland poured over Erl. [ch 34]

The only place unclaimed by this magical landgrab is the house and garden of the 'Holy Freer' – that is, Friar – whose Christianity seals him away (not that he is incommoded by his new situation: 'there he lived happy, contented, not quite alone, amongst his holy things'.) Otherwise Erl becomes a part of the larger kingdom of Elfland, and Alveric and Lirazel can be together forever.

Dunsany's novel achieved belated fame in the 1970s, its Ballantine reissue chiming with the spirit of that decade: L. Sprague de Camp considered it on par with *The Lord of the Rings* 'in terms of its quality and influence' and Arthur C. Clarke thought it cemented Dunsany 'as one of the greatest writers of this century'.[8] In 1977 Bob Johnson and Pete Knight (of folk-rock band Steeleye Span) released a concept album version of the book: Christopher Lee narrates short passages that link the songs: Mary Hopkin sings Lirazel, Frankie Miller sings Alveric, P P Arnold sings the Witch. The record doesn't come anywhere near generating the affect of the book: its uncanny glamour, its balance of traditional storytelling elements with offkilter, unsettling shifts, its evocation of beauty as an asymmetric uncanny. It is, however, an indicator of the way 'Fantasy' flooded into broader culture in the 1970s: a nostalgic pop-song-commodity. In the later decades of the twentieth century, the aftermath of the hippy movement, the growth of environmentalism, and the sense that neoliberal materialism was desertifying the world, the idea of an Anschluss between enchantment and mundanity seemed appealing to many. Not that we travel to fairyland, but that fairyland comes to us. A comparison might be Freddy Mercury, whose rock-band Queen released a musical version of Dadd's *Fairy-Feller's Master Stroke* (so titled, on *Queen II*, 1974): a fine piece of prog-rock that celebrates the verve and detail of Dadd's painting, but which in its camp upbeat energy entirely misses the melancholia of the original.

*The King of Elf-Land's Daughter*'s original publication in 1924, six years after the end of the First World War, two after the secession of Ireland from the UK, positions the fantasy in relation to these historical disruptions: conflicted, desirous change and yet attached to stasis, ultimately reactionary. Dunsany's prose, lusciously descriptive of landscapes and skies, is sometimes over-rich and cloying, the plotting is associative, herky-jerky, moving from element to element in sometimes abrupt and disconcerting ways, but in these ways the writing aspires more to the status of a lyrical poem than a plain narrative. Fairyland is beautiful but changeless, a realm in endless stasis. 'Our' world changes, develops and decays; Elfland does not. Elfland is poetry to Erl's prose. The enchantment is exquisite, lyrical, but also the world of Keats's Grecian Urn, beautiful and wondrous, but incapable of consummation, of growth, of life.

As with Eddison and Dunsany, Hope Mirrlees' *Lud-in-the-Mist* enjoyed only small success on initial publication, and became a much bigger deal when reissued in 1970 as part of Ballantyne list. The novel is set in an imaginary country called Dorimare, a small but prosperous trading nation somewhere between seventeenth-century Holland and eighteenth-century England: 'a rich plain, watered by two rivers, [in which] a considerable variety of scenery and vegetation was to be found'. To the west the landscape becomes 'exotic':

---

[8]Quoted in Gary Westfahl, *The Greenwood Encyclopaedia of Science Fiction and Fantasy Themes*, 1124.

Nor was this to be wondered at, perhaps; for beyond the Debatable Hills (the boundary of Dorimare in the west) lay fairyland. There had, however, been no intercourse between the two countries for many centuries. [ch 1]

The burghers of Lud-in-the-Mist had previously staged a revolution and overthrown the old feudal aristocracy. The last ruler, Duke Aubrey, fled, perhaps into fairyland itself. A senate of respectable burghers now rule the city. But although Dorimare is now modern, many in the population are romantically attached to the idea that Duke Aubrey will return. He figures in the popular imaginary as a kind of Jacobite King-Over-The-Waters, an Arthur whose restoration will supposedly bring universal happiness. The authorities strive to clamp down on this. All dealings with fairyland are forbidden, on pain of death. But fairyland still infiltrates Dorimare in various ways. One, of importance to the story of the novel, is smuggled fairy fruit. People ingesting these comestibles might sing and dance, lose their grip or their minds, speak out of turn, grow silly, uninhibited, run wild or even run off to join the fairies. The fruit is officially banned.

The novel's main character, Master Nathaniel Chanticleer, a respectable burgher and Mayor of Lud, was himself affected by the fairy-uncanny when, as a young man, he picked out a musical instrument in his lumber room: 'a sort of lute ending in the carving of a cock's head, its strings rotted by damp and antiquity'. Playing this for his friends the strings give out 'one note, so plangent, blood-freezing and alluring, that for a few seconds the company stood as if petrified'. This note recurs to Nathaniel at various moments through his life, piercing the dull ordinariness of his regular existence, unsettling him: 'for years that note was the apex of his nightly dreams; the point towards which, by their circuitous and seemingly senseless windings, they had all the time been converging. It was as if the note were a living substance, and subject to the law of chemical changes.'

Before Nathaniel heard this note he had sometimes dreamed of travel and adventures: 'but after he had heard the Note a more stay-at-home and steady young man could not have been found in Lud-in-the-Mist. For it had generated in him what one can only call a wistful yearning after the prosaic things he already possessed.' When his son Luke becomes disaffected – the result, it is rumoured, of him eating the forbidden fairy fruit – Nathaniel takes the advice of his doctor, Endymion Leer, and sends him for a change of air to stay at a country farm. This farm is close to the borderlands of Fairy, and though in itself part of the ordinary, normal world it attracts strange visitors, such as old Portunus the weaver, 'a wizened old man with very bright eyes'. Others see in Portunus only a kindly old fellow 'always ready to lend a helping hand to the maids – to break or bolt hemp, to dress flax, or to spin. And when their work is over to play them tunes on his fiddle.' But Luke notices something else about him that the others don't seem to see: 'sitting by the fire when he thinks no one is watching him roasting little live frogs and eating them'. Portunus' fiddle plays an uncanny music, to which folk are compelled to dance hectic wild dances.

*Lud-in-the-Mist* figures the dynamic between the forces of respectable Lud and the wild, romantic, uncanny, enchanting forces of faerie. Fairyland is fantasy, the uncanny other, the source of romantic wonder; but fairyland is also the past, the pre-Modern.

Nathanial first starts to suspect that Endymion Leer is an agent of fairyland when he hears the 'note' in his voice, and remembers the fellow's antiquarian interests(he is the author of an academic study, *Traces of Fairy in the Inhabitants, Customs, Art, Vegetation and Language of Dorimare*, banned in Lud). 'The past', the narrator tells us, 'was silent and belonged to the Silent People' [ch 12]. The Silent People are the fae: Taylorian porous subjectivity, as opposed to our present's buffered identities. They are Henry James Sumner Maine's 'status' old-world rather than today's 'contractual' levelling.

In Mirrlees' second novel, the non-fantastical *The Counterplot* (1923), a young woman, Teresa Lane, daughter of a well-to-do English family (Mirrlees' self-portrait) observes her family and friends during a summer spent in their country house: their games and love affairs and religious observances. Teresa is fascinated by the potency of fairy tales, in contrast to the banality and emptiness of modern discourse. At one point she reads Calderon's *Autos Sacramentales* (1660) registering her disappointing that it is too in thrall to its religious allegory, 'the characters abstractions – Grace, the Mosaic Law, and so on'. What works for Theresa is a fantasy that is rooted in the materiality of existence:

> I knew, of course, that [Calderon's *Autos*] were written in glorification of the Eucharist and that they were bound to be symbolic, and 'flowery and starry', and all the rest of it – but the unregenerate part of me – I suppose it's some old childhood's complex – has a secret craving for genre. Every fairy story I read when I was a child was a disappointment till I came upon Morris's Prose Romances, and then at last I found three dimensional knights and princesses, and a whole fairy countryside where things went on happening even when Morris and I weren't looking at them: cows being milked, horses being shod, lovers wandering in lanes; and one knew every hill and every tree, and could take the short cut from one village to another in the dark. [Mirrlees, *The Counterplot*, 122]

This is what Mirrlees herself writes in *Lud-in-the-Mist*: 'an *Auto* that was at once realistic and allegorical', as Teresa says here, one that insufflates its allegory with magic. It is one of the great successes of the novel that the reader does indeed come to feel they know every hill and every tree, and could take the short cut from one village to another in the dark. This beautifully detailed and rendered world, its solid ordinariness threaded through with the glamour and terror of fairyland, is also about grace and redemption: temptation in the form of those Edenic fruit; Chanticleer with his cock-crow name facing down three denials before he is able to recover the lost children.

Unlike Lud, Mirrlees' fairyland is not worldbuilt. It is a place, a *locus numen*, but the novel doesn't go there. We are not given its society, the character of individual fairies – their kings and queens, their modes of habitation. They are the Silent People. Though they are drawn into the logic of mythology, and disposed into the story, it is relevant that the narrative structures of the novel are, in effect, modern-ones: a Scottian smuggling adventure, à la *Redgauntlet*; a twentieth-century whodunit like Agatha

Christie. And it is particularly relevant that the numen becomes, at the end, not only absorbed into modernity but commodified and sold around the world. *Lud-in-the-Mist* is not just a novel in which quotidian solidities grow transparent, allowing to glimmer through them the contours of a stranger world – it is a novel about that process, that haunting. Fairyland is delusive. But so, in another way, is modernity. *Lud-in-the-Mist* does not posit a linear supersession of past by present model. There's something more dialectical at work in its juxtaposition of rational Modernity and fae-porous Past, each haunting the other. Fantasy is not an escapism into the magical world of the past, or into marvellous dimension of wonder: it is, precisely, the mutuality of past and present, of the wondrous and the rational, of status and contract, of porous awe and buffered legalist rationality, each construing the other.

# CHAPTER 13
## 1930s–40s: CHILDREN'S FANTASY

The works discussed in the previous chapter, written in the immediate post-war period, represent the first great florescence of fantasy writing, texts that engaged the acuity of disenchantment of industrial war by retreating to an idealized medieval vision of chivalric combat, many specifically set in versions of France. Novels by Dunsany, Eddison and Mirrlees were written into a world devastated by martial destruction, economic slump and the grievous death toll from the worldwide influenza pandemic. This process continued, in a sense, through 1930s and 1940s, although the centre of gravity shifted. The most notable fantasy writing across this period was children's literature. This is, we might say, remarkable: books pitched at children but written by adults and therefore written out of memory, in two senses of the word. There are truths about adulthood only adolescence can access, much as there are aspects of 'reality' only articulable by fantasy.

It was not all children's literature across the 1930s and 1940s, of course. Significant fantasy for adults continued to be written. Eddison elongated his idiosyncratic archaic fantasy project with his Zimiamvian Trilogy (*Mistress of Mistresses* (1935), *A Fish Dinner in Memison* (1941), *The Mezentian Gate* (1958)) – extensions of the mythography and textual strategies of *The Worm Ouroboros*, and novels imbrued with antiquated notions of chivalry, with respect to both warmaking and male courtship of women. There is Conan the Barbarian, pitched somewhere between an adult readership and a juvenile one. In America between 1931 and his death (by suicide, aged just thirty) in 1936, Robert Howard wrote twenty-one short stories about this barbarian warrior. All but one of these were published in magazine *Weird Tales*, and though Conan's chief characteristic is his burly strength, his warrior courage and readiness for a fight – battling men and monsters across the landscapes of 'Hyperborea', a prehistoric version of Europe 'before Atlantis fell' – there is potent weirdness in the telling too. Here is Lovecraft's definition of 'the weird', for Lovecraft was a manifest influence upon Howard's writing:

> A certain atmosphere of breathless and unexplainable dread of outer, unknown forces must be present; and there must be a hint, expressed with a seriousness and portentousness becoming its subject, of that most terrible conception of the human brain – a malign and particular suspension or defeat of those laws of Nature which are our only safeguard against the assaults of chaos and the daemons of unplumbed space …. Therefore we must judge a weird tale not by the author's intent, or by the mere mechanics of the plot; but by the emotional level which it attains at its least mundane point.[1]

---

[1]Lovecraft, 'Supernatural Horror in Literature', *The Recluse* (1927).

It is this, in the words of John Holbo, 'that keeps Conan from just being a bully'. Conan is a 'Cimmerian', as Howard calls the descendants of the Atlanteans, and the ancestor, we are told, of today's Celts: a mighty thewed and dauntless hero, born on a battlefield, grown to superb strength and courage, combative, agile, intelligent, possessed of a sense of honour, blue-eyed, black-haired, his barbarian outfit leaving much of his tanned skin and many of his bulging muscles on display. In addition to being strong, Conan is lithe, canny, repeatedly compared to a panther. His adventures are, in one sense, wish-fulfilment: Howard, who lived with his mother throughout his short life and never left his hometown of Cross Plains Texas and its environs, was a bookish child with a weak heart and precarious mental health, who sought compensation in body-building, boxing and fantasies of implacable strength, dauntlessness, victory and travel. Holbo pinpoints the way such a figure reaches back through time to a more 'authentic' age, freeing the reader, and writer, from the discontents of restrictive civilization: Conan 'spends his time actively slaughtering generally weaker humans', Holbo notes, but 'in the stories he is reactive and just barely holding out in virtue of his panther-like-ness against some foul beast from the stygian pit du jour. So you get fantasy boldness and brutality, freedom from civilization and constraint, without the guilt that tends to attend slaughtering the weak. Such are the moral conveniences that breathless and unexplainable dread affords.'[2] There is something joyous yet silly about the exaggerations of Conan's frame and strength, the sheer ingenuousness of his barbarian appetites and vigour:

> Let me live deep while I live; let me know the rich juices of red meat and stinging wine on my palate, the hot embrace of white arms, the mad exaltation of battle when the blue blades flame and crimson, and I am content. Let teachers and priests and philosophers brood over questions of reality and illusion. I know this: if life is illusion, then I am no less an illusion, and being thus, the illusion is real to me. I live, I burn with life, I love, I slay, and am content. [Howard, 'Queen of the Black Coast' (1934)]

In addition to battling men, Conan wrestles with the unnerving and the terrifying. He might steal a jewel from a strange temple, battle a giant serpent or cleave soldiers on the battlefield, but he also endures a desperate night-fight against Thoth-Amon's demon, and boats upriver on the black waters of the death-river of Zarkheba.

> First there was the blackness of an utter void, with the cold winds of cosmic space blowing through it. Then shapes, vague, monstrous and evanescent, rolled in dim panorama through the expanse of nothingness, as if the darkness were taking material form. The winds blew and a vortex formed, a whirling pyramid of roaring blackness. From it grew Shape and Dimension; then suddenly, like clouds dispersing, the darkness rolled away on either hand and a huge city of dark green stone rose on the bank of a wide river, flowing through an illimitable plain.

---

[2]John Holbo, 'Conan', *Crooked Timber.*

Through this city moved beings of alien configuration. [Howard, 'Queen of the Black Coast']

Conan often swears by 'Crom', his god, a more Lovecraftian deity than Thor or Ares:

Conan's gods were simple and understandable; Crom was their chief, and he lived on a great mountain, whence he sent forth dooms and death. It was useless to call on Crom, because he was a gloomy, savage god, and he hated weaklings. But he gave a man courage at birth, and the will and might to kill his enemies, which, in the Cimmerian's mind, was all any god should be expected to do. [Howard, 'The Tower of the Elephant' (1933)]

This dark sublimity is a quality missing from the Schwarzeneggerized movie versions of the 1980s [*Conan the Barbarian* (1982, directed by John Milius); *Conan the Destroyer* (1984, directed by Richard Fleischer)] and so from the Conan of today's popular imagination. In the original stories, if there is something adolescent, in both a good and bad way, about Howard's muscly hero and his adventures, such juvenility is shot-through with intimations of something profound, a dark sublimity just off the focal-point of the rattling action-filled narrative.

After Howard's death in 1936 his work languished for some years, until republished in volume form in the 1950s. The Gnome Press published a multi-volume edition of all Howard's Conan stories, 1950–7; the first paperback editions were edited by, and in some instances rewritten by, Lin Carter and L. Sprague de Camp between 1966 and 1977. After this, and with the boom in popularity in 'sword and sorcery' of the 1960s and 1970s – discussed below – Conan grew greatly in popularity. L. Sprague de Camp and Lin Carter added many new stories to the Conan canon, and in the 1980s Robert Jordan added another half-dozen novel length stories. These versions are, it must be said, vastly inferior to the originals. Jordan's Conan is a flatter, less interesting character, and the wish-fulfilment fantasy of the conceit runs banally into overpowering strength and insistent sexualization.[3] In one sense this reflects the way this mode of fantasy – barbarian warrior in a perilous land – has moved from its Howardian origins into mere salaciousness, wish-fulfilment narrowing to heterosexual porn, fixated on rape and domination. In this tradition American writer John Norman has published, to date, thirty-eight novels set in the world of 'Gor', starting with *Tarnsman of Gor* (1966) and *Outlaw of Gor* (1967) up to the most recent *Warriors of Gor* (2022) and *Treasure of Gor* (2024). The first half dozen Gor novels were published by Ballantine, the next eighteen

---

[3]Jordan's (non-Conan) *Wheel of Time* novels are discussed below, but this is as good a place as any to note his half dozen Conan novels, with their bragging, Trumpish titles: *Conan the Invincible* (1982); *Conan the Defender* (1982); *Conan the Unconquered* (1983); *Conan the Magnificent* (1984); *Conan the Triumphant* (1983); *Conan the Victorious* (1984). Jordan strips away all the *Weird Tales* weirdness from the original stories, all the dark sublimity and potency. In its place he instead gives us violence and sex, with an egregious focus on naked breasts and spanking.

by DAW, but, after *Magicians of Gor* (1988), as the books became increasingly sexual-explicit and fixated, the violence against women increasingly repellent, DAW refused to publish any more. After a hiatus, Norman took advantage of the possibilities of online e-book publication to resume the series with *Witness of Gor* (2001) and a dozen more books followed. Though they have sold well, the present history has no intention of giving Norman's novels any further attention than this.

Though this is one of the ways in which Howard's Conan stories have fed-through into later fantasy, his original stories have nothing of this noisomeness. Conan certainly engages in what Howard calls 'wenching', but the stories never indulge themselves in the sorts of sexually objectifying and demeaning tactics of those later cash-in works. Howard's Conan has an affinity for women and likes them for themselves. Belit, a pirate queen who becomes Conan's lover, is fierce and capable, for all that she is 'conquered' by Conan's superior strength. Zenobia, a concubine who helps Conan escape from prison in 'The Hour of the Dragon' (1938), is resilient and sensible – when she steals imprisoned Conan a knife he notes with satisfaction that it is a proper dagger, and not a weak fruit knife – and in later stories she becomes Conan's Queen. In fact whilst there is very little male desire expressed in Howard's stories, except occasionally to characterize lecherous villains, there is a good deal of female desire articulated, especially in the novella *Red Nails* (1936). Howard's Conan, though an acme of masculine strength, is also feminized (in a stereotypical way): with his soft 'panther' tread, always looked at and admired by others – and by the narrative voice. He is a 'man not like normal men', moved by instincts and passions rather than reason, and repeatedly manifests an affinity for women, the imprisoned, enslaved. In a way, Conan and women are akin. And through all runs a sublimity of weirdness, a quality none his imitators have managed to replicate: a melancholy fatalism, a sense that, amid all the triumphs, speaks of the limits of life, even, or perhaps especially, for a hero.

The weirdness pedal is pressed more forcefully, though to lesser effect, by American writer and recluse Clark Ashton Smith. In a series of 1930s short stories also published in *Weird Tales*, Smith delineated a far-future Earth that has devolved to medieval fantastika, a world of adventure and marvel that is also filled with dread and morbidities. There is a strong Orientalist, and in places nakedly racist, logic at work here, and a continual striving for intensities that becomes self-defeating. These tales *are* atmospheric, although that atmosphere is pressurized by stylistic excess and fervidities of imagination to the point where it becomes morbidly gloopy, unbreathable. Smith is prone to Poe-like overwriting, his style something dark-pearl nacreous and sometimes simply clogged and fulsome. Smith's adventurers and heroes move through a cosmos of unspeakabilities: 'the skies are haunted by that which it were madness to know; and strange abominations pass evermore between earth and moon and athwart the galaxies. Unnameable things have come to us in alien horror and will come again' [Smith, 'The Beast of Averoigne' (1933)]. But, as with Poe, Gothic excession and gore often tip the writing into the farcical, an aesthetic and imaginative adolescency. In 'The Empire of the Necromancers' (1932) two wizards, Mmatmuor and Sodosma, wander about reanimating corpses, eventually revivifying the entire population of a dead city to serve them. They get their come-uppance whilst reclining on couches of pink and purple, 'with the wan, bloodless dead about them in patient ranks'. Enter the reanimated mummy of a former pharaoh:

> Upheld by the ancient prophecy and the lore of the bright tablets, Hestaiyon lifted the great sword and struck off the head of Mmatmuor and the head of Sodosma, each with a single blow. Then he quartered the remains with mighty strokes. And the necromancers gave up their unclean lives, and lay supine, without movement, adding a deeper red to the rose and a brighter hue to the sad purple of their couches.

'Sad purple' is a nicely ludicrous colour, the shading of the tales.

This balance of adult and children's literature also runs through Tolkien's writing. He worked continually at his 'legendarium', producing through the 1920s and 1930s multiple drafts of material that would, eventually, be published posthumously under the editorial aegis of his son Christopher (twelve volumes issued under the title *The History of Middle-earth* [1983–2002], as well as *The Children of Húrin* [2009], *Beren and Lúthien* [2017] and *The Fall of Gondolin* [2018]). As well as working and revising this work in progress, Tolkien also put out a novel of immense moment to fantasy: *The Hobbit* (1937).

The importance of *The Hobbit* as part of the history of fantasy as a mode can hardly be overstated, both on its own terms, and as the prelude to *The Lord of the Rings*. But it is worth stressing that this is a children's novel, and as such part of a rich seam of children's fantasy written across these decades – in its way richer even than the so-called 'golden age' of children's books (broadly from the 1880s to 1914). Child-sized Bilbo has a succession of fantastical adventures much as Alice did before him, though he comes *from* the underground of his hobbit-hole into adventure rather than tumbling down Alice's rabbit hole. Like Alice, *The Hobbit* is peripatetic and episodic, a string of encounters with talking animals and aloof royalty, with forgetfulness and adventure, interspersed with ballads and poems – parodies in Carroll, pastiche in Tolkien – and where Alice changes size, Bilbo changes visibility.

Tolkien himself, though he took the 'subcreation' of his fantasy world seriously, could be defensive about the, as he saw it, infantile dimension of his work. Writing to his future wife Edith in March 1916 he offers refrain from his 'nonsense fairy language' because 'though I love it so it does seem such a mad hobby!' Edith, fortunately, was content that he continue. Tolkien appreciated childhood in the way a person will who has been forced to grow up too young: first by the death of both parents (he was an orphan by the age of twelve), material hardship in England and then fighting in the Great War. His book for children is, in many ways, grown-up, and his child-sized and childlike hobbit characters are, by mortal reckoning, middle aged; but his book for adults is also a book for children.

A good way of understanding *The Hobbit* is to place it the context of 1930s fantasy writing for children. The landscapes of A. A. Milne's *Winnie-the-Pooh* (1926) and *The House at Pooh Corner* (1928) anticipate in some respects the later imagined worlds of Tolkien, without the latter's scale or grandeur, and without the 'deep history' that

Tolkien took such pains to construct and thread through his storytelling. When Michael Moorcock called *Lord of the Rings* 'epic Pooh' he meant to be disparaging, but actually there is a continuity that runs both ways: dignifying the imagined world of Milne, and capturing the delight and innocence that shine through Tolkien's imagined world, or at least through those parts of it uncorrupted by darkness. For Tolkien as a Christian, took seriously the injunction in Matthew 18:3: 'except ye become as little children, ye shall not enter into the kingdom of heaven.'

Milne's simple hero, living in a den underground; the comfortable roads and fields, the 'wild wood' that marks the boundary where peril and glamour impend – this is the Shire and Mirkwood in nascent form. The fantasyland of 'Pooh corner' is not without its dangers, and the class-allegory by which the Tory Milne deprecated proletarian agitation for social reform in the form of orc-like weasels storming the habitations of the good has struck more than one reader, as it strikes the present study, as reactionary toxicity. But the sheer charm of the Poohverse, its delight, is second to none.

There are particular reasons why Milne and Tolkien rendered their fantasylands the way they did. Milne served in the 4th Battalion, Royal Warwickshire Regiment, on the Somme; and not just the landscape of the Poohverse, its fields and woods, but the specific adventures the stories' characters enjoy, derive in some sense from this experience – Pooh soaring into the sky hanging onto a gigantic balloon, like an observer from a First World War military balloon (the RFC included nineteen balloon companies) or Toad careening around the countryside in his big 'staff' car. Winnie, the titular bear, was based on a toy owned by Milne's young son Christopher Robin Milne (who also appears in the stories) who was in turn named after an actual brown bear, the mascot of the Canadian Fort Garry Horse Regiment, which company won battle honours at Ypres and Amiens. To reconfigure the traumatic events of war into a logic of childish pastoral and delight manifests a therapeutic instinct that informs the way these stories then shine through other generations.

It might seem anomalous to mention the novels of P G Wodehouse here, for he wrote nothing that would by conventional genre metrics be called fantasy. Yet the imagined spaces of his Jeeves and Wooster novels have something of the paradisical quality and affect of Milne's fantasyland. Written notionally for adults, in fact the adventures of the hapless and ingenuous Bertie Wooster and his coolly capable manservant Jeeves iterate a retreat from the demands of adulthood: a common plot involves Wooster 'threatened' with sex (by, for instance, facing the prospect of marriage to one or other young woman) from which predicament he is extricated by Jeeves. Wooster's frank innocence enjoys the simpler delights: delicious food, play, friendship, becoming again as a little child; and the landscapes of the Wodehouse novels are often pastoral *loci amoeni*, country houses in beautiful settings. It helps that Wodehouse is perhaps the greatest writer of comic prose of the century: his range is narrow and he returns over and again to the same stories and locations and characters, but he is in total command of his instrument and he is genuinely laugh-aloud funny. The world of Wodehouse is a fantasy realm in the sense that it is a place of joy and sunshine into which we can escape from the pressures of reality.

André Maurois, an eminent French litterateur (a member of the prestigious Académie Française), also fought in the First World War. Maurois's *Patapoufs et Filifers* ('Fattypuffs and Thinifers' 1930), a book of immense charm and wit, takes its young deuteragonists, Edmund and Terry, through a cleft in a rock and down an escalator to a fantastic underworld in which two nations – the corpulent, gourmand 'Patapoufs' and the gaunt, angular, workaholic 'Filifers' – are at war. France and Prussia being thereby refracted into childhood fantasy, each boy ends up in a different kingdom, rising through the ranks in each and eventually overseeing a peace and union, the creation of 'the United States of the Underground'. Edmund and Terry then return home, to discover that though they spent ten months underground, only an hour has passed on the surface.

If the appalling slaughter of the Western Front becomes denatured and charmed in Maurois's fantasia, something darker underlies Jean de Brunhoff's *Histoire de Babar, le petit éléphant* (1931), the first in a series of titles detailing the adventures of a talking, clothes-wearing African elephant. After his mother is killed by hunters, young Babar travels to a city (unnamed in the stories, but evidently Paris) where he is civilized by a kindly old lady, taught to speak and dressed in clothes. Babar then returns to le Pays des Éléphants to rule it as king, building a city of his own and elevating the elephants around him into quasi-human modes of living. As a whitewash of the French and Belgian expropriation of tropical Africa – the search for, precisely, ivory that resulted in one of the most catastrophic and sanguinary mass-murders in human history – this is offensive.[4] Yet Babar, not Maurois' more charming tale, is the one that enters the logic of commodified mass-culture, becoming like Pooh a 'brand': made into movies, reproduced as toys, copied onto clothes and bags and other products, mass-produced as memorabilia and protected by aggressive copyright reinforcement. This ought not, perhaps, to surprise us.

John Masefield's *The Midnight Folk* (1927) and its sequel *The Box of Delights* (1935) detail a childhood that was old-fashioned even back then: a late Victorian world before electric lights, when travel is by horse and carriage, and fantasy erupts into the comfortably dull life of upper-middle-class Kay Harker. In the first book the pictures on her wall come to life, beckoning Harker into an adventure with pirates and witches and figures out of Arthurian legend, as well as the titular folk: talking cats and other animals. The notional plot, a hunt for lost treasure, is banal, but the affect is much more notable: its nocturnal and dreamlike progression. The Christmas-set sequel concerns a box that can magically shrink and enlarge people. Harker, taking possession of the box and pursued by a wicked magician called Abner Brown, goes on a more wide-ranging series of adventures than the former novel. Masefield's ambition in this novel is, in fact, to fold all the Matter of Britain into a children's fantasia: from King Arthur's knights, through Herne the Hunter and medieval alchemists, classic Punch and Judy shows and the hierarchies of the Anglican church – alongside Alexander the Great, and the siege

---

[4]See Herbert R. Kohl, *Should We Burn Babar?: Essays on Children's Literature and the Power of Stories*; Sika Alaine Dagbovie 'Long Live King Babar! Long Live Bourgeois Imperialism! Racist Elitism in *The Travels of Babar*'.

of Troy – to London (as Geoffrey of Monmouth's 'Troynovant', links Homer to Britain, as founded by Trojan Brutus). There are talking animals, cats and foxes, and a palpable connection with the logic of the Beast fable. The novel strikes in so many directions it becomes fissiparous, but in a manner that builds remarkable charges of enchantment, of ceremonious wonder and fantastical surrealism, a genuine eeriness that will shiver the skin of the most hardened reader.

Barbara Euphan Todd's *Worzel Gummidge* (1936), the first in a series of eleven books about the adventures of two children in company with a sentient and motile scarecrow, is doing something similar, with more focus and resonance. Though styled as bucolic comedy and full of pleasant absurdity and slapstick, the novel generates a pastoral enchantment that carries considerable, and often disorienting heft.

'How old are you?' asked Susan. 'All manner of ages', replied the scarecrow. 'My face is one age, and my feet are another, and my arms are the oldest of all.' 'How very very queer', said Susan. [Todd *Worzel Gummidge*, ch 2]

Much of the series plays the kindly but clumsy Gummidge, and his various magically animated friends, for laughs; but there the books also capture a sense of the long durée of Nature, the deep age of natural processes, 'roots tickling and shooting, rooks lifting in the wind, rabbits here, there, and scattered in a minute'.

Pastoral is also the mode of *The Hobbit* (1937), at least in its early portions. Rather than bringing fantasy into a version of England, Tolkien moves a version of England into his Fantasyland. In our world a 'shire' (from Old English *scir*: a share or cut of land) is divided into 'hundreds'; Tolkien's Shire is divided into 'farthings' – fewer and smaller, and inhabited by 'hobbits', a diminutive folk who live rural life, walking unshod, enjoying food and drink, smoking pipes. Bilbo Baggins, the protagonist, is an upper-middle-class hobbit chosen, for reasons that are somewhat obscure, by the wizard Gandalf to assist a group of dwarfs in their long-distance trek to a distant mountain in order, as with Masefield's novel, to recover some family treasure. The reason specified for the choice of Bilbo, manifestly unsuited though he be, is that the dwarfs number thirteen, an unlucky number; and that Bilbo by turning this into fourteen will bring luck with him. It is also assumed that with no training or apparent aptitude he will prove a skilled thief. In the event this proves true but only because on the way the hobbit chances upon a magic ring that renders him invisible. Bilbo's stealth enhanced by this magical transparency turns him into an excellent burglar.

*The Hobbit* is told in a comfortable, discursive, rather prolix style, with the narrator often interposing himself to address his child readers: an Edwardian style. The opening paragraphs are famous, establishing the haven of bourgeois domesticity out of which Bilbo will be ejected:

In a hole in the ground there lived a hobbit. Not a nasty, dirty, wet hole, filled with the ends of worms and an oozy smell, nor yet a dry, bare, sandy hole with nothing in it to sit down on or to eat: it was a hobbit-hole, and that means comfort. It had a perfectly round door like a porthole, painted green, with a shiny yellow brass knob in the exact middle. The door opened on to a tube-shaped hall like a tunnel: a very comfortable tunnel without smoke, with panelled walls, and floors tiled and carpeted, provided with polished chairs, and lots and lots of pegs for hats and coats – the hobbit was fond of visitors. The tunnel wound on and on, going fairly but not quite straight into the side of the hill – *The Hill*, as all the people for many miles round called it – and many little round doors opened out of it, first on one side and then on another. No going upstairs for the hobbit: bedrooms, bathrooms, cellars, pantries (lots of these), wardrobes (he had whole rooms devoted to clothes), kitchens, dining-rooms, all were on the same floor, and indeed on the same passage. The best rooms were all on the left-hand side (going in), for these were the only ones to have windows, deep-set round windows looking over his garden and meadows beyond, sloping down to the river. [*The Hobbit*, ch 1]

'People considered the Bagginses very respectable', the narrator tells us, not only because 'they were rich', but also 'because they never had any adventures or did anything unexpected'. Smaug is also rich, and never does anything adventurous or unexpected, lying in his own bag-end, the story's cul-de-sac, or cul-de drac. Bilbo travels from 'The Hill' – the only hill, or at least the only hill worthy of the definite article – to The Mountain: the Lonely Mountain. It's a transformation of scale, an access of grandeur, but also of depth: Smaug's tunnels, also a site of wealth and of retirement, but full of smoke and unhospitable to visitors. As wise old magical Gandalf visits Bilbo and extricates him from this hole, with significant consequences, so Bilbo visits the cunning, old, magical dragon, and winds up extricating him from his hole – with immediately destructive consequences. The depth here is temporal as well as physical: 'back' in time from comfortable modernity into the perilous, enchanted realms of an earlier age. The party travels east, out of the imagined fantasy-England into a wider, older magical world of mountains and dangerous forests, of trolls and shape-shifting bear-men. They meet elves, reimagined by Tolkien as an immortal aristocracy of purer and nobler beings whose habitation amongst mortal men (and hobbits) is, as we later discover, a kind of exile. They also meet antagonists: goblins who dwell in holey-spaces under the mountains, sometimes to emerge aboveground to swarm, ugly and malign.

The way Tolkien styles elves, dwarfs, orcs and hobbits has come to be so widely copied by later writers of fantasy novels and games as to become the default way of populating Fantasyland. We take it so much for granted, indeed, that we can forget how idiosyncratic were Tolkien's creative choices. This is a conception of the world as divided between groups that map recoded racial categories – Aryan elves, Jewish dwarfs, middle-eastern 'Southrons' and black-skinned orcs – that correlates these groups with an ethical armature of cosmic 'good and evil'.[5]

---

[5]See Dimitra Fimi, *Tolkien, Race and Cultural History: From Fairies to Hobbits* for a sensitive, detailed account of this aspect of Tolkien's imaginarium.

The adventures are varied and exciting, and each episode moves the story effectively along. Amongst the fairy-tale agents encountered are many elements from the beast fable: a shape-shifter called Beorn who alternates between man and bear, talking spiders of gigantic size, eagles of enormous size and loquacious intelligence – the party find their way into the treasure mountain with the help of a talking crow. The eagles return (in a non-speaking role) in *Lord of the Rings*, but the later book seems to inhabit a cosmos in which the animals are dumb – perhaps Tolkien's reaction to his friend C. S. Lewis's ongoing Narnia fabulations. But the contrast is a striking one. The world of *The Hobbit* thrums with life, a vividness of magical amplitude, that, whilst not entirely absent from the later novel, is less forcefully present. The difference between childhood and adulthood, perhaps.

By the time Bilbo and the dwarfs reach the Lonely Mountain the bourgeois cosiness of tone of the earlier sections is replaced by a more elevated and heroized idiom. The slaying of the dragon does not end the story, for now five separate armies converge on the mountain, and men, dwarfs and elves fight together against an assault by armies of goblins. The battle is won, although at some cost, with dwarf king Thorin slain. Bilbo travels home with enough dwarfish treasure to make him a wealthy man in the Shire. The overall story-structure, therefore, is, as specified in the novel's sub-title: 'There and Back Again': a fort-da pattern: extraversion into the wonder and danger of the outer world, followed by a recuperation into domestic security once again.

*The Hobbit*, taken together with the enlargement and deepening of *The Lord of the Rings*, represents the most significant and influential fantasy text of the century. Another significant fantasy novel of 1937 had, in itself, much less immediate impact, although it led to other things: Noel Langley's *The Tale of the Land of Green Ginger* (later editions shortened the title to *The Land of Green Ginger*), a confection of childish orientalism: Aladdin, from the *Arabian Nights*, has become emperor of China, and his son Abu Ali goes off on a 'hero's quest' adventure through various incidents and overcoming such facetiously named adversaries as Rubdub Ben Thud and Tintac Ping Foo. There is something interesting in building a story around what happens in the world of a fairy tale after 'they all lived happily ever after'. The book was a big enough success that it encouraged MGM to hire Langley to adapt another children's book, L Frank Baum's *The Wonderful Wizard of Oz*, for the big screen.

Baum's Oz novels (discussed above) are important for the history of fantasy, but this 1939 cinematic adaptation of the first of them is much more important. It is according to the US Library of Congress the 'most seen' film of all time; and its cultural dissemination is such that key moments and images have entered the collective imaginary, and even those who have not watched the movie know it.[6] Dorothy Gale, played with forceful ingenuousness by a teenage Judy Garland, is plucked from a life of black-and-white Kansas mundanity and transported to a colourful, enchanted fantasyland when a whirlwind blows her house through the sky to Oz – the windstorm literalizing the 'gale'

---

[6]"To See *The Wizard of Oz* on Stage and Film". Library of Congress; 15 December 2010.

of her surname, pointing up the ambiguous status of her journey as both real travels and interiorized fantastical escapism. The moment when Dorothy opens the door of her monochrome cabin to reveal the technicolour splendour of this new location is one of the greatest *coups de cinema* ever filmed. In Munchkinland, surrounded by a crowd of dancing and singing mini-people, Dorothy discovers that her house has fortuitously landed on and crushed the Wicked Witch of the East. A good witch, Glinda transfers the ruby slippers from the feet of the dead *malefica* onto Dorothy's own, advising her never to take off the shoes, for they have magic power. The dead witch's sister, the Wicked Witch of the West, appears in a puff of smoke and threatens Dorothy (and her dog Toto, who has also come to Oz) with terrible consequences, but for some reason her magic is denatured in Munchkinland and she is forced to withdraw.

Desirous of getting home, Dorothy must 'follow the yellow brick road' to the Emerald City, where the film's titular magician 'the Great and Mighty Wizard of Oz', can assist her. This journey, through a succession of intense colourfield locations – sharply red poppy-fields under bright-blue skies through which the bright yellow road curls like sunlight towards the bright green walls of the movie's Zion – entails Dorothy making three new friends: a living Scarecrow whose head is full of straw and who yearns to supply his intellectual insufficiency with an actual brain; a Tin Man, who lacks a heart and is unable to love; and a Cowardly Lion who is ashamed of his pusillanimity and desires to acquire courage. Dorothy assures them, although it is not clear on what grounds she knows, that the Wizard will grant all these wishes. So the group pass various antagonists – hostile trees with bad faces and clutching arms, the Wicked Witch and her alarming troop of flying monkeys – to reach Oz. Here Oz's head, projected gigantically upon a screen, tells them they must bring him the Wicked Witch's broomstick if they want their wishes granted, so the team set off for her castle. After further adventures Dorothy kills the witch in a startling and gruesome fashion: it transpires that throwing a bucket of water causes the witch literally to melt, her flesh deliquescing in a manner that is, judging by her screams ('I'm melting! melting!' she howls), genuinely agonizing. On bringing the dead witch's broom back to the Emerald City, Dorothy discovers that Oz is not great and mighty after all, but small and mortal: behind a curtain, where is located the machine by which he amplifies his voice and casts a giant projection of his head, he is revealed to be a petty fellow, kindly but fraudulent, a huckster who also comes, coincidentally, from Kansas. He grants the wishes of the Scarecrow, Tin Man and Lion by giving them symbolic indices of their desires – respectively a university scroll, a heart-shaped fob watch and a medal inscribed 'for valor', thereby uplifting them out of their unselfconfidence and revealing that they always actually had 'within them' that which they thought they lacked. Dorothy too, we discover, has always had the power to return home, by clicking the heels of her magic slippers. This she does, repeatedly chanting 'there's no place like home', to awake back in Kansas, once again on black-and-white film stock, where her three Oz companions – and the Wicked Witch too – are revealed to be local farm workers and neighbours.

The film is about home, but in a complicated way; styling domesticity as at once a stifling, oppressive thing from which we yearn to escape, and the place towards which we yearn to return. The movie certainly itself is, as Salman Rushdie says, 'about the joys of going away, of leaving the greyness and entering the colour', but also (as he doesn't say) about the fort-da impetus that makes us want to come back to the greyness.[7] Before the initial whirlwind arrives, Judy Garland sings 'Somewhere Over The Rainbow' (music and lyrics by Harold Arlen and Yip Harburg), a plangent *cri de coeur*, gorgeously delivered by Garland's vocal fusion of strength and vulnerability, a song wholly about the need to overcome the entrapment of mundanity and run off to colour, enchantment, life in its fullest sense. The melody, leaping a full octave between the two syllables of the first word of its title, actualizes that soaring yearning and looks forward to the movie's stormy aerial sequence. Once in Oz's fantasyland the music changes mood: all the remaining songs are upbeat, brisk-tempo, catchy and sing-along, and Dorothy herself is no longer stuck but always in motion, tramping along her golden road. The first such song is the raucous, upbeat paean 'Ding Dong! The Witch Is Dead' (also by Arlen and Harburg). Sung by a Munchkin collective played variously by dwarfs and children, it takes a frankly indecorous delight in the demise and posthumous infernal punishment of the eastern witch:

> Ding-dong, the witch is dead! Which old witch? The wicked witch
> Ding-dong, the wicked witch is dead
> Wake up you sleepy head, rub your eyes, get out of bed
> Wake up, the wicked witch is dead!
> She's gone where the goblins go below, below, below, yo ho.

A sentiment that would have delighted any number of seventeenth-century witchfinder generals, this: Arthur Miller's *The Crucible* as musical comedy rather than tragedy. The Munchkin coroner (played by Meinhardt Raabe) presents Dorothy with the witch's death-certificate. It is, we might think, an unusual move for the authorities to pass such documentation to the deceased's killer rather than her next of kin, and equally unusual for a coroner to be so gleeful at having to certify someone's death:

> As coroner, I must aver
> I thoroughly examined her
> And she's not only merely dead
> She's really, most sincerely dead!

Death bookends the film, the sisters East and West dying at the beginning and the end of Dorothy's sojourn in Oz. Pause the movie, zoom-in on the Munchkin coroner's death-scroll, and you see the date of death recorded as May 6th. L. Frank Baum himself died on 6 May 1919. This is not a coincidence. The studio leaked the story to the press that the tatty jacket worn by Frank Morgan as the Wizard of Oz was bought from a thrift

---

[7]Rushdie, *The Wizard of Oz*, 23.

store, and turned out to be a jacket previously owned and worn by Baum himself. This, it seems, was not actually true, but that the studio promulgated it is significant. The death of the author is the rebirth of the author. These Munchkinland dallyings with death are not morbid: they represent the death of mundanity, of the disenchanted world Dorothy had left behind. And yet as soon as she arrives in her yearned-for fantasy she wants to return home: 'there's no place like home'. This is less paradoxical than it seems. Dorothy, stifled by her buffered sensibility in Kansas, finds her new technicolour porosity in Oz at once marvellous and terrifying. There is a difference between the clean-break demise of the Wicked Witch of the East and the horrifying, prolonged, acid-bath liquefying of her sister.

Fantasyland is colour, just as mundane-land (our world) is black and white. But though the movie revels in the possibilities of its rainbow – indeed, beyond-rainbow – realm, it also spends its length trying to rescue its protagonist from that place, to return her to the home she repeatedly craves. Rushdie finds this a fatal contradiction in the text:

> Are we to believe that Dorothy has learned no more on her journey than that she didn't need to make such a journey in the first place? Must we accept that she now accepts the limitations of her home life, and agrees that the things she doesn't have there are no loss to her?

Rushdie solves this contradiction, at least to his own satisfaction, by referring to Baum's later 'Oz' novels, in which Dorothy does return to Oz: this, he claims, implies that the character's true home is there. We might literalize Dorothy's mantra *there's no place like home* so as to render home precisely *no-place*, that is: utopia. 'So Oz finally became home', says Rushdie. 'There is no longer any such place as home: except, of course, for the home we make, or the homes that are made for us, in Oz: which is anywhere, and everywhere, except the place from which we began.' This, though, is crushingly to oversimplify the valence of 'home', and our desire for it. Dorothy is as much an orphan in Oz as she is in Kansas. The fundamental home from which she has been expelled is irreplaceable *maternitas*. Growing up, which is what this movie is about, is inevitably a journey away from home and therefore from the mother. The first thing motherless Dorothy does when arriving in Oz is to kill a woman old enough to be her mother. The next thing Dorothy does is to steal the older woman's scarlet footwear, the glamour and magic of adult power, red (like Little Red Riding Hood's cape) to symbolize menses, the mark of physical and sexual maturity. But, as Little Red discovered for herself, there are terrors as well as wonders in the woodland of adulthood; and every adult understands the yearning to retreat from maturity back to the lost home, to return to that no-place. There is a place like Oz, but there's no place like home; which is to say, Oz is not home because it is a dream, and Kansas is home, despite its shortcomings because it is real. We dream in order to wake up. That dream from which we do not wake is called death, marked on our death certificate, our habiliments (coats, shoes) passed on to other folk.

Artist and critic David Batchelor considers the moment when Dorothy first opens the door to reveal Oz 'the most famous story of colour's arrival in a monochromatic world'. He connects it to Italo Calvino's meditation on the arrival of colour in the world as such – in a section of *Cosmocomics* (1965) called 'Without Colour' Calvino evokes the early planet as 'a contrastless grey expanses without even the extremes of black and white'. As we all know, it took billions of years before the co-evolution of flowering plants and pollinating insects first brought colour to the landscape. There is, Batchelor thinks, something of that deep resonance, a mythic expressiveness, to this moment in *The Wizard of Oz*, occurring, he calculates 'exactly 16 minutes and 50 seconds after the opening credits'.

> The greyscale landscape of Kansas is not so much modified by colour as utterly obliterated by it – for a while, at least … When colour arrives in *The Wizard of Oz* it comes as a big surprise, as Dorothy literally falls into a new world of colour. It is confusing, disorienting, and it takes a little while to get used to; but it is also a source of wonder, delight, often intense and sometimes explicitly narcotic pleasure. And, at the same time, all this takes place in an atmosphere of childlike innocence.[8]

In a sense colour 'is' fantasy, the pleasure of the eyes, the enchantment of the senses. And *The Wizard of Oz* movie is a dream of colour. Baum's novel doesn't stress the colour transition the way the film does: the narrator talks quite generally about 'a country of marvellous beauty' with 'lovely patches of greensward all about' and 'strange and beautiful sights'. In the novel Dorothy is more struck by the *sound* of water ('a small brook, rushing and sparkling along between green banks, and murmuring in a voice very grateful to a little girl who had lived so long on the dry prairies') than the colour of things. The Munchkins do thank Dorothy for killing the Wicked Witch of the West, as in the movie, but there is no song and dance, no coroner presenting a death certificate like a prize, and the shoes that Dorothy appropriates from the corpse are silver, not red. What the movie does so brilliantly – literally brilliantly as well as metaphorically – is render the transition from mundanity to fantasy, from childhood to adulthood, through death into life, in so vividly coloured a way. There are other differences between book and film. In the novel the Munchkins are described as 'not as big as the grown folk [Dorothy] had always been used to; but neither were they very small. In fact, they seemed about as tall as Dorothy, who was a well-grown child for her age'. By making them so much smaller even than Dorothy, the film adds emphatic force to the transition from reality to fantasy.

*The Wizard of Oz* is a secularized *Pilgrim's Progress*. In Baum's novel, Glinda summarizes Dorothy's way as 'a long journey, through a country that is sometimes pleasant and sometimes dark and terrible'. Dorothy progresses along a road of gold, past temptations and dangers, towards an Emerald Zion (Bunyan knew, as presumably Baum did likewise, that the door that opens in the citadel of Heaven, as per Revelation 4:3 is 'a rainbow that had the appearance of an emerald'). Bunyan's book is presented 'in the

---

[8]Batchelor, *The Luminous and the Grey*, 21.

similitude of a dream', but *The Wizard of Oz* is truer to the dream-logic of its styling. That something will come again out of no-place – there's no-place, and it's like home – is the promise of the work, and is what makes it so powerful and moving.

In 1939 a second great war began, and a tidal shift in world history brought in its wake a shift in fantasy. This, though, took a while to effectuate. Eric Linklater's *The Wind on the Moon: A Story for Children* (1944) engages the war through whimsy: two English sisters, Dinah and Dorinda, are transformed by magic potion into kangaroos and become embroiled in a zoo adventure solving the mystery of an ostrich's missing eggs. In its second half the book swerves into an adventure in a fictionalized Nazi mainland: the girls accompanied by a golden puma and a silver falcon infiltrate the militarized land of 'Bombardy' to rescue the girls' father from the prisons of the nation's evil dictator. The tone is more serious in this second half, and the novel formally enacts a slightly wrenching shift, from whimsy to dark fantasy, that actualizes the war.

Finnish artist and writer Tove Jansson's 'Moomin' books are also informed, but not overshadowed, by the war. After a first volume that only partly relates to the main Moomin story (*The Moomins and the Great Flood*, 1945) Jansson published eight Moomin novels, illustrating them all herself: *Comet in Moominland* (1946: original title *Kometjakten*, literally 'comet-hunt'); *Finn Family Moomintroll* (1948: originally *Trollkarlens hatt*, 'The Magician's Hat');[9] *The Exploits of Moominpappa* (1950: *Muminpappans bravader*); *Moominsummer Madness* (1954: *Farlig midsommar*, 'midsummer danger'); *Moominland Midwinter* (1957: *Trollvinter*); *Tales from Moominvalley* (1962: *Det osynliga barnet*, 'the invisible child'); *Moominpappa at Sea* (1965: *Pappan och havet*); *Moominvalley in November* (1970: *Sent i November*, 'Late November'). The Moomins are trolls, those same beings that are familiar from Scandinavian legend, although Jansson's trolls are a particular tribe, neither frightening nor predatory, but rather epitomes of a kind of welcoming softness: Jansson chose the name *mumin* (transliterated into English as 'moomin' to avoid Anglophones calling them *mummins*) because she considered the letters 'm' and 'u' the softest in speech; and her drawings show rounded, large-snouted, snow-white creatures who are soft without being flabby. Moominmamma wears a red-white striped apron, and Moominpappa wears a top-hat. The books' main character, their child Moomintroll, wears nothing. His best friend, Snufkin, is a humanoid of indeterminate age, a person somehow at once a wise old man and a quirky child, who wears a green robe and large-brimmed felt hat, smokes a pipe and sometimes plays a squeezebox. He is something like a wizard, just as Moomintroll is something like a hobbit. An episode in the middle of *Comet in Moominland*, in which Moomintroll and Sniff travel to 'the Lonely Mountain', encounter eagles and chance upon a golden ring, shows that Jansson has read *The Hobbit*. But though Tolkien was very interested in Scandinavia, Jansson, an actual Scandinavian, takes a rather different approach to the

---

[9]This being the first volume to appear in English translation, the UK publishers took the bizarre decision to remind potential purchasers of Johan Wyss's *Swiss Family Robinson* (1812), a connection entirely unlicensed by Jansson's text, hoping thereby to boost sales. It is regrettable that this title has persisted in anglophone countries.

matter of fantasy. She is less interested in warrior culture, and her ethos of heroism is small-scale, familial and amicable.

Moomintroll has a kind of on-off girlfriend, called Snork Maiden, identifiable by a spread of blonde hair on her big white snouty head, although there is not really any persistent romantic focus in the stories. Rather Moomintroll and his friends, including a kangaroo-like creature called Sniff, a boisterous human girl in a red dress called Little My, a silk monkey and a witch's granddaughter, play and have adventures in the landscape of Moominvalley and beyond. Critics note how Jansson worked autobiography into fantasy: Moomintroll is a gender-swapped version of herself and Snufkin is based upon her onetime lover Atos Wirtanen, although it's also possible to read Snufkin as Jansson herself, and various characters as Tuulikki Pietilä, her eventual life-partner. Jansson was a queer woman in a country in which homosexuality was illegal (Finland did not decriminalize homosexuality until 1971, and it was treated as a mental illness until 1981). Jansson's private code-word for other lesbians was 'ghosts', and there are ghosts, of a sort, haunting Moominworld too: Hattifatteners, floating sock-shaped creatures made in some manner out of electricity. Hattifatteners move in crowds seeking constantly to reach the horizon that constantly evades them; but there is nothing scary or alarming about these ghosts, who drift through the books always on their way somewhere. They recharge their vital force during storms of thunder-and-lightning, and at that time they may inflict electrical burns on people around them, although always inadvertently.

The charm of Jansson's fantasy realm is how inclusive it is, an extended family in which diversity and eccentricity and nonconformity always find a home. Not that Moominworld is denatured or over-safe. There are dangers – the approaching comet in the second novel, the great storm in the eighth – as well as various hostile creatures like crocodiles and bears and insects. But the heart of the novels is a tolerant, hospitable, eccentric and slightly shambolic extended family, a place where children (which is to say: people, for we are all children) can play, from which they can venture out to explore and adventure and to which they can always return. *Comet in Moominland* owes something to Belgian cartoonist Hergé's early Tintin book, *L'Étoile mystérieuse* ('The Shooting Star', 1942): as in the *bande dessinée* a comet approaches Moominworld, threatens to end the world but in the end simply misses and life goes on – although Jansson moves the story from Hergé's bright but hard *ligne clair* realization of actual France into a softer mode of her fantastical version of Finland. Still, towards the story's end, as the comet looms blindingly bright low in the sky, Jansson's illustrations take on a dramatic visual intensity: characters stalk across a huge Gothic stage-set, starkly spotlit. Though there is a profound welcomeness about the Moomin novels, and a beautiful hospitality, they are rarely cosy. The edge of the strange and terrifying that fantasy permits Jansson flavours the novels' sweetness perfectly.

The last novel is the autumnal *Moominvalley in November* (1970), a beautiful, mournful book, about the forlornness of fantasy, the sadness that, I have been arguing, interpenetrates the mode. A group of characters (Mymble, Grandpa-Grumble, Toft, Fillyjonk and the Hemulen) visit the Moomins' house to find the family all away. They occupy the place waiting for their return. Unlike Godot the Moomins do come back, but only at the very end of the story, and the bulk of the story relates the characters' sometimes fractious interactions whilst they wait. Toft is an orphan, and in mourning; Fillyjonk becomes obsessed with putrefaction and decay. Out of the illustrations in a microbiology textbook that happens to be in the house the two somehow summon a gigantic bacterium, 'the Creature', that grows and sparks: 'And it grew and grew, and now there was more lightning, white and violet! The Creature became bigger and bigger. It became so big that it almost didn't need any family.' As a projection of their own bereaved status, the Creature embodies the exhilaration and terror of familial separation and deprivation, and also, in shrinking down again, the inescapable need for reconnection and belonging.

> Toft slumped over the book with his paws clutching his hair and went on describing things to himself, desperately and in a disordered fashion, for he knew that the Creature was getting smaller and smaller the whole time and couldn't really fend for itself. [*Moominvalley in November* (transl. Kingsley Hart), 82]

Frank Cottrell-Boyce calls this 'the wisest and most moving book about mourning I've ever read'.[10] There is an apprehension of sadness woven in with the joy, the roundedness of emotional settlement and unsettlement.

Though she herself valued her other writing, and artwork, it was the Moomin books that made Jansson, as Boel Westin says, 'a megastar in the 1950s'. Indeed, Jansson sometimes resented the disproportionate popularity of these works:

> The Moomins were a huge commercial hit, spawning dolls, clothes, soaps, mugs, theme parks and made her famous around the world. But her creation wore her down: she 'vomited Moomins', she said. Writing the Moomin books, and, from 1954, drawing a weekly Moomin cartoon strip for the *London Evening News*, took her away from her other work. 'By the end I was drawing with hatred'.[11]

As an adult, Jansson knew that earning money was needful, though she somewhat resented that it was through these titles that the money came, rather than from her other 'grown-up' art and literature. But she was, again as we all are, also a child:

> The best known and most frequently quoted of the few things she wrote about her own profession is her shrewd essay from 1961, 'The Deceitful Writer of Children's Books'. Hidden behind her books is a self-centred author who writes children's books as a way of coping with childishness in herself, certainly not to please children. A dangerous writer. A childishness unsuitable for the grown-up

---

[10]'In most fiction, family is what you escape from if you want to fulfil yourself. For Jansson, family is a place of tolerance, where we can fail and become ourselves. Her experience of growing up gay is there in Snufkin, who is all the more loved for being different' [Frank Cottrell-Boyce, 'Five Things to Learn from the Moomins'].
[11]Hogan, 'I Dream of Islands Every Night', 20.

world, a writer looking for something that existed in the past, something she wants to create again. In the words of the deceitful author, she wants to describe and experience 'something lost or unattainable'. The search for this is connected to the arcane secrecy of the Moomin books. It gives form to a certain longing that exists in all of us.[12]

It is this doubled sense that gives these books, in their re-enchantment of disenchanted adulthood via a fantastical recreation of childhood, such purchase. As fantasy, the Moomin books are less engaged with history in a collective, and more with history in a personal, sense. The topography of Moominland is both open-ended and specific, simultaneously a version of Jansson's actual Finland with its myriad islands and valleys, its blanketing winters and great storms – and a dream realm, hospitable to all. We could say that Jansson entered into her own country as if it were a fairyland forlorn, and not altogether forlorn.

Clive Staples Lewis's fantasy writing was also informed by an experience of profound, intense longing, felt from early life, and which he called 'sweet desire' and later 'Joy'. 'Inanimate nature and marvellous literature were among the things that evoked it', he wrote in 1943: 'sweet desire for the unnameable something, desire which pierces us like a rapier at the smell of a bonfire, the sound of wild ducks flying overhead, the title *The Well at the World's End*, the opening lines of Kubla Khan, the morning cobwebs in late summer or the noise of falling waves'.[13] By this point in his career he had established a reputation as a popular theologian, first with a series of broadcasts on UK radio during the Second World War, and then with many published works of Christian apologetics aimed at the general reader. These works tracked Lewis's own conversion, from youthful atheist materialism, via conversations with his friends Hugo Dyson and J R R Tolkien, to his own acceptance of Anglican Christianity: *The Problem of Pain* (1940), *The Case for Christianity* (1942), *The Abolition of Man* (1943), *Miracles: A Preliminary Study* (1947) and the still-bestselling *Mere Christianity* (1952; based on delivered radio talks of 1941–4). This theological context as much as Lewis's detailed, imaginatively engaged expertise in medieval allegory and romance, informed his fantasy writing.

Lewis later identified the origin of *The Lion, the Witch and the Wardrobe* in a dream-like image: 'it all began with a picture of a Faun carrying an umbrella and parcels in a snowy wood. This picture had been in my mind since I was about 16 [that is, 1915]. Then one day, when I was about 40, I said to myself: "Let's try to make a story about it".'[14] An image from one war was rendered into story during another, and bears its imprint. During 'Operation Pied Piper', by which the UK evacuated some 900,000 children out of cities in danger of enemy bombing into countryside locations, Lewis's Oxford house became the home of three London schoolgirls. Prompted by this, Lewis returned to his adolescent image and developed a narrative in which to frame it. The four Pevensie

---

[12]Westin, *Tove Jansson: Life, Art, Work*, 29.
[13]Lewis, *The Pilgrim's Regress*, 7–10.
[14]Lewis, *On Stories*, 53.

children, evacuees lodged in the country house of an elderly professor, discover a magic wardrobe in his attic ('O attic shape! Fair attitude') through which they can access the Fantasyland of Narnia. Lewis had completed the novel by 1947, though it was not published until 1950. Its success led in short order to six sequels: *Prince Caspian* (1951), *The Voyage of the Dawn Treader* (1952), *The Silver Chair* (1953), *The Horse and His Boy* (1954), *The Magician's Nephew* (1955) and *The Last Battle* (1956).

As a young boy, Lewis had been fascinated by the idea that animals might talk. As a grown man, drawing on fabliaux and medieval romances, he began writing Narnia desirous of creating a world hospitable to such bestial loquacity. His first drafts sketched a world in which beavers and horses, wolves and birds all talk. Later Lewis recalled that it was the creation of a talking lion that crystallized his writing: 'suddenly Aslan came bounding into it. I think', Lewis said, 'I had been having a good many dreams of lions about that time. Apart from that, I don't know where the Lion came from or why He came. But once He was there He pulled the whole story together, and soon He pulled the other six Narnian stories in after Him.'[15]

The lineaments of Narnia are, mostly, medieval, high-chivalric, romantic in the old sense of the word. Characters from this era are mixed with figures from classical myth, and aspects of bourgeois modernity also characterize the place – the faun's umbrella, and the parcels he is carrying. The macaronic nature of Narnia's worldbuilding offended Tolkien, who criticized his friend for not taking his fantasy creation seriously enough. He was particularly outraged that, having tossed-in characters from modernity, northern European legend and Greek mythology, Lewis also gives Father Christmas a cameo in *The Lion, the Witch and the Wardrobe*. The charm and indeed force of this impure but vital imaginative amalgamation is diminished in subsequent volumes, where Lewis seeks to explain away, or file off, the ornamentational excrescences of his fantastical imagination, and bring everything within an internally consistent framing superstructure. But the brilliant, inclusive oddness of the original conception remains Narnia's chief glory.

Lewis had previously published three books of science fictional romances. 'The Ransom trilogy' [*Out of the Silent Planet* (1938); *Perelandra* (1943); *That Hideous Strength* (1945)] reconfigures Christian myth and dogma into a set of space-faring *voyages extraordinaires* – to Mars, Venus and back to Earth – that actualize the moral drama of choice, and the pressure of evil. They are, as science fiction, somewhat recherché, in the good and bad sense of that word: often awkward in their mannered stiffness and their repudiation of materialism (this latter being the idiom, one might argue, of science fiction more generally) yet filled with flashes of brilliance and actualizing, especially in the final volume when Merlin reawakens from long slumber and comes alive in the modern world, a dynamic of re-enchantment. Closer to fantasy are the several proselytizing allegories Lewis published through the 1930s and 1940s: *The Pilgrim's Regress* (1933) an attempt, not wholly successful, to 'update' Bunyan, that proceeded

---

[15]Lewis, *Of Other Worlds*, 42.

from a discussion Lewis had with Tolkien and another Oxford Don, Hugo Dyson, one night in September 1931. Tolkien and Dyson were able to impress upon Lewis the notion that Christianity, though mythic rather than strictly historical, was nonetheless a *true* myth. From here it was a short step from Lewis's vaguely theistic worldview to a specific conversion experience into Christian belief.

Lewis, Tolkien and Dyson, together with Charles Williams, Owen Barfield and others, constituted a literary group who called themselves 'the Inklings' (because they were writers – workers in ink – and because they considered they considered themselves to have the start of an idea; and also because they all worshipped Christ, the God from the cradle, in Latin *incunabulum*). Members gathered in the Eagle and Child pub in Oxford to read out sections from their various works in progress. Tolkien read *Lord of the Rings* to the group.[16] Colin Duriez talks of 'Lewis's irrepressible zest for hearing pieces read aloud, and his enjoyment of the give and take of spontaneous, instant criticism'.[17] This speaks to the sense of Lewis's writing, including his fantasy, as *conversational*, a product of discursive interaction and discussion rather than a static disposition. This, it seems to me, is crucial to the nature of the Narnia books, and also to their success.

This sense of an actual conversation is realized in the wittily satirical *The Screwtape Letters* (1942), which presents communications from a senior demon in Hell's vast bureaucracy to a junior, with a view to imparting the best methods for corrupting humanity. *The Great Divorce* (1945), a much more accomplished piece of allegory than the *Pilgrim's Regress*, styles the journey to salvation as a bus journey out of a modern-seeming 'grey city' of perdition into the sky. Lewis's narrator, as Dante met his Vergil, meets George MacDonald, whose *Phantastes* is as much a guiding intertext for Lewis's writing as Bunyan. The vividness with which the characters who travel on this journey acquire brightness and solidity, the passage out of industrialized deracinated modernity into a brilliant spiritual fullness, is the core trajectory of fantasy. Lewis's final significant work of Christian apologetics *Till We Have Faces* (1956), retelling the myth of Cupid and Psyche, was popular upon publication, though its fame has been eclipsed by the Narnia novels.

All this is relevant as the context out of which the Narnia books were produced. As Roger Lancelyn Green noted in 1974, whilst 'the Ransom trilogy and *Till We Have*

---

[16]The story (attested by Christopher Tolkien) is that Dyson, less enthusiastic about some of the group's writing than others, responded to Tolkien beginning yet another reading from *Lord of the Rings* with the exclamation 'oh God, not another fucking elf'. The anecdote is discussed by Philip and Carol Zaleski, *The Fellowship: the Literary Lives of the Inklings*, 358, who note that Dyson was not alone in his animadversion:

> Barfield put [*The Lord of the Rings*] aside unfinished and John Wain poured on the scorn: 'when Tolkien came through the door at a meeting of the Inklings with a bulging jacket pocket I winced because I knew we were in for a slab of Gandalf and Bilbo Baggins and the rest of it. I wished him no harm, but I would have preferred him to keep his daydreams within bounds and not inflict them on us.'

This indexes a belief, shared by many, that fantasy as such is infantile, beneath the notice of adult scholars.
[17]'Tolkien and Lewis, in fact, often met up before the Inklings were in existence and read work in progress to each other. Even when the club was meeting regularly, Lewis and he would meet up together to talk of the things that concerned them, maybe to enjoy a beer, and to share their writings, a habit that was to continue for many years' [Colin Duriez, *C. S. Lewis*, 140].

*Faces* will probably fall out of fashion, be condemned by critics and readers of a different tradition' Narnia is different:

> At present the seven *Chronicles of Narnia*, that unexpected creation of his middle age, which are selling over a million copies a year, seem to be Lewis's greatest claim to immortality, setting him high in that particular branch of literature in which few attain more than a transitory or an esoteric fame – somewhere on the same shelf as Lewis Carroll and E. Nesbit and George MacDonald.[18]

Lancelyn Green, who knew Lewis, has a part to play here, since he actively encouraged Lewis to publish *The Lion, the Witch and the Wardrobe*. And those sales figures, large in the 1970s, are even larger today: Narnia is one of the bestselling of all fantasy series, and remains current. Indeed, for many, Narnia is the core fantasy text of the twentieth-century. British author Francis Spufford's memoir of his childhood reading *The Child That Books Built* (2002) notes:

> my deepest loyalty was unwavering. The books I loved best of all took me away through a wardrobe, and a shallow pool in the grass of a sleepy orchard, and a picture in a frame, and a door in a garden wall on a rainy day at boarding school, and always to Narnia. Other imaginary countries interested me, beguiled me, made rich suggestions to me. Narnia made me feel like I'd taken hold of a live wire. The book in my hand sent jolts and shivers through my nerves.[19]

The first novel in the sequence, *The Lion, the Witch and the Wardrobe*, remains the best-made and most compelling of the series. Four English siblings, Peter, Susan, Edmund and Lucy Pevensie, discover a magical wardrobe in an upper room of the house into which they have been evacuated – magical because it is actually a portal to Fantasyland. Passing through they move, in a splendidly realized, dream-like pun, from fur coats to fir trees. The coats are handy, because the land is snowed-in and wintry, the result of a curse by the narrative antagonist, the 'White Witch', Jadis by name. Edmund (that Lewis has named him after the wicked brother in *King Lear* will alert the more literate readers) turns bad: seduced by the White Witch with some Turkish Delight he betrays his brother and sisters. Narnia is home to Aslan, a great lion, the principle of fantastical heroism and virtue, behind whom the agents of goodness of rally; but the story of the first Narnian book sees Aslan surrender himself to the murderous depredations of the White Witch in order to save Edmund. She kills Aslan, but he comes back to life, and in a big conclusive battle the wintry evil is defeated and the witch killed. At the end of the novel the Pevensie children grow to adulthood inside Narnia, fulfilling an ancient prophesy that 'sons of

---

[18]Lancelyn Green, *C. S. Lewis*, 112.
[19]Spufford, *The Child That Books Built*, 109. Patricia Craig notes of this passage: 'Spufford is only articulating what thousands of equally committed Narnians have experienced to one degree or another' [Patricia Craig, 'Narnia Revisited', 161].

Adam and daughters of Eve' would come to save the land and be crowned its kings and queens. Finally, the now-adult quartet are hunting when they find their original entry point and return to our world, stumbling out of the wardrobe to find themselves children again. Many years have passed in Narnia, but only a few hours in our world.

Lewis told Charles Wrong, one of his Oxford students, that he was not 'particularly interested' in fantasy as a genre, but that 'he happened to have had an idea that he wanted to try out'. 'I had to write three volumes, of course, or seven, or nine', Lewis said. 'Those are the magic numbers.'[20] Scholars have gone to ingenious lengths to explain why the Narnia novels comprise seven titles, but this seems as likely an explanation as any. Michael Ward argues that each of the novels is 'governed' by one of the seven planets medieval man believe to comprise the Ptolemaic solar system, each of which was believed to possess a distinct property.[21] So, according to Ward, Lewis's follow-up novel *Prince Caspian* – in which the four children return to Narnia to find many centuries have passed, and in which they help the rightful heir to the Narnian throne, the titular prince, to combat the evil tyranny of Telmarine – is governed by Mars, the planet of war. The third in the series, *Voyage of the Dawn Treader*, sees Lucy, Edmund and a new child called Eustace Scrub, visit Narnia again, and take part in an ocean voyage: Ward sees this book as a solar work. *The Silver Chair* and *The Horse and His Boy* (a book whose focus is almost entirely on Narnians, rather than on visitors from our world) are governed by Luna and Mercury, respectively. Lewis then wrote what we would now call a 'prequel' to the series: *The Magician's Nephew* is set in Edwardian London, and details how Jadis, originally a magical queen from a dying civilization, comes to London, causing various disruptions, afterward finding her way to the new-fashioned Narnia. This novel features the professor from the first novel as a young man, and the portal in this novel is not a wardrobe, but a magic coppice, 'the wood between the worlds', the wardrobe afterwards being made out of timber from one of its trees. Ward considers this book to exist under the aegis of Venus, the planet of love, and identifies Saturn, the sign of old age and death, as the governing principle for the last Narnia novel, *The Last Battle*. Here Lewis wraps-up his Fantasyland, with a story of false-prophets pretending to speak for Aslan, a final apocalyptic war and, ultimately, the arrival of the true Aslan and the end of all things, with the good and the bad being separated, and the faithful permitted to enter the true heaven, the Platonic form of which Narnia and our world are both mere copies, or shadows. As has already been noted, Lewis specifically namechecks Plato in the last chapter, and, via a violent contrivance, brings the Pevensie children, now grown-up in our world, back into Narnia one last time – the three (not Susan, who is not permitted to enter this ultimate heaven, or at least not yet) are in a railway carriage when a train crash kills them and precipitates them to Narnia and so beyond, 'further up and further in' into ultimate heaven. The last paragraph of the last book includes the mild paradox by which the

---

[20]James T Como (ed), *C. S. Lewis at the Breakfast Table*, 113.
[21]Ward, *Planet Narnia: The Seven Heavens in the Imagination of C. S. Lewis*.

blisses of this ultimate heaven are declared unwritable even as, with a bibliophilic flourish, paradise itself is compared to a book:

> The things that began to happen after that were so great and beautiful that I cannot write them. And for us this is the end of all stories, and we can most truly say they all lived happily ever after. But for them it was only the beginning of the real story. All their life in this world and all their adventures in Narnia had only been the cover and the title page: now at last they were beginning Chapter One of the Great Story which no one on earth has read: which goes on for ever: in which every chapter is better than the one before.

Ward's theory as to the seven may or may not be correct, though it is certainly true that Lewis was imaginatively immersed in nostalgic medievalism that yearned after the enchantment drained-away by the coming of modernity. He very much preferred the old Ptolemaic solar system to the actual, modern one. 'Historically as well as cosmically' he wrote, 'medieval man stood at the foot of a stairway; looking up, he felt delight. The backward, like the upward, glance exhilarated him with a majestic spectacle, and humility was rewarded with the pleasures of admiration.'

> Other ages have not had a Model so universally accepted as theirs, so imaginable, and so satisfying to the imagination ... I have made no serious effort to hide the fact that the old Model delights me as I believe it delighted our ancestors. Few constructions of the imagination seem to me to have combined splendour, sobriety, and coherence in the same degree.[22]

This glory, the medievalized enchantment, is a large part of the power of Narnia as fantasy. But it is also true that the world of Narnia is threaded-through with modernity: the twentieth-century children who come into it are, rightfully, the land's kings and queens. When Lucy first ventures into Narnia alone she discovers a twentieth-century lamppost in the middle of the forest, its gaslight shining. Her next encounter is with Mr Tumnus, a faun out of Greek myth, but one wearing a scarf and carrying an umbrella and returning to his home from (we must assume) a department-store with his purchases under his arm. That there are department-stores in Narnia, or that tea – which Mr Tumnus serves – must be imported from somewhere less wintry, are not considerations the later novels take up. Indeed, as the series goes on, Lewis takes pains and deploys no little ingenuity to round out and smooth off the inconsistencies and irregularities of his worldbuilding. The presence of the lamppost is 'explained' in *The Magician's Nephew*, where the other aspects of bourgeois modernity are simply elided or forgotten. This, it seems to me, is an error. The potency of *The Lion, The Witch and the Wardrobe* derives from the dream-logic of its strange (one might say: surreal, Magritte-like) juxtapositions: an iron streetlamp shining

---

[22] Lewis, *The Discarded Image: An Introduction to Medieval and Renaissance Literature*, 187, 216.

in the midst of a winter wood, fur coats becoming fir trees, umbrellas in medieval castles. Behind this is the surrealist logic of juxtaposing humanity and animality: Christ as a lion rather than a man, the superposition of myth and mimesis.

This juxtaposition is, precisely, the structural logic of allegory. In *The Allegory of Love*, Lewis distinguishes between two aspects of the allegorical:

> On the one hand you can start with an immaterial fact, such as the passions which you actually experience, and can then invent *visibilia* to express them. If you are hesitating between an angry retort and a soft answer, you can express your state of mind by inventing a person called *Ira* with a torch and letting her contend with another invented person called *Patientia*. This is allegory … But there is another way of using the equivalence, which is almost the opposite of allegory, and which I would call sacramentalism or symbolism. If our passions, being immaterial, can be copied by material inventions, then it is possible that our material world in its turn is the copy of an invisible world. As the god Amor and his figurative garden are to the actual passions of men, so perhaps we ourselves and our 'real' world are to something else. The attempt to read that something else through its sensible imitations, to see the archetype in the copy, is what I mean by symbolism or sacramentalism.

It is true, as generations of readers have only belatedly discovered, that *The Lion, The Witch and the Wardrobe* allegorizes Christ's passion, as the last book retells the Revelation of St John. Aslan 'is', in a sense, Christ; his sacrifice redeems sinful humanity, and the book ends with the Satanic Jadis defeated. This, however, is not exactly to say that the story allegorizes the New Testament. What *The Lion, the Witch and the Wardrobe* does is to explore the logic of incarnation, something of central importance to Christians. Aslan doesn't 'represent' or symbolize Christ; he is the form Christ's incarnation would take in a reality populated by talking animals. It is a core part of Christian belief that Christ, as he appeared in our world, was not a 'symbol' for God, he didn't 'stand in for' or 'represent' God; he actually *was* God, incarnated in human form. Some find the way this religious proselytizing is handled in the novel to be sneaky. Laura Miller talks of feeling betrayed when she first spotted it.

> I was horrified to discover that the *Chronicles of Narnia*, the joy of my childhood and the cornerstone of my imaginative life, were really just the doctrines of the Church in disguise. I looked back at my favourite book and found it appallingly transfigured. Of course the self-sacrifice of Aslan to compensate for the treachery of Edmund was exactly like the crucifixion of Christ to pay off the sins of mankind! How could I have missed that? I felt angry and humiliated because I had been fooled.[23]

---

[23]Miller, *The Magician's Book: a Skeptic's Adventure in Narnia*, 6.

But this decoding, as if the work can be exhausted by the extraction of its hidden meaning, does not describe the power of Lewis's fantasy (Miller goes on to say that, after this initial disappointment, she was able to return to the book, to discover that 'it had not lost its power or beauty'). What William Gray calls the illumination of reality by the 'radiance of myth' is the beacon of Lewis's fantasy, and the key to its endurance: rather than producing simple allegories of Christian doctrine, Lewis, in the *Chronicles of Narnia*, 'sought to confront his readers with an experience which, by being presented historically, that is, located (as a "supposition") in this world, powerfully calls into question, transcends and yet glorifies this world – even if only ambiguously and in a glass darkly'.[24] Narnia remains one of the greatest fantasy works ever written.

---

[24]Gray, *Fantasy, Myth and the Measure of Truth*, 151.

# CHAPTER 14
## 1940s–50s: ADULT FANTASY

British artist and writer Mervyn Peake applied to be an official war artist but was rejected, and instead was enlisted into the Royal Engineers. He re-applied to be a war artist repeatedly and was repeatedly turned down. In 1942 he was, following a nervous breakdown, invalided out of the army. He recuperated from his breakdown and in 1943 was finally commissioned by the War Artists' Advisory Committee. He began writing *Titus Groan* at this time, and worked on it, and on its sequel *Gormenghast*, intermittently through the 1940s. Late in the war he was present at the liberation of Bergen-Belsen, and sketched prisoners, some of whom were too sick to be moved and who died before his eyes. The shock of this also worked its way into his writing. *Titus Groan* was published in 1946. He produced a series of brilliant illustrations for various books, including Coleridge's *The Rime of the Ancient Mariner* and Lewis Carroll. His own collection of nonsense poetry, *Rhymes without Reason*, had come out in 1944, to some acclaim – again, the relationship between nonsense, or surrealism, and fantasy has a shaping force on major work in the latter mode. Peake and his family lived (from 1946) on Sark in the Channel Islands, moving back to the British mainland in 1950, the year *Gormenghast* was published.

Peake intended *Titus Groan* (1946) and *Gormenghast* (1950) as the first instalments in a long series. He wrote a third volume *Titus Alone* (1959) and made an abortive start on a fourth (this was eventually completed by his wife Maeve Gilmore, and published as *Titus Awakes* in 2011). But Parkinson's disease collapsed his health, and he died in 1968 at the age of fifty-seven. It's a sad story, and tantalizing where the *Gormenghast* books are concerned. Peake managed only a few, rather scattered paragraphs and scrappy notes for vol 4, *Titus Awakes*, and we have only the title, *Gormenghast Revisited*, for the fifth volume.

In terms of plot the three books are simple enough, although the narrative becomes friable and fragmentary in the third. In *Titus Groan* the title character and heir to the Earldom of Groan is only just born, and has little to do with the story. Instead we get various other bizarre and grotesque inhabitants of Gormenghast Castle, and the rise of ambitious, amoral kitchen boy Steerpike. The elderly Sepulchrave, the 76th Earl Groan, lives for his library. When it is destroyed (his two sisters, Cora and Clarice, are induced to burn it down by the scheming Steerpike) he goes mad, coming to believe he is an owl, eventually dying. Everything in Gormenghast happens according to elaborate and arcane ritual practice, but there is no precedence and therefore no ritual for handling such a demise, and so Sepulchrave's corpse lies in his room until it is devoured by his owls. The first book also gives us Fuschia, Titus's older sister ('a girl of about fifteen with long, rather wild black hair; she was gauche in movement and in a sense ugly of face, but with how small a twist might she not suddenly have become beautiful. Her sullen mouth was full and rich – her eyes smouldered') whom Steerpike seduces. She ends up falling to her death, but Steerpike continues his ascent. 'Steerpike is climbing the spiral staircase of the soul of Gormenghast', Peake tells us, 'bound for some pinnacle of the itching fancy – some wild, invulnerable eyrie best known to himself; where he can watch the world spread out below him, and shake exultantly his clotted wings' [*Gormenghast*, 8]. He plots, manipulates and murders to make himself master of the castle, 'a social climber', in Michael Wood's words, 'who also climbs all over the material castle, bringing a figure of speech to literal life in a way that marks Peake's art'.[1]

In *Gormenghast* Titus grows up. Steerpike continues his ruthless social ascent until he is unmasked, hunted down and slain by Titus himself, in a vividly written vertical chase-and-pursuit through the castle's superstructure of ivy. Having a melodramatically exaggerated villain against which the hero is tested gives these two novels excellent clarity and narrative focus. With Steerpike dead, the next volume, *Titus Alone*, devolves into a peripatetic string of incident, crumbs of plot scattered across the chapters. The book also enacts a shift of mode: out of the Gothic-medieval revenancy of Gormenghast Titus now moves amongst motor cars, high-tech factories and clones: John Holbo talks of the 'sheer, genre-bending weirdness' of this third volume, 'like if spaceships had shown up in *The Return of the King*'.[2] In *Titus Awakes*, Maeve Gilmore continues Titus's peregrinations through modernity: villages, police cells and drunkards' dens. At one point Titus works as an orderly in an insane asylum and looks after Mervyn Peake himself, styled 'the Artist', who has been admitted because his mind is collapsing, and to whom Titus feels a strange connection. This distal novel ends with Titus taking a train to the coast, then a boat to an island, then a smaller boat to a smaller island – Sark – where he encounters the Artist again, now happily with his family. The trajectory is away from home in order to return to home, a resacralized reclamation of belonging. Like Dorothy Gale's Kansas, Gormenghast is simultaneously the site of confinement and restriction from which we yearn to escape, and place to which we yearn to return: the title of the unwritten next volume, *Gormenghast Revisited*, makes this plain.

Peake as artist and Peake as writer cannot really be separated out from one another, and not just because he illustrated his own writing with such panache. He is always an intensely visual writer as well as an intensely self-reflexive one. His prose descriptions read like accounts of illustrations of things rather than direct depictions of things, and there are a great many moments of specific ekphrasis in the novels. Here Steerpike is struck by an illustration in a book. As he looks down upon it, it seems to Steerpike that 'he was the ghost', the image on the page 'truth and actual fact'.

Below him stood three men. They were dressed in grey, and purple flowers were in their dark confused locks. The landscape beyond them was desolate and was filled

---

[1] Michael Wood, 'Eaten by Owls', 12.
[2] John Holbo, 'Titus Awakes', *Crooked Timber*.

with old metal bridges, and they stood before it together upon the melancholy brow of a small hill. Their hands were exquisitely shaped and their bare feet also, and it seemed that they were listening to a strange music, for their eyes gazed out beyond the page and beyond the reach of Steerpike, and on and on beyond the hill of Gormenghast and the Twisted Woods. [*Titus Groan*, 149]

Fuschia's bedroom is an art gallery:

> The walls of her room were hung with pictures once chosen as her favourites from among the scores that she had unearthed in the lumber room. One wall was filled with a great mountain scene where a road like a snake winding around and around the most impressive of crags was filled with two armies, one in yellow and the other, the invading force battling up from below, in purple. Lit as it were by torch-light the whole scene was a constant source of wonder to Fuschia. The other walls were less imposingly arranged, fifteen pictures being distributed among the three. The head of a jaguar; a portrait of the twenty-second Earl of Groan with pure white hair and a face the colour of smoke as a result of immoderate tattooing, and a group of children in pink and white muslin dresses playing with a viper were among the works which pleased her most. Hundreds of very dull heads and full-length portraits of her ancestors had been left in the lumber room. [*Titus Groan*, 83]

This figures almost as a visual manifesto for fantasy itself. The word 'purple' occurs 33 times in *Titus Groan* (not counting the name Fuschia, which is itself a kind of purple); 'grey' occurs 111 times and 'black' 133 times, which gives us some sense of Peake's colour-palette. Over and again the writing generates a distinctive effect via an unusual colour-term: 'Flay began to untie his boots. Behind him his swept cave yawned, a million prawn-coloured motes swaying against the darkness at the entrance' [*Titus Groan*, 445]. Sunlight is 'wasp-gold'; bannisters are 'alternately apple-green and azure'; Steerpike's eyes 'the colour of dried blood'. The novels are a cram of vivid, grotesque, visualized specificities: 'Barquentine put out a tongue like the tongue of a boot and ran it along the wreckage of his dry and wrinkled lips.'

> Whether his face was made of age, as though age were a stuff, or whether age was the abstract of that face of his, that bearded fossil of a thing that smouldered and decayed upon his shoulders – there was no doubt that archaism was there, as though something had shifted from the past into the current moment where it burned darkly as though through blackened glass in defiance of its own anachronism and the callow present. [*Gormenghast*, 159–60]

Through this glass, darkly, is time itself: the dead non-releasing hand of the past. Everything is visualized and as everything non-visual resolves itself into visuality. Take the schoolroom in which Titus must take his lessons:

The air was fuscous with a mixture of smells, including stale tobacco, dry chalk, rotten wood, ink, alcohol and, above all, imperfectly cured leather, but the general colour of the room was a transcription of the smells, for the walls were of horsehide, the dreariest of browns, relieved only by the scattered and dully twinkling heads of drawing-pins. [*Gormenghast*, 49]

Colour and line 'transcribe' the non-visual into the terms of the visual. These are novels about seeing, intensely: about seeing every detail. The northern dialect English word *gorm* means 'heed, pay attention' (it is more recognizable today in its negative form, 'gormless'). Gormenghast means, as it might be, how close attentiveness, how vision, leaves us aghast. 'Ghast' is terror, is that which is terrifying: it is the idiom of Gothic to pay close heed to the terrifying. It's there in the rambling, Dickensian opening sentences of the first novel:

Gormenghast, that is, the main massing of the original stone, taken by itself would have displayed a certain ponderous architectural quality were it possible to have ignored the circumfusion of those mean dwellings that swarmed like an epidemic around its outer walls. They sprawled over the sloping earth, each one half way over its neighbour until, held back by the castle ramparts, the innermost of these hovels laid hold on the great walls, clamping themselves thereto like limpets to a rock. These dwellings, by ancient law, were granted this chill intimacy with the stronghold that loomed above them. Over their irregular roofs would fall throughout the seasons, the shadows of time-eaten buttresses, of broken and lofty turrets, and, most enormous of all, the shadow of the Tower of Flints. This tower, patched unevenly with black ivy, arose like a mutilated finger from among the fists of knuckled masonry and pointed blasphemously at heaven. At night the owls made of it an echoing throat; by day it stood voiceless and cast its long shadow.

Those owls, who eventually devour the Lord of Gormenghast, are there at the beginning with their giant eyes, their seeing in the dark. *Were it possible to ignore* indeed.

At the same time, there is a kind of contradiction at the heart of the books. Gormenghast is an edifice of stasis: ultra-conservatism and unchangingness is in a sense the whole point of the castle, and its society. Yet it is a place where there is the most amazing grotesque diversity and variety. When Titus leaves it and enters modernity he encounters many things, but a kind of flatness, a sameness enters the telling. Both *Titus Alone* and *Titus Awake* are attenuated productions, compared with the hefty, rich massiveness of *Titus Groan* and *Gormenghast*. This seems to me an intriguing contradiction. Steerpike is brilliant, talented (and ruthless) but he is also strangely disengaged. As Michael Wood notes: Steerpike – the name glances at Dickens's Steerforth – is a model of the unfeeling, intelligent person. He has, among many other qualities, 'an unusual gift. It was to understand a subject without appreciating it'. He plays music brilliantly but without emotion. He doesn't grasp, but seeks to undo 'the ancientry of the tenets that bound the anatomy of the place together'. The most eloquent tribute to him is that

Fuchsia, the wild child, almost falls in love with him and when she discovers the extent of his criminal career, considers suicide out of despair at her folly. Ritual, the idiom of Gormenghast Castle, is the substitute for original thought and, more to the point, of original feeling. We could go further: ritual and the reification of the past are more than a restraint upon feeling, they are a substitute for it. This relates then to 'history' as such, and therefore to fantasy as a mode.

In France Julien Gracq published *Le Rivage des Syrtes* (1951: the title means 'The Sandbank Coast'; the book has been translated into English as *The Opposing Shore*), a fantasia set on the border between two imaginary kingdoms who have been at war for three hundred years – although at the time of the story an uneasy ceasefire is in place: the civilized but stagnant principality of Orsenna and, across the water, the mysterious, savage land of Farghestan. As with Gormenghast, architecture becomes landscape, and vice versa: ancient structures of great size under moonlit skies:

> Cut off from the city by waste stretches where one divined the traces of its former gardens, the Aldobrandi palace loomed up at the tip of one of the fingers of the open hand, and its isolation on the right of the passage through the lagoons and at the end of the widened canal seemed to me a singular figuration of the temper of the easily offended race which had built the place in its own image. This pleasure dome, cast like a sneer upon the fever-ridden waters, still recalled something of the stronghold, the fortress … The moon had risen, and a dome of mist hovered over the lagoon. [*The Opposing Shore* (translated Richard Howard), 73]

Dome and dome. This is a novel of waiting, in which little happens but much is anticipated, like a prelude to a never-written narrative: a tone poem: spare, humourless and existentially enigmatic. It stands, we could say, not as an exploration of disenchantment, but of a kind of hesitant fear of re-enchantment: the volcanic barbarian nation, threatening to invade, represents the potential of a potent de-buffering of existence for the sterile life of Orsenna. The novel's point-of-view main character, Aldo, goes about his life amongst the ruins of antique traditions and decayed formalities, like Titus, though without the noble bloodline or prospect of inheritance. He does have a position of some, obscure authority within the fortress, a posting that is also a kind of exile from the main city of Orsenna. Maria Boletsi brackets this novel with Cavafy's 1898 poem 'Waiting for the Barbarians', and also with Dino Buzzati's *Il deserto dei Tartari* ('The Tartar Steppe' 1940), Samuel Beckett's *Waiting for Godot* (1952) and Coetzee's later Cavafian fantasia *Waiting for the Barbarians* (1980). In all these works, she says, 'the theme of waiting for the arrival of the other becomes an anaphora, an act of beginning ceaselessly renewed through the repetition of promises not carried out, not kept'. This stasis is iterative, she argues, 'in the Derridean sense of the word'.[3] The border between the two nations, a stretch of water

---

[3]Boletsi, *Barbarism and Its Discontents*, 145–6.

that is always the same as itself, looks forward to, without ever actualizing, the terror and bliss of transcendence: 'as if I had been given the power to pass beyond, to slip into a world filled with intoxication and trembling. This world was the same, and this endless stretch of empty water desperately resembled itself everywhere one looked' [*Opposing Shore*, 185]. The water that always resembles itself is the rebus of both the monotony of existence and, paradoxically, its imminent 'throbbing' cataract of visceral energy. Gracq, a friend of Breton, worked on the edge of surrealism and is fond of a kind of textural disorientation of description that (like Oppenheim's pelt-lined teacup) achieves striking surrealist effects: 'amid these moon-varnished waters bristling with reeds, the sea spread before me like a wide margin of dark fur' [33]. In Enrique Vila-Matas's novel *Dublinesca* (2010) a Barcelonian publisher called Riba is obsessed with *Le Rivage des Syrtes*:

> He'd published lots of important authors, but only in Julien Gracq's novel *The Opposing Shore* did he perceive any spirit for the future … establishing five elements he considered essential for the novel of the future. These essential elements were: intertextuality; connection with serious poetry; awareness of a moral landscape in ruins; a favouring of style over plot; a view of writing that moves forward like time. It was a daring theory, given that it put forward Gracq's book, usually considered antiquated, as the most advanced of all novels.[4]

Gracq's book *is* antiquated in many ways, archly over-written, positioning a kind of decayed romanticism of dying expectation against the blankness and sterility of actual modernity; but the novel is also advanced, as Vila-Matas's Riba says. It is in this, rather than in any (as it might be) in-text magical or supernatural element, that it figures as fantasy. The landscape in ruins is the externalization of morality (a public or historical morality) as well as an estranging, surrealist-existentialist stage-set full of stark, moonlit beauty. The barbarians for which we are ecstatically awaiting are ourselves, our phantasmic past, the reach of history across time.

Peake is a similar, if prior case. A fundamentally Gothic writer, his architecturalized landscape, his buildings cast as territories, are landlocked, surrounded by mountains, intricately cyclopean structures perduring into technological modernity. Gracq's topographies are more like Giorgio De Chirico's paintings of arcades and corridors, of stagey public squares, stark lit and membraned by shadow. A Roman something that subsists in a world of steam-trains and aeroplanes, as Gormenghast is a Gothic something subsisting into the same modern world. *Titus Groan* actually does move away from Gormenghast, but it makes no difference. Aldo doesn't leave his fortress (or at least, doesn't fully cross over into Farghestan) but the distant intimation of transition hypnotizes the stolidity of his world. Bit Gracq and Peake are in touch with, or in mourning for, a Romantic fullness, a visceral expressiveness as absence, for what Gracq in a 1950 pamphlet called *La Littérature à l'estomac*. In a sense, Gracq's 'opposing shore' is

---

[4]Vila-Matas *Dublinesque*, 8.

Peake, and Peake's is Gracq. This a distinct mode of fantasy, picking up from Kafka and feeding through, later in the century, into significant works. A clutch of British writers have written notable fantasy in this tradition: Christopher Priest's *Indoctrinaire* (1970), M John Harrison's *The Pastel City* (1971), Brian Aldiss's *Malacia Tapestry* (1976), Mary Gentle's *Rats and Gargoyles* (1990) and China Miéville's *Perdido Street Station* (2000) some of which are discussed below. Why this should be so predominantly a British mode is a question to which I shall return.

## Commercial fantasy

Fantasy as a commercial vehicle was not entirely self-sufficient during the 1940s and 1950s – unlike science fiction, which was entering its Golden Age, supported with a great many decades-old, genre-specific magazines and selling well. The first fantasy-specific magazine does not arrive until 1949, when the US Mystery House, a subsidiary of Lawrence Spivak's Mercury Press, set up *The Magazine of Fantasy* as a companion title to their successful crime imprint *Ellery Queen's Mystery Magazine*; but almost at once, it was decided that fantasy on its own was not, at this point, enough to sustain a monthly publication, and the publication was renamed *The Magazine of Fantasy & Science Fiction*. In time this would become one of the most important venues for fantasy short-fiction and serialized novels, but, in Mike Ashley's words, its initial 'impact on the field was more diffuse and less immediate'.[5]

Fantasy did have, in this commercial sense, a recognizable generic identity and a fanbase, but it was nascent. American writer Jack Vance wrote a series of loosely linked short-stories under the general title *The Dying Earth* (1950). Regarded now as one of the most influential fantasy works (voted 16th on the Locus Magazine's 1987 'All Time Best Fantasy Novels', based on a poll of subscribers), in 1950 Vance couldn't place any of its constitutive stories in magazines, and they were bundled together and issued as one volume by Hillman, an obscure paperback publisher. It was not until the mid-1960s that the appetite for fantasy of Vance's type enabled him to write, and sell, more 'Dying Earth' stories. These were collected as *The Eyes of the Overworld* (1966; further volumes followed: *Cugel's Saga* [1983] and *Rhialto the Marvellous* [1984]). Gene Wolfe, writing in the 1980s, by which time Vance was famous, recalls when he was not, and records the potency and influence he had upon him:

[T]here was a time when I could put my hand flat on the front of a tattered paperback called *The Dying Earth* and feel the magic seeping through the carboard. Turjan of Miir, Liane the Wayfarer, T'sais, Chuun the Unavoidable. Nobody I knew had so much as heard of that book, but I knew it was the finest book in the world.[6]

---

[5]Ashley, *Transformations: The History of Science Fiction Magazine, 1950–1970*, 20.
[6]Wolfe, *Castle of Days*, 211.

The 'Dying Earth' series is set in the very far future of Earth, where science has exhausted itself and magic has re-asserted its dominance. The Moon has vanished from the sky, and the Sun is burning down. Various populations live in this world, decadent societies, religious fanatics, enterprising rogues and adventurers. Monsters and demons throng the wilderness, themselves the consequence of magical castings. For these stories Vance invented a magic system that was later adopted by the *Dungeons and Dragons* game and so became widely disseminated. Magic spells require memorized syllables, of which the human brain can only accommodate a certain number at any one time: when the spell is cast the syllables vanish from the caster's mind. It is also possible to summon creatures called 'sandestins' to undertake magical actions, although this can be a dangerous business for the summoner.

Vance's career was lengthy and important, and some of his later work is discussed below; but the distinctive excellence of his fantasy imagination is perfectly manifest in these early works. Elegant, intricate, witty, with a baroque distinctiveness that grows more distinct as Vance's career developed: varied, exciting adventures, and a gorgeously estranging wondrousness of invention. He has a liking for amoral, resourceful characters and writes an elegant, intricate, witty, estranging prose. 'As Vance's created worlds became richer and more complex, so too did his style', John Clute and Malcolm Edwards note.

> Always tending towards the baroque, it developed into an effective high-mannered diction, somewhat pedantic, and almost always saturated with a rich but distanced irony. Vance's talent for naming the people and places in his stories (a mixture of exotic invented terms and obscure or commonplace words with the right resonance) increasingly generated a sense that dream ethnographies were being carved, almost as a gardener would create topiary.[7]

## The Lord of the Rings

J R R Tolkien, to whom this study has previously several times adverted, had been working slowly throughout the 1940s and into the 1950s on the novel that was eventually published as *The Lord of the Rings*. Publishers Allen & Unwin expressed interest in a sequel to *The Hobbit*, which had been one of their more successful titles. Tolkien wanted his whole legendarium published in a two-volume set: *The Silmarillion* as vol 1 and the entirety of the 1,000-page *Lord of the Rings* as vol 2. But in post-war Britain, economically depressed, rationing still in place and the price of paper very high, this was not a commercially viable proposition. Allen & Unwin agreed to publish the book, but on a profit-sharing basis (so, no author advance payable to Tolkien: a cheaper option for the publisher) and in three volumes, with publication staggered so that if the first or second volume flopped they need not proceed with the third. *The Fellowship of the Ring*

---

[7]John Clute and Malcolm Edwards, 'Jack Vance', 982.

duly appeared, 29 July 1954, priced at 21 shillings – a guinea: a high price for one third of a novel. The whole business was, indeed, a very risky undertaking from the publisher's point of view: 'Allen & Unwin did not expect *The Lord of the Rings* to sell, for it was bulky, unconventional, and did not appeal to any one "market", being neither a children's book nor an adult novel.'[8] That they went ahead with the project at all is remarkable. The firm's founder and director Stanley Unwin later recalled.

> We were all of us at Museum Street [Allen & Unwin's London office] *Hobbit* fans and were longing for a sequel, but when we learnt that it was a work of enormous length, primarily intended for adults, upon which Tolkien had been engaged for over twenty years, we were some of us rather aghast. But my son was not intimidated either by the appearance or length of this formidable manuscript. He pronounced it a work of genius which we simply must find a way of publishing, even if it meant issuing it in three volumes. I was away in Japan, and wrote at once agreeing to its acceptance even if it involved a loss of as much as £1,000. When on my return I was able to read a set of proofs I recognized at once that we were backing a certainty and that there would be no question of losing money. It was a book for all time, which will be selling long after my departure from this world.

He goes on:

> When we published the first two volumes, we confidently anticipated following them up immediately with Volume 3, of which we had the complete text of the story. But the author was not ready with all the supplementary material, and there was what seemed to all an interminable delay. Volume 2 [published 11 November 1954] had left readers in agonizing suspense, and never in over fifty years of publishing have I received so many letters from the public – some intensely humorous, more resentful, but all complaining that they could endure the suspense no longer, and complaining of our cruelty in delaying the publication of Volume 3. The burden of answering all these letters was such that we were as thankful as our correspondents when the production of Volume 3 was finally completed.[9]

*The Return of the King* finally appeared on the 20 October 1955, nearly a year after the appearance of *The Two Towers*. The gamble paid off, in two stages. Through the remainder of the 1950s the book sold consistently if not spectacularly, making its publisher (and author) a modest profit. It won, somewhat belatedly, the 1957 'International Fantasy Award'. Then, in the 1960s, the book took off in the United States on a wholly different scale. Houghton Mifflin, the US hardcover publisher, had omitted to copyright the work in America, a loophole Donald A. Wollheim, science fiction editor of the paperback

---

[8]Humphrey Carpenter, *J. R. R. Tolkien: A Biography*, 215.
[9]Stanley Unwin, *The Truth about a Publisher*, 300–1.

publisher Ace Books, decided to exploit. In 1965 he published a cheap paperback edition in three volumes, unauthorized by Tolkien and without royalties being paid to him. This sold very well, but also generated a backlash from Tolkien fans that further increased the visibility of the book (eventually Ace Books withdrew their edition and made a small payment to Tolkien). Later that same year Ballantine Books published a paperback edition, authorized by Tolkien, which became a huge success. *Lord of the Rings* was a 'campus novel', and then a hit outside universities as well. By December 1966 the novel was number one in *The New York Times*'s paperback bestsellers list, a position it held for months. Joseph Ripp calls the post-1965 commercial popularity of *The Lord of the Rings* 'truly staggering': 'lifetime global sales total more than 50 million copies, and the book has been translated into more than thirty-eight languages: if you say it is the biggest selling fiction creation of all time, you'll find it difficult to find anyone able to say you're wrong.'[10] Another spike in sales followed the release of the Peter Jackson movies: in 2005 Houghton Mifflin calculated that 'more than 25 million Tolkien books have been sold in the past three years'. Sales continue strongly today.

One aspect of the success of Tolkien's fantasy has been its adaptation into other media. Indeed, its cultural penetration, and its influence in shaping the generic lineaments of fantasy as a genre, depends as much upon such adaptation as upon the original novels. After the film rights were sold in the 1960s the plan was to make a movie starring The Beatles. This came to nothing, but American animator Ralph Bakshi's 1978 movie was notable, and two decades later *The Lord of the Rings* film trilogy (2001–2, directed by Peter Jackson) was a huge global success. On TV, a live-action special of *The Hobbit* was produced in the Soviet Union in 1985. More recently Amazon have spent, reputedly, a billion dollars making the TV series *Rings of Power* (2022), a prequel to *Lord of the Rings*. The BBC broadcast a radio adaptation in twelve parts in 1955 and 1956, and in 1981, BBC Radio 4 produced a new dramatization of *The Lord of the Rings* in twenty-six half-hour instalments. The first parody of *Lord of the Rings* appeared in the first flush of the book's breakthrough: Henry Beard and Douglas Kenney's *Bored of the Rings* (1969) is a scattershot, intermittently funny mockery of Tolkien's novel that remains in print to this day, and has been followed by less funny books, not written by Beard and Kenney, lumbered with titles like *The Soddit* (2003) and *The Sellamillion* (2004). Numerous computer and video games have been inspired by Tolkien's works. The first video games set in Middle Earth began appearing in the 1980s. *Lord of the Rings: Game One* (1985), *Shadows of Mordor: Game Two of Lord of the Rings* (1987) and *The Crack of Doom* (1989) are text-adventure games for early computers that enable players to work through the storyline and worlds of the novel. Dozens of video game adaptations followed through

---

[10]Joseph Ripp, 'Middle America Meets Middle-Earth: American Discussion and Readership of J. R. R. Tolkien's *The Lord of the Rings*, 1965–1969', 277. 'From 1965 onward, and during a time when the focus of American culture generally became increasingly fixed on youth, masses of college-aged readers swelled the ranks of, and ultimately became entirely identified with, Tolkien's audience. Indeed, both the book's immense popularity and the association of *The Lord of the Rings* with young adults stem from a period during which it was frequently mentioned alongside the later stages of Beatlemania and the incipience of hallucinogenic culture.'

the 2000s, with the game-trilogy *Guardians of Middle-earth* (2011), *Middle-earth: Shadow of Mordor* (2012) and *Shadow of War* (2017) being especially successful. These games allow players to move freely through a richly detailed and vividly imagined three-dimensional rendering of Middle Earth, fighting orcs, pursuing quests and forging their own rings of power. To this must be added the sheer imitative influence this novel has had, the vast number of fantasy titles written and published that take *The Lord of the Rings* as a template, that rewrite and rework the fundamentals of this novel as constitutive of their own works of fantasy fiction. This becomes a major element in fantasy writing in and after the 1960s, with some works – often very popular, commercially successful works – de facto plagiaries of Tolkien, retreads and midrashim.

What is it about this novel that made it so shapingly successful as fantasy? In terms of story, *Lord of the Rings* retells *The Hobbit* on a larger scale and at much greater length: a hobbit joins a group embarking upon a lengthy quest, travelling out of the Shire, through mountains (where they encounter orcs) and into a magical forest inhabited by elves, and finally coming to a single mountain. A key difference is that, in *The Hobbit*, the band of adventurers is travelling to the mountain to find golden treasure, where in *Lord of the Rings* they are going to *lose* a specific piece of golden treasure – the ring of invisibility that Bilbo chanced upon in the earlier novel, now revealed to be a magical artefact of immense, malign power, that must be destroyed to save the world, which can only be unmade in the volcanic fires that forged it. The war that erupts into *The Hobbit* at the end is threaded through the whole of *Lord of the Rings* – it is the same war, still being fought a generation later – and there is much more antiquarian or pseudo-antiquarian matter in the telling than is the case with the earlier novel: footnotes, quoted songs and ballads from an earlier epoch in the imaginary history of the realm, recent historical and deep historical elements and related, embedded into the ongoing narrative or referenced in passing, and a book-concluding series of appendices that include lengthy annals-style chronologies, thousands of years of invented history, languages, alphabets and runes, anthropological and other data. The novel comes with two prefaces, one in the voice of the author detailing the circumstances out of which the novel was written, another styled as a historical essay 'Concerning Hobbits', sketching the history of these diminutive peoples, their manners and mores, their pipe-smoking and their level of technological advancement: 'they do not understand or like machines more complicated than a forge-bellows, a water-mill or a hand-loom, though they were skilful with tools'. They are, in other words, a pre industrial revolution, eighteenth-century community: with their waistcoats, bathtubs and indoor plumbing, their tea-kettles and small-town respectability, 'English' in many ways, non-feudal though classbound. In the novel Frodo is of a higher social status than his companion, his former gardener Sam, who figures to him somewhere between friend and servant. The point of this worldbuilding is to contrast the comfortable, bourgeois world of the Shire with the wider world of Middle Earth, which is variously medieval (Gondor), Anglo-Saxon (Rohan) or wilderness. When Frodo leaves Bag End to go on his adventure, just as Bilbo did before him, he leaves modernity and enters the older, perilous and enchanted realms of faerie and heroism.

This in-text movement from modernity into the past is Walter Scottian, as is the style and form of *The Lord of the Rings*: the discursive, somewhat prosy style, the inset ballads and poems, the way a texture of lived-experience is created through detail and digression, through appeal to historical authority – in Tolkien's case, pseudo-historical – in prefaces, footnotes, appendices; but most of all the central *shape* of the story. The narrative *Waverley* (1814) and *Lord of the Rings* share is a there-and-back-again journey, through a landscape peopled with various tribes (in Scott: English, Borderers, Lowland Scots, Highlanders; in Tolkien, hobbits, men, elves, dwarfs, orcs and ents) and different cultures and, in some cases, languages. Scott's stories are full of descriptions of mountains and battles, above all the elegiac sense of an old world passing away. More, in several places in *The Lord of the Rings* Tolkien reworked and adapted specific famous elements from Scott.[11] Tolkien grew up reading the *Waverley* novels, as did all his class and generation; it is not surprising that his sense of how a narrative novel of adventure should be written drew heavily on Scott.

Into this form Tolkien inserts elements from older sources – the ambulant forest of *Macbeth*, dragons and warriors from *Beowulf*, dwarf and wizard names from the Elder Edda, other story-elements from northern folk-tales and Märchen. The magic ring is adopted from the story of Gyges, or Wagner – modulated and augmented by his own imaginative inventiveness. Stylistically the book opens in a Scott-like discursive idiom leavened by the various touches of alterity. The book's opening sentence, 'When Mr. Bilbo Baggins of Bag End announced that he would shortly be celebrating his eleventy-first birthday with a party of special magnificence, there was much talk and excitement in Hobbiton', could have come from any nineteenth-century novel, save for the made-up placename and the slightly disorienting note of 'eleventy-first'. We discover that, like biblical patriarchs, hobbits are longer-lived than regular humans, going through adolescence in their twenties and entering adulthood at 33; but even so an age of 111 is remarkable (credited not to Bilbo's resilience but of the effect of the magic ring he still carries). Throughout *Fellowship* this familiar, even chatty tone reverts us to a version of recent modernity that is only occasionally diverted into strangeness and enchantment.

---

[11]Two particular examples: Tolkien's monstrous 'Black Riders' draw on the *Schwartz Reiters* (faces like 'grinning, ghastly monsters … they rode on black chargers, and smeared with black ointment their arms and accoutrements') that chase Quentin and the fair Isabelle across the spacious medieval landscapes of *Quentin Durward* (1823). And the episode in which the Fellowship attempt, and fail, to cross the haunted mountain Caradhras is based on the opening of *Anne of Geierstein* (1829): 'a small party, two Englishmen and an Italian boy, together with their mule, trying to cross the Alps into Switzerland. One snowy peak they must pass, Mount Pilatus, is occupied by a malevolent spirit, supposedly the angry unquiet ghost of Pontius Pilate himself. The younger Englishman, Arthur, defies the mountain: '"How the accursed heathen scowls upon us!' [he] said … while the cloud darkened and seemed to settle on the brow of Mount Pilatus. 'Vade retro! Be thou defied, sinner!"' At his words a wind starts up. There are, as we might say, fell voices on the air. '"A rising wind, rather heard than felt, seemed to groan forth, in the tone of a dying lion" … The party's attempt to cross the mountains becomes increasingly difficult, through blizzard and rockslide: "the evil spirit was peculiarly exasperated at the audacity of such strangers as ascended the mountain." They also pass "dismal lake", within the murky waters of which exists "a form", an evil creature that on occasion emerges' [Roberts, 'Crossing Caradhras: a Second Note on Tolkien and Scott'].

But the tone changes as the book proceeds, and the adventure moves deeper into its perilous fairyland, shifting from the discursive forms of the nineteenth-century novel and older, archaic styles and idioms, the latter becoming more prominent a feature of the text as the novel goes on: from "'Lawks!' said Merry' in Book 1, to 'Didst thou think that the eyes of the White Tower were blind? Nay, I have seen more than thou knowest' in Book 6.

Once Frodo reaches Rivendell a fellowship of nine individuals is formed, comprising the four hobbits who have travelled out of the Shire, two men (Aragorn, and a warrior from Gondor called Boromir), an elf and a dwarf – Legolas and Gimli – all led by the wizard Gandalf. The fellowship walks hundreds of miles south from Rivendell and moves through the orc-infested mines of Moria, where Gandalf is killed by a fire-demon called a Balrog. The survivors pass on to the lands beyond, coming ever closer to Mordor. Boromir, his heroic nature poisoned by the influence of the ring, of which he is increasingly covetous, betrays the company, and tries to steal the ring from Frodo so as to claim its power. Frodo evades him by means of the ring's invisibility, and Boromir redeems himself as the party is attacked by a party of orcs, fighting them off at the cost of his own life. Frodo and Sam leave the group to try to find their way to Mount Doom and there destroy the ring; Gollum, who craves the ring from which he has been dispossessed, has been shadowing the journey of the Fellowship, and now reveals himself to the hobbits, promising to guide them to their journey's end – in fact planning to betray them and steal the ring back. The remaining members of the Fellowship travel into the ancient forest of Fangorn where they meet a reborn Gandalf. Saruman the White, the leader of the order of wizards, has betrayed his trust in a search of power and allied himself with Sauron. Gandalf, mystically resurrected on a mountain-top, takes his place, becoming Gandalf the White. He leads the abbreviated fellowship to Rohan, an Anglo-Saxon realm where the horselords are threatened by Saruman's army of orcs, and thereafter to Gondor, a medieval kingdom centred on a beautiful, towering white city Minas Tirith, where Sauron's army orcs is attacking. The final battle of good versus evil arrives, whilst Frodo and Sam make their way through the mountains, past the terrible giant spider Shelob, into the blasted land of Mordor itself and finally up the slopes of Mount Doom. The story ends with a 'eucatastrophe': a term Tolkien's coined in 1944 for a particular kind of narrative shape, a particular kind of happy ending: *eu* meaning good, *catastrophe* in its original Greek sense of a narrative about-turn, a sudden switch. For a story properly to be eucatastophic it needs to have more than just a happy ending (although it does need that). It needs to be tending implacably towards tragedy, to frame a sense of inevitable disaster, for 'good' to be facing overwhelming odds and certain defeat, such that the final triumph of good is both sudden and unexpected – or (because this is also part of Tolkien's understanding of the eucatastrophe) both unexpected and *not* unexpected. This latter is so because, on a deeper level, the eucatastrophic ending chimes with something deep inside us, something Tolkien understood in spiritual, religious terms, and which he believed to be true about the cosmos. So, it seems as if Sauron's victory is unstoppable, the struggling forces of good are powerless to prevent it, until at the last minute the ring is destroyed and Frodo and Sam are rescued from certain death. This is one story. So far as Tolkien was concerned the greatest story – the Christian passion – was also eucatastrophic. This is the story God is telling, through the medium of His creation. Which is to say, Tolkien thought this was the deep structure of the universe as such.

'Eucatastrophe' is everywhere nowadays, an absolute mainstay of contemporary popular storytelling. Defeat seems inevitable – as the soldiers die, one by one, in the face of deadly and implacable German advance at the end of *Saving Private Ryan*, as Captain America stands, bruised and alone, before Thanos's slavering, bloodthirsty hordes in *Avengers: Endgame*, as Harry Potter limps, exhausted, hounded, doomed to die before Voldemort's inevitable triumph – right up to the moment when victory is snatched with a flourish from defeat's jaws. But its presentday ubiquity should not distract us from the innovation of Tolkien's narrative conception.

The novel's shift from Scottian discursiveness to medieval archaism actualizes the way this imaginary world moves its characters back into history: to medieval and Dark Age Europe. Fantasy, as this study argues, is a way of 'doing' history, and fantasy novels are in a particular way historical fiction. Lukács's *The Historical Novel* (1937 in Russian, 1962 in English translation) takes Walter Scott as the paradigmatic historical novelist, not because he was the first person to write a historical novel (he wasn't), nor because he was in his day very popular and influential (he was, but that's not what interests Lukács). Rather he identifies in Scott's *Waverley* novels a dramatization of the dynamic of history as such. The typical Scott novel goes like this: there's a protagonist not in himself notable or important, a (fictional) individual living at a time of (actual, historical) flux, who meets various real historical characters in the course of his peregrinations. Generally this individual – let's call him Waverley, after the protagonist of Scott's first and series-naming novel – is torn between supporting the old and supporting the new. The old is the romantic, thrilling, charismatic but outmoded and unviable past; the new is the practical, bourgeois, in many ways unappealing but viable and inevitable present-future. In *Waverley* (1814) this dyad is: the romantic, doomed Jacobites on the one hand and the Whiggish Hanoverian succession, which is the future, on the other. Waverley 'wavers' between the two, hence his name: drawn first to the cause of Bonnie Prince Charlie, he ends the novel a respectable Hanoverian-supporting laird. And, with variations and tweaks, that's Scott's basic paradigm for all his novels. What Lukács thinks important about this is that Scott (writing decades before Marx though he was) intuitively grasped that history is a dialectical process by which older social-cultural theses come into conflict with antithetical present-day forces and are sublated into a synthetic future. That, in other words, Scott is writing about the dynamic of history itself, his stories and characters illustrations of that dynamic. Scott's historical periods are always in flux, always illustrative of process, rather than being static period backdrops. 'Through the plot of the historical novel', says Lukács, 'at whose centre stands the hero, a neutral ground is sought and found upon which the extreme, opposing social forces can be brought into a human relation with one another'. Where Shakespeare's histories (say) focused on figures of world-historical importance, kings and caesars, Scott's protagonists are ordinary people, removed from the centres of historical power. In Scott's novels, the big names of history 'can never be central figures of the action. The important leading figure, who embodies an historical movement, necessarily does so at a certain level of abstraction. Scott, by first showing the complex and involved character of popular life itself, creates this being which the leading figure then has to generalize and concentrate in an historical deed.' Accordingly 'the struggles and antagonisms of history are best represented by "mediocre" heroes who, in their psychology and destiny, always represent social trends and historical forces.' In this context, 'it matters little whether individual details, individual facts are historically correct or not … Detail is only a means of achieving historical faithfulness, for making concretely clear the historical necessity of a concrete situation.' At the same, time, Lukács insists that historical fiction written entirely 'from below', dealing only with proletarian experience without any middle class or aristocratic characters, cannot capture the totality of historical experience as such.[12]

All of this has its bearing on the way Tolkien styles his fantasy novel, and because of the scale of the success and influence of that novel, a continuing relevance to the way fantasy as a mode has been written through the later twentieth and twenty-first centuries. A mediocre hero, Frodo, wavers between the larger historical forces at war in his world, and also between the older, romantic, glamorous but doomed past and the inevitable coming of a flatter, less enchanted but also less perilous modernity – although, unlike a Scottian hero, Frodo cannot, ultimately, adapt to his place in the triumphant modernity: too haunted and possessed by what he has been through, he finally leaves Middle Earth altogether for the mystic, unseen 'Undying Lands' across the western ocean.

Another specific Scottian feature is the story's reliance on disguise. In the Waverley novels, characters repeatedly go about incognito, kings and princes disguised as traders, physicians, beggars. Whilst there is much disguising and hiding of self in the first volume of *The Lord of the Rings*, this is not, significantly, maintained through the rest of the book. Frodo and his companions leave the Shire under false pretences, and a pseudonym. To cover the fact that they are porting the dangerous ring, and perhaps throw the Black Riders off their scent, they tell people that Frodo is moving to a new house, at Crickhollow on the far side of the Brandywine river. Indeed Merry and Fatty Bolger actually buy an entire house, furnish it with all mod cons ("A bath!" cried Pippin. "Oh blessed Meriadoc!'" [ch 5]) and fully stock its larder. The first portion of the journey is the hobbits making their way to this house – a fake domicile, because Frodo has no intention of staying there. As soon as they arrive Frodo reveals his true purpose to the others: he is leaving immediately for Rivendell.

Disguise, subterfuge and misdirection run through Book 1. Bilbo plans a Birthday Party that is actually a farewell party, during which we discover that Bilbo has been lying to everyone about how he came by his magic ring. We discover that Gollum is not that individual's name: he's actually called Sméagol. Frodo travels under the pseudonym 'Mr Underhill', by which name he books into *The Prancing Pony* at Bree. Here he and the other hobbits are met by a dangerous-looking and mysterious man called Strider, who is

---

[12]György Lukács, *The Historical Novel*, 34–5.

actually called Dúnadan, although he's actually-actually called Aragorn. Much of chapter 10 is given over to the hobbits' suspicion of this hooded, hidden figure ('a strange-looking weather-beaten man ... A travel-stained cloak of heavy dark-green cloth was drawn close about him, and in spite of the heat of the room he wore a hood that overshadowed his face; but the gleam of his eyes could be seen as he watched the hobbits'). It is not until Bilbo receives a letter from the absent Gandalf, confirming Strider as friend not foe, that the tension is relaxed. 'Why didn't you tell me that you were Gandalf's friend at once?' Frodo asks him. 'It would have saved time.' In reply Strider reveals that he was not sure that the hobbits might not have been Sauron's agents in disguise:

'I had to study you first, and make sure of you. The Enemy has set traps for me before now. As soon as I had made up my mind, I was ready to tell you whatever you asked. But I must admit', he added with a queer laugh, 'that I hoped you would take to me for my own sake. A hunted man sometimes wearies of distrust and longs for friendship. But there, I believe my looks are against me'.

The theme is: appearance versus reality (as in Shakespeare). Sauron looked fair, but was wicked. Aragorn looks hard and dangerous and suspicious, but is good. A related pairing might be Saruman, who appears 'white' but is dark-hearted, and Gandalf, 'grey' but with the, as it were, whiter soul. My point is that this element of *Fellowship* notably falls away in the second half of Fellowship, and throughout the rest of the novel. The 'disguise' plot elements are a Scottian touch, but also a marker of modernity, the divided self, the confusion of disenchantment.

Then, on their journey further into the wider world, Frodo and Sam encounter a character called Tom Bombadil: a strange individual who plays no part in the ongoing story (beyond rescuing the hobbits from a barrow wight). Tom is entirely disengaged from, indeed oblivious to, the war of the ring. He is in fact an anthropomorphic representation of the land itself, a genius loci. Living a joyful life in the country with his wife Goldberry, singing and roaming about. He is potent with the magic of place. Whatever you might say about Tom Bombadil he is in no way in disguise. He is entirely, authentically himself: what you see is what you get, frank and open and direct. He hides nothing; he is. Insofar as the ring embodies this principle of disguise (for becoming invisible is another, very effective mode of disguise) it's significant that, alone amongst all the many characters in the novel, it has absolutely no effect upon Tom – he puts it on and does not vanish, his blue eye gleams through the ring of it, and he hands it easily back to Frodo.

It seemed to grow larger as it lay for a moment on his big brown-skinned hand. Then suddenly he put it to his eye and laughed. For a second the hobbits had a vision, both comical and alarming, of his bright blue eye gleaming through a circle of gold. Then Tom put the Ring round the end of his little finger and held it up to the candlelight. For a moment the hobbits noticed nothing strange about this. Then they gasped. There was no sign of Tom disappearing!

Arguably contemporary Tolkienian (and post-Tolkienian) fantasy are more expressive of the Lukacsian dialectic than Scott himself, since the whole premise of fantasy is a complicated desire to return to an enchanted past, in a world that has been comprehensibly disenchanted by modernity (by science, by capitalism, by Protestantism). Fantasy is in deeper love with this pre-modern past even than was Scott. And yet fantasy can see how unviable this feudal, warrior, hierarchical shame-culture is in actuality. Modernity's 'disguising' has something to do with the shift from a shame-culture to a guilt-culture. In the former, ethics depends upon outwardness: everyone knows that Orestes is guilty of the murder of his mother, and his atonement is performed in public, where everyone can see. Nowadays though, motivated by guilt rather than shame, there is a disjunction between what's happening inside us and the face we put on when we go out into the world. Raskolnikov is no Orestes. Our social being as such becomes, as it were, a disguise, hiding the inner reality. For Freud this is a simple description of humanity, over and above questions of crime and punishment.

Out of the Shire disguise ceases. When the fellowship meet a Balrog, it is not anything else disguised: it is itself. When they meet Galadriel she is simply Galadriel. Tempted by Frodo's ingenuous offer of the ring, she resists the temptation saying: "'I pass the test", she said. "I will diminish, and go into the West and remain Galadriel."' She is who she is, and so is everyone else the hobbits meet on the far side of the Misty Mountains. One way of putting this would be to say that disguise is the index of privacy, and the ability to have a private life is something the characters lose as they leave the Shire. At the same time, the wider world of the novel is one in which enchantment abuts the mundane and the ordinary. Subjectivity is not buffered away from the world, but porous.

The landscapes and rendering of Middle Earth come at this from several angles. We might, as readers, be surprised by the relative ignorance of Éomer, a nobleman of Rohan, concerning Lothlórien, the elf-inhabited woodland a few miles north of the Rohanian plains. Aragorn tells him that the fellowship 'passed through Lothlórien, and the gifts and favour of the Lady go with us' [452]. Éomer is amazed:

> The Rider looked at them with renewed wonder, but his eyes hardened. 'Then there is a Lady in the Golden Wood, as old tales tell!' he said. 'Few escape her nets, they say. These are strange days! But if you have her favour, then you also are net-weavers and sorcerers, maybe.' He turned a cold glance suddenly upon Legolas and Gimli. 'Why do you not speak, silent ones?' he demanded.

There are two layers here. If we take this on terms of politics, the realm of international relations, of a continent-spanning war, of state power, and armies, and diplomacy and realpolitik, then it is baffling that a Prince of Rohan has only the haziest, fairy-tale sense that a huge, powerful polity exists, a few miles north of Fangorn and their own territory – as if a medieval English prince had heard of Scotland only through rumour and old-wives-tales. But this little speech by Éomer articulates a different logic, a different and distinctly pre-Modern apprehension of the world: a place in which the woodlands are haunted by strange, supernatural powers, forces perhaps for good, perhaps for evil: fairies and bogies, monsters and elves. Éomer speaks here (in Charles Taylor's terms) out of an unbuffered sensibility, in which the strange glamour and wonder and terror of the woods are not material or political. But he also speaks, and as the novel goes on increasingly so, as an important member of a national-political entity, itself soon to ally with another national-political entity in order to make war on a common enemy, and in those terms what he says strikes an odd note.

The first half of *The Two Towers* is a book artfully and eloquently passing from the tower of Death to the tower of Life: Gandalf, dead, revivifies; Theoden, a living corpse, is returned to youth; trees, rooted and insentient, are transformed by Tolkien's imagination into roving, powerful Ents. According to what I am arguing is the dialectical dynamic of the novel, the second half of the same book traces the opposite trajectory; from Life to Death, or some ghastly state in between which is not yet dead but not quite life. It does not seem to me either irrelevant or random that the main characters of the first book of *The Two Towers* move, broadly, east to west; where in the second book Frodo, Sam and Gollum move, broadly, the opposite way, from west to east. One way of thumbnailing this would be to invoke Coleridge's famous phrase: *Nightmare Life-in-Death*. Gollum is a major figure in this section partly because he embodies this Coleridgean fate: a creature who has lived far beyond his natural span of life and is more profoundly damaged and miserable as a result than is easily described. The theme of the book hits home most powerfully in Chapter II, 'The Passage of the Marshes'. This is introduced by a clever little glance back to *The Hobbit*'s riddles. As he guides them through the dead marshes, Gollum sings a little song:

> The cold hard land they bites our hands, they gnaws our feet,
> The rocks and stones are like old bones all bare of meat
> But stream and pool is wet and cool: to nice for feet!
> And now we wish —

This is where the rhyme stops, although (as with Lewis Carroll's 'Fury Said To A Mouse') we can fill-in the unuttered final couplet ourselves: 'For some nice fish/All fresh to eat'. Instead of this, Gollum mocks his companions: '"Ha! ha! What does we wish?" he said, looking sidelong at the hobbits. "We'll tell you ... He guessed it long ago, Baggins guessed it."' Then he quotes again the riddle from *The Hobbit*: 'Alive without breath as cold as death never thirsting, ever drinking; clad in mail, never clinking. [*Lord of the Rings*, 646]. The original ichthyic answer to this is joined, in this chapter, by a second, more eerie possibility: for these words perfectly describe the warriors ('they lie in all the pools', says Frodo, dreamily: 'pale faces, deep deep under the dark water ... grim faces and evil, and noble faces and sad/ Many faces proud and fair, and weeds in their silver hair. But all foul, all rotting, all dead' 653). They cannot be the actual corpses of those slain in that antique battle, as Sam points out ('that is an age and more ago ... the Dead can't be really there'). But whatever they are, they turn the very landscape into a place in which some grisly remnant of life clings to death.

As with the warriors alive-without-breath beneath the waters of the Dead Marshes (and as with Gollum himself), so with Frodo: stung by the monstrous gigantic spider Shelob at the end of the book, and so mortified by this wound that Sam initially believes him a corpse. He's not; he is a poisoned body in which life still clings. Shelob, also ancient, is also more Death than Life (the 'stench of death' is about her, we're told; and 'little she knew of or cared for towers, or rings, or anything devised by mind or hand, who only desired death for all others, mind and body' [751]).

The nightmare of Life-in-Death is very different, indeed profoundly so, from Death-in-Life. The former is a kind of violation. The latter is natural; a ripeness; the grain of existence. 'I say unto you', as Jesus declares in the Gospel of John: 'unless a grain of wheat falls into the ground and dies, it remains alone; but if it dies, it produces much grain.' He has just brought Lazarus back from the dead when he says this, and is looking forward to his own crucifixion and rebirth. That's also what's going on with all the fish, in this book. Fish are Gollum's staple. He not only eats fish, he has become fishy – like Caliban in *The Tempest*, a monstrous companion with a fishy reek: 'a very miserable creature he looked, dripping and dank, smelling of fish (he still clutched one in his hand); his sparse locks were hanging like rank weed over his bony brows, his nose was snivelling' [674].

A finely observed moment in the novel happens when Sam tries to fry the fish that Gollum has caught, to the latter's horror: 'Spoiling nice fish', he screeches; 'scorching it!' Gollum, we might say, prefers gravlax to fish-and-chips. Which is to say: Gollum, here, is Nature to Sam (and Frodo's) Culture. What Lévi-Strauss argues in *The Raw and the Cooked* about the raw/cooked axis that, symbolically speaking, cooking marks the transition from nature to culture. To cook food is to mediate nature and society, life and death, heaven and earth. The cook, according to Lévi-Strauss, can be viewed as a cultural agent whose function is to 'mediate the conjunction of the raw product and the human consumer, making sure the natural is at once cooked and socialized'.[13] Sam, the most gregarious of hobbits, is precisely the right actant, here. And actually the moment when Gollum objects to the spoilation of his lovely natural raw fish by exposure to the cooking-fire of culture is interesting in another way, too. One vector of raw to cooked is *history as such*. The differential of 'past' and 'present' is anachronism, an event, object or type of person from the now that is out of place in the then. We would be startled to read a medievalized fantasy tale in which a character brought out an iPhone. Gandalf can race across Rohan riding Shadowfax, but we would revolt if he caught a steam-train. On the question of anachronism, as also consistency, Tolkien took pains to work everything into a harmonious whole. As we have seen, he objected to his friend C. S. Lewis's more macaronic approach to worldbuilding. When Thorin gives Bilbo a suit of mithril chain-mail, we feel it to be a fitting gift in terms of the medievalized logic of the story; were Thorin to hand him a gift-wrapped box from Bloomingdale's, or Marks and Spencer, we would look askance. This is to restate Lévi-Strauss's point. Anachronism mediates the

---

[13]Lévi-Strauss, *The Raw and the Cooked*, 336.

shift *from* the raw *to* the cooked – from the pre-modernity of fantasy to the bourgeois 'civilized' settlement of the now. What Father Christmas gives the children in *The Lion, The Witch and the Wardrobe* are suitably medieval donations: potions, weapons. But that it is Father Christmas, that Late Victorian invention, dressed in the livery of Coca Cola, who is pulling these gifts out of his sack brings us crashing into the modern age. This is not accidental: Lewis's novel is much more centrally about the link between disenchanted modernity and enchanted fantasy – a connection literalized in the wardrobe portal after which the novel is, in part, named. We think of Tolkien as avoiding this kind of anachronism, but actually he doesn't. True, he does not foreground the disjunction the way Lewis does, and he put much labour and care into fitting together his imagined world according to logics of internal-consistency and artistic vision. But anachronism is still very much a part of *Lord of the Rings*. Two in particular stand out, in the sense that a medieval individual would find them perfectly incomprehensible. One is tobacco, in which pleasurable vice hobbits indulge. When Aragorn, Legolas and Gimli finally catch up with Merry and Pippin, they are sitting beside Isengard smoking their pipes. With this detail Tolkien at least has other characters remark upon the strangeness and novelty of the activity, marking it as, at the least, unusual in its world. But here, in the second half of Two Towers, we get Sam Gamgee musing about the deliciousness of Fish 'n Chips.

> 'Po – ta – toes', said Sam. 'The Gaffer's delight, and rare good ballast for an empty belly … But be good Sméagol and fetch me the herbs, and I'll think better of you. What's more, if you turn over a new leaf, and keep it turned, I'll cook you some taters one of these days. I will: fried fish and chips served by S. Gamgee. You couldn't say no to that.' [*Lord of the Rings*, 649]

Gollum, of course, rejects the cooked modernity in favour of his raw antiquity: 'Yes, yes we could. Spoiling nice fish, scorching it. Give me fish now, and keep nassty chips!' Fish and Chips popping up in Middle Earth are hardly less egregious an anachronism than Lewis's department-store packages and Father Christmas. What in-world Walter Raleigh, we might ask, sailed beyond the sea and brought back tobacco and potatoes? (And sailed where? The place the Americas would occupy, were Middle Earth a kind-of Europe, is taken by the Undying Lands). Fish and Chips are pre-eminently cooked. The re-enchanted premodern is never hermetically sealed away from disenchanted modernity, in fantasy.

We can constellate the presence of fish in this fantasy with the use of the 'fish' rebus amongst early Christians. Christ telling his followers 'I will make you fishers of men' [Matthew 4:19]; the Greek for fish, ἰχθύς, serving as an acronym (Iesus CHristos Theos Uois Soter: it's in use to this day). Tolkien, writing his medievalized fantasy novel, draws on medieval romance as well as Old English epic. The Holy Grail quest – the Sangraal – is one such, expressly inverted here. In the Holy Grail story, the knights and companions of King Arthur go on a quest to discover and retrieve the Holy Grail, a magic metal item. They do so because the health of the kingdom is magically bound up with this object. In *Lord of the Rings* the king (Isildur's heir, and king to be) and his companions undertake a quest to lose, rather than to find, a magical metal item, and do so because the health of the kingdom is magically bound up with it. It's a clever inversion and works amongst other things to express a spiritual dimension to do with kenosis, of letting-go and emptying – to do with sacrifice and passivity ('passion', as the Christian synonym has it). We could contrast the grail, a cup, capable of containment, a symbol of fertility and wholeness, with the ring, which has, as it were, the sides of a cup without any bottom, through which the contents would simply drain away.

Timothy Morton situates Tolkien in terms of both the longer tradition of 'Romantic nationalism' and environmental art:

> As the idea of world (Welt) became popular in German Romantic idealism, so the nation-state was imagined as a surrounding environment. The idea of the nation as 'homeland' … demanded a poetic rendering as an ambient realm of swaying corn, shining seas, or stately forests. Nature appeared sublime 'there' and yet fundamentally beyond representation, stretching beyond the horizon and back into the distant, even pre-human past. It was a suitable objective correlative for the *je ne sais quoi* of nationalist fantasy. Walter Scott's invention of historical novels, realist fictions generating an entire world in a bubble of past-tense narrative, did as much for environmental nationalism as explicitly Romantic criticisms of modern society and technology.[14]

They go on to read Tolkien in this light.

> The Shire, in J R R Tolkien's *The Lord of the Rings* depicts the world bubble as an organic village. Tolkien narrates the victory of the suburbanite, the 'little person', embedded in a tamed yet natural-seeming environment. Nestled into the horizon as they are in their burrows, the wider world of global politics is blissfully unavailable to them. Tolkien's work embodies a key nationalist fantasy, a sense of 'world' as real, tangible yet indeterminate, evoking a metonymic chain of images – an anamorphic form. *The Lord of the Rings* establishes not only entire languages, histories, and mythologies, but also a surrounding world. If ever there was evidence of the persistence of Romanticism, this is it.

In this, and with all its contradictions, *Lord of the Rings* is truly a summation of tradition from Romantic art, Scott, Victorian Arthuriana, MacDonaldsian and Morrisian fantastical apprehension. Writing in 1967 Tolkien insisted that 'Faery might be said indeed to represent Imagination … esthetic: exploratory and receptive; and artistic; inventive, dynamic, (sub)creative. This compound – of awareness of a limitless world outside our domestic parish; a love (in truth and admiration) for the things in it; and a desire for wonder, marvels, both perceived and conceived – this "Faery" is as necessary

---

[14]Morton, *Ecology Without Nature*, 97.

for the health and complete functioning of the Human as is sunlight for physical life'.[15] As William Gray glosses, this 'view of "Faery" or fantasy, as essential to human completeness' is an expression of Tolkien's fundamentally Coleridgean, High Romantic theology of 'sub-creation', 'a theology shared with Lewis and echoing MacDonald's'.[16] This is not to veil the question asked above ('what is it about this novel that made it so shapingly successful as Fantasy?') behind a cloud of unknowing, or to evade the interpenetration of the work by political, historical striations and problematics: the bourgeois ideological centring, the masculinism, the racialized rendering of good and evil into distinct in-world species, the conservatism and hierarchies. But it is to accept the force with which the novel captured the imaginations, and hearts, of so many readers – the present author included. This is not, fundamentally, a question of narrative, although, as John Clute notes, Tolkien was 'pervasively concerned with narrative, and a master in the techniques of telling a secondary-world tale'. In his essay 'On Fairy Stories' (1937) Tolkien itemizes four elements that are necessary to 'the fairy tale', which we can take to be fantasy as such: Fantasy; Recovery; Escape and Consolation. Clute suggests that 'oddly, these four elements do not constitute and narrative analysis of Fantasy', though they have sometimes been thought to.

> Fantasy incorporates Tolkien's arguments about the nature of the secondary world. Of the 'recovery of freshness of vision' ... he intends his audience to understand that that the washed vision of Recovery returns us to a capacity to see things as we are meant to see them. 'Escape' is not 'the flight of the deserter' but the 'escape of the prisoner'. The prison – he make clear by example – is the modern world; the secondary world may be imaginary, but it is at times preferable to think oneself inside such a world ... By 'Consolation' Tolkien means the Eucatastrophe – the happy event – which properly ends the fairytale and which all-importantly defines the fairytale as something requiring an ending.

In all this, as Clute says, Tolkien is working to 'enforce a trust in the reader that what is being told is a truth'; that 'what is so deeply engaging for readers of Lord of the Rings is the sensation that they are being brought to *recognize* the "true" nature of fictional characters' – and world – 'and they are doing so within the implacable security of a technique that not waver from the instillation of belief'.[17] This belief, this faith, this 'reality' of a re-enchanted world, is the compelling strength of Tolkien's recovered, escapist, consoling fantasy.

---

[15]Tolkien, *Smith of Wootton Major*, 101.

[16]Gray, *Fantasy, Myth and the Measure of Truth*, 151. Gray adds that 'this is made explicit in the declaration of faith at the end of 'On Fairy Stories' [1939] where 'Fantasy' does not so much refer to a literary genre as to 'a quality of strangeness and wonder in the Expression ... Fantasy remains a human right: we make it in our measure and in our derivative mode, because we are made: and not only made, but made in the image and likeness of a Maker'.

[17]John Clute, 'J R R Tolkien', in Clute and Grant (eds) *The Encyclopaedia of Fantasy*, 953–4.

# CHAPTER 15
## 1960s–70s: THE BOOM

### Sword and Sorcery

Asked to provide the introduction to a 1995 reprint anthology of Fritz Leiber's *Lankhmar* stories, Michael Moorcock recalled the commercial climate of 'sword and sorcery' fantasy writing in the early 1960s, when he himself first began publishing. He credits Cele Goldsmith Lalli (1933–2002) – editor of *Amazing Stories* from 1959 to 1965, and *Fantastic Stories* from 1958 to 1965 – with midwifing the mode.

> Cele Goldsmith (later Lalli) is one of the great editors of science fantasy and, with Judith Merril, godmother to the American sf New Wave of the 1960s. She published all the Young Turks, most of them for the first time, in the magazines she edited … Lalli had a liking for what one of her contributors [Leiber himself] had christened 'Sword and Sorcery' and she commissioned a young John Jakes to write her a series of Conan-like adventures, *Brak the Barbarian* [1968]. She published an early fantasy of mine called 'Earl Aubec and the Golem', which she retitled 'Master of Chaos' [1964]. She published the first Roger Zelazny story – and published many more. She published Thomas M. Disch and J. G. Ballard and Samuel R. Delany and all the exciting talents which helped create that wonderful sea-change of the 1960s. She also liked Philip K. Dick and Keith Laumer, but I think her favourite writer, whose talent stood so far above the majority of his more financially successful peers, was Fritz Leiber.[1]

For some, Leiber's importance as a writer of twentieth-century fantasy rivals Tolkien's. Moorcock certainly thinks so: where (in his words) 'J. R. R. Tolkien, an obscure academic, published a peculiar trilogy with a William Morris/Anglo-Saxon ring to it [that] became the core of a somewhat unhealthy cult', Leiber was, simply, 'the best living Fantasy writer'. Lalli coaxed Leiber out of a writer's-block-induced semi-retirement, and in doing so brought him to a new, large audience.

Leiber began publishing in the Pulps before the war but after he serialized his 1943 novel *Conjure Wife!*, a contemporary-set fantasia in which witchcraft is revealed as a secret art known to all women, he began to dry up, although 'dry' is perhaps the wrong word, since his alcoholism proved an increasing impediment to working as a writer: 'I began to run into difficulties', he later recalled going through a 'period of indecision

---

[1]Moorcock, 'Introduction' *Ill Met in Lankhmar.*

and anxiety' about his writing, exacerbated by and in turn further exacerbating his alcoholism (his 'heavier drinking').[2] He continued writing, but the magazine market was increasingly inhospitable to serialized novels, preferring standalone stories, and his writing career languished. Until, that is, Lalli resurrected it in the 1960s. The kind of work he was doing, as Moorcock, had to create its own audience.

> Few recognised the tradition in which we wrote and the public for our work numbered a few thousand throughout the world. The works of most of our predecessors – whether commercial writers like Howard, Burroughs and Merritt or literary writers like Dunsany and Cabell – were largely out of print and hard to find. In those days the kind of supernatural romance which dominates today's best-seller lists had virtually no commercial market. Leiber had done no better with his first *Gray Mouser* book than I had done with my first *Elric* book ... So Cele Goldsmith, when she commissioned Fritz Leiber to write a new series of *Fafhrd and Gray Mouser* stories for *Fantastic*, was taking a big gamble with her circulation figures.

Leiber's naming of the mode linked it to the work of Robert Howard:

> Howardian fantasy-adventure is ... a field which I feel more certain that ever should be called the sword-and-sorcery story. This accurately describes the points of culture-level and supernatural element and also immediately distinguishes it from the cloak-and-sword (historical adventure) story – and (quite incidentally) from the cloak-and-dagger (international espionage) story, too! The word sorcery implies something more and other than historical human witchcraft, so even the element of an alien-yet-human world background is hinted at. ... At any rate, I'll use sword-and-sorcery as a good popular catchphrase for the field.[3]

Though Leiber's first Fafhrd and the Gray Mouser story was published in the 1930s ('Two Sought Adventure' just squeaks into that decade, appearing in *Unknown* in August 1939), it makes sense to consider his work, and Sword and Sorcery more broadly, in the context of the 1960s and 1970s. The novelette *Ill Met in Lankhmar* (1970), perhaps the best, surely the most characteristic, of the 'Gray Mouser' tales, won both Hugo and Nebula Awards, a high point in Leiber's reception. It was collected along with two other stories detailing the early adventures of Fafhrd and the Gray Mouser, as *Swords and Deviltry* (1970): other stories, either earlier magazine pieces reprinted or new tales specifically written, were collected in the volumes *Swords in the Mist* (1968), *Swords against Wizardry* (1968), *The Swords of Lankhmar* (1968), *Swords against Death* (1970), *Rime Isle* (1977), *Swords & Ice Magic* (1977) and *The Knight and Knave of Swords* (1988).

---

[2]Leiber, *The Ghost Light*, 350–51.
[3]Don Herron 2023, *The Pulp Net* https://thepulp.net/pulp-articles/three-sought-adventure/ Accessed March 2023.

Fafhrd is a huge, muscular barbarian from the northern lands: seven-foot tall, skilled at swordsmanship fond of hearty singing, quaffing, carousing and fighting: in many ways a 'Conan' type. The Mouser is much smaller: five foot, and slender, talented equally with the rapier and the dagger, a romantic and somewhat mercurial thief and former wizard's apprentice. 'The Unholy Grail' (1962; collected in *Swords and Deviltry*) relates how his former wizard-master, Glavas Rho, was murdered by the magic-hating autocrat Duke Janarrl, how Mouser took his revenge upon the Duke, before running off with his toothsome daughter. The Gray Mouser retains some, though small, skill at magic throughout the stories. Both Fafhrd and the Mouser are charming rogues, turning their hand to whatever scheme, robbery or adventure comes their way. The mainline of Leiberian storytelling is a peripatetic Walter-Scottian adventure-romance mode, something like *Quentin Durward* or *The Talisman* with added supernatural (magic, wizardly, monstrous) elements, though Leiber's approach is more archly knowing, wittier self-reflexive. Some of Fafhrd and the Mouser's many adventures lean into the absurdist, or comic; some embody a more Jacobean grand guignol. Sometimes the tales switch from one to the other – in 'Ill Met', for instance, a 'what-larks!' night-time jaunt infiltrating the Lankhmarian Thieves Guild in disguise turns dark, when, on returning home, Fafhrd and the Mouser discover the Guild has had their two girlfriends garrotted and left their corpses to be half-eaten by rats. The two return to exact a furious revenge with their swords.

Perhaps the most significant influence of Leiber on the mode was his importance for Terry Pratchett, whose first Discworld novel (*The Colour of Magic* 1983) overlapped with Leiber's later career. Pratchett issued a half-hearted denial that his city of thieves, sorcery and adventure, Ankh-Morpork was in any way based on Lankhmar, but clearly the two characters appearing in *The Colour of Magic* under the pseudonyms 'The Weasel and Bravd' were the Gray Mouser and Fafhrd. Pratchett's richer comic imagination, and his vastly superior command of comic prose as an instrument, developed something greater, more capacious and more humane, out of Leiber's legendarium: Discworld is discussed below.

David Langford rightly zeroes-in on Leiber's 'stylish wit', the sinister, magical shop in 'Bazaar of the Bizarre' (1963), 'a personified Death who repeatedly tries to harvest the elusive duo' and above all the City of Lankhmar itself, 'with its eccentric Overlords, Silver Eel tavern, Thieves' Guild, exotic pleasure-areas like the Plaza of Dark Delights, countless warring temples in the Street of the Gods (with a piquant distinction between these "Gods in Lankhmar" and the feared, unworshipped "Gods of Lankhmar") and general sense of sleazy, colourful inexhaustibility'.[4]

Through the 1960s and into the 1970s 'sword and sorcery' fantasy boomed. L. Sprague de Camp, for one, wrote a great many examples of the type. *The Tritonian Ring* is a selection of linked short stories, fixed-up into a single paperback volume in 1968, bearing the cover-caption 'Thrilling Sword and Sorcery for Fans of Tolkien's *Lord of the Rings*!'

---

[4]Langford, 'Fritz Leiber' in Clute and Grant (eds) *Encyclopaedia of Fantasy*, 573–4.

The book concerns the quest of Prince Vakar to save his sinking continent, Poseidonia, from the wrath of antagonistic gods: a lively peripatetic series of adventures, with headless zombies, gorgons, giant crabs and octopus-headed creatures. The violence is gruesome ('he struck right and left, slicing open torso and reaching arms, spraying blood … looking across the shambles, Vakar saw the king lying with his head staved in' [*Tritonian Ring*, 154]), the misogynistic objectification of women more so: – at the court of Queen Porfia, Vakar 'felt an urge to leap up and seize' his hostess, since 'she had a form that practically demanded rape of any passing male' [56]. As the story proceeds, Vakar is accosted by the erotic importuning of naked amazon queens, naked satyr-women ('quite human except for the horse-tail and pointed ears') and even naked puritans – although the latter start off clothed: 'she blinked her large dark eyes at him. "I cannot endure these fanatical notions of order, and I burned with passion for you from the moment I saw you – oh, take me! You shall never regret it!"' [151]. He does, and with various others too, although in the end he marries Queen Porfia, having resisted his, as de Camp believes, perfectly natural urge to rape her. Indeed she extracts a promise from him that he will stick with her in the longer term:

> I speak of other kinds of love, not merely carnal love, which for all its delights both of us know for a sly deceiver. Oh, I know you would give me a tumultuary time beneath the drugget; but how about the long pull? [De Camp, *The Tritonian Ring* 202]

Fantasyland as a venue for this kind of heterosexist male wish-fulfilment continues in De Camp's *The Goblin Tower* (1968) and its sequels *The Clocks of Iraz* (1971) and *The Unbeheaded King* (1983). In this series an adventurer called Jorian, hired to steal a magical artefact by the wizard Karadur, fights and beds his way across de Camp's imagined realm of 'Novaria'. One intriguing twist is that this location is the mortal prelude to an afterlife in 'our' world; but the story itself is if anything more calcified and sexist than *Tritonian Ring*: 'she was naked, holding the dress in her hands. The light was now strong enough for Jorian to perceive that she was a comely wench … "let us find a comfortable bed amongst this cargo, for there is scant romance doing it standing up"' [*Goblin Tower*, 82]. *Scant romance* is the keynote. The swordplay adheres to melodramatic cliché, as with this piece of dark-and-stormy-night combat:

> The swords met with a whirl and a multiple clang, which was lost in a roar of thunder. The two powerful men stood on the bridge glaring into each other's eyes, cutting, thrusting, and parrying. For an instant they backed off, then they were at it again, clang-tzing-zip-clang. [*Goblin Tower*, 247]

British writer Michael Moorcock rarely stoops to clang-tzing-zip-clang, and may indeed be what John Clute calls him, 'the most important UK Fantasy author of the 1960s and 1970s, and altogether the most significant UK author of sword and sorcery'; though there are limitations as well as exhilarations in his extensive output.[5] Moorcock, a man who takes writerly prolificity to extremes, has assembled a bibliography that runs to multiple hundreds of novels. Initiated into the pulp-market of writing at speed in the 1950s, by the 1960s and 1970s he would write a whole novel in a week or, if he is to be believed, sometimes in a single weekend. But the quantity of outputs matters less than the fact that each book iterates variations on a single theme and story, aggregating into a megatext ergative of fantasy as such. Moorcock coined the term 'multiverse' to describe what he was doing, and not only do all his stories take place in that location, most of his fantasy heroes are versions of the same individual, 'the Eternal Champion', an individual who appears and reappears across time, space and dimension to continue the fight against entropy, and in defence of valour, love and life.

Speed of composition sometimes results in sketchy or ragged prose, and there are many repetitions across Moorcock's oeuvre. At the same time his prodigality granted him an access to a kind of unmediated subconscious, an unmannered and undiluted flow of fantastical ideas and situations, something a more considered or revisionary writer could not achieve. We could call this rawness – and Moorcock's prose is often raw, his characters and plotting crude – as against the cooked blandness of much other fiction. In his later writing, he has been more conventional in his writing approach, but in his 1960s and much of his 1970s work he comes close to automatic writing, not excluding the value of mere accident, the contrivance of jokey juxtapositions and puns, which connects him to the tradition of the Parisian Surrealists, as to Joyce and Burroughs, harnessing the elements of fantasy to a repeated, ritualist game-playing of near constant creation. That Moorcock's fecundity finds its greatest expression in a vision of decadent exhaustion and entropic decline is not a paradox: his imagination casts (often) into the far future, the terminal beaches and decaying end-times, in order to reach back into medievalized and earlier history; his vigour is put at the service of stylish aristocratic languidness, his inventiveness framed by a multiversal eternal recurrence.

The most famous version of Moorcock's Eternal Champion is Elric, albino emperor of the ancient realm of Melniboné and bearer of the sentient blade Stormbringer, a demon in broadsword-form that devours the souls of those it kills. Elric first appeared in the novella *The Dreaming City* (1961), bringing an armada to besiege the dreaming city of Imrryr in order to recover his lover Cymoril, kidnapped by his cousin, Yyrkoon. Elric's fleet is destroyed by dragons, forcing him to make his way through hidden caves into the city, to confront his cousin; but his cursed sword instead kills Cymoril. Elric, distraught, attempts to throw Stormbringer into the ocean but instead of sinking it hovers over the waves. Elric retrieves it, accepting that he is bound to the cursed sword and it to him by unbreakable magical force. The sword figures largely in two following novels *The Stealer of Souls* (1963) and *Stormbringer* (1965). *Elric of Melniboné* (1972) is the first of several prequel tales, along with *Elric: The Sailor on the Seas of Fate* (1976), *The Weird of the*

---

[5]Clute, 'Moorcock', in Clute and Grant (eds) *Encyclopaedia of Fantasy*, 656.

*White Wolf* (1977) and *The Vanishing Tower* (1977). With all the paraphernalia of various magical Fantasyland, these novels' version of decadence has a distinctly of-its-decade quality. Elric himself is, in effect, a rock star: his skin 'the colour of a bleached skull' and 'the long hair which flows below his shoulders milk-white. From the tapering, beautiful head stare two slanting eyes, crimson and moody, and from the loose sleeves of his yellow gown emerge two slender hands, also the colour of bone' [Moorcock, *Elric of Melniboné* (1972)]. Constitutionally languid, he must ratchet up his energy with illegal drugs in order to 'perform' as ruler, warrior or lover, and the singing sword he carries is somewhat like a guitar: 'Elric's fingers played nervously with the pommel of his runesword. "Can an ultimate God – exist – or not? That is what I need to know, Shaarilla."' [*The Weird of the White Wolf* (1977), 77]. The rock-star logic means that Elric must be both creator and destroyer, supporter of civilization against anarchy – Moorcock's preferred terminological dyad is 'law and chaos' – and also the force that brings civilization crashing down: his name, after all, is a version of Alaric, the king of the Goths who sacked Rome in AD 410. He parses a rock-star popular celebrity and also an outsider strangeness, a Bowie-esque alienness. Absolute ruler of a 100,000-year-long empire ('el-ric', like Alaric, must etymologically be the *all-reich*, the all-ruler) and eternal wanderer and loner.

Less well-known than Elric, though prior to him in terms of being identified as 'the eternal champion', is Lord Erekosë, wielder of the radioactive sword Kunajana. *The Eternal Champion* (1962; expanded into a novel of the same title in 1970) opens with Erekosë dead, resurrected by necromantic magic as 'John Daker', a twentieth-century man dragged out of his comfortable life by dark enchantments. The world into which Daker awakes is a war between humanity and 'Eldrens', and Erekosë promises total war: 'You will spare none?' asks the beautiful Princess Iolinda; and Erekosë replies: 'None! None! I want it to be over. And the only way I can finish it is to kill them all. Then it will be over – only then! And when the last Eldren dies, when the whole world is ours, then I will bring it to you and we shall be married'. Genocide as dowry, the kind of gesture that would be offensive if it weren't framed in so artificial and sketchy a fashion. A further iteration of the Eternal Champion is prince Dorian Hawkmoon, son of the stern but fatherly Count Brass, both of whom adventure across a far-future Europe that has reverted to a magical medievalism, plagued by monsters and mad gods. The Hawkmoon novels constitute a quartet [*The Jewel in the Skull* (1967), *The Mad God's Amulet* (1968) *The Sword of the Dawn* (1968) *The Runestaff* (1969)], followed by a trilogy concerned with the adventures of his father: *Count Brass* (1973), *The Champion of Garathorm* (1973) and *The Quest for Tanelorn* (1975). The topographical identifiers of Hawkmoon's Fantasyland are only slightly morphed from ours: there is the 'Dark Empire of Granbretan', ruled by King-Emperor Huon, who preserves his immortal life within a fluid-filled sphere in the empire's capital, Londra. Hawkmoon, from 'Germania', defends mainland Europe against these 'British' hordes as they swarm across the giant channel bridge. A jaded nihilism is here the characteristic of this mirror-image Second World War:

> the great power of the Lords of the Dark Empire was that they valued nothing
> on all the Earth, no human quality, nothing within or without themselves. The

spreading of conquest and desolation, of terror and torment, was their staple entertainment, a means of employing their hours until their spans of life were ended. For them, warfare was merely the most satisfactory way of easing their ennui. [*The Sword of the Dawn* (1968), 5]

With flatfooted playfulness, Moorcock ties this fantasyland to the real world of the 1960s: the people of Granbretan worship a quartet of ancient gods, who once ruled the land before the Tragic Millennium, the Beatles as were: 'Jhone, Jhorg, Phowl and Rhunga', themselves existing under the doubled avatars of Churchill and Harold Wilson, 'Chirshil, the Howling God' and 'Aral Vilsn, the Roaring God, the Supreme God, father of Skvese and Blansacredid, Gods of Doom and Chaos' [*The Runestaff*, 106–7]. The fossilized whimsy of apotheosing these Wilsonian economic policies ('credit squeeze' and 'balance of credit') date the book badly, and jar with the dominant mode of the quartet, which is a more timeless heroic swashbuckling. Hawkmoon carries a magical sword that can summon Pictish and Celtish warriors from the dawn of time to assist his martial aims. 'Hawkmoon lifted up the Sword of the Dawn. "I warn you, Count, this blade I bear is no ordinary instrument! See how it glows with rosy light!" he grinned and raised the rosy sword high in the air. "I summon *the Legion of the Dawn!*"'

The Count screamed and came forward again, but Hawkmoon raised his booted foot and kicked him in the chest, sending him reeling back against the dais. Then Hawkmoon recovered his sword and when Shenegar Trott ran at him again, blind with anger, he ran directly on to the point of the Sword of the Dawn, dying with an obscene curse on his lips and one last, backward look at the Runestaff. [Moorcock, *The Runestaff*, 72]

The titular staff is a 'mysterious artifact said to control all human destinies' which Hawkmoon serves, and which he must retrieve from a fabled city across the ocean in 'Amarehk'. It's all jolly, phallic play, men's magic staffs and swords pouring out glamour and power and domination, but for all their inventiveness and readability, their very ingenuousness – thrown into starker contrast by the occasional gestures towards the mannered wit of Beatle-divinities and the like – the books tend towards a kind of flatness and repetition. Aware of this, Moorcock increasingly works to open up his fantasy realms to other dimensions, bringing in characters from other novels, parsing everything as a carnivalesque multiverse. Another version of the Eternal Champion is the 1960s counter-cultural figure Jerry Cornelius, by turns white-skinned and black-, male and female, polymorphously and perversely multiform: a spy, flâneur and urban adventurer. Cornelius first appears in the 'Cornelius Quartet' [*The Final Programme* (1969), *A Cure for Cancer* (1971), *The English Assassin* (1972), *The Condition of Muzak* (1977)], ludically and rather self-consciously experimental texts that flirt with the, in the 1970s, modish trappings of *nouvelle roman* and Burroughsian cut-up, rather in hock to the counter-culture that birthed it. To the rebuke 'there's more to life than drugs and sex, Mr. Cornelius', Jerry replies 'There's more than life to drugs and sex'; adding: 'it's better than nothing'. The best of Cornelius is the trilogy of novels known collectively as *Dancers At The End of Time* [*An Alien Heat* (1972), *The Hollow Lands* (1974), *The End of All Songs* (1976)], an ultra-decadent civilization of bored immortals existing millions of years in the future at the 'end of time', created not begotten, capable of time-travel, listlessly devoted to parties and distractions from their existential ennui: 'they found pleasure in paradox, aesthetics and baroque wit; if they had a philosophy it was a philosophy of taste, of sensuality. Most of the old emotions had atrophied, meant little to them'. The complication of a love story between Jerek with Mrs Amelia Underwood, a time-traveller from the nineteenth century, gives the trilogy much of its shape. Moorcock later styled a personal myth of composition in which Cornelius was the product of a terminal authorial enervation. A 2012 reissue of *An Alien Heat* includes an introduction in which Moorcock recalls the mid-1960s – at which point, we might note, his immensely prolific career had barely started:

I had been editing *New Worlds* for some months and had published several science fiction and fantasy novels, including *Stormbringer*, when I realized that my run as a writer was over. About the only new ideas I'd come up with were miniature computers, the multiverse and black holes, all very crudely realised in *The Sundered Worlds*. No doubt I would have to return to journalism. 'My career', I told my friend J G Ballard, 'is finished'. He sympathised and told me he only had a few SF stories left in him, then he, too, wasn't sure what he would do.

At this point Moorcock wrote, in nine days (or so he claims), the first Jerry Cornelius novel. The buried story in *Dancers At The End of Time* is that Jerek is a sort of experiment, fashioned to escape the eternal decay of time, and the deleterious effect time-travel has upon the immortals, a sort of psychopomp to break through to newness. This vigour is the dialectical presence of exhaustion, and vice versa.

All these various 'J.C.' names recall Jesus Christ, not as singular agent of passion and redemption but as the recurring figure of an endlessly ongoing process of salvation. The flipped 'C.J.' gives us Prince Corum Jhaelen, the hero of two trilogies of high fantasy: the first 'Swords' trilogy [*The Knight of the Swords* (1971), *The Queen of the Swords* (1971), *The King of the Swords* (1971)] and the second [*The Bull and the Spear* (1973); *The Oak and the Ram* (1973); *The Sword and the Stallion* (1974)]. The setting here is a mythic-magical version of prehistoric Earth: humanity, 'upstart man', is on the rise. Corum himself is an elf-like being, the last of his race, who wages an ongoing war against Lord Arioch of Chaos and his bestial hordes. Though a poet and a thinker, Corum spends most of these novels in action mode:

He struck out with his fist as a pigthing clambered after him. A dog-thing leapt at him. It wore a helmet and a breastplate but its muzzle was full of long teeth which snapped at his arm. He swung the sword and broke that muzzle in a single, smashing blow. Hands which had turned into claws and paws grabbed at him, tore at his cloak, his boots. Swords stabbed and clubs struck the stone at his feet as a whole-mass of the creatures began to climb towards him. [*Queen of Swords*, 95]

The multiverse intrudes in the form of an interdimensional traveller, Jhary-a-Conel – Cornelius again. Corum defeats Arioch only to encounter the gigantic form of the Queen of Swords herself, divine avatar of Chaos: 'the monstrous, beautiful furious face of the Queen of Swords rose higher over the horizon … "AH! CORUM! DREADFUL ASSASSIN OF ALL I LOVE!" The voice was so loud that it made Corum's ears throb with pain. He staggered backwards against the battlements' [153].

The sardonicism of this, the juvenile glee at all the violence, the hectic churn of travel and plotting, pull rather against the potential of wonder and sublimity: but the verve with which fantasy is evoked achieves something memorable nonetheless. The cascade of activity is not wholly structureless: anarchic energies kept in check by order, order enlivened by effulgence. Nor is the rendering a total desublimation of the aesthetic: the torrential energies of fantastical activity touch on tremors of horror and eschatological dread, and also a kind of enchanted euphoria, an ecstasy of enhanced, transcendent consciousness. But the enchantment of this open-ended multiversal Fantasyland degrades under the sheer repetitive weight of the retelling.

The mode is variousness, working a pastiche melange of prior sources into hectic tessellation. And though there were few writers with the volume of output, or sheer heroism of logorrheic intensity of Moorcock, there's no doubt that the 1960s and 1970s saw an algae bloom of related work.

Poul Anderson's *Three Hearts and Three Lions* (1961), the first in a long series of fantasy works by a prolific, long-lived author, belongs under this aegis. This novel reworks Mark Twain's *A Connecticut Yankee in King Arthur's Court* (1889), although without the humour, and replacing Twain's satirical critique of the horrors of modern war with a militaristic valorization of the heroic soldier and the Just War. Holger Carlsen, a member of the Danish resistance fighting the German occupation of his country, tangles with strange Nazi technology in a battle fought at Elsinore ('Hamlet's home town' the novel tells, in case we didn't know). As a result, he is transported to a parallel universe, a medievalized European realm. Carlsen must resume his combat on a more existentially prime level, as the forces of 'Law' battle the forces of 'Chaos' – Anderson, who published the first short story version of this novel in 1953, may claim precedence for establishing 'Law versus Chaos' as a fantasy concept, something Michael Moorcock, 'Sword and Sorcery' and especially *Dungeons & Dragons* and other RPGs, have wholeheartedly adopted. Kitted-up as a chivalric knight, accompanied by the dwarf Hugi and the beautiful swan maiden Alianora, Holger enjoys peripatetic adventures and quests, aiming at once at victory in the fantasy war, to win the heart of Alionara and to find a way home to 'our' world. The amalgam of tough-guy adventure narrative and medievalized cod-archaisms, especially of dialogue, makes for a sometimes tonally dissonant blend. The latter in particular is not beyond mere ridiculousness: "'Tis Alianora, the swan-may." Beer gurgled down the dwarf's throat. "Hither and yon she flits throughout the wood and e'en into the Middle

World sometimes. Aaaaah!'" [*Three Hearts and Three Lions*, 29]. But the story rattles along, and the book enjoyed notable success.

The storytelling idiom here is pastiche. The novel unabashedly recycles the Matter of France, Arthurian romance, Norse mythology, witchcraft: in this realm, with indiscriminate panache, all these myths and legends are 'real', as are the character of Spenser's *Faerie Queene* and Shakespeare's *A Midsummer Night's Dream*. Eventually Holger comes to understand the intertextual primacy of Twain's book as the original upon which his own adventure is merely a variant, and is able, by 'taking a crib' from the book, 'from literature – the *Connecticut Yankee*' [150], to win the day. Whether the explicit embracing of this notion, of fantasy as a palimpsest of jumbled-together prior texts, remits the novel from the pitfalls of mere cliché is the question. We could say it is playful, a game of spot-the-source (Mirkwood is mentioned, though with madcap adulteration of the Tolkienian source: 'there in Mirkwood do the Pharisee lairds hunt griffin and manticore' [44]). Alternatively, we might say it is plagiaristic, tired and tiresome. Certainly the gender politics of the novel are clichéd in a more substantively malign manner:

> Holger decided he had troubles enough without a hysterical female on his hands. He pulled her around, shook her, and said between his teeth, 'I have nothing to do with this. Hear? Now will you come along like a grown human being, or must I drag you?' [75]

Alianora's response: 'she gulped, stared at him with wide wet eyes … "I'll come wi' ye," she said meekly'. The novel ends as she finally declares her feelings ('I love ye, Holger'), although this moment is swamped, rather, by the fact that this is the precise time Holger finally understands who he is: namely, a version of what Moorcock would later call 'The Eternal Champion'. He rides off into the dawn, abandoning her in preference for other adventures, quests and battles. Sequels by Anderson and other writers detail his peregrinations and adventures and his eventual return to Alianora. From them we also discover that he converts to Catholicism. This final touch speaks, I suppose, to a Taylorian 'de-buffering' of Holger's sensibility: a return to the old religion and the enchanted world which it frames. It is not clear that the novel, though it is lively, readable, full of incident – actually communicates this sense. There's something pat, a strange combination of frantic and stale, about the texture here.

Anderson is usually better than this. Sandra Miesel finds in Anderson's many fantasy novels what she calls a 'mortal shield' against entropy.[6] This, if we translate the terminology out of thermodynamics into questions of the diminishing of enchantment, speaks to his achievement in his greatest and most influential novel, *The Broken Sword* (1954), which as Miesel notes

---

[6]'In Anderson's basic formula, a man acts for love of a Cosmic Woman, and their love begets the Hopeful Child. The family bond is the sturdiest defence against entropy' [Miesel, *Against Time's Arrow: the High Crusade of Poul Anderson*, 60].

makes Faerie a preternatural domain coexisting with historical reality, but ordinarily hidden from human eyes. When the elves and trolls wage war in tenth century England, mortals only see stormy weather. Faerie shelters all the fabulous but soulless beings famed in myth and legend. As in the medieval view, it is a state belonging neither to Heaven nor hell, an alluring refuge for men unwilling to choose between those Powers.

*The Broken Sword* exists in two versions: as published (and broadly ignored) in 1954 – it was Anderson's first novel – and as revised and republished in 1971 as part of the Ballantine list. Comparison of the two reveal the later Anderson pruning the sometimes overdense boscage of his prose, trimming away adjectives and adverbs and toning-down the use of archaic terminology. In a preface added to the 1971 edition he said 'I would not [now] myself write anything so headlong, so prolix, and so unrelievedly savage. This young, in many ways naive lad who bore my name could, all unwittingly, give readers a wrong impression of my work and me'. Michael Moorcock has repeatedly acknowledged the influence of this book upon his own fantasy writing. It is, he says, 'the best story of its kind'.

> The strong Scandinavian influence is combined with a sophisticated view of Alfheim perhaps owing something to Spenser. His Elf-lords are both more attractive and more sympathetic than his human characters. Unlike most generic fantasy Anderson's story is a true tragedy. A human child is exchanged for a troll-born changeling. Scafloc the human is raised in Faerie, amongst the immortal, sardonic elves. He falls under the power of his own evil sword. Valgard the changeling becomes a bewildered, alienated berserker in the world of men, betraying and killing in his desperate quest for a world where he can feel at home. The tragedy begins to play itself out, inevitably. This superb tale is Anderson's finest dramatic achievement.[7]

Calling the novel tragedy might imply that there is more of catharsis in the story than is actually the case. Enduring, not prevailing, is man's lot in *The Broken Sword*. This 'unrelievedly savage' novel provides the starkest possible contrast to Operation Chaos. It is a brutal, tumultuous saga that epitomizes Tolkien's definition of the Northern heroic spirit: 'uttermost endurance in the service of indomitable will. Here Fate, the force that sunders ties of blood, faith, and reason, proves too mighty a foe for the bravest and truest of lovers to survive. Only courageous death bears witness against entropy'.[8] Anderson's 1971 preface implies that he only read *Lord of the Rings* after writing *The Broken Sword*, which is a remarkable consideration for a book so in tune with Tolkienian fantastical ethos and so richly provided with Tolkienian elements and touches. But one does not wish to call Anderson a liar.

---

[7]Moorcock, *Wizardry and Wild Romance*, 88.
[8]Miesel, *Against Time's Arrow*, 15.

## Earthsea, Prydain and others

The single best fantasy novel of the 1960s is not so shy of its influence. Asked by her publisher to write a book for older children Ursula Le Guin revisited and reworked some short stories she had previously written set in a fantasy archipelago. The resulting work, *A Wizard of Earthsea* (1968), together with its five sequels, remain some of the most celebrated of all the works of post-Tolkienian fantasy. Margaret Atwood calls the book a 'wellspring' of modern fantasy. Amanda Craig praises it as 'the most thrilling, wise and beautiful children's novel ever'.[9] It owes much to Tolkien, although it is also its own thing, distinctive, wondrous, beautiful.

The story is set upon a spread of islands in what appears to be a global ocean on a world that lacks continents – or perhaps the sea goes on forever, beyond the reach of the archipelago. The title character is Duny, known as 'Sparrowhawk', who grows up on a small island in the north-east of Earthsea. When he manifests magic power – he summons a fog that baffles and defeats an invading force of Viking-like 'Kargad' raiders – he is trained, first by a local wizard, who gives him his 'true name', Ged, and afterwards travels to the school for wizards in the centrally located island of Roke. The 'true name' conceit is crucial, for magic in this realm is radically nominalist, and knowing the true name of a person or a thing gives a wizard power over it. On Roke Ged improves his skills, but, youthfully arrogant, he also undertakes a magic duel with a rival student, thereby inadvertently unloosing a hideous entity from some other dimension. The shadow-being attacks Ged, wounding and scarring him, before rushing away. This incursion is very dangerous, for the shadow-entity is malign, and has the power to possess and hollow out people turning them into wraiths. If it can do this to Ged, with his prodigious magic ability, it could make him into a dreadfully, perhaps apocalyptically harmful figure. So Ged flees from the shadow creature until, travelling from island to island, having adventures on each, he comes to understand that he must turn the tables, and pursue the entity. This he does, eventually passing beyond all the islands and across the deep sea. Here he finally encounters his nemesis. The entity has evolved. When it first emerged from the rip in reality Ged's improvident spells had wrought 'it had no head or face, only the four taloned paws with which it gripped and tore' [*Wizard of Earthsea*, 61]. By the end of the novel it has acquired a human form, mimicking Ged himself – it is, we realize, Ged's Jungian anima, his shadow-self. As such, it possesses the same 'true name' as Ged who, naming it, defeats it.

Many languages are spoken across Earthsea, but there is one aboriginal 'true' language: the language out of which the world was originally spoken into being. Only dragons, the other intelligent species with whom humans share the world, speak this tongue. Wizards learn it as part of their training. Knowing the true name of something enables magic, although the usage is difficult and draining, and wizards do not undertake it trivially. We are several times told that any magic act entails the risk of upsetting the cosmic

---

[9]Craig, 'Classic of the month: A Wizard of Earthsea', *The Guardian* (24 September 2003).

'balance', which wizards in all things serve. In Tolkien, wizards are rare, individuals not fully integrated into human society, beings (in fact) of a different species. There is no larger population of wizards, cunning men, or – for that matter – witches, sorceresses, wizardesses in Middle Earth. But in Le Guin's Earthsea wizards are common. They are human, like everyone else, and live not apart but within human communities, with a social role to play and a broad level of acceptance. The ability to wield magic exists on a spectrum, with many people able to cast certain spells, and only a few wizards have access to the bigger, more fundamental or impressive magic. Women are able to cast spells as well, although, in a ratio inferior to men: 'weak as woman's magic, wicked as woman's magic' is a proverb in this world, and in *A Wizard of Earthsea* the struggle between good and evil is explicitly gendered. Le Guin's re-examination and reconfiguring of the sexist logic underlying this structure of belief inform subsequent novels in the Earthsea sequence, *The Tombs of Atuan* (1970) and *The Farthest Shore* (1972). After a pause, the series was continued in *Tehanu* (1990), *Tales from Earthsea* and *The Other Wind* (both 2001), by which time we come to understand that women's magic is revealed as neither weak nor wicked, though it is different to men's.

There is a seriousness, an absolute belief, in the way Le Guin renders her world, and it compels the reader, draws her into Earthsea not as a merely ludic or flippantly rendered fantasia but a genuine location. The attention to detail, as much anthropological (a pseudo-anthropology that draws on and mimics real-world anthropological research – Le Guin's parents were both anthropologists) as mythographic, as much linguistic as geographical. The Earthsea books are careful to construe their world as a believable, lived-in space, the existence of magic, dragons and wraiths notwithstanding. Not that Le Guin is po-faced in her worldbuilding. On the contrary, she plays a number of games with her source material. On Roke, the master wizard displays how magic works to Ged:

> The Master Hand looked at the jewel that glittered on Ged's palm, bright as the prize of a dragon's hoard. The old Master murmured one word, 'Tolk', and there lay the pebble, no jewel but a rough grey bit of rock. The Master took it and held it out on his own hand. 'This is a rock; *tolk* in the True Speech', he said, looking mildly up at Ged now. 'A bit of the stone of which Roke Isle is made, a little bit of the dry land on which men live. It is itself' [*Wizard of Earthsea*, 43]

The stuff out of which the islands of Earthsea are made is *tolk*: knowing its true name means that a wizard can manipulate it, for instance turn it into a jewel – although this alters only its accidence, not its essence. A little later we discover that the 'True Speech' word for sea is: *inien*. Le Guin is saying that Earthsea is *tolk-inien*, that is, Tolkienian: an elegant way of acknowledging her major influence.

Other kinds of games with words are at play in these novels. Ged is first introduced to us as 'Duny', and after he acquires his 'True Speech' name Ged he is known to most by the name 'Sparrowhawk'. (it is not a good idea to let too many people know your true name, lest they use magic against you). 'Dun', from the Middle English *dunne*, means brown soil, and the colour thereof; *ged* is a word for pike or luce, and a sparrowhawk, obviously, is a bird – three names covering three of the four elements, earth, water and air. The fourth, fire, is the province of the dragons. In *Tehanu* (1990) the titular girl-child has passed through fire, and been scarred by it (her father, a wandering vagabond, had pushed her into a campfire and left her for dead). She is revealed at the end to be half-human half-dragon, and so to command draconic magic power. She ends the novel living with elderly Ged (and Tenar, the heroine of *The Tombs of Atuan*) under the name Therru, which we are told means 'flame'. *Tehanu* was published under the rubric 'The Last Book of Earthsea' (although other books did subsequently appear) and there is a nice harmony in a conclusion that homes 'flame' with earth/water/air Ged.

Another intertextual game in *A Wizard of Earthsea* concerns the door of the School for Wizards on Gont. When Ged first comes to the school he cannot get inside: 'it seemed to him that he had passed through the doorway, yet he stood outside on the pavement where he had stood before'. He is told by the doorkeeper that he must say his true name in order to pass, which he does. The door is made of two substances, somehow both at once: 'the door through which he had come was not plain wood, but ivory without joint or seam', yet 'the door that the old man closed behind him was of polished horn, through which the daylight shone'. [*Wizard of Earthsea*, 35] When he leaves the school at the end of his education, he steps back through 'the door of horn and ivory' [74]. The allusion, of course, is to Vergil's gates of the underworld in *Aeneid* 6, and behind that to the gates of dreaming in Homer's *Odyssey*. Le Guin, who is too scrupulous in her worldbuilding to leave this detail as it is (since Earthsea has no elephants), adds a gloss: the ivory is actually 'a tooth of the Great Dragon'. In Homer and Vergil there are two separate gates: one of horn, through which 'true dreams' pass out into the mortal world, and the other of ivory, through which come deceptive dreams. By combining them Le Guin suggests that Ged, trained in the ways of magic and passing out into the world, is somehow both 'true' and 'false' – a dualism very much of a part with Le Guin's vision in the novel. This is more than the 'balance' (what the novel calls 'the Balance and the Pattern which the true wizard serves'): it is a way of talking about fantasy as such, as a mode: its bivalve truth and unreality, its admixture of mimesis and fantastica.

Le Guin's use of this detail in *A Wizard of Earthsea* is more Vergilian than Homeric: for she is more interested in the border between the lands of the dead and the living than in dreams as such. In Earthsea the realm of the dead, with desert lands and lightless cities under unfamiliar constellations, lies alongside the realm of the living, separated by a low wall. In *Wizard*, Ged travels into the dead lands, as wizards can, chasing a young girl who has died. He lets the girl go and returns to the boundary wall only to see his shadow-being waiting on the other side. 'Either he must go down the hill into the desert lands and lightless cities of the dead', the novel tells us: 'or he must step across the wall back into life, where the formless evil thing waited for him'. He chooses life, but there is always that balance between the truth – of power, of desire, of life itself – and falsehood. In this I differ from Francis Spufford's account of the novel:

> Later, I discovered and cherished Ursula Le Guin's *Earthsea* novels. They were utterly different in feeling [to Tolkien], with their archipelago of bright islands

like ideal Hebrides, and their guardian wizards balancing light and dark like yin and yang. All they shared with Tolkien was the deep consistency that allows an imagined world to unfold from its premises solidly, step by certain step, like something that might really exist. Consistency is to an imaginary world as the laws of physics are to ours. The spell-less magic of Earthsea gave power to those who knew the true names of things: a beautifully simple idea. Once I had seen from the first few pages of the first book, *A Wizard of Earthsea*, that Le Guin was always going to obey her own rules, I could trust the entire fabric of her world.[10]

I would put it slightly differently. Le Guin is indeed careful in her worldbuilding: taking care in the craftsperson sense that her imaginary world coheres and works according to its specified logic, and also having a care, in the Heideggerian *Sorge* sense of the word, for the power of words and the worlds they create. But at the same time Le Guin is *in*consistent, untruthful, in her worldbuilding – openly, directly so. Part of Ged's training upon Roke involves him studying under the 'Master Namer', a wizard 'who was called by a name that had no meaning in any language, Kurremkarmerruk'. This sage lives in a tower and devotes his time to compiling a huge list of all the names in the True Language. Pupils come to learn these names: 'writing down lists of names that must be learned before the ink faded at midnight leaving the parchment blank again'. From Kurremkarmerruk, we discover that true names proliferate endlessly, a kind of Derridean *différance* that surely leaves magic as such no place on which, finally, to stand and leverage the actual world. It is not enough to know that the True Name of sea is *inien*: 'he who would be Seamaster must know the true name of every drop of water in the sea'. Quite the task!

> Here is the reason. The sea's name is *inien*, well and good. But what we call the Inmost Sea has its own name also in the Old Speech. Since no thing can have two true names, *inien* can mean only 'all the sea except the Inmost Sea'. And of course it does not mean even that, for there are seas and bays and straits beyond counting that bear names of their own. So if some Mage-Seamaster were mad enough to try to lay a spell of storm or calm over all the ocean, his spell must say not only that word *inien*, but the name of every stretch and bit and part of the sea through all the Archipelago and all the Outer Reaches and beyond to where names cease. Thus, that which gives us the power to work magic, sets the limits of that power. A mage can control only what is near him, what he can name exactly and wholly. [48]

Of course, this is impossible: the 'exact and whole' naming is on these terms baldly unachievable. How to turn a cup of brine to clear potable water – a magic act Ged himself manages – without naming every single drop, every saline molecule, every atom? Yet Ged does perform the magic. The magical 'system' in Le Guin's novel, her worldbuilding,

---

[10]Spufford, *Child That Books Built*, 84–5.

both is and is not consistent, at one and the same time. It is true-horn and false-ivory, it is the 'good' Ged and his wicked shadowy anima, combined into one person as at the novel's end. This is the whole point of her story.

Much-loved, and still current, is American author Lloyd Alexander's 'The Chronicles of Prydain': a five-book series written for younger readers, set in a magical version of medieval Wales. In an author's note Alexander declares 'Prydain is *not* Wales', thereby confirming how largely he has drawn on Welsh history, mythology, language and geography – for stationed there during the war, he had fallen in love with the country and its culture. Alexander initially intended simply to retell Welsh and Arthurian myth for a young readership but discovered that he couldn't: 'I found I had been kidding myself', he later wrote. 'I didn't want to retell anybody's mythology. What I really wanted to do was invent my own, or at least use my own in some way'.[11] This own use explains his insistence that Prydain and Wales are not the same thing (and, technically, the name Prydain is cognate with *Britain* rather than Cymru), but the books draw so heavily on the *Mabinogion* and the collection of legendary stories *The Myvyrian Archaiology of Wales* (1801–3), and recreate expertly the beauty of Welsh landscape and atmosphere, that we can locate them in that re-enchanted principality. In *The Book of Three* (1964) Taran, assistant pig-keeper at Caer Dallben, discovers that one of his swine, Hen Wen, has magic oracular powers. The book is a Bildungsroman, in which Taran's dreams of becoming a great hero are set against his actual development and maturity as, on account of his remarkable pig, he is drawn into the war against the Death-*brenin* Arawn, Lord of the Underworld, who, as per the titular pot of the series' second volume *The Black Cauldron* (1965), is using a magic crochan to enslave and reanimate the souls of the dead. With his zombie army Arawn is a potent and compelling antagonist. Taran's journey out of obscurity and to importance includes him meeting and befriending Princess Eilonwy, a young girl his age, a poet-king called Fflewddur Fflam, the Dwarf Doli and, for comic relief, a sidekick character called Gurgi, a simian creature somewhere between animal and person. Writing *The Castle of Llyr* (1966) – in which Taran and Eilonwy are separated, and Taran must rescue her – Alexander decided that the third portion of his trilogy needed two books rather than one, and, having reason to believe (wrongly) that he would soon die, wrote *The High King* at speed. This was not published until later, since his publishers decided that the transition to this title was too abrupt and requested he write a linking tale. He did so: *Taran Wanderer* was published in 1967 and *The High King* in 1968. Upon the conclusion of the series, Taran has defeated Arawn, is crowned High King of Prydain and marries Eilonwy.

It was remarked, upon first publication, that Eilonwy is a female character with more agency and pep than was usual in the mode,[12] although a twenty-first-century

---

[11]Quoted in Jill Wheeler, *Lloyd Alexander*, 19.

[12]'Eilonwy, a feisty orphan princess with flowing red-gold hair ... was born at a time when the feminist movement of the sixties was simmering but had not come to full boil. But Elionwy was a stride ahead of her time and helped to introduce a new breed of female character ... she became the prototype for Alexander's subsequent female protagonists – and the female characters of other authors writing in the seventies and eighties' [Michael O Tunnell, 'Eilonwy of the Red-gold Hair', 558].

perspective is more likely to be struck by her limitations and passivity. She has magic powers, or at least magic potential, but in *The Castle of Llyr* she succumbs to the witch Achren who uses her for evil ends, and later surrenders her magic artefacts and powers in order to save her companions. She mourns this: 'I'll only be just a girl', she says, to which Gwydion replies: 'that is more than enough cause for pride'. Taran, on the other hand, goes from strength to strength. He is at once a humbler Frodo and an Aragorn, and Gurgi is somewhere between Sam and a friendlier Gollum:

> Under a chill, grey sky, two riders jogged across the turf. Taran, the taller horseman, set his face against the wind and leaned forward in the saddle, his eyes on the distant hills. At his belt hung a sword, and from his shoulder a silver-bound battle horn. His companion Gurgi, shaggier than the pony he rode, pulled his weathered cloak around him, rubbed his frost-nipped ears and began groaning so wretchedly that Taran at last reined up the stallion. 'No no!' Gurgi cried. 'Faithful Gurgi will keep on! He follows, kindly master, oh yes, as he has always done! Never mind his shakings and achings!' [*The High King*, 7]

The whole series is written in this plain style, which well captures both the stark sublimity of the world and its magic, and the homelier, person and comic moments. Wide-ranging, full of incident, magically charming, the books never lose sight of the central group. There is a pleasing sense of community here, through which they strengthen the group as a whole by sharing their individual weaknesses, with an attractive emphasis on humility, service and honour. But the books have a sharp-edged glamour, a darkness and violence that strengthen what might otherwise be too safely cosy a series of adventures. Here Taran finally defeats Arawn, who has taken the form of a gigantic snake.

> Taran swung the flashing sword with all his strength. The blade clove the serpent in two. A horrified gasp came from Eilonwy. Taran looked up as the girl pointed to the cloven serpent. Its body writhed, its shape blurred. In its place appeared the black-cloaked figure of a man whose severed head had rolled face downward on the earth. Yet in a moment this shape too lost its form and the corpse sank like a shadow into the earth; and where it had lain was seared and fallow, the ground wasted, fissured as though by drought. Arawn Death-Lord had vanished. [*The High King*, 256–7]

The Disney corporation adapted the first two books into a movie *The Black Cauldron* (1985; directed by Ted Berman and Richard Rich): an expansive piece of hand-drawn animation that flopped so badly it nearly sank the company. The adaptation necessarily simplifies the complexity of the books and elements of 'Disneyfied' cuteness and kitsch mismatch the source material; but it remains a visually rich and involving piece of fantastika with some enormously striking scenes.

The failure of this movie, and that of the big-budget adaptation of Robert Howard's *Red Sonja* (1985, directed by Richard Fleischer) in the same year, persuaded movie producers that fantasy was not a commercially viable cinematic mode – unlike science fiction, which (as with the *Star Wars* and *Star Trek* franchises, *The Terminator*, *E.T.: the Extra-Terrestrial*, *Back to the Future*) produced many of the highest-grossing movies of the 1980s – and (*Jurassic Park*, *Independence Day*, further *Star Wars* and *Terminator* movies, *The Matrix*) of the 1990s too.[13] The question as to why SF should score so lucratively with filmgoers across these decades, and fantasy so poorly, is an interesting one, and I return to it below.

British author Susan Cooper also drew on Welsh legends, though in less comprehensive manner than Alexander, for her 'Dark Is Rising' sequence of books, beginning with *Over Sea, Under Stone* (1965) and continuing, after a hiatus, with *The Dark is Rising* (1973), *Greenwitch* (1974), *The Grey King* (1975) and *Silver on the Tree* (1977). The hiatus is significant: the first book was never intended as the first in a sequence. It was written as a standalone to be entered into an Edith Nesbit tribute contest, such that its characters are a trio of 'Nesbit-esque' children, Simon, Jane and Barney Drew, on holiday in Cornwall. Helped by the Merlin-figure of Oxford Professor Merriman Lyon the three find a treasure map, decipher it and eventually uncover the Holy Grail, despite being pursued by forces of darkness. It is charming and whimsical, but is tonally at odds with the darker, more powerful later novels. Those books treat a similar (and indeed related) story: an ordinary British child who discovers a wondrous and dangerous fantasy realm erupting into ordinary life, in a more focused, even stately manner. Linda Bachelder puts it well when she describes the novels as 'written in an exquisite style, treating a beautiful rural life with reverence while finding under it an exciting and satisfying sub-structure of universal meaning'.[14] In *The Dark is Rising*, Will Stanton, who (with six older brothers and six uncles) is the seventh son of a seventh son, discovers on his eleventh birthday that he is one of an ancient magical folk called 'the Old Ones', destined to wield the powers of The Light in the ancient struggle with The Dark. The telling does not complexify the starkness of this moral divide, but its vividness and directness, and the integration of Arthurian legends, add brilliance and grandeur – especially in *The Grey King*, where Will joins forces with a lonely local boy, Bran Davies, who turns out to be King Arthur's son and a version of the Celtic god Bran the Blessed. They face the terrifying Grey King, the oldest and most powerful of the Lords of the Dark. From his grim castle Cader Idris he issues 'the Breath of the Grey King', filling the mountains and valleys with fog, tricking unwary travellers to their deaths over hidden precipices and slopes. Though he cannot leave his fastness, he has human followers, and an army of 'Milgwn', giant spectral grey foxes that walk in the fog and leave no trace, go unnoticed by mortals (though both Bran and Will can see them) and attack with the force of great hounds (*milgwn* is Welsh for 'greyhounds'). Jennifer Bryan notes how *The Grey King* exemplifies a shift in the focus of Arthurian retellings more broadly: 'not only the turn toward fantasy' as such, but a 'return to pre-romance

---

[13]Each of the titles listed here was the highest-grossing movie of the year in which they were released. See 'Highest Grossing Movies by Year', IMDB [2023] https://www.imdb.com/list/ls090455617/

[14]Bachelder, 'Young Adult Literature: Looking Backward', 87.

versions of the legend; the growing focus on Merlin-figures, as wizard-heroes displace knights and kings' and 'the detachment of Arthurian elements from standard narratives to become mythic archetypes', together with a focus on '"the medieval" as the location of the lost secrets of modern culture'.[15] A later movie adaptation of the second book, *The Seeker* (2007, directed by David L. Cunningham) can be ignored: wrenching the setting to America and so losing the potency of the book's eloquent legendary specificity, it smothers Cooper's distinctive fineness with a commercial blandness of tone. Cooper herself disowned the adaptation.

British writer Alan Garner's *The Weirdstone of Brisingamen: A Tale of Alderley* (1960) owes much to Tolkien. Two London children, Colin and Susan, are staying with friends of their mother in this location whilst their parents are overseas. Susan possesses a tear-shaped jewel, unaware that it is the titular magic 'weirdstone'; and the two become embroiled in an adventure with wizards, dwarfs and monsters, as varying forces – the dark spirit Nastrond, a shape-shifting sorceress called Selina Place and an evil wizard Grimnir – pursue them to seize the gem. The book's contemporary impact had to do with its relative newness in the world of children's fiction. To read it in the larger context of twentieth-century fantasy is to be struck by a certain amount of over-familiarity, as well as by a sluggish over-explained plot and a distracting tendency to lapse into archaic language. Garner intended the work as the first volume in a trilogy, and published the second, *The Moon of Gomrath* in 1963, as well as a fine 'portal fantasy' novel *Elidor* (1965), but he grew to dislike the mode, calling *Weirdstone* 'a fairly bad book', aborting the trilogy and moving to more naturalistic fiction.[16] Garner's attentiveness to his local land and culture, parochial in the best sense, has made him a darling of the literary establishment – *Treacle Walker* (2022) was shortlisted for the Man Booker prize – although his mimetic writing lacks something of the intermittent potency of his first works.

That potency is topographic. In 1968, Garner distinguished between stories in which magic and the supernatural 'impinges on the real world' and 'self-contained fantasies of the Tolkien type':

> if we are in Eldorado, and we find a mandrake, then OK, so it's a mandrake: in Eldorado anything goes. But, by force of imagination, compel the reader to believe that there is a mandrake in a garden in Mayfield Road, Ulverston, Lancs, then when you pull up that mandrake it is really going to scream; and possibly the reader will too.

The Cheshire and Manchester locality of Garner's writing, the precisely and vividly rendered real-world world of Alderley Edge, informs the fantasy penetratingly. This is about enchantment, the temenos of holy spaces and the transcendent folded into the mundane, as Neil Philip notes:

---

[15]Bryan, 'Memories, Dreams, Shadows: Fantasy and the Reader in Susan Cooper's *The Grey King*', 30.
[16]Quoted in Neil Philip, *A Fine Anger: A Critical Introduction to the Work of Alan Garner*, 123.

The physical backgrounds of all Garner's books are important elements in the stories, be it Manchester and suburban Alderley in *Elidor* ... or Alderley Edge in *The Weirdstone of Brisingamen*, *The Moon of Gomrath* and the *Stone Book* quartet (in which Chorley is simply an old name for Alderley). In 'Aspects of a Still Life' Garner writes of his childhood experience of the Edge that 'on that hill, the universe opened'; the process of argument from the particular to the general, from the thing intensely known to the thing intensely felt, lends his early fantasies an inner strength which sharply distinguishes them from the outwardly similar productions of lesser talents.[17]

Peter Beagle's *The Last Unicorn* (1968) was reprinted almost immediately, in 1969, as one of the initial ten titles in the Ballantine Adult Fantasy list. The titular unicorn leaves her enchanted forest to find out what happened to all the other unicorns. In the world – recognizably our modern, which is to say twentieth century, world – she encounters various people and has various adventures, accompanied by a small group of people she meets on the way: particularly a sort-of wizard called Schmendrick, whose control over his own magical powers is hazy and intermittent, and a bandit's wife called Molly Grue. The unicorn is for a time imprisoned in a carnival and put on display with various other monsters and wonders; but she escapes and she, Molly and Schmendrick make their way to a fantastical city by the sea for a show-down with the terrifying Red Bull, who threatens to destroy her. Michael Weingrad reads the novel as a specifically Jewish fantasia. 'Beagle's depiction of the unicorn's melancholy quest for the rest of her kind borders on secular post-Hasidic parables of God discovering what has become of His Jews in the wake of the Shoah', he notes.

> 'Wherever she went,' Beagle writes, 'she searched for her people, but she found no trace of them.' Though the novel cannot be reduced to allegory, its language is infused with suggestive parallels to God and the Six Million. The unicorn repeatedly refers to the other unicorns as her 'people.' 'How terrible it would be.' She says ominously, 'if all my people had been turned human by well-meaning wizards – exiled, trapped in burning houses. I would sooner find that the Red Bull had killed them all.' When the unicorn leaves her timeless forest she enters into history and is shocked and saddened by what she discovers, not least that human beings are no longer able to recognize her.[18]

That thrust is magic, I think; and one of things that give Beagle's novel its power is the skill with which it not only describes but evokes magic, the way it re-enchants the world. Beagle's ethnicity notwithstanding, we could read *The Last Unicorn* as a specifically Christian fable: Weingrad concedes that 'some of the novel's resonances are Christian'

---

[17]In Philip, 25.
[18]Weingrad, 'The Best Unicorn'.

('the medieval unicorn was a symbol for Christ' he says, rightly) and he does note that in the second half of the tale the unicorn is transformed into a human woman. But he denies that this makes it a novel about incarnation in the Christian sense: 'this fairy tale incarnation doesn't follow the Christian story; the now-human unicorn does not herself atone or make sacrifice, and we are reminded that, unlike Jesus, "she is a story with no ending, happy or sad"'. This, though, is to give too great a priority to the specific narrative-elements of the passion story, and so misses the really crucial part of it: incarnation as such as a means of reconnecting the mundane and the divine. There are a great many Jewish specific references in Beagle's novel of course (Weingrad mentions 'Molly Grue making "bricks without straw" or the Sodom-like town of Hagsgate whose citizens warn "we allow no strangers to settle here"'). Schmendrick, charming, good-hearted, a bit inept, comical, is a figure from the rich tradition of Jewish comedy. But we can wonder how central these are to the novel's magical through line, its beautiful generative evocation of the numinous reilluminating the world.

What *The Last Unicorn* certainly does is inject a distinctly North American tone into the largely European tradition of fantasy. Beagle is not alone in this, in the sixties. John Bellairs's *The Face in the Frost* (1969) possesses considerable whimsical charm, and remains a significant if small-scale genre masterpiece. Ursula Le Guin described it as 'an authentic fantasy by a writer who knows what wizardry is all about'. Set in a fantasyland distinguished from England (which its wizard deuteragonists have visited) and itself divided into northern and southern territories, a place of small towns, villages, farms, a degree of old-world courtesy mixed with suspicion at the profession of wizards. It is, in other words, the dis-united states of America, Mason-Dixon refracted through a pre-industrial magical lens. The tone of the book is chirpy, amusing, and the events shift from comic misadventure to uncanny, queasily disturbing nightmare. Two elderly wizards, Prospero ('not the one you're thinking of') and Roger, run up against the machinations of a malign sorcerer named Melichus. Prospero's house is besieged by minions of evil (the two escape by shrinking themselves down and sailing a boat through the sewer pipe) and a series of peripatetic adventures ensue before our heroes are able to vanquish evil by means of a magical glass globe. Prospero becomes separated from Melichus and believes him dead; in one nightmarish episode he overnights in what appears to be a regular inn, with a regular landlady. But in the night he shakes himself, with difficulty, out of soporificity and discovers the inn is a magical tar-pit.

> He looked up at the woman again and stepped back with a gasp. The woman's eyes were gone. In her slowly rising head were two black holes … Now the woman's voice, mechanical and heavy: 'Why don't you sleep? Go to sleep.' Her mouth opened wide, impossibly wide, and then the whole face stretched and writhed and yawned in the faint light. With a cry, Prospero shoved the melting thing aside and got to the door … the walls were sagging, bulging, stretching wildly – one door fell before him and tried to wrap itself around his leg. [Bellairs, *The Face in the Frost*, 94]

'*The Face in the Frost*', Bellairs later said,

> was an attempt to write in the Tolkien manner. I was much taken by *The Lord of the Rings* and wanted to do a modest work on those lines. In reading the latter book I was struck by the fact that Gandalf was not much of a person, just a good guy. So I gave Prospero, my wizard, most of my phobias and crotchets.

He also speaks of: 'a fable pitting logic against chaos' adding: 'I am on the side of the latter, since I know no one who uses logic who does not use it as a hammer. And chaos is more the rule in life anyway'.[19] But Bellair means 'chaos' in a particular, idiosyncratic sense. His fantasy is in love with the comfortable eccentricities of a version of Shire-ish gentlemanliness – Bellairs was sojourning in Bristol when the idea for *The Face in the Frost* first came to him, and, Tolkien influence aside, there is an outsider's engagement with Englishness in the novel. Prospero 'lived in a huge, ridiculous, doodad-covered, trash-filled two-story horror of a house that stumbled, staggered, and dribbled right up to the edge of a great shadowy forest'. But the real chaos is not this paraphernalia, but the glutinous dissolution of meaning as such, the disconnection of all from all, hinted at, though not specifically attributed to the malignity of Melichus. Dawn Heinecken argues that 'echoing changing discourses about masculinity at work in the late sixties and seventies, Bellair's novels propose a new form of manhood for young readers at the same time they continue to tie femininity to loss, lack and unspeakable desires'.[20]

In Joy Chant's *Red Moon and Black Mountain* (1970), three siblings from 'our' world, Oliver, Penny and Nick Powell, are walking in the woodlands of northern England when they fall – like Alice – into a fantasyland called Vanderei. The oldest boy Oliver finds himself amongst steppe-dwelling horse-lords who adopt him: he grows to adulthood, forgetting his mundane origins and even his name. In a strange time-dilation, his younger brother and sister remain children, and are raised by the princess In'serinna of Rennath, a fairy-tale medieval kingdom:

> That night Penelope slept in a canopied bed, in a small tower room whose walls were plastered white and painted with flowers, after a bath in a wooden tub in front of a log fire. She woke far into the morning to a breakfast of porridge and milk and honey, and they dressed her in fresh clothes, a blouse of white silk and a skirt of dark green, the stiff sleeveless tabard embroidered with bright yellow flowers. Then the Princess came to her, clothed all in white and gold, and kissed her and asked her how she liked Rennath; and she answered that she liked it well. And In'serinna led her down and took her to her father and presented her. Penelope curtsied, the king raised her and greeted her gravely, and courteously, and presented to her his sons, Argerth the Throne Prince, Prince Veldreth, and Prince Garon. [*Red Moon and Black Mountain*, 128]

---

[19]Quoted in Anne Commire, *Something About the Author*, 20.
[20]Heinecken, 'Haunting Masculinity and Frightening Femininity: The Novels of John Bellairs', 118.

The adventure of the story concerns a quest and battle against the Sauron-like antagonist Fendarl: 'he was not only King of Bannoth, but also a Star Enchanter … a Black Enchanter'. [41] But though many elements of the worldbuilding and plotting are familiar, the novel raises itself beyond derivativeness by the fineness of its prose, its beautifully evocative imagined realm, and by an immanent moral seriousness. The style is formal without being stiff or mannered, the reader's immersion in what is, at root, a child's fantasy – playing at princess, riding horses – complete. Chant added two more titles, to bulk up a trilogy: *The Grey Mane of Morning* (1977) and *When Vioha Wakes* (1983), in which the matriarchal logic of Chant's imagined world is most fully explored.

C J Cherryh has said of her first published novel *Gate of Ivrel* (1976) that, having been writing since her teens, this 'was the first time a book really found an ending and really worked, because I had made contact with Don Wollheim at DAW, found him interested, and was able to write for a specific editor whose body of work and type of story I knew'. The reference to an ending is a little odd, since this book, on its own, doesn't really end – indeed two sequels followed in short order, carrying on the narrative directly [*Well of Shiuan* in 1978 and *Fires of Azeroth* in 1979]. It is, however, one of the best-written fantasy novels of its decade: stark, absorbing, a fantasyland quest with real friction through a believable, immersive world, and a fascinating main character. The story is set on the world of Andur-Kursh, a pre-medieval world of clans, warriors, horses, honour, life a hardscrabble existence in a chill, Nordic landscape of mountains and plains. Humans share the world with regular animals and also certain kinds of monster, haunting the wilderness. There is a caste of folk with supernatural powers, witches and wizards called here 'qujalin'. There are remote places, with strange structures erected upon them, which are considered cursed. Handsome young Vanye, the illegitimate son of a Nhi lord called Rijan, is banished for killing one of his brothers. In exile, he encounters the beautiful Morgaine, who appears through one of the 'gates' with which the wilderness is dotted. He believes her to be a qujalin witch-queen, and agrees to serve her. In fact, she is a regular woman whose 'magic' is actually technological (a phaser, a sophisticated medical pack and a 'sword' that is actually an atom-bomb). A hundred years before the story began, Morgaine had raised an army of a thousand warriors from the land of Koris against a wicked king called Thiye, but the latter used magic to 'raise a mighty wind' that slew every last one of these soldiers – actually what he did is open a gate onto interstellar vacuum, sucking a chunk of the atmosphere of the world out into space and dragging the army with it. Morgaine flees on horseback, rode into a gate in the far south. No time passes for her, though a century rolls by in Andur-Kursh. Now she rides out again, meets Vanye and puts him under an oath to serve her for a year and a day as her *ilin*. There are complicated honour-bound reasons why Vanye must agree to this, though he doesn't want to, for he is thereafter, in effect, her slave. He wants to ride south to more temperate lands, but Morgaine is determined to travel to the far north and finish what she started with Thiye.

Cherryh's novel is under 200-pages long but feels longer, in part because of her spare, stark style: the details of life on this gruelling world are well chosen – struggling on horseback over snow-blocked mountain passes, building fires in woodland to keep oneself warm and alive, but not too large a fire (you don't want to attract the attention of the monsters who live there). Notable is the twist the novel offers on what this study has been arguing is one of the main structural functions of fantasy – the Walter Scott dynamic, the Lukácsian dialectic, in which romantic older worlds (feudal, heroic, shame-culture, honour, status cultures) clash with inevitable modernity (bourgeois, respectable, Whiggish guilt-culture, contract-rather-than-status worlds), the interaction dramatized by a 'waverley' figure who wavers between the two worlds, though he (usually a he) really belongs in the latter. In *Gate of Ivrel*, Morgaine is literally from the former – she's been gone a hundred years, and speaks an English full of ostentatious archaism – and Vanye is the 'modern'; but actually Morgaine is the future, the coming of modernity as such, and Vanye a relic of an outmoded feudal honour-status-romantic past.

## Multi-volume series

Through the 1970s the popular success of Tolkien in the 1960s was consolidated via a considerable number of new fantasy works written in more-or-less straight imitation of *Lord of the Rings*. Large numbers of readers, switched-on to fantasy by reading that novel and *The Hobbit*, looked around for other things to read in the same mode and were disappointed to discover that Tolkien had written almost nothing else. The Ballantine list, discussed above, was one way of catering to this new demand: the list made many pre-Tolkien fantasy titles newly available, together with some fantasy titles from the 1960s. But 1970s authors also began writing new-minted Tolkienian fantasy of various kinds, and various quality – though few of these exercises in pastiche Tolkieniana have any real merit – and some were very successful in commercial terms.

Katherine Kurtz, *Deryni Rising* (1970) was the first book included in the Ballantine List that was not a reprint of a prior publication. Its importance is less grounded in the novel itself, for it is not very good, and more with a new phenomenon that it represents. As a stand-alone it is weak, but as the first instalment in a lengthy series of connected books – there are as I write, in 2024, twenty-eight *Deryni* books in print – it represents something significant. Over time, and with the accretion of many new volumes, this series generates by sheer persistence and extension, something complex and involving. The titular Deryni are a race of humanoid warrior-sorcerers, with telepathic and other magical powers, who once ruled over the human populations of 'Gwynedd', Kurtz's version of early medieval England and Wales. Their power overthrown centuries earlier, their people outcast and persecuted, the Deryni are starting to re-emerge and integrate into human society again as the series opens. Kurtz approaches fantasy as a historical-novelistic undertaking. Kari Spelling argues that, though 'unequivocally fantasy' it is, she says, 'written more in the mode of the historical fiction of the time than its companion books on the Ballantine and other lists'.

It is closer to the complex and thoroughly researched novels of Dorothy Dunnett, Maurice Druon, and Zoe Oldenbourg than the fantasy that surrounded it ....

Its treatment of magic too was dramatically different. This is a world of highly formal, ritual magic, without sorcerers, or demons, or exoticized and stereotypical 'witchdoctors'. It is set against a background of closely observed and detailed faith, which is closely intertwined with every aspect of her characters' lives.[21]

This grows as the series augments itself, itself an interesting reflection on the way long series fiction can work. The first novel *Deryni Rising*, a pulp melodrama with medieval-magical trappings, displays none of this complexity. Teenaged Kelson Haldane, inheriting the crown, must protect himself and his kingdom from the Deryni usurper who murdered his father. The narrative is direct, and though there are gestures in the direction of court politics and church power, the world of the novel feels pasteboard, the characters stereotypes, the good heroic in look and deed, the wicked decadent, devious, orientalized (the sorceress Lady Charissa, 'the Shadowed Lady of the North', attended by dark-skinned Moors: 'the lady sat motionless on the pillow, a slender, pale figure shrouded in richest velvet and fur, delicate hands encased in jewelled doeskin gloves'.) The novel is not long, and the story not complicated. In the sequel, *Deryni Checkmate* (1972) – also a Ballantine List novel – young Kelson, learning how to reign, leans on his champion and adviser Duke Alaric Morgan: Duke of Corwyn, Lord General of the Royal Armies. But the fact that Duke Alaric has Deryni blood in his veins makes him a focus of suspicion. Again the whole is built from cliché, the plotting hackneyed melodrama. But as Kurtz adds more and more instalments to the series, bringing in more detail, more characters, elaborating backstory, more of the topography and society and culture of Gwynedd, the thin soup of her melodrama becomes inspissated into a richer fantasy embodiment. A second trilogy [*Camber of Culdi* (1976), *Saint Camber* (1978), *Camber the Heretic* (1981)] is set 200 years before the first, and enriches the sense of the larger historical context of the series. A third Deryni trilogy [*The Bishop's Heir* (1984), *The King's Justice* (1985), *The Quest for Saint Camber* (1986)] flesh-out the reign of King Kelson. In the later novels, it comes to seem as if everyone has Deryni blood, and that, rather than a cipher for an oppressed minority, magic is the defining feature of life as such.

Kurtz was not the first writer to turn a successful single book into a lengthy series of titles, but it was during the 1970s that fantasy saw a shift towards a franchise logic, where what had been presented as complete in one novel, or three, expanded. Works that had been complete in trilogy form, such as *Earthsea* or *Lord of the Rings*, were re-opened, and added-to – the former by Le Guin herself, the latter, posthumously to its author, by Tolkien's son, who edited from his father's papers first *The Silmarillion* (1977) and then a long sequence of other material: *Unfinished Tales* (1980) a twelve-volume *History of Middle-earth* (1983–96), *The Children of Húrin* (2007), *The Legend of Sigurd and Gudrún* (2009), *Beren and Lúthien* (2017) *The Fall of Gondolin* (2018) and *The Fall of Númenor*

---

[21]Sperring, 'Matrilines: The Woman Who Made Fantasy: Katherine Kurtz'.

(2022). The fantasy title becomes a brand, a location, a set of characters and an open-ended process to which new volumes can always be added.

This process can be seen in the two most commercially successful fantasy series of the decade, Terry Brooks's *Shannara* (beginning with *The Sword of Shannara*, 1977) and Stephen Donaldson's trilogy *The Chronicles of Thomas Covenant, the Unbeliever* (1977–9). In both cases, an initial work was followed by a great many additional volumes – as of 2023, there are ten *Thomas Covenant* and a frankly egregious forty-two *Shannara* titles in print.

Terry Brooks's *The Sword of Shannara* achieved its success because of, not despite, its extreme proximity to Tolkien. Tom Shippey notes 'the dogged way' the novel 'follows Tolkien point for point', including multiple 'analogues' for Tolkien characters such as Sauron (Brona), Gandalf (Allanon), the Hobbits (Shea and Flick), Aragorn (Menion), Boromir (Balinor), Gimli (Hendel), Legolas (Durin and Dayel), Gollum (Orl Fane), the Barrow-wight (Mist Wraith) and the Nazgûl (Skull Bearers), among others. He also finds plot similarities to events in Tolkien's novel such as *The Fellowship of the Ring*'s formation and adventures, the journeys to Rivendell (Culhaven) and Lothlórien (Storlock), Gandalf's (Allanon) fall in Moria (Paranor) and subsequent reappearance, and the Rohirrim's arrival at the Battle of the Pelennor Fields (Battle of Tirsys), among others. 'What *The Sword of Shannara* seems to show', Shippey argues, 'is that many readers had developed the taste for heroic fantasy so strongly that if they could not get the real thing they would take any substitute, no matter how diluted'.[22] *Sword of Shannara* is Young Adult writing, issued before publishers quite realized the commercial potential of the mode; a quest and adventure in which likeable characters pass through varied exciting adventures, marvellous, monstrous, arriving at a satisfying conclusion. But as with Kurtz's Deryni, what starts as derivative and pat develops, as the series continues, into something deeper and more interesting.

Stephen Donaldson's 'Chronicles of Thomas Covenant, the Unbeliever' trilogy [*Lord Foul's Bane* (1977), *The Illearth War* (1978), *The Power that Preserves* (1979)] is somewhat less Tolkien-derivative. Covenant, a man in our world, suffers from leprosy, which has rendered him bitter and alienated from humanity. He is transported to 'the Land', a beautiful, enchanting and harmonious fantasy realm, though under threat from malign forces. Here his physical illness can be healed, although the focus of the series is more on his mental, or spiritual, delinquencies: he is destined to be the saviour of the Land, and to grow out of his alienation into a fuller being. A distinctiveness of *Lord Foul's Bane* is the way it elaborated its charming, hippyish location of 'The Land' only to flag-up horriblenesses of a kind Tolkien would never countenance – so, for example, Thomas Covenant starts his sojourn in The Land by raping the first woman he meets. It was the first intimation of what would later be known as Grimdark, although it doubtless would read as thin stuff to today's more committed, Sadean Grimdarkster. Still, this sense that Donaldson was adding 'edge' to the naïveté and blandness of conventional fantasy was a large part of its appeal to the fantasy reader of the 1970s.

---

[22]Shippey, *Tolkien*, 319–20.

The success of the series led to a sequel second trilogy [*The Wounded Land* (1980), *The One Tree* (1982), *White Gold Wielder* (1983)] and then to an elongated third instalment in the sequence [*The Runes of the Earth* (2004), *Fatal Revenant* (2007), *Against All Things Ending* (2010), *The Last Dark* (2013)]. All titles were bestsellers, and drew a large fan base, although the books are not good: dense, blockish works of a thickness and soddenness of style. 'The Land' is elaborated, detailed, reverberated, clogged and overwritten – 'over' in the sense both of prolixity, and also stylistic pretentiousness and indulgence. David Langford talks of Donaldson's 'knurred and argute vocabulary', an attempt to elevate the idiom of fantasy writing that crashes precipitously into the ceiling of the ludicrous (Langford quotes this line from *White Gold Wielder*: 'they were featureless and telic, like lambent gangrene. They looked horribly like children'). Nick Lowe invented his game of Clench Racing with Donaldson in mind:

> The rules are simple. Each player takes a different volume of *The Chronicles of Thomas Covenant*, and at the word 'go' all open their books at random and start leafing through, scanning the pages. The winner is the first player to find the word 'clench'. It's a fast, exciting game – sixty seconds is unusually drawn-out – and can be varied, if players get too good, with other favourite Donaldson words like wince, flinch, gag, rasp, exigency, mendacity, articulate, macerate, mien, limn, vertigo, cynosure.[23]

This style characterizes the novels to the end of the series. The Narnia-esque temporal relationship between 'The Land' and our world means that centuries pass there for every few years here, such that Thomas Covenant, and in later novels his companion Linden Avery, coming and going, is involved in millennia of fantasy history, evil defeated only to recur, the eco-metaphor 'Earthpower' magic waxing and waning.

Another series, whose augmentation was curtailed only by the death of its writer, is Roger Zelazny's *Amber* series, a work of extremely capacious fantasy worldbuilding spread across two five-book sequences, the 'Corwin cycle' [*Nine Princes in Amber* (1970), *The Guns of Avalon* (1972), *Sign of the Unicorn* (1975), *The Hand of Oberon* (1976), *The Courts of Chaos* (1978)] and the 'Merlin Cycle' [*Trumps of Doom* (1985), *Blood of Amber* (1986), *Sign of Chaos* (1987), *Knight of Shadows* (1989), *Prince of Chaos* (1991)]. *Nine Princes in Amber* opens like a hardboiled noir thriller. A man wakes, amnesiac, injured, in a private clinic in the United States, at some point in the late twentieth century. The man, Corwin, is a tough guy: smart, capable and ruthless. Though he can't remember who he is or how he got there, he senses that he's in danger. He manages to escape the clinic, defeat the goons sent to kill him, to gather allies and start for home. This Dashell Hammett or Raymond Chandler style of opening is Zelazny's misdirection: Corwin is not a private dick but a prince, a high-born figure from 'Amber', the Platonic Form of The World, of which a million other worlds – including our Earth – are mere shadows.

---

[23]Lowe, 'The Well-Tempered Plot Device', 3.

Amber was ruled by King Oberon but he has been deposed, or perhaps has merely absented himself, and his nine sons, the nine princes of the first novel's title, are fighting one another to succeed him. During the course of his adventures, Corwin meets most of his brothers (and a few of his many sisters), battling some, allying himself with others, seeking to supplant his brother, Eric, who sits on the throne of Amber.

Amber is a kingdom of High fantasy, full of magic and wonder. There are several routes, or portals, to it from our world. For instance: one might walk the shadows, passing through the many other worlds which both exist in their own right and can to some degree be shaped by the imagination of Amber's princes and princesses. It is also possible to use certain magic cards, 'trumps', the artwork upon which work as sorts of doors directly to the places represented. But one cannot walk the shadows in Amber, for Amber is real, not shadowy. Corwin, assisted by his brother Bleys, passes from world to world, recruiting an army as he goes, so as to storm the citadel of Amber itself: 'the assembled troops were not quite men – all of them around seven feet in height with very red skins and little hair, cat-like eyes and six-digited hands and feet'. These people consider Corwin and Bleys gods, a faith of which the two brothers take rather cynical advantage. Corwin has spent many centuries on our world – we discover he fought in Napoleon's army, and at the Siege of Stalingrad too (the crappy yet cult-popular movie *Highlander* [1986, directed by Russell Mulcahy] plagiarizes various elements of Zelazny's novels). Zelazny-as-writer is promiscuous with his idiom. Looking back, later in the novel, on the situation in which he found himself at the story's beginning, Corwin addresses the reader: 'Well, take it like this: I had awakened in a hospital bed and learned that I had recovered all too soon. Dig?' This kind of slang jars against the other main style the novel inhabits, a High fantasy medievalized flourish:

> Amber, Amber, Amber – I remember thee, I shall never forget thee again, I guess deep inside me I never really did, through all those centuries I wandered the Shadow Earth, for often at night my dreams were troubled by images of thy green and golden spires and thy sweeping terraces. I remember thy wide promenades and the decks of flowers, golden and red. I recall the sweetness of thy airs, and the temples, palaces, and pleasances thou containest, contained, will always contain. Amber, immortal city from which every other city has taken its shape. [ch 5]

The friction between this fruity archaism and the informal 1970s idiom works to destabilize and vivify the inertnesses of what might otherwise be yet another cod-medieval fantasy realms. Fantasy as a genre is oversupplied with cliché castles, fair maidens, bold knights and feasts by torchlight, but not with noble princes driving automobiles whilst chased by T-Rexes across deserts under purple skies. Moreover, as the novels proceed we come to understand that Zelazny is playing a richly complex game of literary intertextuality. As Amber is the prototype of all worlds, all the mythological and literary wonders of our world are revealed as its shadows: Shakespeare's plays, often referenced, are as marvellous as they are *because* they imitate Amberian originality, the myths and legends of King Arthur (among many) likewise.

## Animal fantasy

1970s fantasy saw a burst of popularity in anthropomorphized animal stories, most, though not all, children's literature. Roald Dahl's vulpine fantasia *Fantastic Mr Fox* (1970) pits its roguish title character against three ghastly human farmers. We rejoice in the protagonist's larcenous outwitting of the humans. The 2009 animated film version (directed by Wes Anderson) emphasizes the bohemian carefree stylishness of Mr Fox, voiced of George Clooney – a modern Aesopian fabulation in which foxy cunning and daring are valorized. The other side of the predator/prey divide provided one of the single most successful fantasy novels of its decade: Richard Adams's *Watership Down* (1972). Here a group of talking, thinking rabbits must leave their burrows (evicted by human property development) and quest across the English countryside to find a new home. The story reframes the English landscape into an animal *Odyssey* and *Iliad* – the rabbits, after they reach the titular downland that will be their new home, must battle the forces of General Woundwort, a fascistic ruler of a rival rabbit tribe, a ferocious and terrifying piece of characterization. There is nothing cutesy about Adams's rabbitdom. The novel is a vital, often brutal and intense reimagining of Englishness through a beast-fable fantasia. The core appeal remains that bestial life is more authentic, more connected to the natural world, and more enchanted than the currency of human life. There are supernatural elements in the story: the rabbits know to leave their original home because of the visionary powers of a rabbit called 'Fiver', his name a reflection of that which transcends mundanity: being four-toed, rabbits count according to a quaternary numerical system, and 'five' is an inconceivability to them. But it is the brilliantly rendered animal being-in-the-world that brings this novel mythically alive. The telling construes allegory, as beast-fable traditionally does: a conservative vision of battling the depredations of industrialized modernity that reinstalls fantasy into English rural actuality.[24]

Adams, an unknown, initially found it hard to obtain a publisher for *Watership Down*, and little was expected of it in commercial terms. Yet the novel proved one of the biggest successes of the decade. An animated movie version, directed by Martin Rosen in 1978, was also very successful – the theme song 'Bright Eyes', written by Mike Batt and sung by Art Garfunkel, topped the UK charts for months and was 1979's bestselling single. For a year or so the work was inescapable, a testament to the reach of its fantasy. Adams's follow-up novel *The Plague Dogs* (1977; also filmed, in 1982) has a more tragic cast. The title characters are two dogs upon whom torturous experiments have been performed by pitiless human scientists in an English animal testing facility. The hounds escape and

---

[24]'*Watership Down* is a beast fable, a fantasy, a mythological tale, an epic, a political/Utopian novel, and an allegory' [Robert Miltner, '*Watership Down*: A Genre Study', 63].

have various adventures. There is a great emphasis on suffering and disillusionment, and a persistently applied and heart-wrenching emphasis on the cruelty and nastiness with which humanity treats the natural world. A red fox the dogs encounter and befriend is killed; the book ends with the dogs swimming out to sea searching for a fabled 'Isle of Dogs', of which they have heard and which they consider a canine utopia – though they worry this may turn out to be another Isle of Man. They swim to their deaths, although Adams's publishers, thinking this ending too downbeat, persuaded him to modify it (it was restored in the animated movie version).

Adams also wrote two connected fantasy novels in more conventional High fantasy, post-Tolkien idiom: *Shardik* (1974) and the enormous *Maia* (1984), this latter more than a thousand pages of lubriciously described sex, indulgence and feasting. *Shardik* is set in the 'Beklan Empire', a Fantasyland with an Eastern European or Russian flavour. At the edges of the story is a war of imperial expansion, which everyone assumes will be a straightforward and rapid victory, but which – Adams was writing during the latter stages of the Vietnam War – proves the empire's undoing. Shardik is a gigantic bear, driven out of woodland by a forest fire, and afterwards worshipped as a god by the Beklans. A bear is also at the heart of Canadian author Marian Engel's *Bear* (1976), in which the ursine and the erotic combine in an intense, furry-focused tale of a lonely woman who travels to the remote wilds of Ontario for work, only to enter into a sexual relationship with a bear. Though it sold many copies and won the 1976 Governor General's Literary Award, its unashamed bestiality rendered it, in Donna Coates's words, 'the most controversial novel ever written in Canada'.[25] Animal fantasy continued a popular mode through into the 1980s, with both William Horwood's *Duncton Wood* (1980) and Brian Jacques's *Redwall* (1986) enjoying prolonged popular success, and provoked many sequels (they are discussed in the following chapter).

It is worth pausing briefly to consider what these novels are doing. In medieval fabliaux, talking animals tend to embody specific non-animalian characteristics: lions are brave, monkeys are tricksters, oxen are strong and so on. In the 'Reynard the Fox' stories (popular in France through the twelfth and thirteenth centuries), the fox embodies wiliness and cunning, and his opponent Isengrim the wolf is greedy and slow-witted. The projection of human qualities into these 1970s fantasy titles is more complex. Often, not just human-level consciousness and language skills but human dress, trappings and social codes are transferred onto populations of, as it might be, badgers, rabbits or mice: a pre-industrial bourgeois modernity. Yet the projection also tacitly expresses the belief that animals live with more immediacy and authenticity than we humans do. Styling human agents as animals and detailing their adventures is to connect with something unbuffered, a greater degree of existential enchantment.

Animals and monsters also figure largely in Michael Ende's *Die unendliche Geschichte* ('The Neverending Story' 1979), another bestselling fantasy book of this decade. A lonely, bookish boy in our world, Bastian Balthazar Bux is able to enter an enchanted

---

[25]Coates, 'Bear (Novel)', *Canadian Encyclopedia. Historica Canada* (2 June 2006).

kingdom through a magical book: the place is called, with nominalist overdetermination, 'Phantásien' – that is 'Fantastica'. The story is an exercise in, and in many ways a celebration of, wish-fulfilment: Bastian is a short, overweight child, bullied by his school-fellows and neglected by his father after the death of Bastian's mother. Entry into the book identifies him with a boy called Atreyu, who is heroic and adventurous figure, befriended and loved, moving through an enchanted world of marvels, monsters and magic. Atreyu must go on a quest to save the kingdom by finding and naming its ruler, the nameless Childlike Empress. He meets Fuchur the Luck Dragon who flies with him; he loses his horse Artax in the Swamps of Sadness, overcomes a werewolf called Gmork (who is also, in 'our' world, a substitute teacher who torments Bastian). When Atreyu looks into a mirror the face he sees looking back is Bastian's (although Bastian is also, eventually, transported physically into Phantásien). The Childlike Empress is reached and given a new name. In the movie adaptation (directed by Wolfgang Peterson, 1984 – the film was a hit, although Ende disliked it), this is where the story ends. The novel, though, goes on: Bastian is given a magical medallion called Auryn, and instructed to do as he wishes by way of restoring Phantásien back to full existence. Instead of doing his duty in this manner, he wishes himself tall handsome and strong, and in doing so forgets his true self, which must be rediscovered and recovered through subsequent adventures in order to save both him and the realm.

In the first half of the novel the threat is that Phantásien will be consumed by Nothing; in the second half, as Bastian loses his sense of self, the danger is amnesia. At the end, Bastian forgets everything, including his name, and falls to the ground weeping, where Falkor and Atreyu find him and restore him through the power of their friendship. The novel ends with a baptism:

> But then he jumped into the crystal-clear water. He splashed and spluttered and let the sparkling rain fall into his mouth. He drank till his thirst was quenched. And joy filled him from head to foot, the joy of living and the joy of being himself. He was newborn. And the best part of it was that he was now the very person he wanted to be. If he had been free to choose, he would have chosen to be no one else. Because now he knew that there were thousands and thousands of forms of joy in the world, but that all were essentially one and the same, namely, the joy of being able to love. [*Neverending Story*, 386]

Ende's Christian faith was complicated by an interest in Eastern mysticism, a political commitment to Humanism and his engagement with German mystic traditions; but the core through line of the book is essentially Bunyanesque in its framing of faith.[26] It's also a self-reflexive text, a book about a book, and about books. In the first German edition,

---

[26] 'The *Neverending Story* is, above all, a profoundly religious text, although there is not a word in it that is specifically religious'; Kath Filmer 'Religion and Romanticism in Michael Ende's *The Neverending Story*', 60. There is a critical tradition for reading Ende's novel as an Anselmian fable, in which 'Nothing', conceived as a theological cancellation, or the antithesis of God: see for instance Joel R Gallagher, 'Nothing According to Anselm and Michael Ende's *The Neverending Story*'.

the text is at first printed in red ink, until the reader reached the parts set in Phantásien, which are printed in green. The first letters of each of the twenty-six chapters printed in green are the twenty-six letters of the alphabet in order.

## Viriconium

A rather different fantasy masterpiece straddles the end of the 1970s and the coming 1980s: M John Harrison's Viriconium series: *The Pastel City* (1971), *Storm of Wings* (1980), *In Viriconium* (1982) and *Viriconium Nights* (1985). This is Peake-influenced writing that draws also on the Vancean tradition of 'Dying Earth' far-future science-fantasy, a world of intricate urban solidity in which medieval knights in armour ride to war under royal banners, whilst robot-eagles and high-tech airships fly overhead. The prelude to *The Pastel City* notifies us that our 'morning' culture has given way to a succession of 'afternoon' cultures (including one that conquered the galaxy, but which then declined and collapsed), and which in turn gave way to the 'evening culture' of the city of Viriconium – which will, we intuit, in turn eventually give way to desuetude and the end of things.

It is the development of the whole series here, rather than any one title, that is significant. The first volume runs along familiar generic grooves: a decadent sword-and-sorcery cavalcade of adventure and mood. The elderly lord tegeus-Cromis, writing poetry in his tower on the shores of a great lake, first hears and then sees for himself that the great city of Viriconium has fallen to the 'men-wolves' of the north, led by warrior-queen Canna Moidart. Cromis was once a member of a band of heroes, though the band has dispersed, some members having died, the rest grown old. Now Cromis must, as it were, get the gang back together to save Viriconium. What lifts *The Pastel City* is its iconicity, the arresting expressive oddness of its imaginative inhabitation of this tradition. Here Cromer and his comrades defend a knoll against a horde of lupine northerners.

> It was the second hour after dawn. A cold, peculiar light filtered through the low cloudbase, greying the dead faces on the corpse-heaps, striking mysterious reflections from their eyes. The wind keened in off the Waste, stirring bloody hair and fallen pennants. Four wallowing Northern airboats hung beneath the clouds like omens seen in a dream. The entire valley was a sea of Northmen, washing black and implacable against one tiny eyot of resistance. Out among the corpse-heaps, black, huge figures moved on a strange mission, a mechanical ritual a thousand years old. The geteit chemosit had lost interest in the fight. Their triplex eyes glittering and shifting as if unanchored to their skulls, they stalked from corpse to corpse. They performed their curious surgery on the lifeless heads – and robbed each Viriconese, like the dead smuggler in the Metal-salt Marsh – of his brain. With a wild yell, the Northerners threw themselves at the knoll, and it shook beneath the onslaught. [*Pastel City*, 80–81]

At first, these brain-harvesting machines are presented as mere vampiric horrors, revenants from an earlier epoch moving about a world that can do nothing but be horrified by them. Later we discover that the brains of the dead are being harvested such that bodies can be regrown around them and the fallen soldiers resurrected. These reborn golems, or zombies, appear as important characters in the later Viriconium novels. But they are also tropes for Harrison's imaginative process: extracting the cortices of dead fantasy writing and returning them, strangely, strikingly, to life. The second Viriconium novel *A Storm of Wings* (1980) starts as if it will be a familiar sort of quest-adventure novel, only deliberately to interfere with the usual genre fixtures and fittings. Alstath Fulthor, the very first of the Reborn Men to be resuscitated from his thousand-year-long death, leads a band of heroes northwards on a mission to save the city, which is collapsing in on itself, prey to strange new religions, to nihilisms, a string of grisly murders. But the quest does not follow the sorts of conventional lines a reader might expect. The work is at once genre fantasy and Modernist experimentalism, and foregrounds the surrealism that, as this study has been arguing, bridges mainstream Modernist art and the pulp traditions of genre writing.[27]

Viriconium is, to appropriate T S Eliot's phrase, the 'Unreal city'; a prose rendering of the surrealism of Salvador Dalí, or de Chirico's cityscapes. Whilst Harrison, and later 'New Weird' writers, owes much to Peake and Lovecraft, Viriconium is a different kind of *urbs phantastica* to Gormenghast, or to Kafka's Castle. Peake's structure has a massy, architectural solidity and heft. Viriconium is more often described with a phantasmic uncanny evanescence, as if it is a ghost city haunting itself, ill self-met by moonlight: 'the City caught its breath; the blue hollow lunar glow, streetlight of some necrotic, alternate Viriconium flickered' [*A Storm of Wings*, 25]. It is 'a perfect mirage of the City, pastel towers tall and mathematical, cut with strange designs' under 'a sky filled with mica; the wind stooped like a hawk'. Its inhabitants, en masse, seem less substantial than the weather blowing through its streets:

> Fulthor could only stare into Viriconium, where at night in a lunar chiaroscuro of gamboge and blue, the long processions wound silently from one street to another, to the accompaniment of a small aimless wind. The weather deteriorated as he watched, a raw air piling up against the massif of the High City and filling the Low with damp. Beneath a thick grey sky the watery plazas took on a wan and occult look. The walls seeped. [*A Storm of Wings*, 80]

This is fantasy as deliquescence. 'Up near the vaulted ceiling a salmon-coloured layer of light had begun curdling into grey muculent lumps and strings which floated about like bits of fat in a lukewarm soup, bumping one another gently'. This, though it looks like a writer pushing his fauvist descriptions of light-effects too far into weirdness, is actually

---

[27]Nick Freeman's essay '"All the Cities That Have Ever Been": *In Viriconium*' persuasively makes the case for the immanent presence of Eliot's *Waste Land* to Harrison's series.

one of the novel's characters: legendary astronaut and lunar explorer Benedict Paucemanly who has spent a century imprisoned on the moon and can no longer retain his original form. He pulses, separates into floating blobs and recoalesces painfully. When solid or semi-solid he speaks strangely, gibberish and insight mingled, trying to tell us something, haunting the world from which he had departed. Paucemanly is the novel Harrison has written, its queasy, striking, unnerving, confusing accumulation of fantasy tropes and dream images. At the end of the novel, the city itself melts, or seems to, in an 'incandescence': 'all the shabby dependencies of the plaza of unrealized time – all slumped, sank into themselves, eroded away until nothing was left in Hornwrack's field of vision but an unbearable white sky above and the bright clustered points of the chestnut leaves below'. Hornwrack thinks: 'something lies behind all the realities of the universe and is replacing them here, something less solid and more permanent'. 'Then', the narrator adds, 'the world stopped haunting him forever'. A paragraph break and we're given: 'It is so hard to convey simultaneity'. In the novel's epilogue Viriconium is still there ('its achingly formal gardens and curious geometries, its streets that reek of squashed fruit and fish … its histories make of the very air around it an amber, an entrapment'), and in the superposition of actual metropolises and phantasmal cities it endures, into *In Viriconium* (1982) and through the collection of short fiction *Viriconium Nights* (1985), through plague, Arthurian motifs, Tarot cardplay, fewer instances of chivalric swordplay and more Parisian-style artists and allusions to Baudelaire. In *Viriconium Nights*, simultaneity judders and dislodges. One of its stories 'The Luck in the Head' stages a *théâtre de l'absurde* performance, a procession of 'Mamma Vooley', a Mère Ubu satire of 1980s Margaret Thatcher. The character Crome, a kind of reversion of tegeus-Cromis from the earlier volume, sets out to assassinate this ruling figure, but finds himself in the middle of a bizarre *Wicker-Man*-esque ritual, folk horror, in which dancing crowds of Mamma Vooley supporters hand him the murder weapon ('" … this murder weapon is making me ill," said Crome. "What must I do?"'). A man emerges from a hole 'dragging behind him a wicker basket of earth and excrement'. A choir sings in early Elizabethan style, 'renunciative cantos above the whine of the cor anglaise and the thudding of a large flat drum'.

> Soon Mammy Vooley was pushed into view at the top of the steps, in a chair with four iron wheels. Her head lolled against its curved back. Attendants surrounded her immediately, young men and women in stiff embroidered robes who after a perfunctory bow set about ordering her wisp of hair or arranging her feet on a padded stool. They held a huge book up in front of her single milky eye, then placed in her lap the crown or wreath of woven yew twigs which she would later throw to the dancing boys.

We can say that this is indicative of fantasy becoming 'more political' in the 1980s, but that's a thin way of putting it. Fantasy has always been political. The insertion of a satirical caricature of Margaret Thatcher into a fantasy story, as here, is an ideological gesture in a specifying, deictic way, an approach liable to stale as the times move on. 'The

Luck in the Head' hauls the stories away from the difficulty of conveyed simultaneity back into the linear limitations of political-satirical allegory. The 1980s, that decade of materialism, it too shinily brittle, too parched, to coalesce into myth in the way needful for a story, and a figure, like this. The lapse into a kind of absurdist positivism denatures the fundamental strangeness, the capacity to exist in superposed doubts and surrealities, that characterize *Viriconium* at its best.

# CHAPTER 16
## 1980s–90s: EXPANSION AND IMITATION

Fantasy – comprising heroic fantasy, sword and sorcery, Gothic fantasy and the fantastical iterations of children's literature – saw a small florescence after the First World War, as readers reactively retreated from the horrors of modern mechanized warfare into tales of chivalric *guerre-courtois*; and, more broadly, as readers sought to reverse the Weberian disenchantments of modernity. Such fantasy was a vigorous if small-scale cultural discourse through the following decades, predominantly a children's literature in the 1920s and 1930s, an adult mode through the 1940s and 1950s. After the 1950s, when Tolkien and Lewis published their respective major fantasy series, and then through the 1960s and 1970s the paperback success, especially of Tolkien, launched fantasy as a global phenomenon. The Ballantine Adult Fantasy List drew on and shaped this to create a sense of what the mode was. Through the 1970s authors wrote fantasy novels to take advantage of the new demand for this kind of writing, books that were, as with Brooks' *Shannara* series – patently derivative of Tolkien. With the 1980s and 1990s the number of such works expanded exponentially. A very great many fantasy novels were published across these decades, some derivative retreads of Tolkien, others bringing more originality to the mode, reimagining and recreating it in various way.

The sheer number of notable fantasy titles across these decades presents a chronological account such as this one with a problem. To notate them all would turn the chapter into a protracted and barren list of names. Selection is requisite, although, as James Gifford notes 'the establishment of a canon' is always 'an apt reflection of the works that are most intelligible to the prevailing critical paradigms that seek to analyse literary history'.[1] He says so to discuss why literary High Modernism has so often been excluded from critical histories of fantasy, but the case also applies here. Though there is some innovation and originality in the 1980s and 1990s fantasy, some sense of a genre moving out from the shadow of Tolkienian influence, there is also an immense deal of frankly derivative, sub-Tolkienian stuff. The sheer repetitiveness of fantasy as a mode has an interesting aspect to it; as if there is something compulsive, almost neurotic, in its cultural production: Lady Macbeth washing her hands over and over. What, we might wonder, are 'we' trying to scrub away with this repetition? Straightforward plagiary of Tolkien tropes, worldbuilding and eucatastrophic narrative structures; assertive repudiations of Tolkien, informing 'Grimdark', violent, torturous, sexually explicit Fantasylands, but versions of fantasy which nevertheless are definitionally structured by Tolkien, photographic negatives of the original vision. There is also the question of

---

[1] Gifford, *Modernist Fantasy*, 14.

length as such: fantasy novels are often longer than other kinds of novel, and tended to become increasingly elongated as the genre developed towards the end of the century: long individual novels aggregated into trilogies, trilogies of trilogies, series running into the dozens, scores or more instalments. Great cliff-faces of pagination.

There are thousands of fantasy titles that ring only limited changes on an extremely repetitive formula: a young protagonist, often born into a low station in life (a pig-boy or farm-hand, a street-kid or urchin), undergoes a series of adventures that brings him or her – though typically, in the twentieth century, a him – into the 'large' historical events in his imaginary fantasy kingdom: a war between the forces of good and evil that entails both physical military engagement and a superstructure of magical folderol; a quest around or 'Cook's tour' of the fantasyland map is enacted, in which the various different nations, peoples or tribes are brought before the reader. The *differentia inter gentes* is often represented in racialized or pseudo-racialist terms: 'Aryan' elves, Semitic dwarfs, negroid orcs or barbarians, Mongol-like steppe-dwellers and so on. There are kings and princes, queens and princesses, wizards and witches, there may be priests and monks and priestesses, there will be a hierarchical pseudo-Medieval society, and the physical world-architecture will be early modern (castles, hovels, inns, horses, sail-ships and so on), although some of the exigencies of modern technology will be supplied by magic (orbs that enable communication at a difference, wands that shoot lethal spells as a gun shoots bullets, magic swords and staffs) or by such monstrous fauna as inhabit the world: as it might be, the lack of medieval aeroplanes supplied by humans riding dragons, or giant birds or other flying creatures.

Diana Wynne Jones summarizes many of these timeworn tropes in her hilarious *Tough Guide to Fantasyland* (1996), a book which parodies both the 'Rough Guide' series of real-world travel-books (in format) and, in content, the many clichés of fantasy worldbuilding and writing. It starts with an absurd map ('the empty inland parts will be sporadically peppered with little molehills, invitingly labelled "Megamort Hills," "Death Mountains," "Hurl Range," and such'), and includes entries that style the typical fantasy novel 'quest' as a tourist trip. Entries are cross-references via capital letters: BANDITS are 'employed by the Management to make the early stages of the Tour more interesting' and SCURVY ('Despite a diet consisting entirely of STEW and WAYBREAD, supplemented by only the occasional FISH, you will not suffer from this or any other deficiency disease'). Jones is especially good on the gaps in generic fantasy worldbuilding:

> INSECTS are practically non-existent, possibly as a result of the WIZARD'S WAR (see also ECOLOGY). Parasitic insects such as LICE and bedbugs have mostly been stamped out – although fleas are still popular – and only HOVELS occasionally manifest houseflies. Small numbers of bees must exist, since honey is often served, and so must silkworms, because so many persons wear silken garments. Otherwise, almost the only recorded insects are the mosquitoes all Tourists complain of in the MARSHES. (in *stinging clouds* [Official Management Term])

That this generic repetitiveness has its funny side is undeniable. But it may be that something more is going on. On the level of culture, Hillel Schwartz notes how immanent 'the copy' is in twentieth-century life:

> Repetition, replication, simulation are the enabling and disabling myths of our culture of the copy. Boon and bane, they steal from us that for which they are the guarantors: insight, integrity, inheritance. Like placebos, they please us as they deceive us. In kriegspiel or newsreel, pageant or experiment, events must take place twice to take place at all.[2]

Nonetheless, there is, Schwartz argues, no going back. Ours now is a culture of the copy: 'authenticity can no longer be rooted in singularity, in what the Greeks called the *idion* or private person. That would be, in our culture of the copy, *idiocy* – as it was for the Greek geographer Pausanias of the second century' [Schwartz, 312]. The modern English sense of 'idiot' is an individual of low intelligence, a fool; but this sense is rooted in the old Greek sense: ἰδιώτης (*idiṓtēs*), 'a private citizen, one who has no professional knowledge, a layman', from ἴδιος (*ídios*, 'one's own, pertaining to oneself, private'). Fantasy that once was 'idiotic' in this root sense – I'm talking about such idiosyncratic (another word from the same root) private mythologizing as underpinned Eddison's *Worm Ouroboros*, or indeed informed Tolkien's drafting of Middle Earth – has become, now, general, collective, a shared discourse. Tolkien lived long enough to see, and to regret, his idiosyncrasy seized by the populace, reappropriated, often (as he saw it) misinterpreted and abused. This, however, is the logic of fantasy as a contemporary mode.

One sign of this is the rise to popularity of *collective* apprehensions of fantasy. In place of the solitary figure sitting reading her book, we have the group playing a game of *Dungeons and Dragons*, or video games, or gathering in fandoms and cons, dressing-up as favourite characters, sharing their engagement online. Shwartz's study has much more to say about twins than about trilogies, or indeed more promiscuously duplicated copying than that. But something fundamental is carried over. There is, the Freudian and the critic of society can both agree, reassurance in repetition. We play games in which we engage the same or similar actions over and over again (this is especially true of video games). We read novels that are the same or similar to the novels we love. We flee the icy individualism of modernity into a fantasy of a collective, organic and enchanted social past.

This brings us to gaming. Sword & Sorcery is by its nature a playful, ludic mode. In the case of the tabletop game *Dungeons and Dragons* – developed in its first iteration by Gary Gygax and Dave Arneson, and published in 1974 by 'TSR Inc' – play is actualized in the social iteration of the sword-and-sorcery text. Players adopt characters, and embark upon adventures that involve both a map (functioning as a game-board), pieces, dice and other gameplay paraphernalia, overseen by a quasi-author, a 'dungeon master',

---

[2]Schwartz, *The Culture of the Copy*, 246.

who sets up, coordinates and narrates the adventure. Adventures can happen anywhere in a capacious and expansive fantasy realm, and players can encounter any manner of monsters, wizards, fantasy creatures, magical weapons and artefacts, but often D&D 'campaigns' will focus on the titular dungeons, explored at length and mapped-out in great subterranean detail. Plays can interact with what they encounter in many ways, their success or otherwise being determined by dice-rolls. The game rapidly became immensely, and globally, popular.

D&D success fed the format back into literature. The first tie-in novelization was Andre Norton's *Quag Keep* (1978), in which a group of D&D players find themselves propelled into an 'actual' fantasy realm. Since the early 1980s TSR(Inc) has published or licensed hundreds upon hundreds of D&D novelizations.[3] Two of their licensed authors, Laura and Tracy Hickman, developed an adjunct game called 'Dragonlance' in the early 1980s, set in a fantasy realm called 'Krynn' dominated by dragons – reportedly the TSR(Inc) marketing department believed 'that the company should do more with dragons. We had plenty of dungeons, they said, but very few dragons.'[4] For inspiration, Hickman admits 'I remembered McCaffrey's *Dragonriders of Pern*. There it was. I wanted to create a world where fighters on dragonback fought other fighters on dragonback.' The Hickmans helped develop the game, and, as with 'original' D&D, its popularity swiftly led to tie-in novelizations, many of them written by Hickman and his long-term collaborator Margaret Weis. At present, there have been nearly 200 'Dragonlance' novels published, with sales in the many hundreds of millions. Edward James and Farah Mendlesohn call Hickman and Weis 'hacks', pointing to the tired shuffling and reshuffling of overfamiliar generic counters and tropes in which these novels indulge, their exhaustion-by-repetition of the 'quest narrative' format across so very many titles.[5] Hack is overharsh, although the books, lacking the element of individual engagement, reaction and in-story feedback of actual gameplay, do tend to a more procrustean and limited praxis. Yet despite their conventionality, these novels are, as befits their provenance, playful. In the words of Jared Shurin:

> *Dragonlance* has done more than almost any other post-Tolkien property in influencing fantasy. Its narrative and conceptual tropes can be found in every nook and cranny of the genre, and much of the modern low fantasy resurgence can be traced back to (or through) *Dragonlance* as well.[6]

The first trilogy of novels – *Dragons of Autumn Twilight* (1984), *Dragons of Winter Night* (1985) and *Dragons of Spring Dawning* (1985) – concern a group of friends having adventures together in a Tolkienian-derivative world: Tanis half-elf, Sturm Brightblade,

---

[3]TSR(Inc) list eighty-five separate authors of D&D novelizations, all of whom have written a multiple, and some a great many, novelizations.
[4]Margaret Weis and Tracy Hickman, *Realm of Dragons: The Worlds of Weis and Hickman*, 46.
[5]Mendlesohn and James, *Short History of Fantasy*, 123–4.
[6]Shurin, 'Underground Reading: *Dragonlance Chronicles*'.

Caramon, Raistlin, Flint, Tasslehoff Burrfoot (a hobbit in all but copyrighted name: in the story his 'race' is called the kender) and the beautiful Kitiara Uth Matar. They tangle with a puritanical religious cult called 'The Seekers' who, in league with the Dragon Highlords, are themselves questing for the magic Blue Crystal Staff with which they can rule the world. The group battle lizardmen 'Draconians', befriend centaurs, fight-off undead zombies, fly on the back of Pegasus-y flying horses, locate the magical 'Disks of Mishakal', are sold into slavery, are freed by elves (the beautiful elven princess Laurana Kanan is in love with Tanis and wants to marry him, although Tanis himself is in love with Kitiara). They fight dragons, ally themselves with dwarfs, encounter a mysterious figure called 'the Everman' who flees almost as soon as spotted, travel to the port-city of Tarsis, watch as a dragon army entirely destroys Tarsis (Weis and Hickman claim to have based this scene on documentary footage of the Luftwaffe bombing London during the Blitz), split up, come back together, encounter certain magical orbs, artefacts capable of controlling dragons, and afterwards break these, fight in a dream dimension (in which they have visions of their own deaths), get involved in an elf civil war, and take possession of newly forged 'dragonlances' with which the draconic armies can be fought. The group voyages, visits an underwater city inhabited by sea elves, meets mages, encounters a rare group of 'good' dragons and end up fighting over the magical 'crown of power' in the ancient city of Neraka. When the book is over, the reader need not despair: literally hundreds of sequel volumes await her, telling variations and reiterations of this story, these circumstances, alternate versions of these characters, restaging this vibe.

Related, if not in the same league in terms of commercial success, are Steve Jackson and Ian Livingstone's 'Fighting Fantasy' books, a series that ran to forty plus titles. The first of these *The Warlock on Firetop Mountain* (1982), published by UK children's imprint Puffin as a paperback, was the first 'gamebook' in the Fighting Fantasy series. Each volume consists of a series of non-sequential, numbered paragraphs in which the reader is positioned in a fantasy-realm adventure or quest, and given a numerated set of options as to how she wishes to proceed after every paragraph. Depending on the reader's choice the story might be shorter or longer, might end in triumph or failure. The use of standardized plot-points, fixtures and fittings of traditional fantasy is enlivened by the element of choice, and the fact that no two readings of the book need be the same. Flipping excitedly back and forth from paragraph to paragraph was a formative experience for the present author, although the format was only successful – and it was, for a decade or so, extremely successful – until video gaming came along to replace it. Reprints in the twenty-first century have been pitched at the nostalgia market, although the rise of gaming, considered in the next chapter, has rendered it redundant.

Few mega-series, multipart *romans-fleuves*, have been as long as the ongoing *Dragonlance* series, but fantasy in the 1980s and 1990s was characterized by many long-series books. Hugh Cook's *The Wizards and the Warriors* (1986) was the first in a planned sixty book sword-and-sorcery sequence, although in the event declining sales meant that only ten were published (Cook has subsequently posted a large amount of additional material online). Similarly elongated is Raymond Feist's 'Riftwar' series, beginning with *Magician* (1982), another example of a fantasy novel that began life as

*Dungeons-and-Dragons*-style gameplay. The major premise of this series is that two worlds, a medieval quasi-European realm called 'Midkemia', and a quasi-oriental world called 'Kelewan' (influenced by M. A. R. Barker's role-playing game *Empire of the Petal Throne*, 1975) come into conflict. While studying at the University of California San Diego, Feist and his friends would play their own D&D-style game set in Midkemia, and Feist wrote up the lengthy, 800+ page *Magician* based in part upon this gameplay. Repetition is the modus operandi, not just repeating elements from these games and other fantasy writing, but Feist repeating himself: some thirty 'Midkemia' novels are now in print, mostly disposed into successive trilogies, and the same things come round and round again.

*Magician* construes a commonplace fantasy storyline: a boy from a humble background (Feist's is called Pug) goes on a series of adventures as he grows in importance, eventually achieving eminence, in this case, as the titular magician. We might call this a Bildungsroman, except Bildungsroman traces the evolution of character, and it would overdignify Pug to describe him as a study in character. He's a type, as all Feist's figures are, subject neither to growth nor development so much as to inconsistency. Midkemia is a medievalized land of kings and wizards, of trolls and dragons, elves and dwarfs. Such alterations as Feist makes to Tolkienian source material do not move us very far: not giant spiders, but giant ants; not Gondor but 'Krondor', not Thorin but 'Tholin' dwarf-lord. Then again, the east-meets-west culture-clash major premise of the series is something not found in Middle Earth: for no sooner has Pug's story gotten underway in *Magician* than strange warriors wash up on the shore, first a mystery to be investigated, then a series of battles to be fought, and ultimately a world-wide war. It transpires that a portal, the series-titular 'rift', has been opened between medieval Europe and medieval Japan – that is, between Midkemia and Kelewan – such that warriors from the latter place have invaded the former. The rest of the novel, and indeed the series, details the development of this war and its eventual resolution. Where this major premise is concerned it is worth noting that with Feist (born in the 1940s) we are only a generation away from American writers penning hysterically racist fantasias about the 'yellow peril'. *Magician* is, to its credit, nothing like this: the world and culture of Kelewan are respectfully detailed, and the culture clash eventually resolved. Then again, later novels in the Riftwar sequence revert to a too-familiar moral bivalve, with our heroes battling various 'evil' forces, including a near-immortal wizard called Macros the Black, a Genghis-Khan-esque mass-murdering warlord called Murmandamus and a gigantic magic power known as 'The Enemy', a sort of condensation of the ancient magic race of dragon-lords called the Valheru.

The magicians in this world are all male. Indeed, in a later books characters travel back in time through the multiverse to the origin of the universe only to discover that on every imaginable world magicians are male. The same can be said for almost all figures in authority in both Midkemia and Kelewan. A patriarchal social and sexual logic generally obtains. Mieke Claessens has broken down the balance of male and female characters in eight novels (i.e. across the first twenty-five years of *The Riftwar Cycle*) noting that male characters outnumber female five-to-one: 'at best, female characters form 30% of the cast, with equivalent dialogue. Furthermore, female characters are often marginalised, put in traditional roles or are victims of sexism'.[7] Claessens also quotes Feist's offhand response to criticism of the lack of female magicians in his Fantasyworld from 2000: 'it's a male domination thing, certainly. We never explored the historical reasons behind it, just set it in place as a social "norm".' Rarely has the embedded nature of structural sexism, the way ideology masquerades as nature, been so laconically expressed.

For some of the Riftwar series Feist collaborated with Janny Wurts, a more skilled writer of prose than he and an individual with an imagination less encumbered by cliché. Particularly notable is their 'Empire Trilogy', set in Kelewan/fantasy-Japan: *Daughter of the Empire* (1987), *Servant of the Empire* (1990), *Mistress of the Empire* (1992). The underlying story of this series (the *fabula* rather than the *sjuzhet*) is similar to *Magician*: a kid – here, seventeen-year-old Mara – overcomes adversity, passes through various adventures and eventually achieves power and prominence. The key difference is not just that Pug exists in a fictionalized medieval Europe and Mara in a fictionalized medieval Japan, although that clearly is a difference. It's that Pug's 'power' is the arbitrary exteriorized folderol of 'magic', a manifestation of the jejune belief that power means the ability to manipulate externalities at a distance. Mara's 'power' is power as it actually manifests, in the world: control over interpersonal dynamics, attracting or compelling obedience from other human beings, being able to get them to do what you want them to, or to support you doing what you want: which is to say, power as politics, not a sparks-and-levitation conjuring trick, indexing human intersubjectivity. That's what Mara works towards and finally achieves in these novels, using the structures of belief of her society and her own resourcefulness and determination to bend people, and eventually the whole of her society, to her will. This is a good story, a better one than in *Magician*: there's an attractive cleverness in the way Mara uses her disadvantages – her youth, her vulnerability, her femaleness in a highly structured patriarchal society – as weapons against her combatants, turning the honour-code hierarchies and warrior-logic of her world against her adversaries. And, setting questions of cultural appropriation aside, it's refreshing to turn from a Yet-Another-Medieval-Europe fantasy world to one based on an Eastern society and culture. Not that the novels are flawless. The pace sometimes slows and stagnates, and the prose is sometimes awkward and tangled. The inclusion of the interspace rifts, and the presence of Midkemia on the far side of them, mandated by the fact that this is a Riftworld novel, is a rather wrenchingly introduced.

Also significant is Wurts's solo-authored 'War of Light and Shadow' series, beginning with *Curse of the Mistwraith* (1993) and continuing, to date, with nine further volumes. This is a world in which 'light' and 'shadow', good and evil, compete, on the material but also the magical plane. There are two half-brothers who embody these two modes and around whom the story is constructed: Arithon s'Ffalenn, wielder of elemental shadow magic, able to generate darkness, conjure cold, summon eidolons and illusion, and Lysaer s'Ilessid, possessed of elemental light magic and dedicated to justice. Both men are more than five-hundred-years old, having drunk from a magical fountain

---

[7]Claessens, 'The Presence and Role of Female Characters in Raymond E. Feist's *The Riftwar Cycle*', 2.

that grants five centuries of extra life to imbibers. This novel concerns the titular 'Mistwraith', which evil, magical entity has swaddled the land in fog and blotted out the sun. Lysaer and Arithon, together with seven sorcerers, known as 'Fellowship of Seven', must combat this evil. The fantasy is Nominalist, like Le Guin's Earthsea, magic being primarily a matter of naming, and knowing true-names: 'since the effectiveness of any arcane defense stemmed from Name, no spell could perfectly thwart what lay outside of the grasp of true seeing; to balk an essence wrought of mist and multifaceted sentience posed a nearly impossible task, like trying to fence darkness with sticks' [*Curse of the Mistwraith*, 355]. As this quotation suggests, nominalism entails a kind of essentialism, just as the 'good versus evil' moral superstructure entails a reductive binarism.

At a mere seven volumes, the 'Gandalara Cycle' of Randall Garrett and Vicky Ann Heydron seems, in the context of 1980s fantasy series, almost meagre. In *The Steel of Raithskar* (1981) first-person narrator Ricardo Emilio Carillo, an elderly and infirm university professor in our world, is taking a cruise in the Mediterranean when a giant fireball crashes into the ship, as is typical of these sorts of cruises. Ricardo passes through 'heat, pain and blinding light' to awaken in the body of a young and vigorous man called Markasset, in the cod-Arabian fantasy-land of Gandalaran. Markasset launches himself into a series adventures, alongside his companion, the beautiful female illusionist Tarani. There's also a giant, intelligent cat named Keeshah with whom Ricardo shares a telepathic bond. In *The Steel of Raithskar* Ricardo is suspected of stealing a sacred jewel called the 'Ra'ira' and must prove his innocence via the expedient of questing-about, fighting people with swords and generally getting to know his new land, riding his cat-friend like a horse. There are giant white apes, beautiful princesses, a desert land, mysterious magicians, an 'All-Mind' overpower: all very *John Carter of Mars* in flavour. In the later volumes, Ricardo travels to the land from where the giant intelligent cats come, and also meets the draida, 'dog-like in the same sense that the sha'um were cat-like'. So all readerly pet preferences are catered for.

Much of the appeal of this series is in the imaginative excitement in riding giant intelligent cats around a varied fantasyland adventure arena. Although earlier chapters have looked at various examples of 'talking animals' fantasy, cats hold a special place in the affections of many fantasy fans. Andrew Lloyd Webber's stage-musical *Cats* (1981) might be so bracketed. Taking as libretto a very freely adapted version of T S Eliot's poetry collection *Old Possum's Book of Practical Cats* (1939), Lloyd Webber's narrative posits our world from the point of view of intelligent singing-dancing cats. The two pertinencies of the presentation are a kind of frenetic energy, when younger cats sing and dance to up-tempo numbers, conveying the liveliness and ardour of catkind, and pathos: the latter especially during the song 'Memories' when the once young and beautiful, now old and decrepit, cat Grizabella gives genuinely poignant voice to her diminishment.

Cats figure largely in fantasy in the last two decades of the century. Shirley Rousseau Murphy's ongoing series of 'Joey Grey' novels (beginning with 1996's *Cat on the Edge* and currently sixteen-novels long) concerns a cat that, having magically learned how to read and write English, uses his skills to solve a series of murder mysteries. Gabriel King's *The Wild Road* (1997) and its sequel *The Golden Cat* (1998) see a cast of intelligent cats fight supernatural forces of darkness and quest in service of an ancient prophesy. Tad Williams's *Tailchaser's Song* (1985) is more systematic in its worldbuilding and less whimsical. The titular protagonist is Fritti Tailchaser, a ginger tom cat characterized as brave and intelligent, who lives in a felinocentric world in which human beings (known as 'M'an') are marginal, if dangerous, beings. Tailchaser's story is a familiar from genre fantasy: an unassuming character goes on a magical quest and battle forces of supernatural evil, with the difference that the protagonist is a cat. Williams develops a cat-language, cat-mythology and legendarium, cat deities, although the story itself underserves this carefully worked-through imaginative superstructure.

Williams is better known for his more traditional Tolkienesque trilogy *Memory, Sorrow and Thorn*, [*The Dragonbone Chair* (1988), *Stone of Farewell* (1990) and *To Green Angel Tower* (1993)]. These lengthy novels – the last so long that its half-million words had to be split between two separate, hefty volumes upon paperback publication – detail the rise of Simon Mooncalf from his lowly status as a kitchen boy in the castle of dying High King Prester John, to saviour of the realm. Williams calls his Middle Earth 'Osten Ard', his elves 'Sithi', his wizards 'mages' and his Old Forest 'Aldheorte forest', folding into his story magic swords of power, enigmatic prophesy, wicked sorcerers, various quests, enchanted scrolls, intelligent wolves, trolls and all the paraphernalia of an enchanted pseudo-medieval Europe. What makes his trilogy different to the, by the late 1980s, excessively over-familiar fare of post-Tolkien heroic fantasy is the detail: the novels give us great shovelfuls of specific detail, a textual strategy Tolstoyan in ambition if not in execution. It means that the series is slow to start, several hundred pages of scene-setting and authorial throat-clearing that a reader will tend to find either immersive or else frustrating and offputting. Eventually a larger story emerges from the welter of minutiae: Ineluki the Storm King, undead ruler of the Sithi, blights the land with the power of his dark wrath, forcing the scattered remnants of humanity to rally at the 'Stone of Farewell'. Simon, rising from servitude and adolescence into an important adult role as master of the 'League of the Scroll', is caught up in the final battle of good against evil. Williams is attempting, in this trilogy, to use sheer bulk to give his story impact, weight, heft. What other fantasy series do in thirty short volumes he is attempting in three, by dint of extending those three to three thousand pages. The commercial success of the books suggests that many readers have been persuaded that he succeeded.

*Memory, Sorrow and Thorn* may have eclipsed *Tailchaser's Song* in terms of Williams's reputation, but animal-based novels, reflecting the continuing influence of *Watership Down* continued a major element in 1980s fantasy. Two series in particular merit attention. The success of English author William Horwood's *Duncton Wood* (1980) rode the coattails of Richard Adams's success. Horwood swaps out rabbits for moles, but otherwise follows the *Watership* template: a quest to repair terrible danger in which the loveable protagonists venture out from safety of underground in to an above-world of danger – human roads are cacophonous rivers of death (moles, often killed upon them, call cars 'the roaring owls') – driven by the tyrannical mole Mandrake, whose very name evokes terror amongst moledom. *Duncton Wood* is rather more brutal, and contains more sex, than does *Watership Down*, and Horwood's talpean characters are rather more anthropomorphic than Adams's rabbits. Despite lacking opposable thumbs, they have a complex, literate society of many books written by 'scribemoles', including seven holy texts, dedicated to certain godlike standing stones ('and if there were seven books, there must be a seventh Stillstone, for each of the six books in Uffington had its counterpart in a Stillstone, as the special stones associated with the seven books were known, whose location in the deepest parts of Uffington was a secret known only to the Holy Mole and the masters' [*Duncton Wood*, 181]). The first novel is long, over-detailed and often implausible – as when moles travel easily, despite the great distance, the many roads that must be crossed and the owls that must be evaded, from Duncton in Sussex to mid-Wales and back. But it was popular enough to lead to five sequels, disposing the series into two trilogies: first *Duncton Quest* (1988), in which characters from the first novel must face-down an invasion of 'warrior moles' from the north, and then *Duncton Found* (1989), in which a mole messiah called the Stone Mole arrives to redeem the world. The follow-up trilogy *Duncton Tales* (1991) *Duncton Rising* (1992) and *Duncton Stone* (1993) is set a century after the events of the first books, and concern a fanatical religious mole-cult called the 'Newborn', that provokes a religious war. The focus on religion becomes more intense, and indeed strident, as the books go on: a Lewisian allegory of Christian sacrifice, atonement and redemption.

Brian Jacques's *Redwall* novels – beginning with *Redwall* (1986) and comprising, with a repetitious productivity characteristic of these decades, twenty-two titles, with another dozen or so offshoot books – are less mono-species. The first novel opens on young Matthias, a novice mouse-monk at Redwall Abbey, which establishment is besieged by the army of Cluny the Scourge, an evil one-eyed rat. In his quest to save the Abbey, Matthias encounters, and sometimes makes common-cause with, foxes, adders, sparrows, shrews, badgers, cats, otters and others, eventually killing Cluny by dropping the abbey bell on him, crushing him. The remaining sequels and prequels elaborate a set of stories too complex to summarize neatly here, but throughout there is a commendable theme of creatures overcoming their species-differences to unite in the fight against wickedness. One notable aspect of the novels is that these animals, despite dressing in human-style clothes and inhabiting infrastructure that only humans could have constructed, never encounter *Homo sapiens*. There are none of *Duncton*'s 'twofeet' here.

Nature is at the heart of Robert Holdstock's *Mythago Wood: A Fantasy* (1984), a book considered by some the greatest fantasy novel of the century.[8] The story is set immediately after the Second World War; demobbed, and recovering from the physical and mental wounds of war, Stephen Huxley comes to stay with his brother George on the outskirts of Ryhope Wood. The woodland is enchanted: time operates differently within it, and though it seems from the outside only a few square miles in extent, inside it is much larger. To walk towards the centre of this wood, a place called Lavondyss, is to find the trees becoming larger, more ancient and more estranging. The wood generates 'mythagos', emanations of the collective unconscious of the humans who live

---

[8]See Paul Kincaid, *Robert Holdstock's Mythago Wood: A Critical Companion*.

thereabouts that take the form variously of people, animals and monsters, each the materially embodied 'myth imago, the image of the idealized form of a myth creature' [*Mythago Wood* 39–40]: King Arthur, Robin Hood, Cúchulainn, Herne the Hunter, characters from Greek myth or fairy tales. Holdstock's novel stages the interaction of its human characters with these mythagos, and in a wider sense the interaction of modern mundanity with fantasy as such, the ancient, enchanted past. It is, in part, a reversion of Arthurian legend: Stephen falls in love with a mythago Guinevere, although she is also Guiwenneth of the Green, a manifestation of the Earth goddess. Holdstock's sequels [*Lavondyss* (1988), *The Hollowing* (1993)] carry the story and its characters through the 1950s and 1960s, and deepen the Arthurian element: *Merlin's Wood; or, The Vision of Magic* (1994) is set in Brittany, the magical woodland of Brocéliande, whose mythagos include Merlin and Vivien. And in *Avilion* (2009) Stephen is living in Ryhope Wood with Guiwenneth, raising their two children, half-human half-mythago beings, haunted by the end of Arthur and his battle with his son Modred. But myth is polysemous in all Holdstock's novels. His buffered modern characters experience the porosity of magical engagement, the wonders and the terrors of the aboriginal enchanted world. Kincaid notes that Mythago Wood 'defied the conventions that had grown up around fantasy':

> At its most basic it tells the story of a quest, that most typical of fantasy tropes; yet there is no return from this quest, the land is not healed, the hero is not restored … everyone who enters the wood is transformed utterly, and so becomes the hero and villain of their own story. And the stories arrive at no conventional ending, nothing is settled forever, nothing is explained.[9]

Arthurian fantasy more conventionally conceived saw a significant resurgence in the 1980s. Marion Zimmer Bradley's *The Mists of Avalon* (1984), a bestselling feminist retelling of the Arthurian cycle from the perspective of Morgaine, is a euhemerist work, explaining away the magical or supernatural elements of the myth. But most Arthurian works fully inhabited the fantastical. The movie *Excalibur* (directed John Boorman, 1981) includes the magical lady of the lake, Merlin as an active sorcerer – an eccentrically memorable performance by Nicol Williamson – and Morgana (Helen Mirren) as sorceress. Boorman, ambitiously, attempts to cover the entire legendary cycle in one film, from Arthur's birth to his passing after the Last Battle, and though this makes the movie a little overlong, it is filled with visually brilliant, vehement set-pieces. The repeated assertion, articulated by several characters, that the king and the land are one, as much as the valorization, through the titular sword, of warfare as spiritually and aesthetically glorious, and the focus on Arthur himself as supernaturally chosen to lead – not to mention the soundtrack, which draws heavily on Wagner – contributes to a whole that could be accused of valorizing fascism.[10] Nikolai Tolstoy's *The Coming of the King* (1988) was the first volume in a projected but uncompleted trilogy, a quasi-Arthurian fantasy that lards dense and

[9]Kincaid, *Robert Holdstock's Mythago Wood: A Critical Companion*, 4.
[10]Roberts, *Silk and Potatoes*.

sometimes estranging Norse and Celtic elements into a peripatetic, rather unstructured whole. In Tolstoy's telling Merlin postdates Arthur, the king whose coming is adverted in the book's title is not Arthur but his descendent Maelgun. Much of the book is given over to the hallucinatory spirit-journeys Merlin, more shaman than wizard, undertakes into the otherworld. There's a lot of unleavened research into Celtic and Norse mythology and culture dumped into this novel: untranslated names and concepts, archaic flourishes of prose. There is also a quantity of revolting, scatological detail.

Much more beguiling is Jack Vance's late career fantasy trilogy: *Lyonesse* (1983), *Lyonesse: The Green Pearl* (1985) and *Lyonesse: Madouc* (1989). These books manage, with Vance's characteristic lightness of touch, wit and invention, to cover many of the stereotypes of fantasy in an attractively fresh manner. The main locus is the contract between the rather dour, medievalized human kingdom of Lyonesse itself – located in the legendary continent supposedly west of France, and doomed to sink beneath the waves (although Vance's story doesn't include this element) – and the world of fairy that borders and intersects it. The former element lends itself to stories of political machination, and such Arthurian elements as the search for the Holy Grail; the latter to Grimms' fairy-tale-like delight and enchantment. The contrast is nicely elaborated. The novel opens in the human realm, properly downbeat:

> On a dreary winter's day, with rain sweeping across Lyonesse Town, Queen Sollace went into labor. She was taken to the lying-in room and attended by two midwives, four maids, Balhamel the physician and the crone named Dyldra, who was profound in the lore of herbs. [*Lyonesse*, 1]

The fairy world is far livelier and more colourful. Here is the puck-like Falael, 'with the girl's grace and the boy's body':

> Falael assembled an orchestra of hedgehogs, weasels, crows and lizards and trained them in the use of musical instruments. So skilfully did they play and so melodious were their tunes that King Throbius allowed them to play at the Great Pavanne of the Vernal Equinox. Falael thereupon tired of the orchestra. The crows took flight; two weasel bassoonists attacked a hedgehog who had been beating his drum with too much zeal, and the orchestra dissolved. [*Lyonesse*, 206]

Vance's eye for charming detail, as with that poor hedgehog, is expert and brilliant throughout. If the larger story loses some of its architectonic coherence as a result, it doesn't diminish the achievement of the whole.

## Gemmell

The reputation of British author David Gemmell inheres the notion that his books represented a return to 'classic' fantasy at a time when the mode was becoming increasingly diverse and decadent. 'Classic' here means: an early medieval world of kings and empires, of warriors, monsters and magic, a plainly told story of adventure and battle. It also means a distinctly masculinist vision, gendered notions of strength, soldiery, honour. *Legend* (1984) combines its northern-European world with the story of the Spartans holding Thermopylae against the Persians. The people of the 'Nadir' (a word that means, of course, the lowest point) have united under the ruthless leader Ulric, who leads a vast army to invade the northern land of Drenai. Only an Alamo-style stand by the warrior 'Druss the Legend' and his small force at the fortress of Dros Delnoch can prevent them, keeping the invading army back long enough for the Drenai general Magnus Woundweaver to muster an army and preserve the realm. The odds are entirely against Druss, and his courageous struggle at this forlorn hope gives the story tremendous narrative tension and readability. Gemmell later claimed that he wrote the book in the 1970s to distract himself from a cancer diagnosis and its debilitating treatment: Ulric's horde was the disease, and Druss's embattled heroism at Dros Delnoch was Gemmell's refusal to succumb to the sickness. The novel dramatizes resistance as martial heroism, projecting the struggle of the individual onto the big screen of a fictionalized history; and there is, in that, the dynamic of bourgeois individualism and an older, feudal and heroic code. Success encouraged Gemmell to write another twenty-three novels in this series, for though Druss dies at the end of *Legend* he reappears in a number of prequel novels. In one of these, *The First Chronicles of Druss the Legend* (1993) an elderly warrior called Shadak passes to young Druss the 'code', which he must follow, and which thereafter defines Druss's actions.

> The true warrior lives by a code. He has to. For each man there are different perspectives, but at the core they are all the same. *Never violate a woman, nor harm a child. Do not lie, cheat or steal. These things are for lesser men. Protect the weak against the evil strong. And never allow thoughts of gain to lead you into the pursuit of evil.* [Gemmell, *First Chronicles*, 130]

In a later novel, *White Wolf* (2003), an older Druss passes this 'code', word for word, onto a younger warrior called Rabalyn: 'the axeman leaned back and closed his eyes. When he spoke it was as if he was reciting a prayer' [207]. The second sentence, there, is indicative of Gemmell's prose, innocent as it is of the proper use of the subjunctive – syntactical over-correctness is not what Gemmell gives us. It would not, we can imagine, be *manly* to be too precise about grammar. It also styles a set of moral obviousnesses – that rape, child abuse, lying and theft are wrong – as if they are hieratic profundities. In fact what Gemmell's 'code' does is foreground the contradiction at the heart of the concept of 'hero' as it appears in these novels, and Fantasies like them. These are books that supply their readers with the fantasy of superabundant strength, bravery and force, by making a tacit deal with bourgeois values, such that the hero with whom the reader identifies and is also decent in a legalistic, modern sense. Homer's Achilles would have disregarded Druss's 'code' with disdain, a mere impediment to the achievement of his *kleos*. Nietzsche's 'blond beast' Übermensch would look with contempt on anyone bound by such slave-morality. Which is to say, Gemmell's fantasy (in the generic sense) is precisely the compromise of archaic and modern values that fantasy as a mode more broadly is. Trapped in the coils of civilization and its discontents, we yearn to express ourselves violently, to maim and kill. Druss, and Gemmell's various other heroes, enable readers vicariously to do this whilst also providing them with the contractual escape-clause that the people on the receiving end of such violence *are bad*, and that we therefore are licensed in violating them. There is, at root, a patriarchal logic at work in these stories – patriarchal in the strict sense. A repeated trope sees an older father-figure mentoring or training a younger male warrior, initiating him into this 'code' of violence according to the buried oedipal logic of the whole. The antagonist is a 'dark figure', and the violence a symbolic castration of the father-figure the young man both reveres and resents:

> Rolling to his left, Waylander lunged upright with knives in his hands as a dark figure leapt at him, He blocked the downward sweep of the sword, catching it on the hilt-guard of his left-hand knife. Dropping his shoulder, he stabbed his attacker low in the groin; the man twisted as he fell. [Gemmell, *Waylander* (1986), 210]

The question of ultra-violence in fantasy comes, increasingly, to the fore through the 1980s and 1990s, and we shall return to it. But it would misrepresent Gemmell to characterize him as a sadistic or Grimdark author. With the thirty novels he published between 1984 and his death in 2006 he attracted a large, devoted fanbase. Those novels are all, more or less, variants on the same basic adventure story template, but it was a story that people loved, and the creation of the David Gemmell Award for fantasy in 2009 indexed the affection in which his writing, and he himself, was felt. The awards ran until 2018, rewarding what a popular vote considered the 'best' fantasy novel of the year written in this 'classic', Gemmellian manner. The prize, fittingly, was an axe.

Matthew Oliver brackets Gemmell with Leiber, as writers who 'reveal the illusions created by conventions as a social necessity'.

> By operating on the fringes of subgeneric distinctions, both Gemmell and Leiber are able to use one set of conventions (cynical war fiction and sword-and-sorcery action-adventure respectively) to comment on another (epic idealization). Consequently, at foundational moments for the fantasy genre writers like Gemmell and Leiber create a language for fantasy out of a fundamental tension: a self-consciously artificial 'magic' which nonetheless forms social bonds.[11]

For Oliver, Gemmell suggests a fantastical world and deflates it with mundanity – he might have said 'violence', a textual strategy of the Grimdark fantasy of the twenty-first

---

[11] Matthew Oliver, *Magic Words, Magic Worlds*, 199.

century – where Leiber 'teases with a mundane world and then upends it with the irrational fantastic', a textual strategy Pratchett follows through upon.

## Prehistory

Fantasy set in prehistory made a significant mark upon the decade. Samuel Delany's 'Nevèrÿon' sequence, a mix of short stories, novellas and novels [*Tales of Nevèrÿon* (1979), *Neveryóna* (1983), *Flight from Nevèrÿon* (1985), *Return to Nevèrÿon* (1994)], is located in a prehistorical Fantasyland, a carefully detailed representation of early history: slave-owning societies, the first cities, trade, war – although this is also, as its nomenclature suggests, a 'never never land' of magic, enchantment and dragons: 'Did you see the dragons, earlier tonight, flying against the moon? ... you know the fabled flying dragons are cousins to the tiny night lizards that scurry about the rocks on a spring evening' (*Tales of Nevèrÿon*, 156). The first narrative, 'The Tale of Gorgik', concerns a young man of Kolhari, the major port of Nevèrÿon who is sold into slavery, working first in an obsidian mine, then purchased by the royal vizerine Myrgot as her lover. Freed, he serves in the army, and then becomes an outlaw, fighting to free slaves. A light-skinned man in a majority dark-skinned world – most slaves are light-skinned – Gorgik's tale explores questions of race, power, sex and communication. 'The Tale of Old Venn', set in an archipelago off the main Nevèrÿon, sees the supersession of barter economics with money. In 'The Tale of Small Sarg' a young barbarian prince is captured and sold into slavery: bought by Gorgik, the tale dramatizes Hegel's master–slave dynamic through Gorgik and Sarg's sexual relationship. This, as the later books make explicit, is 'magic', the enchantment to which fantasy approaches.

> The purport of magic is so simple, it's odd that it is not as obvious as... But then, what was obvious to Venn was not obvious to Belham. Still, in any encounter there is always a stronger side and a weaker side – and both sides always have power. But because there is magic loose in the world, the stronger had best pay attention to the weaker if the stronger wishes to retain its position. You are not in a terribly strong position. I am not in a terribly weak one. We are not arguing, you and I, about which of us holds which place. You want to know my reasons for bringing you here. I want to know your reasons for coming. It only seems fair to me to ask, since you, at this point, know so much of me!
> [*Neveryóna*, 159]

'The Tale of Dragons and Dreamers' brings characters from the earlier tales together. The volume reflects upon itself in its final section, a critical-theoretical appendix 'Some Informal Remarks toward the Modular Calculus': modular because a fantasy text models reality, and calculus because the relational semiotics of representation must be calculated by the writer. Delany engages with literary and critical theory throughout the *Nevèrÿon* series, quoting Lacan, Derrida, Susan Sontag and others as epigraphs to stories, and foregrounding the intertextuality of his own literary praxis. As Kathleen L. Spencer argues in *Nevèrÿon* Delany is simultaneously presenting fantasy and deconstructing it.[12] The novel comes with pastiche academic introduction and afterword by fictional professors, pre-interpreting the stories according to the lights of postmodern semiotics. And the stories themselves reconfigure the standards of fantasy writing into recursive signifiers.

> In Nevèrÿon the dragon, that staple of fantasy, undergoes a similar postmodern transformation. To Ursula Le Guin the dragon is a symbol of fantasy, the imagination, a 'beautiful non-fact' that may lead to 'truth'. Most fantasy writers, including Le Guin, strive to present dragons as concrete and credible. But in order to establish their 'authenticity', Delany foregrounds the 'reality': their inauthenticity. They become not so much multiple signifiers as figures for the Derridean signifier itself, their meaning in constant play, their 'truth' forever deferred. In the scene that closes *Tales of Nevèrÿon*, a flying dragon is explicitly called 'a mysterious sign'. Its flight is difficult, doomed never to be repeated.[13]

The second volume *Neveryóna* is subtitled 'The Tale of Signs and Cities'. A young girl called Pryn, unusual in her culture in that she can read, plays the part of Isolde: she flies by dragon to Nevèrÿon where she joins Gorgik's campaign against slavery. The novel contrasts the simple mountain world from which comes with the complexity and richness of city life. And cities, as the modernity – the future – of this world connect with actual modernity, as the dialectic of fantasy sublates disenchantment and enchantment. *Flight from Nevèrÿon* (1985) includes a novel-length episode titled 'The Tale of Plagues and Carnivals'. A sickness afflicts the city of Kolhari, a state of affairs that the story specifically parallels with the early years of the AIDS epidemic, in 1980s New York. The juxtaposition actualizes the passage from mundanity to fantasy, the portal between the two worlds being autobiographical metafiction. Delany writes from the position of a black gay man living in New York in the 1980s, which is significant because of the autobiographical aspects of *Plagues and Carnivals*, in which the narrator, Chip (a fictionalized persona of Delany), navigates between the fantastic Nevèrÿon and 1980s New York. Both worlds experience and attempt to manage the effects of plague – in New York, it is AIDS; in Kolhari (Nevèrÿon's capital city), there is a strange plague (essentially an unnamed AIDS) that affects certain groups of people, namely homosexual men.[14]

A simpler, though not simplistic, novel is Jean M Auel's *The Clan of the Cave Bear* (1980). A prehistoric adventure set in Ukraine 25,000 BC, the novel follows a young

---

[12]Kathleen L. Spencer, 'Deconstructing *Tales of Nevèrÿon*: Delany, Derrida, and the "Modular Calculus, Parts I-IV"', 59.

[13]Sylvia Kelso, '"Across Never": Postmodern Theory and Narrative Praxis in Samuel R. Delany's *Nevèrÿon* Cycle', 292.

[14]Kala B. Hirtle, 'Rhetorically (De)constructing AIDS', 319.

human girl as she grows up as part of a tribe of Neanderthals. The book was a huge success, with more than twenty million copies sold worldwide. Five sequels followed, comprising what Auel calls the 'Earth's Children' sequence [*The Valley of Horses*, 1982; *The Mammoth Hunters*, 1985; *The Plains of Passage*, 1990; *The Shelters of Stone*, 2002; *The Land of Painted Caves*, 2011] and a big-budget movie was made of the first book in 1986 (directed by Michael Chapman, and starring Daryll Hannah). The film flopped, and the series has not endured as culturally significant or present into the twenty-first century. In the first novel five-year-old orphan Ayla, a Cro Magnon human, is taken in and raised by a Neanderthal tribe, the titular clan. The novel is her bildungsroman, and a tale of her difference: Auel speculates that Neanderthals possessed a capacious race-memory at the back of their brains (their heads growing larger and larger as this memory augments, which eventually leads to a situation in which Neanderthal babies can no longer pass through the birth canal, and so the species becomes extinct). Sensitive, cultural, barely speaking – they communicate through sign language – their problem is their lack of adaptability. Ayla, on the other hand, possesses a large frontal lobe, which enables her to intuit, invent, experiment and develop in ways the Neanderthals cannot: she improves the clan's hunting by inventing the spear thrower, develops basket-weaving, invents the sewing needle which she also adapts to life-saving surgical stitching, and improves fire-lighting by the use of flint and pyrite. Auel is fond of her Neanderthals, and the novels develop a commendable feminist throughline in which the challenges of this austere and dangerous environment of European prehistory are met and overcome by Ayla's resourcefulness and skill. The novels dramatize the shamanistic religions of the time, touching on questions of visions and telepathy, leavening purely materialistic explanations (to which Auel, as narrator, is drawn) with the possibilities of something supernatural. This is less a fully articulated armature of magic and the transcendent, and more an index of the books' love for their time and place, the sense that this is a more authentic and, in the fantasy sense, more enchanted world in which to live. Hardship and danger are not glossed-over, but neither is the wondrous and (often sexual) epiphanic quality of life in this imagined realm. *Clan of the Cave Bear* construes a similar Lukascian/Walter Scott dialectic: the old world that is passing away, the new world that is coming, and a character 'wavering' between them, much as we see in Tolkien and his successors.

The other major fantasy publication of 1980 did not, on its initial release, enjoy anything like Auel's level of commercial success, although it and its three sequels have grown in status and importance as the decades have passed, to the point where some consider them the most important fantasy novels of their decade. This is Gene Wolfe's *The Shadow of the Torturer* (1980), the first novel in the series *The Book of the New Sun* [followed by *The Claw of the Conciliator* (1981), *The Sword of the Lictor* (1982) and *The Citadel of the Autarch* (1983). A fifth volume, *The Urth of the New Sun* (1987), transitions the continuing story – carried-through into the four-volume *The Book of the Long Sun* (1993–6) and the two-volume *The Book of the Short Sun* (1999–2000) – into science fiction, and so these works are not considered here. The books are fantasy in the idiom of Jack Vance's *Dying Earth* series, iterating a baroque dynamic of death and rebirth.

The story follows the life of Severian, a journeyman torturer exiled from his guild who quests through the fantastical landscapes of Wolfe's 'Urth', carrying with him his executioner's broadsword *Terminus Est*, Latin for 'it is the end'. Severian wears clothes of 'fuligin', a darker-than-black fabric the mere sight of which inspires terror among the common folk (early in his travels he buys a cloak from a rag-shop to cover this gear and so disguise himself and travel unnoticed). It is not immediately clear after what he is questing although, as the series goes on, a world-redeeming end-point comes into view. The plot of the books is intricate, involving many digressions and side-quests, stories-within-stories: at one point the text shifts into playscript, and the characters put on a theatrical performance. Severian meets and re-meets many different characters, so much so that a full summary here would be dense, over busy. Nor would it capture the texture of Wolfe's work, which is detailed to a purpose, fluently rendered, easy to follow: Wolfe pays attention to the details, none of which are merely arbitrary, all of which have a place in the larger pattern of the book's construction, narrative and symbol, theme elaborated in small as well as large.

The sun is dying, and civilization is in decay. Severian, an apprentice in the guild of torturers, falls in love with Thecla, a noblewoman. She is a prisoner of the state, caught-up in political machinations of the Autarch, the absolute ruler of the Commonwealth of Urth ('she's a pawn in the Autarch's game', we are told. 'Her sister, the Chatelaine Thea, has fled the House Absolute to become his leman. They will bargain with Thecla for a time at least' [*Shadow of the Torturer*, 58]). She is due to be executed in a particularly cruel manner: tortured with a suicide-provoking device that will drive her to mutilate herself with her own hands until she dies. Severian, out of pity, smuggles a knife into her cell, allowing her to abbreviate her suffering. In doing so he violates his oath to his guild. Severian, expecting to be executed for his disobedience, is instead sent to the remote city of Thrax to act as public executioner. On the way to his new appointment he fights a duel, and connects with an ambiguous woman called Agia, who steals a magical thorn, 'the claw of the conciliator', from a religious sect and hides it amongst Severian's things. Severian later wears this thorn around his neck as a talisman. Severian falls into a lake of death, and is rescued by a young woman called Dorcas, who has also come, somehow, out of the lake. Moving on, Severian executes various criminals, meets a green-coloured man who claims to have travelled from a future in which the sun has been renewed and humans live by absorbing sunlight directly into their skin. To balance this hint of a redeemed future, later in his adventures Severian meets a different future time-traveller, who has come from a dead world overtaken by ice. Severian develops feelings for Dorcas. He encounters a revolutionary agitator called Vodalus and enters his service. He fights savage man-ape creatures in a cave and eats a magical substance that means he becomes incapable of forgetting – the absolute nature of Severian's memory is the basis of the first-person narration that constitutes the whole book, although his memorious perfection does not mean that he is necessarily a reliable narrator. He fights shape-shifters, witches and bat-monsters. Eventually he arrives at Thrax and takes up his duties as torturer and executioner. Dorcas, now his lover, grows doleful, shunned as the partner of so reviled and feared a figure. Severian encounters a terrifying monster called the Alzabo, which acquires the memories of those it devours. He discovers that the 'claw of the conciliator' has the power to heal wounds and even to revive the dead.

In the final volume northerners called Ascians (the name means: 'shadowless') are invading, and soldiers of the Commonwealth, Severian among them, are resisting. It is revealed, after the manner of a Walter Scott novel, that the Autarch, the supreme ruler, has been in the novel for a while now, disguised as someone else. When he is fatally wounded he instructs Severian to consume his flesh such that, with the help of the blood of the Alzabo, he will be able to absorb his Autarchian memories – for Severian, we learn, is to be the new Autarch of the Commonwealth. Severian does this and discovers that the Autarch's mind contains hundreds of consciousnesses, acquired this way, which Severian now absorbs. Wandering the coast he has a spiritual epiphany:

> What struck me on the beach – and it struck me indeed, so that I staggered as at a blow – was that if the Eternal Principle had rested in that curved thorn I had carried about my neck across so many leagues, then it might rest in anything, and in fact probably did rest in everything, in every thorn on every bush, in every drop of water in the sea. The thorn was a sacred Claw because all thorns were sacred Claws; the sand in my boots was sacred sand because it came from a beach of sacred sand. … everything had approached and even touched the Pancreator, because everything had dropped from his hand. Everything was a relic. All the world was a relic. I drew off my boots, that had traveled with me so far, and threw them into the waves that I might not walk shod on holy ground. [*Citadel of the Autarch*, 258]

Severian makes his way back to the city and assumes the role of Autarch, abolishing the torturer's guild and making plans to renew the dying sun (which task he accomplishes in 1987's *The Urth of the New Sun*). Where as torturer he had worn clothes of fuligin, he now dons a robe of argent, 'the color that is more pure than white'.

In all this, every element has its place in the larger patterning of the text: narrative elements, aspects of character, symbolism and moments of poetic beauty. Wolfe is fond of recherché vocabulary and formalisms of expression, but unlike Stephen Donaldson's pretentious and distracting prose, Wolfe's terminology is always precise, always appropriate. He is a consummate stylist. 'Wolfe's prose continually charms, amazes, and seduces us with its lyricism, its eccentric lingoes and vocabularies (as often drawn from arcane and ancient sources as from modern science), and its surprising use of metaphor.'[15] He finesses his meaning, preferring to signify by inflection and suggestion than direct statements. This means that some find him obscure, although in fact he is rarely so: a properly attentive reader will decipher what things are and how things fit

---

[15]Larry McCaffery, 'On Encompassing the Entire Universe', 335.

together. At the end of *Citadel of the Autarch*, Severian as narrator advises the reader still unclear about any aspect of the story he has just told to read it again; and rereading Wolfe is always an enrichment of his work and world.

Memory and the workings of memory are at the heart of the novel: individual memory, and collective memory, the ways in which the past is apprehended by the present. Fantasy as a mode is about this, of course: a fantasy kingdom, evoked in a fantasy novel, is a way of creatively remembering history: recalling in the sense not just of adverting to but in the sense of interpellating these worlds into now. Wolfe's *New Sun* series are complexly apprised of this, and Wolfe explores what memory is, how it means. Having a narrator with a flawless recall sets the intermittencies of memory into sharp relief. Severian not only remembers what has happened, but also remembers how he *used* to remember what had happened, and so sees the difference between the way he used to see things and the way he sees them now. For most of us memory is a decay, but it is also the reconfiguring of what is lost. Wolfe's Urth is a fantasy reimagining of Byzantium, with elements from other cultures and periods mixed in – it is, as it were, a 1980s memory of medieval Constantinople that is also a notional far-future's memory of now. Towers might be traditional erections of stone, or they might be antique spaceships repurposed for habitation. Early in the first novel, Severian encounters a picture – we deduce, of Neil Armstrong, standing on the surface of the moon in 1969, although this is not specified – from his world's deep past.

> The picture showed an armored figure standing in a desolate landscape. It had no weapon, but held a staff bearing a strange, stiff banner. The visor of this figure's helmet was entirely of gold, without eye slits or ventilation; in its polished surface the deathly desert could be seen in reflection, and nothing more.

> This warrior of a dead world affected me deeply, though I could not say why or even just what emotion it was I felt. In some obscure way, | wanted to take down the picture and carry it – not into our necropolis but into one of those mountain forests of which our necropolis was (as I understood even then) an idealized but vitiated image. It should have stood among trees, the edge of its frame resting on young grass. [*Shadow of the Torturer*, 49]

This image works, in the texture of the novel, to situate our present as the story's distant past. But it is beautiful, its estrangement of the over-familiar image repurposing it: saying things about striving, adventure, the quest, about the hero, and about the desolation of a dead world and the springtime renewal of a renaissing one. The astronaut becomes the fantasy knight.

John Crowley's *Little, Big: or, The Fairies' Parliament* (1981) is a large, complex book about, at its heart, the interaction between contemporary humanity and the kingdoms of Fairy, which exist, we discover, in a kind of topographical fold, or series of folds, within our regular world. The story opens with Evan 'Smoky' Barnable, an innocuous young man from an unremarkable family who works in as a clerk in 1980s New York City. He befriends another clerk, George Mouse, and through him meets Alice Dale Drinkwater, known as Daily Alice, a scion of the ancient, wealthy Drinkwater family. He falls in love. To marry Alice Smoky must walk into the countryside north of the city and find the family home, Edgewood, though it is not on any maps: a big house set in large grounds. He manages this, and meets Alice's family, about whom there is something uncanny, something other-worldly.

Then the story flashes back to the building of Edgewood, at the beginning of the twentieth century: wealthy American John Drinkwater marries a much younger English girl called Violet Bramble and builds the house for her. Violet, we discover, is in communication with the fairy folk, who are hidden in the interstices of our world. Drinkwater becomes increasingly fascinated by her visions and communications, and the nature of the fae. He revises and republishes his book *The Architecture of Country Houses* multiple times, turning it from a conventional architectural description into a disquisition of fairy spatiality: Drinkwater believes that 'space' is actually a vast, perhaps infinite series of concentric spheres, with the corollary that each sphere, as we go inwards towards the centre, is actually and counter-intuitively larger than the one before. In the centre of this nested geometry live the fairies, a kind of parallel evolutionary life-form, unnoticed by science because they have left no material artefacts in the fossil record. The novel then fleshes-out the family tree of John and Violet's children. Through their mother the family inherit the ability to see, and sometimes interact with, the fairies. They possess a magical pack of tarot cards that can predict and in some cases determine the future. The Drinkwaters think not of 'history' or 'family history' but of 'Story', which folds back upon the novel itself, whose story Crowley is shaping and we are reading.

The novel tells the stories of the family's generations, against a backdrop of a collapse-of-society dystopia. New York is decaying, and poverty and crime are everywhere. A charismatic politician, Russell Eigenblick, becomes president of the United States, promising to wage war on the mysterious forces that, he claims, are behind the general decay and ruination. In a bizarre turn we discover that this person is actually a reincarnation of Holy Roman Emperor Frederick Barbarossa, who has been re-awoken not to help humanity but to protect Faerie from human depredation. Auberon Drinkwater comes to understand that President Eigenblick is the emissary of the fairies, and that what is at stake in the ongoing war is the rolling-back of human civilization and the restoration of the wilderness.

> The Wild Wood: yes. There had been a time, Auberon knew, say when Frederick Barbarossa was emperor of the West, a time when it had been beyond the log walls of tiny towns, beyond the edges of the harrowed land, that the forest began: the forest, where there lived wolves, and bears, witches in vanishing cottages, dragons, giants. Inside the town, all was reasonable and ordinary; there were safety, fellows, fire and food and all comforts. Dull, maybe, more sensible than thrilling, but safe. It was beyond, in the Wild Wood, that anything could happen, any adventure could be had; out there you took your life in your hands. [*Little, Big*, 338]

The unbuffering of modernity. This second half of the novel has something in common with Gene Wolfe's contemporaneous *Book of the New Sun* series; and more directly of Hope Mirrlees' *Lud-in-the-Mist* and Dunsany's *King of Elfland's Daughter*, though it is bigger, shaggier and more baroquely constructed than either of those two. As America descends into civil war, the fairies, who can see the future (but have a much hazier sense of 'the transitory forms of the present' and are almost entirely blind to the past) prepare to retreat further into their wildness. The novel's subtitular fairy parliament is called to facilitate this migration – it happens at Edgewood, at Midsummer, and is attended by the entire Drinkwater family. Daily Alice departs for fairyland, and the rest of her relatives agree to follow her, to take the place of the retreating fairies, all except Smoky, who elects to stay ('I was never really part of this, you know', he tells the family). So he stays, and mends the magic orrery that provides electrical power for the house. But then, at the last moment, Sophie manages to persuade him to come along after all, and so he goes. Or tries to: as he steps out of the house, he dies, of a heart-attack:

> But Smoky heard nothing now but the wind of Revelation blowing in him; he would not, this time, escape it. He saw, in the blue midst of what entered him, Lilac, turning back and looking at him curiously; and by her face he knew that he was right. The Tale was behind him. 'Back there', he tried to say, unable himself to turn in that direction; back there, he tried to tell them, back to where the house stood lit and waiting, the Park and the arches and the walled garden and the lane into the endless woods, the door into summer. If he could turn now (but he could not, it didn't matter that he could not but he could not) he would find himself facing summers house, and on a balcony there Daily Alice greeting him, dropping from her shoulders the old brown robe to show him her nakedness behind the shadow of leaves: Daily Alice, his bride. [*Little, Big*, 619–20]

His funeral doubles-up as the wedding of Auberon and Sylvie. Then there is a coda, entitled 'Once Upon a Time': a description of now empty Edgewood decaying into the wilderness, although still shining with light (because Smoky mended the orrery-generator) which, since electricity is a rare thing in the socially collapsed human world in which the novel concludes, makes the place a legend.

The book is baroque, not in the sense of rococo over-ornamentation and kitschy artifice, but in the sense for which Gilles Deleuze argues in *The Fold* (1988). For Deleuze the Baroque does not comprise what we associate with Bernini, Borromini, or Le Brun:

> The Baroque state reveals identical traits existing as constants within the most diverse environments and periods of time. Baroque designates a trope that comes from the renewed origins of art and has stylistic evidence that prevails in culture in general. Under its rubric are placed the proliferation of mystical experience, the birth of the novel, intense taste for life that grows and pullulates, and a fragility of infinitely varied patterns of movement. It could be located in the protracted

fascination we experience in watching waves heave, tumble, and atomize when they crack along an unfolding line being traced along the expanse of a shoreline; in following the curls and wisps of color that move on the surface and in the infinite depths of a tile of marble.[16]

This is worth quoting not only as a gloss upon *Little, Big*, but as a commentary upon fantasy as a mode. Everything is folded, infolded in Crowley's novel, and the art of the Baroque – the pleats and flexes of the painting, the curlicues and grace-notes of the music – captures this. This is Deleuze's reading of Leibniz's monads:

> If the differential mechanisms of our clear perceptions are checked, then the minute perceptions force selection and invade consciousness, as in drowsiness or in giddiness. A dust of colored perceptions falls on a black backdrop; yet, if we look closely, these are not atoms, but minuscule folds that are endlessly unfurling and bending on the edges of juxtaposed areas, like a mist or fog that makes their surface sparkle, at speeds that no one of our thresholds of consciousness could sustain in a normal state. But when our clear perceptions are reformed, they draw yet another fold that now separates the conscious from the unconscious, that joins the tiny edges of surface to a great area, that moderates the different speeds, and rejects all kinds of minute perceptions in order to make from all the others the solid fabric of apperception: dust falls, and I see the great fold of figures just as the background is unfurling its tiny folds. [Deleuze, *The Fold*, 93]

To call this fairy-dust is not entirely a facetious comparison on my part: for though he doesn't mention fairies, part of Deleuze's argument is that the transcendent, miraculous and spiritual worlds (which Leibniz, devout Lutheran, identified with the God of Protestantism) are folded complexly into the material, mundane, ordinary worlds. It is not a matter of simple revelation, or of one magisterium subsuming the other; it is a striated and pleated surface. This is also Crowley's sense of things: magic, faerie, is there, but tucked away, easy to miss. Or to put it another way, we mundane beings are tucked away in the logic of wildwood and fairy glamour. Crowley's universe is one radically folded, fairyland into mundane reality and vice versa, just as his novel folds a wide range of story-elements and allusions – Grimms' tales, Carroll's *Alice*, *A Midsummer Night's Dream*, Barrie, *Wind in the Willows*, the Cottingley Fairies – into its cinched textual surface. The two sizes specified in the novel's title are not opposed, but complementary. Alice, named for Carroll's heroine, whose own size keeps changing, who shrinks down and shoots up, who interpenetrates her wonderland and is interpenetrated by it, thinks so:

> Daily Alice couldn't tell if she felt huge or small. She wondered whether her head were so big as to be able to contain all this starry universe, or whether the

---

[16]Tom Conley, 'Translator's Introduction', Gilles Deleuze *The Fold*, x–xi.

universe were so little that it would fit within the compass of her human head. She alternated between these feelings, expanding and diminishing. [*Little, Big*, 207]

The house at Edgewood is a TARDIS-like structure, not just a combination of different architectural styles but of different topographies and dimensions, all folded into one another. The architectural enfoldment is also the principle upon which the book is structured: the reader passes from chamber to chamber, some tiny, some vast, each linked to the preceding in a way that feels intuitively right rather than linear or conventionally emplotted. Dreams are folded into the novel, just as they are into life, and as in life what dreams work is the pliable tucking-away of whole universes into our minds. Stories within stories, worlds within worlds, oak and thorn double-helixed around one another. Crowley is working towards a form that enables him not just to denote but to embody, formally and evocatively, the way marvellousness and ordinariness are intertwined, one with the other. His success in this is the splendour of *Little, Big*.

## Discworld

The appearance of Terry Pratchett's *The Colour of Magic* in 1983 inaugurated, without fanfare, one of the most important fantasy works of the later century. Pratchett's 'Discworld' series ran to forty novels until his premature death in 2015 – a forty-first *The Shepherd's Crown*, was published posthumously. 'Discworld' is a flat, circular world, supported by four elephants that in turn are carried on the shell of a titanic turtle, travelling through space. Its geography runs from a huge central mountain outwards, past four main continents to a rim-encircling sea. There are many countries and cities, although the main is 'Ankh-Morpork'. This fundamentally unserious premise – a flat-earth carried upon a cosmic turtle – is treated very seriously, worldbuilding-wise, by Pratchett, precisely in order to ground a series of ludicrous stories and comic characters. It perhaps looks contradictory to say Pratchett treats his comedy seriously, but it is in this that his genius resides: a writer of comic prose to rival Wodehouse, the creator of rounded, believable, beloved characters as the ground of character-comedy, an ingenious and rigorous extrapolator of comic premises, joyfully rather than satirically, and spinning both stories and, with each book, increasingly capacious, hospitable worldbuilding.

The early Discworld novels are amusing exercises in pastiche, somewhat limited by their focus on parodying fantasy conventions and figures. The joke in *The Colour of Magic* (1983) is that, rather than being a dignified mage, the wizard Rincewind is a coward and a fool, although a beguilingly likeable one. He pairs with a parodic version of Howard's Conan of Cimmeria, 'Hrun, the Barbarian, of Chimeria', who is strong and brave but very dim. The second novel *The Light Fantastic* (1986) includes a rather sharper parody of Conan in 'Cohen the Barbarian', an irascible Jewish nonagenarian, his scrawny body still dressed in leather cloak and loincloth, who, in a nod to the premise of fantasy as a genre, is grumpy that the heroic age is over, and that he has survived into a kind of bourgeois modernity where mighty battles and heroic quests happen rarely except in stories. *Equal Rites* (1987),which concerns a coven of witches in the Discworld provinces, introducing the character of Granny Weatherwax, marks a step-up in quality. Pratchett is no longer content simply to parody fantasy clichés; he is now inhabiting and more fully exploring his imaginative creation. The same year saw *Mort* (1987): a richly funny and thoroughly immersive story about a simple country lad who becomes the apprentice to Discworld's 'Death', an anthropomorphized figures to talks entirely in capital letters. Death, it seems, is tired of his job and believes himself ready to hand his scythe and responsibilities to somebody else.

At the end of the 1980s the Discworld novels entered a golden period. *Wyrd Sisters* (1987) plays with the story-frame of *Macbeth* to bring the witches to the fore. *Guards! Guards!* (1989) concerns the 'City Watch' of Ankh-Morpork, under their captain, the grumpy, hard-bitten but good-hearted Sam Vimes. Through a great many subsequent novels these two groups, the witches of the countryside under Esme Weatherwax, and the City Watch under Vimes, constellate a series of deeply funny, absorbing, properly fantastical, sharply intelligent and deep-hearted stories. Sometimes Pratchett hangs a story on the hook of modern 'real world' technologies coming to Ankh-Morpork, although since our planet (which, under the name 'roundworld' is also an aspect of the Discworld cosmology) operates on science and Discworld operates on magic, such things are suitably and comically adapted. For instance, *Moving Pictures* (1990) is about the invention of cinema, although the cameras and projectors used do not use chemically activated celluloid but rather miniature demons and sprites living inside the boxes. *The Fifth Elephant* (1999) parodies telegraphy, via a complicated system of semaphores and *Raising Steam* (2013) locomotives.

*Small Gods* (1992) fleshes out and actualizes the intriguing notion that divinities' magnitude and power correlate directly to how many people believe in them. *Lords and Ladies* (1993), one of Pratchett's funniest novels, also contains a beautifully nuanced representation of elves as embodiments of an uncanny, glamorous and dangerous otherness. As the series developed, Pratchett used Discworld as a lens to write about various cultures: *Pyramids* (1989) riffs on ancient Egypt – in Discworld called 'Djellibeibi' (playing at once on the British candy 'jelly babies' and the upset-stomach British colonists attributed to foreign food 'Delhi-belly'). *Interesting Times* (1994) concerns 'the Aurient', a version of Far East and *The Last Continent* (1998) Australia. Pratchett also engages in thorough-going generic appropriation: *Carpe Jugulum* (1998) has much fun with the traditions of vampire literature, *Feet of Clay* (1996) with golems and *The Wee Free Men* (2003) pixies.

It is hard to convey Prachett's skill as a comic writer via quotation, since much of it depends upon a sense of timing that only works in situ. He is capable of pointed witticisms and one-liners, but his best effects happen at greater length. Here a bandit chief and his gang attempt to hold-up a carriage containing several wizards ('octarine' is 'the colour of magic', a hue not visible in our world.).

He knocked on the coach door. The windows slid down.
'I wouldn't like you to think of this as a robbery,' he said. 'I'd like you to think of it
more as a colourful anecdote you might enjoy telling your grandchildren about.'

As wizard's staff poked out. The chieftan saw the knob on the end.

'Now then,' he said pleasantly. 'I know the rules. Wizards aren't allowed to use magic against civilians except in genuine life-threatening situa—'

There was a burst of octarine light.

'Actually, it's not a rule,' said Ridcully. 'It's more of a guideline.' He turned to Ponder Stibbons. 'Interesting use of Stacklady's Morphic Resonator here, I hope you noticed.'

Ponder looked down.

The chieftain had been turned into a pumpkin although, in accordance with the rules of universal humour, he still had his hat on. [*Lords and Ladies*, 115]

After Ridcully relieves the bandit crew of their belongings (three hundred dollars; 'we're in pocket on the trip!') and the carriage rolls away, the pumpkin 'develops a mouth'. The spell will wear off in a few hours. 'Roll me into the shade, will you?' the chieftan orders his men. 'And no one say anything about this ever again.'

There are signs of the sheer joyful energy of Pratchett's comic and fantastical invention waning in the later books, but the series as a whole remains a monument to the capacity of fantasy to enchant the world, and a testament to the capacity of laughter to achieve precisely that. At the same time, and though it might look on its face like a mere contradiction in terms, Pratchett is a deeply serious comic writer. Above his moral vision animates his novels with something approaching greatness. He was a moral writer above all, before he was a comic one, before he was a worldbuilder, or a creator of character, or a popular metaphysician about gods or existence or death or anything like that; important though all those elements were to his writing. Nor can his moral purpose, and his anger, be separated out. As *Wyrd Sisters* notes of Granny Weatherwax:

Granny Weatherwax was often angry. She considered it one of her strong points. Genuine anger was one of the world's greatest creative forces. But you had to learn how to control it. That didn't mean you let it trickle away. It meant you dammed it, carefully, let it develop a working head, let it drown whole valleys of the mind and then, just when the whole structure was about to collapse, opened a tiny pipeline at the base and let the iron-hard stream of wrath power the turbines of revenge. [*Wyrd Sisters*, 198]

Granny Weatherwax's ethical philosophy, as articulated in *Carpe Jugulum* (1998) – 'sin is when you treat people as things. Including yourself. That's what sin is' – is essentially a restatement of Immanuel Kant's ethical philosophy. Kant grounded his ethics in the idea that we must always treat other people as ends in themselves, and never as means to an end. It might, I suppose, look wrongheaded to call Pratchett's ethics 'Kantian'. Kant's most famous moral concept is his 'categorical imperative': act only according to that maxim whereby you can, at the same time, will that it should become a universal law. Perhaps calling him Kantian does a sort of violence to Pratchett's ethical vision. We could, for instance, argue that the most Kantian, in the sense of the most universalizing, creatures in all of Discworld are the Auditors of Reality. These beings first appear in *Reaper Man* (1991), where we're told they 'see to it that gravity operates and that time stays separate from space' (and where we learn they have conversations with one another without speaking: 'they didn't need to speak. They just changed reality so that they had spoken'). The Auditors hate mess and unpredictability and they particularly hate life because it is messy and unpredictable. They would much prefer a cosmos made up of lifeless balls of rock circling stars in mathematically predictable orbits. Indeed, they would like to eliminate humanity, although they can't simply do so because it is 'against the Rules' (the Auditors can't break the Rules because, in a certain sense, they *are* the Rules). They can use proxies, though, and do so to try and extirpate the messiness of life. This drives the plots in *Hogfather* (1996), where they try to eliminate the titular Santa-Claus-alike because he's so messy and irrational, and *Thief of Time* (2001), where their plan is to stop time and so deprive humanity of its necessary element. In terms of sheer dedication to this mass genocide, the Auditors are perhaps the most evil characters in the Pratchettverse, although in fact we're told that they lack the imagination to be truly evil.

But this analysis, I'd argue, misrepresents Kant, and so misses something crucial about Pratchett's moral vision. It's true that for Kant morality must be derived by what he calls pure practical reason; that is, it can't be based on the selfish or partial reasons people might come up with for their actions, what he calls 'dependent incentives'. Pure reasoning chooses actions because those actions are good in themselves; good without any ulterior justification, good because derivative of transcendental law. But if that sounds inhuman, it shouldn't. Kant argues this not because he wants to subordinate human will to some tyrannical universal necessity, but on the contrary because this seems to him the only way to ensure that individual people treat other individual people as ends in themselves, rather than as means to an end. We can put it this way: morality is the business of deciding which actions are permissible and which are impermissible. When you make a choice to act, you are in effect indicating you believe what you are doing to be permissible. If you steal, then in effect you're giving permission to others to steal from you. If you kill another person, then you're giving permission to others to kill you. The ethical imperative is a reciprocal rather than an absolute frame, and by universalizing this individual reciprocity, Kant gives it rational and categorical force. And the sheer rational force of acting ethically is something to which Pratchett often returns. In *Maskerade* (1995), Weatherwax reminisces:

> There was a wicked ole witch once called Black Aliss. She was an unholy terror. There's never been one worse or more powerful. Until now. Because I could spit in her eye and steal her teeth, see. Because she didn't know Right from Wrong, so she got all twisted up, and that was the end of her. The trouble is, you see, that if you do know Right from Wrong, you can't choose Wrong. You just can't do it and live. So if I was a bad witch I could make Mister Salzella's muscles turn against his bones and break them where he stood ... if I was bad. I could do things inside his head, change the shape he thinks he is, and he'd be down on what had been his

knees and begging to be turned into a frog … if I was bad. I could leave him with a mind like a scrambled egg, listening to colors and hearing smells … if I was bad. Oh yes'. There was another sigh, deeper and more heartfelt. 'But I can't do none of that stuff. That wouldn't be Right. [*Maskerade*, 123]

Choice seems much less open-ended when you think rationally about right and wrong. Weatherwax does not claim to have all the answers, but she does understand that 'right' is not the same thing as 'nice', and that doing the right thing very rarely coincides with doing the popular thing. That's the main plot of *Witches Abroad* (1991), in fact. Indeed, it's the main plot of many of Pratchett's novels.

Pratchett's strongest characters, in the sense of most memorable, most loved, and most often the bellwethers for the novels' ethical dramas, are also his strongest characters in terms of ego. 'Granny Weatherwax was not lost', we're told in *Wyrd Sisters*. 'She wasn't the kind of person who ever became lost. It was just that, at the moment, while she knew exactly where *she* was, she didn't know the position of anywhere else.' That's both funny, and a neat piece of characterization, although it describes the sort of person we might find rather alarming in real life. Sam Vimes has some of this quality, too: a grounded, or centred, sense of his own grasp on right versus wrong, whatever other insecurities or insufficiencies he might admit to. And Tiffany Aching, despite her youth, likewise. The 'ego' here means: Pratchett's fondness for strongly rendered, pungent and memorable and positive characters. The really telling thing, I think, is how rarely he does the opposite: how undersupplied the Discworld books are with full-on moustache-twirling melodramatic villains. That's sometimes seen as a problem. Amanda Craig argues that Pratchett supplies 'a lifelong source of pleasure and happiness', but, she thinks, 'this comes at the price of not showing us "the darkness"'.

> There is a bullying father here, and spite and sudden death, but none of it disturbs. Other great fantasy authors from Tolkien to Robin Hobb leave us in no doubt that the torture, rape and murder in their worlds, described in chilling detail, are real and terrible, like the lust for power and sex that inspires them: but the filth of the city of Ankh-Morpork is down to dirt and poor plumbing. We are so used to the way George RR Martin or Joe Abercrombie or even Ursula le Guin show us fantasy worlds riven with cruelty, that perhaps the kindliness of Discworld is more subversive than it seems. It is, in essence, a humanist's creation in which laughter, as Nabokov said, is the best pesticide, and humour as potent as swords.[17]

The strength of Pratchett's writing is the way he grounds his fantasy in this strategy of ethically universalizing the moral particular. Rather than seeing Kant's categorical imperative as a top-down quasi-tyrannical imposition of moral order on the universe, we could see it as exactly the opposite. After all, it takes as axiomatic that nobody is

---

[17]Craig, '*The Shepherd's Crown*: review', *The Guardian* (30 August 2015).

outside the moral world – that is to say, it fundamentally repudiates one of the oldest moral fix-ups in human history, the one where the world is divided into 'us', who deserve to be treated ethically, and 'them', the outgroup, the Others who fall outside of the protection of justice, and can be treated in ways beyond the ambit of morals. Kant isn't having that, and neither is Pratchett. This manifests, for Pratchett, in a refusal to take the dramatically easy way of demonizing one or other outgroup. Really, nobody is beyond the pale in Discworld. No group is demonized, actual demons least of all. This same impulse manifests for Kant in an ethical rule that obtains categorically, not only to those like us, or whom we like. One final point is worth making here: Pratchett's strategy for communicating ethically with his readers was fundamentally story-based: he tells us stories, and we are amused, and intrigued, and moved, and in that process we are called-forth into actualized ethical situations, made to think through the business of what it means to act well and to act badly, to consider consequences and otherness and so on. I suppose it's true that actual Kantian moral philosophers are thin on the ground nowadays, but one of the most important and celebrated interventions into ethical thought of the last ten years or so was Barbara Herman's *Moral Literacy* (2008), which is not only thoroughly Kantian, but which explores how morals are a mode of existential literacy, something we learn and practice, and something for which stories are the ideal mode. Herman doesn't discuss Pratchett, but she could easily have done. Doing the right thing, Pratchett says, over and over, is not a passionless matter of obeying an inhuman universal duty; it is always particular, always passionate, and above all always funny.

## Commodified fantasy

The books discussed above, though all notable, are not necessarily characteristic of the main current of fantasy publication during the 1980s and 1990s. A great many series of fantasy novels were published across these years, and most were derivative and imitative books, re-presenting the Tolkienian figures and fittings in commodified form: extruded fantasy product rather than genuinely written fiction. Nonetheless, many of these books were bestsellers, their commercial success speaking to the existence of a large audience of fantasy fans eager for precisely such product. The mismatch of success and quality is in itself interestingly indicative of a wider cultural logic, but it has a particular valence for fantasy: readers chasing 'enchantment' in amongst increasingly reified and repetitive-iterative copies of copies. Looking back in 2001 over what had happened to fantasy over the thirty years since *A Wizard of Earthsea*, Ursula Le Guin noted:

> Commodified fantasy takes no risks: it invents nothing but imitates and trivialises. It proceeds by depriving the old stories of their intellectual and ethical complexity, turning their action to violence, their actors to dolls, and their truth-telling to sentimental platitudes. Heroes brandish their swords, lasers, wands, as mechanically as combine harvesters, reaping profits. Profoundly disturbing moral choices are sanitized, made cute, made safe. The passionately conceived ideas of the great

storytellers are copied, stereotyped, reduced to toys, moulded in bright-colored plastic, advertised, sold, broken, junked, replaceable, interchangeable. What the commodifiers of fantasy count on and exploit is the insuperable imagination of the reader, child or adult, which gives even these dead things life – of a sort, for a while.[18]

Piers Anthony's Xanth series, starting with *A Spell for Chameleon* (1977) is ongoing: the forty-seventh title, *Apoca Lips* was published in 2023 and more are to come, with the conveyer-belt regularity of an iterated product. Xanth is a realm powered by magic, promiscuously supplied with all the figures of fantasy and fairy tale: dragons, centaurs, witches, demons, magicians, harpies, zombies, nymphs, ogres, pixies, fairies and talking animals. Every citizen has one particular spell that only they can cast, although in *A Spell for Chameleon* it seems that humble village boy Bink lacks this ability. But in fact he is destined for greatness, and access to world-changing magical potency, his quest to uncover his powers of enchantment comprising the story of the book. In the follow-up, *The Source of Magic*, the King of Xanth sends Bink on a quest to discover where the land's magic actually comes from.

The early Xanth novels are inventive and colourful, whimsical and fast moving, aimed at middle grade readers and full of puns. Indeed in Xanth puns are actualities, not merely stylistic drolleries: foldings together of magical possibility. Everything is alive in Xanth, except the storytelling: for the longer the series has gone on the deader and more repetitive they have become, and the punning becomes more and more grating (eighteenth-century wit John Dennis's 'he that would pun, would pick a pocket'). The titles alone warn us off: *Centaur Aisle* (1982), *Heaven Cent* (1988), *Roc and a Hard Place* (1995), *Faun & Games* (1997), *Knot Gneiss* (2010). More, the sexual politics of the books has drawn justifiable ire. Women are sexually objectified throughout, rape and sexual assault are common and presented as no big deal, male characters lust after underage girls with impunity. The titular heroine of the first novel Chameleon is defined, as per the magic logic of Xanth, by her one magic ability: every month she transforms, on a cycle tied to her menses, from a clever but ugly woman to a beautiful but very low-IQ one. In the story she hopes – at least, when in her intelligent-but-ugly phase (for her beautiful incarnation manifests such mental retardation as not to be in any sense a thinking person) – to find magic that will even out the cycle, leaving her moderately clever and moderately beautiful. But Bink persuades her that he loves her as is, because it affords him the opportunity for greater variety than would a conventional monogamous relationship – although he only has sex with her when she is physically beautiful and has the mind of a child. The novel sees nothing wrong with this, by definition, non-consensual relationship. This sexism reaches a nadir in *The Color of Her Panties* (1992), a book that quite lives up, or down, to its wince-inducing title: Mela Merwoman's panties are often on display, because she has inadvertently gotten dressed in a 'Freudian slip', an

---

[18]Le Guin, *Tales from Earthsea* (2001), xii-xiii.

undergarment that repeatedly embarrasses its wearer. In later Xanth books the underage girls and sexism are toned down, and Anthony has reacted defensively to accusations at the books' sexual inappropriatenesses. The titles trudge through their annual or biannual appearance, diminishing their returns.

Scottish writer Michael Scott Rohan's 'Winter of the World' series – two trilogies, the expansion of which was interrupted by the author's illness and death [*The Anvil of Ice* (1986); *The Forge in the Forest* (1987); *The Hammer of the Sun* (1988); *The Castle of the Winds* (1998); *The Singer and the Sea* (1999); *Shadow of the Seer* (2001)] – are set in an icebound, pseudo-Norse world. Young Alva-Elof, orphaned when pseudo-Vikings raid his town, becomes an apprentice blacksmith and learns to craft magical weaponry. The storytelling takes him on adventures in all the various locations identified in the generic map with which each volume is supplied, rising in importance and the myth of Wayland's Smithy is reinhabited and retold.

Terry Goodkind's 'The Sword of Truth' comprises twenty-one lengthy novels in which an improbably omnicompetent, handsome and upstanding forest ranger, Richard Cypher, wielding the magic sword of the series' title, fights the evil tyrant Darken Rahl so as to prevent him and his minions taking over the generic Fantasyland world. Richard is in love with the beautiful female magician Kahlan Amnell, and she with him, but a magic curse means that men who have sex with Kahlan die immediately, so the two lovers cannot be together. The first volume, *Wizard's First Rule* (1994), is indicative of the whole series: a stew of fantasy clichés rendered into dreary, flabby prose: quest, monsters, wizards, fights, this and that, plus the element that Goodkind adds, to make his book stand out from the rest of the fantasy crowd: a great deal of sexualized torture and violence. Partway on his quest Richard is captured by a wicked 'Mord-Sith' called Denna. She is a sexual sadist and tortures him for hundreds of pages, all described in painstaking and indeed painsgiving detail. Torture is designed to break Richard. Richard is unbroken. Later in the story a different Mord-Sith tries to rape Kahlan. She overcomes him with her magic, then cuts off his testicles and makes him eat them. We might call this 'Grimdark', but that's not really the flavour of the novel: for the world of the text is otherwise entirely derivative of lighter, more brightly coloured prior fantasy writing, Richard and Kahlan are utterly upstanding, righteous, uncynical; 'good' and 'evil' are distinct, exteriorized qualities in this world: there's none of Grimdark's moral grey areas, none of its realpolitik, or moral pragmatism. The violence in this novel is its own thing: it is, in point of fact, the novel's kink, the fetish of a writer at once excited and revolted by the sadistic drives he believes to be universals. Goodkind's hard right-wing political views directly inform his writing: the titular 'Wizard's First Rule' (each volume cites a different rule) is 'people are stupid'. This contempt for humanity, an Ayn-Randian disdain for the vulgar herd, the mass, the ordinary folk – you and me, that is – licences the intimately described horrors the novelist inflicts upon the 'people', and therefore the 'good' violence of men like Richard that counters it. Goodkind fans, of whom there are many, might object that I am permitting my own political views to interfere in the business of properly disinterested critical engagement, but ideology aside it must be admitted that Goodkind was a very bad writer of English prose, capable of manifold ineptnesses and prone to a level of repetition indicative of notable authorial laziness.

Not all fantasy authors were as bad at the business of writing prose as was Goodkind. Robin Hobb (the pen-name of American author Margaret Astrid Lindholm Ogden) writes well, and her fantasies are absorbing and imaginatively rich. Her 'Farseer Chronicles' [*Assassin's Apprentice* (1995), *Royal Assassin* (1996), *Assassin's Quest* (1997)] were successful enough to lead to a number of related fantasy trilogies and series, amongst them 'The Liveship Traders Trilogy' (1998–2001), the 'Tawny Man Trilogy' (2001–3) the four-volume 'Rain Wild' series (2009–13) and the 'Fitz and the Fool Trilogy' (2014–17). Set initially in and around the late-medieval realm of the Six Duchies, the series, as it continues, shifts attentions to the naval world: waterborne trade, pirates, battles, exploration and sea-serpents. In this world, in addition to regular sailships, there are 'liveships', constructed of magical 'wizardwood', which come to sentience once three generations of a ship's owners have died on board, thereby transferring their memories to the craft. Each ship has its own personality. In *Ship of Magic* (1998) the newly 'quickened' Liveship *Vivacia* must cross the perilous water of the Rain River and discover what happened to the Liveship *Paragon* – now known as the *Pariah*, after it apparently drowned its crew – which is beached blind and lonely on the river's far shore. The books are skilfully enough put-together to avoid becoming 'Thomas the Tank Engine with Ships Instead of Trains' and the (human) characters Hobbs draws are less one-dimensional-typological, and more complex and more interesting than is often the case in this mode of writing. But as the series continues the worldbuilding adds new elements and fleshes out backstory – dragons, the ancient 'Elderlings' whose magic still litters the world, the coming logics of an early modernity – with a proliferation that becomes increasingly centripetal and uncontrolled. Nor does she always balance the idioms of the pre-modern and the modern with any finesse. In *Blood of Dragons* (2013) characters exclaim 'hark!', do not or cannot use contractions like 'don't' and 'can't', and say things like 'she is like the fire inside a blue opel! Like glittering blue steel she is!' [510]; but they also drink coffee and have curtains on their windows and say things like 'good plan!' and 'don't – just don't –', chatting on like bourgeois moderns. So the dialectic of fantasy works, crudely and rather distractingly, through these novels.

Dragons remained popular throughout the decade and beyond, usually embedded in medieval stories in which humble characters grow into important figures in realms riven by magical war, as in Kate Elliot's *King's Dragon* (1997) and its many sequels, or Christopher Paolini's *Eragon* (2002), a clumsy and derivate book written when its author had yet to reach the age of majority which, published by Paolini's parents' company, proved extraordinarily popular, a success it is rather hard to link to the book's actual quality.

As a young man Guy Gavriel Kay assisted Christopher Tolkien in editing and publishing Tolkien's posthumous *Silmarillion* (1977). Kay's own writing began somewhat derivatively with his trilogy *The Fionavar Tapestry* [*The Summer Tree* (1984) *The Wandering Fire* (1986), *The Darkest Road* (1986)], a portal fantasy in which five college students, Kim, Paul, Kevin, Jennifer and Dave, travel from our America to Fionavar, 'the first of all worlds', a magical land of men, dwarfs and giants, of orcs (here called urgach) and elves, of dragons and gods. The three men and two women are summoned by a wizard called Loren Silvercloak to help battle the 'dark lord' Rakoth Maugrim and his evil hordes. Given the stakes, and the subsequent trauma and suffering the five endure (Paul is crucified upon the Yggdrasil-esque Summer Tree, Jennifer is raped and impregnated by Rakoth) the group continues to agree to leave our world for Fionavar with a surprising nonchalance. As the 'prime' world from which all others are copied, Fionavar contains not only explicit Tolkienisms but elements from Arthurian legend, and also Norse and Celtic mythologies. The whole is over-busy, everything including the fantasy-kitchen-sink thrown in, and the first two volumes swap awkwardly between real and fantasy worlds, but in the third, set entirely in Fionavar, the story achieves some climactic momentum. Towards the end Jennifer is revealed as an incarnation of Guinevere, and meets both Arthur and Lancelot. Maugrim is a god and cannot by killed, but a twist at the end, during the last battle, undoes him: a magic dagger of tremendous power, called Lökdal, can only be used to kill those one loves. Were you to use it to kill without love in your heart, you would yourself die. At the last moment in the last battle, Darien, the son of Jennifer and Rakoth Maugrim, gives his father the dagger and, whilst the dark lord is momently distracted, steps forward onto the blade, killing himself and Maugrim together. This has the form of a clever twist, but it is predicated upon a series of magical arbitrarinesses that end up simply as contradictory – for instance, that Maugrim is an unkillable immortal but that there is an artefact that can kill him. The familiar Tolkienian and fantasy elements are mostly effective, if a little exhausted; details invented by Kay are less so, and sometimes parley incongruousness into ludicrousness: for instance, adding evil swans to the army of darkness, or giving Darien the power to shoot lasers from his eyes ('he let his eyes burn as red as they could go. With this blast of fire he incinerated the swan' *The Darkest Road*, 304). Kay as author is unembarrassed by how much he owes to Tolkien, arguing that such derivativeness is inevitable: 'to be successful in fantasy', he insists, 'you have to take the measure of Tolkien – work with his strengths and away from his weaknesses'.[19] Kay's later novels have pursued a different strategy, adapting a selected historical and geographical situation into fantasy. *Tigana* (1990) is set in a fantasy version of Renaissance Italy, 'The Peninsular of the Palm' shaped roughly like a hand, rather than the Italic foot. *A Song for Arbonne* (1992) reworks the Albigensian Crusade in medieval Provence and *The Lions of Al-Rassan* (1995), set in an analogue of medieval Spain. More recent works depart from Europe: Justinian I's Byzantium is behind *Sailing to Sarantium* (1998) and *Lord of Emperors* (2000), where *Under Heaven* (2010) and its various sequels take place in a Fantasy-land version of Tang Dynasty China. In all these, actual history is mildly estranged, enchanted, and characters put through the paces of familiar fantasy plotting, questing, battling and politicking.

Married couple David and Leigh Eddings co-wrote a number of fantasy novels, 1980s and 1990s bestsellers, although (until 1995) only David's name appeared

---

[19]Quoted in David Pringle, *Modern Fantasy*, 252.

on the title pages. Their first work, the multi-volume 'Belgariad', was written as a trilogy, although the publisher Del Rey preferred to issue five slimmer rather than three fatter volumes [*Pawn of Prophecy* (1982), *Queen of Sorcery* (1982), *Magician's Gambit* (1983), *Castle of Wizardry* (1984), *Enchanters' End Game* (1984)]. This is by-the-numbers fantasy that owes much to the Eddings' reading of Tolkien.[20] We follow journey of a young farm boy, Garion, who rises to greatness when caught up in the battle between good and evil that is ravaging his cod-medieval land, and which has to do with certain magic orbs created by the gods at the beginning of time. These magic balls, each containing a soul, are being fought over, with the evil god Torak commanding his army recruited from 'the monstrous races'. The novels open with a summary of these events, written in *Silmarillion*-pastiche ('the evil God Torak … used the Orb to break the earth asunder and let in the sea, and the Orb burned him horribly and he fled into Mallorea') but the novels themselves are written in a meat-and-potatoes discursive style, modern-sounding dialogue, plain accounts of action and repetitive descriptions of place that speak to a hurriedness of composition and a careless absence of revision.

> The shape of the city perched atop the crag began to emerge. The walls were as black as the sides of the pinnacle, and black turrets jutted out from them, seemingly at random. Dark spires rose within the walls. There was a foreboding, evil air about the black city of the Grolims. It perched, brooding, atop its peak. [Eddings, *Magicians Gambit* (1983), 268]

Early in his adventures Garion meets Belgarath the Sorcerer, a seven-thousand-year-old individual known as 'the Eternal Man'. The series is, confusingly, not named after him, but instead after the name Garion assumes when he himself becomes king: Belgarion.

For many, the 'clean' flavour of the *Belgariad* novels is central to their appeal: simple prose, clear-cut divisions of good and evil, a forward-moving plot, no explicit sex or excessive violence. The happy family life portrayed at the start of *Pawn of Prophecy* exists to provide something valuable for the forces of evil to threaten and so to set the narrative stakes, but it is also appealing on its own terms. The sense the books dramatize, of decency being threatened by vast, demonic forces of wickedness, takes on a peculiar force when we understand that both the Eddings spent time in prison for child abuse. Gifford's *Modernist Fantasy* treats David Eddings serious as an academic Modernist and reads the *Belgariad* and other Eddings' fantasy writing as informed in part by his own academic work on High Modernism. Reflecting on his subsequent discovery of the Eddings child abuse, Gifford wrote:

---

[20]Eddings later expressed disdain for 'Papa Tolkien' and claimed that he only imitated him out of commercial exigency. Having 'doodled' a first draft of the *Belgariad* in the 1970s he abandoned it: 'years later I was in a bookstore … and spotted one of the volumes of *The Lord of the Rings*. I muttered "is this old turkey still floating around?" Then I picked it up and noticed that it was in its *seventy-eighth* printing!! That got my immediate attention and I went back home and dug out the aforementioned doodle' [Eddings, *The Riven Codex*, 11].

Eddings' *Belgariad* novels … earned millions, tens of millions during his fantasy writing career. Those books are also symptomatic. They depict an idyllic childhood, serenely innocent children, a woman like his wife who experiences her happiest moments in life while gently holding a child, there's a direct juxtaposition of his own alter-ego in the books and an abuser, and a failed marriage saved by the birth of a son, and the tremendous gentleness this awakens in his parents. In short, I now read Eddings' later fantasy novels as an impossible attempt at atonement, a desperately failed wish put to paper, and a tortuously painful digging out of his and his wife's shame.[21]

The biggest 'classic Fantasy' sequence of the decade was Robert Jordan's *The Wheel of Time*, the first volume of which, *The Eye of the World*, was published in 1990. Originally planned as a trilogy, commercial success, and Jordan's self-indulgence, extended the work across eleven volumes. Jordan's fantasyland is a retread of Middle Earth: the 'third age' of a quasi-European landscape divided between bourgeois societies and older pre-modern ones, a great city 'of the White Tower' instead of Minas Tirith and a Volcanic 'Mount Dhoom'. There are humble folk living in small villages menaced by sinister dark riders and trollish orcs, here called 'trollocs'. There are colour-coded wizard castes, blue, white, brown, grey and so on, including 'Black Ajahs' who serve the dark lord. As in Tolkien the world is caught in a great war between the forces of evil, led by 'the Dark One' and the forces of good. For the sake of variation, Jordan rings some superficial changes: for example, his wizards are exclusively women, the truth-telling 'Aes Sedai'. And despite some medieval touches, the pseudo-historical period is Early Modern European, into which orientalized dangers intrude. The books elaborate its global 'magic system' at great length and complexity, with many rules and exceptions, magical artefacts, portals, prophesies and the like, although this horror vacui systematization is not nearly as effective as the non-systematic, broader brush gestures towards the magical sublime we find in Tolkien. In Jordan's world magic is a kind of standing-reserve, an aquifer that can be tapped by various people, deriving ultimately from the One Power that turns the mighty wheel of existence from which the series takes its title – but with this hitch, that although women (or: some women) can access this magic without compromising themselves, when men do so it inevitably drives them mad and turns them to evil. The novels also give us a pseudo-militia called 'the Children of the Light' who, like New England Puritans, have taken opposition to the Evil One to self-defeatingly extremist, fundamentalist lengths, and who kill all Aes Sedai they encounter as, in effect, witches. Later volumes add-in an invading Eastern civilization, the Seanchan: fleshed-out in greater detail than Tolkien's Southrons, though just as orientalized: a horde of mysterious, inscrutable folk from the east who are offhandedly violent, untrustworthy, fanatically devoted to their leader and bent on world domination.

The novel's gender-swapped Gandalf, Moiraine and her Strider-like warrior companion al'Lan Mandragoran come to the distant village of Edmond's Field. Here the

---

[21]James Gifford, 'On Reading Monsters'.

main characters are living a humble life: young Rand al-Thor, a sheep farmer, and his friend Thom (rather than Sam) together with their friends Mat and Perrin (not Merry and Pippin). The village is attacked by trollocs and dark riders. Moraine, who believes one of this group is the prophesied 'dragon reborn', the hero who will lead the battle against the Dark Lord, hurries them away to safety, along with a young girl with healing powers called Nynaeve and a young lupine-shapeshifter called Perrin. From here the adventures spool out at immense length, characters travel all over the map (with which each volume is of course supplied), separate, reunite. Some narrative tension is provided in *The Eye of the World* (1990) by a studied uncertainty as to which of the various friends actually is 'the dragon reborn', although this is resolved by the end of the book (it is Rand).

The hook, here, is of ordinary young people 'levelling up' into greater power and importance, a naturally appealing fantasy for young readers. With each of the first few volumes our point-of-view characters gain in status and magical potency until the achieve world-saving importance and cosmic valence. This, though, is achieved after only a few volumes, where the story's denouement was delayed for more than a dozen chunky instalments. This hyper-extended narrative plateau, this endless recapitulation and treacly slow-down of pace, is amongst the most extraordinary in contemporary fiction. Volume 2 *The Great Hunt* (1990) introduces a magic horn (of greater potency than the one Boromir blows) and stages an encounter between Rand and one of his nemeses, Ba'alzamon. This diabolical individual informs Rand 'I shall destroy you to your very soul, destroy you utterly and forever … do you not know I can destroy you utterly? Die worm!' As he stabs him with a staff, Rand reciprocates with a knife. The writing strains for an intensity that is beyond Jordan's skills: 'Rand screamed. Ba'alzamon screamed and the dark behind him screamed' [Jordan, *The Great Hunt*, 666]. Neither individual is killed, so the combat can be restaged in *The Dragon Reborn* (1991). Elements from Arthurian legend and Wagnerian opera ('the Maidens of the spear') are inserted. Ba'alzamon presides over his evil minions like a Bond villain disposing of unsatisfactory underlings:

> 'You have been given tasks. Some of these tasks you have carried out. Others you have failed. You!' … The man screamed and began to quiver like a file struck against an anvil. [*Dragon Reborn*, 411]

Boingg! With *The Shadow Rising* (1992) the momentum of the series begins a pronounced deceleration. As individual volumes grow longer (some are over a thousand pages) less and less actually happens to move the narrative onwards. Instead characters are shuffled about, fixtures, fittings and costumes are described at enormous length, women tug on their braids and adjust their skirts. The impending final battle between the Dark Lord and the Dragon Reborn is continually deferred. In the seventh volume *A Crown of Swords* (1996) a parching drought afflicts the world, which can only be ameliorated with a magic bowl. Nynaeve, Elayne and Mat go looking for this bowl, which they finally find at the end of volume 8, *The Path of Daggers* (1998) – otherwise the story treads water for one and a half thousand pages. In *Winter's Heart* (2000) the story freezes altogether, as winter grips the land, and nothing happens. Towards the end Rand, the Dragon reborn, manages to 'cleanse' the reservoir of magic, known as 'saidin', such that men, previously unable to access it without going mad, can now do so. But, to quote an earlier study, though 'the cleansing of saidin is "the big event" of the novel'

> actually it is not an event at all. It is on the contrary a kind of un-event. What is 'cleansed' in this interminable text is *narrative itself*: drama, plot, narrative interest … the *Wheel of Time* series, despite launching itself with conventional narrative stylings, increasingly sheds it narrative momentum as it goes on. Each volume covers less ground, goes slower, dissipated so-called 'narrative interest' in a welter of pointless details and endlessly proliferating characters. What Debord calls 'neosemioticist narrative' replaces sequential developmental progression with a frozen constellation of semiological placeholders.[22]

Nonetheless, the longer the series went on the more popular it became. It has, as of 2023, sold 100 million copies worldwide, and been adapted into comic books, a collectible card game, into both video and roleplaying games, and latterly has been restaged as a hugely expensive ongoing set of television series, produced by Sony Pictures and Amazon Studios (2021-present). The books have legions of dedicated fans. Of course familiarity has a value; readers aware of the books' deep derivativeness are not discouraged by it, and readers who had never before read a fantasy novel connect at second hand, in Jordanian-diluted form, with at least something of the splendour of the original material Jordan is appropriating. Once a book-series achieves the momentum very large sales provide, that momentum will tend to carry the sequence through to the end, even in the teeth of deteriorating quality, not least because readers are by now invested in finding out what happens. The first few volumes are fairly good, and the later volumes are very bad indeed, but having read those earlier volumes readers will be motivated to swallow the badness and continue. But perhaps the truth is something else. American critic David Moles suggests that what fans take pleasure in is the very vast, intricate *repetitiveness* the series provides:

> you don't find that level of mechanical complexity very often outside of a role-playing supplement … you can't dismiss the trainspotting, stamp-collecting aspect [of the books], the sheer plethora of implied, distinct collectable figurines and playsets, the number of possible 'which would win in a fight, X or Y?' matchups. I'm not sure there's anything in print fiction to match it.[23]

Manifestly the stylistic inadequacies of these books, their vastness, derivate repetitiveness, do not discourage millions of fans from imaginatively playing in the imaginative theme

---

[22]Roberts, *Sibilant Fricative*, 256.
[23]Quoted in ibid, 267–8.

parks they represent: a wish-fulfilment world more colourful than our own, furnishing an idealized nostalgic past that does not deprive us of present-day bourgeois creature-comforts, parlayed through honest-to-goodness melodramatic emotional intensity.

On Jordan's death only eleven volumes of a promised twelve had been completed. The estate retained American author Brandon Sanderson – no stranger to immensely long fantasy composition, in which cardboard characters jostle through massively elaborate magic-systems and derivative Fantasylands – to write the final missing volume, which exercise he completed in not one but three corpulent volumes: *The Gathering Storm* (2009), *Towers of Midnight* (2010) and *A Memory of Light* (2013). Such story as inhabits these books does not need two and a half thousand pages to work itself Out. The best that can be said is that Sanderson's dissipating episodic prolixity is slightly less enervatingly prolonged than Jordan's. The series does, at least, come to an end.


## Pullman

But though Jordan's was the 'biggest' fantasy of the 1990s, it was neither the best nor the most important. That was Philip Pullman's *His Dark Materials* [*Northern Lights* (1995; published as *The Golden Compass* in North America), *The Subtle Knife* (1997), and *The Amber Spyglass* (2000)]: a beautifully written, superbly imagined, wonderfully immersive trilogy, powerfully engaged with the core storying of fantasy. Its invention is macaronic, but creatively rather than derivatively so, using the vehicle of multiple dimensions, through which the main characters travel, to assemble a wide range of fantastical types and figures, together with elements from the Western, from the realist novel and from science fiction. There are talking polar animals, witches, ghosts, angels, various kinds of monster and bizarre life forms – like the elephantine 'mulefa' who, in a nod to the 'wheelers' from Baum's *Oz* books, move around on foot-mounted wheels.

*Northern Lights* opens in an alternate version of Oxford, a steampunk realm of elegantly crafted machinery and zeppelins, where university dons are people of power and influence. There is a caricature version of the Catholic Church, 'the Magisterium', which rules according to a repressive logic. The book's hero, Lyra Belacqua, is a young girl growing up under the care of the University. Pullman loves Oxford, and its alt-Edwardian bourgeois comforts and securities are the 'Shire' from which Lyra must leave to have her adventures, a quest that progresses her through different lands to the sublimities of frozen north. The first volume's titular northern lights are, in this universe, manifestations of a cosmic ectoplasm, called 'Dust', that informs and enmagics the world.

In the world of the novel everybody has a 'daemon', a sort of exterior soul – not that person's soul as such, for the individual him- or herself retains subjectivity and intelligence, and yet an emanation of the individual. These daemons are bestial manifestations. A child's daemon swaps its shape between many different types of animal, although at puberty the daemon's form fixes, such that the nature of a person's daemon tells you something integral about that person: an individual of notable bravery might have a lion as daemon, a fundamentally devious person might have a snake and so on. Daemons have material as well as spiritual existence, and can roam away from their people, although only within a limited circumference. The novel's focus is on the child's experience of this companion: a magical literalization of the imaginary friend many children invent for themselves, superintelligent independent animal pet.

At first Lyra believes herself an orphan, though she later realizes that two powerful antagonistic adults, the handsome Lord Asriel, warrior-don of Jordan College Oxford, and the beautiful but villainous Marisia Coulter, are actually her father and mother. Mrs Coulter has developed a torturous technology that can sever a child's daemon, leaving the subject in effect lobotomized. There is also a mystery associated with the particulate substance 'Dust'. The Magisterium teaches that Dust is the source of sin, but Mrs Coulter (drawing on Lord Asriel's research) realizes that it is a powerful emanation from and creator of conscious life, a kind of spiritual radiative fundamental. Her cruel surgery, separating daemons from their people, is performed in order to access and control Dust, for her own uses.

In the second book *The Subtle Knife* the action shifts to our world, and Pullman introduces the second of his deuteragonists: a young English boy called Will Parry. In this realm Dust is studied as dark matter. Various characters from the first book are able to cross over from the 'Brytain' of *Northern Lights* and back. Will acquires the titular knife, which can open a portal between worlds, and so meets Lyra. The two become companions and ultimately fall in love, although the trilogy does not give them the satisfaction of a pay-off in which they can be together. A third parallel universe is introduced, a spectacular Italianate city by the sea called Cittàgazze, into which Lyra and Will stumble – this place is void of adults, who have all been preyed upon by Spectres who, by devouring their daemons, kill them, although these Spectres do not attack (and are invisible to) children. Cittàgazze is a kind of crossroads of alternate realities, from where the story moves into other realms: although it is revealed that Spectres are generated by the creation of the subtly knifed portals that permit such travel in the first place.

These are novels deeply engaged in the core activation of fantasy: the passage from materialist bourgeois modernity to an enchanted alterity, the process of history and the liquidization of the religious. As far as this last thing is concerned, an anti-religious address runs hotly through the writing, a critique of organized religion as oppressive of human happiness and retrogressive on human development and a wider animadversion to God as such. Pullman's Magisterium has no redeeming features. Early in *Northern Lights* a witch (witches in this universe are uniformly virtuous) asserts: 'every church is the same: control, destroy, obliterate every good feeling.' And that *every church* is the increasing focus of the books. Pullman's apparent anti-Catholicism reveals itself, as the series goes on, as a less sectarian anti-Christianity (in his fantasy version of Europe a historical 'Pope John Calvin' moved the heart of the church from Rome to Geneva, keeping the faith from splitting in two) and, then, an absolutist anti-theism.

In *Amber Spyglass* Lyra and Will pass from realm to realm and through Hell itself until they finally encounter the evil god – Metatron, also known as Enoch – who (as in gnostic theology) rules the universe. Lord Asriel and a reformed Mrs Coulter have followed their daughter on this journey and they sacrifice themselves in order to drag Metatron into the abyss. After this Lyra and Will discover the original God, 'the Authority', whose power had been usurped by his regent Metatron, and who has been trapped thereafter in a magical crystal. In a strange scene, the two adolescents in-effect unplug this ailing deity from his life-support, letting him die and freeing the universe from theology altogether. 'He must be so old', says Lyra. 'I've never seen anyone suffering like that – oh Will, can't we let him out?'

> Will cut through the crystal in one movement and reached in to help the angel out. Demented and powerless, the aged being could only weep and mumble in fear and pain and misery, and he shrank away from what seemed like yet another threat. 'It's all right', Will said. The shaking hand seized his and feebly held on. The old one was uttering a wordless groaning whimper that went on and on, and grinding his teeth, and compulsively plucking at himself with his free hand; but as Lyra reached in, too, to help him out, he tried to smile, and to bow, and his ancient eyes deep in their wrinkles blinked at her with innocent wonder … His form began to loosen and dissolve. Only a few moments later he had vanished completely, and their last impression was of those eyes, blinking in wonder, and a sigh of the most profound and exhausted relief. [*The Amber Spyglass*, 367]

This denouement, together with Pullman's public assertions of his own atheism, not to mention his anticlerical reimagining of the passion, *The Good Man Jesus and the Scoundrel Christ* (2000), has given the trilogy the reputation as an anti-religious tract. Alan Jacobs praises the books (Pullman, he says, has 'prodigious skills as a storyteller; in imagination and narrative drive, he has few peers among current novelists') but registers disappointment 'at how often, in *The Amber Spyglass*, the tale's momentum is interrupted by polemical anti-theistic scolding'.

> Decent, compassionate folk regularly denounce religion and God, while the monsters who run the Church utter scarcely a word in their own defense – just to make sure that no reader comes to a conclusion Pullman doesn't want. Pullman the storyteller has also been cheated – by Pullman the village atheist. Powerful alternative versions of the biblical narrative can only be told by people who are passionately theological: Pullman invokes Milton and Blake as his models, but he could scarcely be less like them. Pullman's oft-professed materialism and anti-supernaturalism clash not only with Milton but still more with Blake, who, when he looked at the sun, saw not 'a round disk about the size of a guinea' but 'a multitude of the heavenly host crying Holy, Holy, Holy is the Lord God Almighty.'[24]

---

[24]Jacobs, 'The Devil's Party'.

Jacobs is not alone in his animadversion, and is more generous with his praise of Pullman's skills than some. But a point is being missed here. In the way Tolkien's *Lord of the Rings* is a 'profoundly Catholic work' not despite but *because* it itself contains no churches, temples, priests or religious rituals, so *His Dark Materials* is not an anti-religious text although it often, especially in its last volume, indulges in anti-clerical rant and atheist militancy. What makes the trilogy sing, what brings it alive, is its openness to the wondrous. It is, like many classic fantasy novels, fascinated with the relationship between transportative pre-modern religious subjectivities and 'buffered' modern bourgeois sensibilities; its case against the church – as sexually prudish, using concepts of sin to oppress and harm people, as prideful and overmighty – is not an attack on the transcendent wonder and magic of the pre-modern world in which that church was dominant, but on the contrary on the uses of domineering political power characteristic of buffered modernity. Suffusing throughout is 'Dust', the particulation of transcendence itself. Pullman suggests his 'Dust' is a metaphor, but saying so does not detranscendtalize it. Fantasy as such is a metaphorical literature, because it aims to represent the world without reproducing it. Late in the story, an angel explains the nature of Dust, and the history of the cosmos's Divinity, to Lyra:

> Balthamos said quietly, 'The Authority, God, the Creator, the Lord, Yahweh, El, Adonai, the King, the Father, the Almighty – those were all names he gave himself. He was never the creator. He was an angel like ourselves – the first angel, true, the most powerful, but he was formed of Dust as we are, and Dust is only a name for what happens when matter begins to understand itself ... The first angels condensed out of Dust, and the Authority was the first of all. He told those who came after him that he had created them, but it was a lie'. [*The Amber Spyglass*, 28]

That the universe is not the handiwork of a creator God does not mean that the universe is not wondrous. On the contrary, Pullman's cosmos is immanent with magic and wonder. 'Dust is only a name', perhaps; but in the New Testament God is only a word, the Λόγος (logos), out of which are made worlds, and books, both. Christian critic Tony Watkins reads Pullman's trilogy against the grain of its manifest hostility to 'the Church' to uncover a latent work of deep-dyed spiritual positivity.[25] Watkins considers Pullman a 'dualist'. I would go further: Dust is *Geist*, and the whole of *His Dark Materials* is enspirited.

There is also the question of sex. After the death of God, Lara and Will, in a reformed Edenic situation, sexually consummate their relationship. But it is the nature of the multiverse Pullman has created that people can only inhabit different realities to the one in which they are born for a short time, so the two cannot remain together. More, the 'subtle knife' that cuts interdimensional portals creates demonic dust-devouring creatures every time it acts, so they are denied the chance even to meet from time to time. Pullman

---

[25]Watkins, *Dark Matter: Shedding Light on Philip Pullman's Trilogy, His Dark Materials*.

has defended this ending against complaints from his readers, who wanted a 'happy ending' for the couple: 'it's a stronger ending than if they'd stayed together, and part of the reason for its superiority to the happier ending, I think, is that it's true to the formal pattern of the whole story: things splitting apart.'[26] Jenny Turner identifies what she calls 'the three great works of modern English fantasy: Tolkien, C.S. Lewis's Narnia books and Philip Pullman's magnificent *His Dark Materials*', works that she says share a fascination with 'mortality, sex, mutability, Genesis and Revelation'. But she praises the way Pullman brings his child-characters through puberty and into adulthood, because – she argues – sex is a mode of ending, necessary to the proper mytheme of fantasy.

> In Lewis and Tolkien, the scope for sexual activity is stunted by the authors' Christian beliefs, and/or conservatism, and/or psycho-sexual hang-ups. In Pullman, on the other hand, sex is allowed to happen, and shown to bring with it enormous losses. It is also made clear, however, that it has to happen, and that it is good that it does. … when, in Pullman, sex is permitted, it is impossible to feel that soggy, yearny nostalgia you feel at the end of *The Lord of the Rings*, with Frodo and pals passing through the curtain of rain, or at the end of Lewis's *The Last Battle*, with poor old Narnia dark and broken and Susan, with her disgusting lipstick and her nylons, shut out. Sex happens because it has to happen: there wouldn't be much of a human race without it. And the existence of sex acts like a sentry – like Milton's cherubim at the gates of Eden – preventing you from indulging that favourite fantasy that maybe what has been done can be undone.[27]

## Angels

Pullman's engagement with the angelic was very much of its decade. Harold Bloom, *Omens of Millennium: The Gnosis of Angels, Dreams, and Resurrection* (1996) – a work of criticism rather than fiction – takes seriously the belief, which Bloom considers widespread in North America, that an angelic dimension interpenetrates our mundane one. The book is Bloom's clearest expression of the Gnostic metaphysics that have shaped his writing since his youth, and which explain his affinity for the poetry of William Blake and Percy Shelley. What makes the argument of this work so pertinent to the present study is the way it rearticulates the thesis of Weberian disenchantment, against which fantasy as a mode reacts, in, precisely, mythic-fantasy terms:

> The transcendent stranger God or alien God of Gnosticism, being beyond our cosmos, is no longer an effective force; God exists, but is so hidden that he has become a nihilistic conception, in himself. He is not responsible for our world

---

[26]Pullman, *Dæmon Voices: Essays on Storytelling*, 35.
[27]Turner, 'Reasons for Liking Tolkien'.

of death camps and schizophrenia, but he is so estranged and exiled that he is powerless. We are unsponsored, since the God of this world, worshipped (as Blake said) by the names of Jesus and Jehovah, is only a bungler, an archangel-artisan who botched the False Creation that we know as our Fall.

To find your angel is not necessarily to find yourself, though most quests for the angels seem nowadays to suppose that a guardian angel is rather more like a dog or cat than like a husband or wife. You acquire an angel in the expectation that this addition to your household will give you perpetual and unconditional love.

This dignifies and deepens what might otherwise be thought of as a mere fad, an attempt to inject some novelty into increasingly over-familiar modes. 'Angelic' fiction certainly saw a flurry of textual production in the 1990s. Pullman's great *Dark Materials* trilogy is, in a way, an example of this; as is Terry Pratchett and Neil Gaiman's *Good Omens* (1990) – this latter later turned into a doublet of BBC /Amazon TV series in 2019 and 2023. The comic richness of Pratchett enlivens Gaiman's story of a 'Revelation of St John'-style apocalypse. In the book the two 'angelic' characters (strictly one angel, Aziraphale, and one demon, Crowley, although the latter, for all his sneery posing and dressing in black, is a fundamentally good-hearted supernatural being) are secondary characters to the main story of an ordinary English kid who discovers he is the antichrist. The first TV series gave Aziraphale and Crowley much more screen time, trading off the superb chemistry of the two actors, Welshman Michael Sheen and Scot David Tennant, and the second series was almost wholly the Aziraphale and Crowley show. Their homosocial bond, by turns mutually supporting and sparkily bickering, grows in the TV adaptation (though not in the original novel) into a rather touching love story, and the various mundane issues that provide ostensible plot movement are actually merely the backdrop for this affective coming-together. Gaiman returned to angels in *Neverwhere*, a 1996 BBC TV series he wrote and co-produced and which he later novelized. Richard Mayhew, a young resident of the 'actual' London, discovers that there is an Alice-in-Wonderland 'underground' London, called London Below – much of which is subterranean, although parts are superposed upon the unnoticing world of the regular metropolis – populated by magical characters, monsters, humans who have 'fallen through the cracks' and ruled over by an angel, called (as with the rather tiresome punning naming-convention to which the story cleaves) 'The Angel Islington'. This angel harbours the secret that he was previously charged with overseeing Atlantis, a duty he spectacularly failed.

Sharon Shinn, *Archangel* (1996), the first of a lengthy and successful series, details the romance of a mortal woman, Rachel, and the archangel Gabriel. The books' notable commercial success does not reflect its literary quality. Notionally set on a distant planet, the book parleys a Biblical fetish – realms called Gaza, Bethel and Jordanna all ruled by angels, not the giant eye-studded interlocking wheels or six-headed monsters of Ezekiel, but handsome young men in sexy leather clothes. Into this world various beautiful young human women, proxies for the reader, are positioned. The sex is treated with all propriety but the eros finesses the possibility of something more sublime and transcendent. Michael Moorcock's *The War amongst the Angels* (1996), the third in a loose trilogy, brings angelic warfare into the Moorcockian 'Eternal Champion' multiverse. *Final Fantasy VII* (developed by Japanese video-game company Square, 1997) blends science-fictional and fantasy worldbuilding into its gameplay, its main antagonist, Sepiroth, is an angelic superbeing – *VIII* (1999) and *IX* (2000) soon followed, each title bigger, more capacious and more expensive than the last. More artistically substantial is David Almond *Skellig* (1998) – winner of the Whitbread Children's Book of the Year and the Carnegie Medal – in which ten-year-old Michael discovers, in his parent's garage, a creature who might be an old tramp or an angel whose wings have been amputated. The tension between real and fantastical, expertly balanced on Michael's consciousness, is beautifully worked-through.

## Harry Potter

The first of J. K. Rowling's seven 'Harry Potter' novels, *Harry Potter and the Philosopher's Stone*, appeared without fanfare in 1997. These novels would go on to become the most popular and successful fantasy works of their era. Success built as the series developed, each of the titles doing better than the previous ones: the books as a whole have sold more than 600 million copies, have been translated into eighty-four languages, and spawned a global media franchise including films, video games and a theme park north of London. The release of later volumes became, each time, a major event: bookstores opening at midnight on the day of release, fans queuing round the block, dressed as their favourite characters. Part of the reason for this is that the books appearance coincided with the rise of online forums and the internet, spaces in which fans would congregate in large numbers of discuss and enthuse over the books. Credited with 'getting kids reading again', Rowling's popularity and range are hard to overstate. For a time it felt as if nobody was reading anything else. So completely did Harry Potter references and comparisons saturate social media, that a reaction hashtag 'Read Another Book' spread across various platforms.[28] When movie adaptations of the novels began appearing in the following decade (discussed in the following chapter) Rowling's fantasy world achieved a remarkable, global cultural penetration. Fans not only read, they wrote 'Harry Potter' fan-fiction, extending the story-universe, reworking and adding. A very large amount of this has been published on the online non-profit repository 'Archive of Our Own' (often shortened to AO3).[29] The success is its own thing, a reflection of the global appeal of this Fantasyland world.

---

[28]'*Read Another Book*: a catchphrase intended to criticize people who use the Harry Potter series to compare real-world events to that of the books, frequently appearing as a hashtag in such posts across a number of social media platforms online' https://knowyourmeme.com/memes/read-another-book Accessed February 2024.

[29]The resource was established in 2008, and has grown to the point where it now has over 6 million registered uses, and hosts an astonishing 12 million distinct works of fan-writing across 60,000 fandoms, from short-stories and poems to entire novels. Currently the five most popular fandoms on the site are: *Harry Potter* (with 442,105 distinct works posted to the site), *Star Wars* (222,929), Sherlock Holmes (133,629), J R R Tolkien (94,058) and George R. R. Martin's *A Song of Ice and Fire* (84,994). That is, Rowling's seven novels have inspired the creation nearly half a million pieces of original writing [https://archiveofourown.org/media, Accessed 31 December 2023].

Harry Potter is an ordinary English boy. His parents having died when he was a baby he is being raised by his aunt and uncle, the Dursleys, who mistreat him – they force him to sleep in a cupboard under the stairs, and repeatedly denigrate him in favour of their biological son, the unpleasant and corpulent Dudley. They also keep from him his true nature, for in reality Harry's parents possessed magical powers, which Harry has inherited. In the world of the novels communities of witches and wizards live alongside ordinary non-magical human beings ('muggles'), hiding in plain sight and keeping their magical ways secret. Though her sister was a witch, Harry's aunt is not – the inheritance of magical powers being a genetically capricious matter – and she hates and fears magic, hence her horribleness to Harry. He eventually discovers his nature, and is invited to transfer from his regular English education to Hogwarts School of Witchcraft and Wizardry, an exclusive boarding school run out of a castle in the Scottish Highlands. This is where wizards and witches are educated in their various crafts, and the proper use of their powers. Harry travels to his school by train, the 'Hogwarts Express', which leaves London King's Cross from 'Platform 9¾', a departure point reached via a magic portal in the wall of the station (the actual station now has a *Harry Potter*-themed display between its actual platforms 9 and 10, at which visitors from around the world come to pose for photographs). On the way to the school, Harry meets what will become his two best friends: Ron Weasley and Hermione Grainger. Ron comes from a large family, all of whom are magical, though according to the rather inchoate economics of the magical world they are relatively poor. (Given that witches and wizards can use their wands to make pretty much anything appear, come or go, it is not obvious why any of them would be indigent. But by the logic of the story magical people do not use regular money, but rather their own unfakeable golden currency, which is kept in a special magical banking system run by goblins.) Though Hermione's parents are both unmagical muggles, she has inherited notable magical abilities.

Each of the books details a different year in Harry's time at school, the characters ageing as they go, ending the series as adults. In many ways the books are part of the tradition of English public-school writing that began with Thomas Hughes *Tom Brown's School Days* (1857) and Dean Farrar's *Eric* (1858), rehearsing many of the same story moves – although Hogwarts is a magical school, where attention is on such subjects as how to cast magical charms, mix magical potions, transfigure oneself and 'Defence against the Dark Arts'. As with this tradition much emphasis is placed on school sports: in this case a kind of airborne hockey game called 'Quidditch' in which contestants fly around on broomsticks attempting to score goals or catch a hurtling magical amulet known as a 'snitch'. In *Harry Potter and Philosopher's Stone* Harry learns the world of his school, makes friends, admires the kindly headmaster Dumbledore, fears the sinister black-clad Potions Master Snape – who had known and despised Harry's father when the two of them had been at the school a generation earlier, and who has passed his animosity across to the son – and learns the truth of his orphandom. An immensely powerful, evil wizard called Voldemort, so terrible that his name is not to be spoken, and who must euphemistically be called 'He-Who-Must-Not-Be-Named', had learned that Harry was the 'chosen one' prophesied to overthrow him. In attempting to kill baby Harry, Voldemort killed both Potter parents, his killing spell aimed at the baby ('Avada Kedavra', a twisted abracadabra) rebounding, leaving Harry with a zigzag scar on his forehead and destroying Voldemort himself.

At the end of the first novel Harry must leave his wonderful new environment and new friends to return to the Dursleys, to mundanity and misery, although with each new school year he returns to the enchantments of Hogwarts. Though access to Hogwarts happens via a magic railway-station portal, in fact we discover that fantasy beings are distributed widely through the mundane world: giants, basilisks, unicorns, hippogriffs and phoenixes, trolls, fairies, leprechauns and mermaids, ogres, ghouls and werewolves. There are many species of dragon, and a race of gigantic intelligent spiders inhabit the forest in the school grounds. The banking system is run by Semiticized goblins, and a race of subservient, though magically potent, creatures called 'house-elfs' work as a servant class. It is just that we 'muggles' do not notice this interpenetration of our mundanity by the marvellous; or if we do, witches and wizards cast spells that obliterate our memories. The books do not explain why witches and wizards seek to hide the magical elements of the world, including themselves, away from human perception. Vastly more powerful than human beings they surely have nothing to fear from us. But here we are: magic and enchantment is hidden in the interstices of our world, in a way that manifests the textual logic of fantasy as a mode.

In *Harry Potter and the Chamber of Secrets* (1998), Harry's second year at school, we learn that Voldemort has not been vanquished and is planning a magical resurrection. At the head of an army of dark wizards, 'death eaters' and myriad monsters, he could overrun the world and rule it as Dark Lord. *Harry Potter and the Prisoner of Azkaban* (1999), the best of the books, marks a shift away from the childlike, whimsical tone of the earlier two volumes, towards something more tenebrous, more seriously conceived. This book introduces 'dementors', wraith-like beings that feed on happiness, leaving their victims drained of all joy – a brilliant allegorization of the operation of depression – who act as guards of 'Azkaban', the prison in which witch and wizard malefactors are detained. One such, a psychotic murderer called Sirius Black, escapes, with a view to finding and killing Harry; although the twist in the story is that he is neither mad nor a criminal, and indeed becomes Harry's adult friend and protector. Each of the subsequent novels ramps up the cost of Voldemort's dark encroachment. At the end of *Harry Potter and the Goblet of Fire* (2000) Voldemort is reborn, and one of Harry's schoolfriends, the handsome and popular Cedric Diggory, is killed. In *Harry Potter and the Order of the Phoenix* (2003) followers of Voldemort take over Hogwarts and Sirius Black is killed; in *Harry Potter and the Half-Blood Prince* (2005) Dumbledore himself is killed, by Snape, and Harry and his friends flee the school. It transpires that Voldemort has rendered himself unkillable by distributing his soul across a number of magical artefacts, called 'horcruxes' – Latinity might suggest, *horcruces* as the correct plural of the singular *horcrux*, but Rowling chooses a different word – each of which must be located and destroyed if Voldemort's invulnerability is to be overcome. In the final novel, *Harry Potter and the Deathly Hallows* (2007), Hogwarts becomes the site of a final battle between the forces of magical good and evil, Harry is killed and not-killed, and Voldemort finally defeated.

The first three novels in this series are short, the last four very lengthy. One can, in fact, locate the moment that Rowling's extraordinary success became so effectual to the finances of her publisher Bloomsbury that no one dared tell her to edit-down her drafts, for fear that she would take her series to another press. The novels become increasingly capaciously hospitable to influence as they go on, ingurgitating all manner of prior texts: the idea of a magical school from Le Guin's Earthsea and Jill Murphy's *The Worst Witch* series of novels (1974–2018), elements from Tolkien, Lewis, Edith Nesbit, T H White, Chaucer's *Pardoner's Tale*, Elizabeth Goudge's *The Little White Horse* (1946), British folklore and many other sources. The books have been criticized on these grounds as derivative: British author A S Byatt dismissed them as a 'secondary secondary world, made up of intelligently patchworked derivative motifs from all sorts of children's literature … written for people whose imaginative lives are confined'.[30] But this is to miss the point of what is Rowling is doing. The hospitality of the works to influence is the point, and her fantasyland is one into which readers can lose themselves. More, there is a profound moral narrative at work: the wizarding world divided between 'pure blood' fanatics, who despise the unmagical and express in-effect racist views against those witches and wizards, like Hermione, whose bloodlines are not 'pure': the offensive term 'mudblood' stands-in for racial slurs too familiar from the real world. Voldemort is the fascistic leader of this faction, against whom the novels' forces of good stand as inclusive, diverse, supportive, motivated by love and community, by courage, sacrifice and determination. The (in the world of the story) literal enchantments, the spells and magic and transformations in which the story traffic, are aspects of a profounder re-enchantment, an enmagicing of the world as such.

Rowling's books benefit from their scale, and the decision to track the main characters, Harry, Ron and Hermione, from childhood through adolescence and into adulthood. They are eloquent and effective *Bildungsromanen*. Harry misses his absent parents, idolizes them, discovers that they were not perfect and finally grows to succeed them. In *Prisoner of Azkaban* Rowling introduces a magical device called a 'time turner', the winding of which reverses time to some hours earlier (depending on how far the device is wound). Hemione, keen to advance her schooling, is secretly using this device to turn back time and so double up her lessons. But the device is used to work the plot forward, then rework it. Menaced by dementors on the banks of a lake, Harry sees his father's 'patronus' (a kind of spectral emission cast by a wizard's wand, each one distinctive to the individual) come to save him. Later, in order to redeem the events of the story, Harry and his friends use Hermione's time-turner to relive the day. Rehearsing events, reconceptualizing influence, folding together past and present, all this is put at the service of a profound and moving observation about the nature of growing up. In the words of Wendy Doniger:

---

[30] A S Byatt, 'Harry Potter and the Childish Adult'.

Harry is haunted by his mother's dying screams, but now that he is older he moves on, in Lacanian fashion, to come to terms with his father. Thanks to a wonderfully complex and subtle episode of time travel that traces a Möbius twist in the chronological sequence, Harry encounters himself in the loop where past and present come together and overlap. The first time he lives through this period, he sees, across a lake, someone he vaguely recognises: perhaps his father? No, his father is dead, but that person sends a silver stag which saves him from present danger. When he goes back in time, he runs to the same place to see who it was, and there's no one else there: he is the one who sends the stag to save himself in the future. ... The moment when Harry realises that he mistook himself for his father is quite powerful; and it is, after all, the only real kind of time travel there is: each of us becomes, in adulthood, someone who lived some thirty years before us, someone who must save our own life.[31]

After *Harry Potter and the Prisoner of Azkaban* introduced time-turners into the world of the novels, some fans wondered why they couldn't be used to put an end to Voldemort before he ever became Voldemort. You'd have to give the device 250,000 turns or so, but that's a small exertion to undertake to prevent all the horrors that the dark lord unleashes on the world. So why is the time-turner used only for trivial, and never for world-saving, purposes? A related issue with this device is why it appears only in *Prisoner of Azkaban*, and vanishes from the later novels. Such a trinket could come in very useful in the final battle fought in *Deathly Hallows*, after all, and its disappearance rather smacks of an author, anxious not to paint herself into an impossible corner plotting-wise with one too many magical get-out-of-narrative-jail-free cards, nudging this extraordinary item under the carpet with her toe. Rowling is not unaware of such fannish questions. In *Harry Potter and the Cursed Child* (a spin-off play written by Jack Thorne from an original story written by J. K. Rowling, Thorne and John Tiffany, first staged in 2016) Rowling introduces a previously unmentioned 'Croaker's Law' that limits time-turners to a maximum backtime-travelling of five hours: any longer, we're told, would create ripple effects that would harm either the time traveller or time itself (although in fact the plot of *Cursed Child* depends upon an extraordinary and illegal time turner that takes us back many years, so at the same time as filling that worldbuilding divot Rowling gouges out another). As for the 'why not use time-turners in the battle of Hogwarts?' puzzle – for even five hours would provide immense strategic advantage in war – in *Half-Blood Prince* Hermione reads a newspaper account of an accident at the Ministry of Magic, in which a cabinet containing all the time-turners in the world has been destroyed. On account of the turners' special properties, the cabinet falls, shatters and repairs itself endlessly in a temporal short-circuit, that happens to keep them conveniently out of the way of the remainder of the plotting Rowling has to do.

---

[31] Wendy Doniger 'Can You Spot the Source?'

Rowling hasn't plugged all such internal coherence gaps (why is Hermione in *Prisoner of Azkaban* so tired all the time? We're told it's because, using the time-turner, she's doing twice as much school-work. But, given that she has a time-turner, why doesn't she use it to do twice as much school work *and* get twice as much sleep?) – but to pursue this kind of nitpicking is to miss the point. Hermione's time-turner has its manifest role in the plot, but it has a much more resonant and powerful latent role in the thematic through-line of *Prisoner of Azkaban* as a novel, which is why it appears in that novel only, and isn't needed for later instalments. That success has much more to do with the way these novels express a complex of, fundamentally, affective and existential truths, things that chime deeply with its readership of children and of adults both: to do with friendship and solidarity, with school and love and loss, and especially to do with parents and children. The novels are littered with ingenious trinkets and amusing spells, but most of these remain mere narrative garnish unless – like the time-turner – they express something deeper.

Another problem Rowling-as-writer has, in terms of boxing herself into a corner, is how very over-surveilled her world is. The story needs its mysteries to remain mysterious until the proper point in the narrative when they can be revealed with the conjurer's flourish and the satisfied 'ahh!' of the audience. Disguises must not yet be penetrated, hidden people and things have to remain hidden a while longer, and so on. Yet magic allows anyone and everyone to see, pretty much, everything. There is, for instance, a magical chart called 'the Marauder's Map', which shows the true identity and location of everybody in Hogwarts. No magical countermeasure, not Animagus disguises, Polyjuice Potion or Invisibility Cloaks, can fool the map. But key figures (an evil wizard called Peter Pettigrew who has transformed himself into a rat, and Voldemort himself) nevertheless manage somehow to evade detection. It's not just maps. An important thread in the novels is that certain characters are granted access inside the minds and memories of other characters. It takes what in conventional novels would be 'eavesdropping' to a new level of psychological intimacy. There are two main iterations of this. One is a magical artefact called 'the Pensieve', used to re-play the memories of others, most notably when Harry gathers tears from the eyes of dying Snape and, by dropping them in the Pensieve, not only learns but, it seems, experiences the secret history of Snape's whole life: his love for Lily Potter, how he was bullied at school, and the double-game he played at Dumbledore's prompting to keep Harry safe. Another example is even more intimate: the direct connection of mind to mind, primarily dramatized via the link that exists between Harry himself and Voldemort. This link is actualized via Harry's forehead scar, which grows more painful as the connection strengthens. It's a major narrative strand in the series, in fact: Voldemort tries to use the connection to possess Harry, and when he can't plants false visions into Harry's mind. Finally Harry learns to use the connection to surveil Voldemort and to track down his horcruxes. In *Deathly Hallows* Hermione scolds Harry for looking into Voldemort's mind: 'Harry, You are not supposed to let this happen anymore! … what good is it to watch him kill and torture, how can it help?' [*Deathly Hallows*, ch 27]. Harry's reply ('because it means I know what he's doing') is only part of the answer. Something far more crucial is represented by this linkage. Hogwarts School is a Panopticon-like space, in which the pupils are under continual surveillance by not only their teachers, but by prefects, by ghosts and house-elves and even by the portraits on the wall. And yet, despite being so thoroughly surveyed, Hogwarts is also a place of invisibility, of hiding, rebuses of secrecy as such: many hidden rooms, secret paths and veiled elements. And that's as we might expect: it's part of Rowling's inheritance of the Gothic, where the actual structure at the heart of the story (castle, monastery, stately home) literalizes the symbolic structures of society and, especially, of family, in order to dramatize the truth that such structures are built on secrets. Secrets, and the uncovering of them, are most of the plot-thrust of the Harry Potter novels. More, these various lesser secrets (and their uncovering) are constellated around, and in various ways reflect upon, one core secret: the 'big' secret that the series works through. That secret, in a nutshell, is: Abraham and Isaac. Which is to say: the mystery (in the strong sense of that word) of why the old are called upon to sacrifice the life of the young, to kill the favoured child, the chosen one. And why they do so without any apparent qualm.

Snape, despite outward hostility towards Harry Potter, has actually been protecting him, because he loved Harry's mother. His allegiance to Voldemort is a sham, in service of a scheme hatched by Dumbledore finally to defeat the dark lord. But that scheme depends upon Voldemort killing Harry, since part of Voldemort's soul had inadvertently become trapped inside Harry's head. By killing Harry, Voldemort will be destroying himself.

> 'So the boy ... the boy must die?' asked Snape quite calmly.
>
> And Voldemort himself must do it, Severus. That is essential.
>
> Another long silence. Then Snape said, 'I thought ... all these years ... that we were protecting him for her. For Lily'.
>
> 'We have protected him because it has been essential to teach him, to raise him, to let him try his strength', said Dumbledore, his eyes still tight shut. ... Snape looked horrified. 'You have kept him alive so that he can die at the right moment? You have used me. I have spied for you and lied for you, put myself in mortal danger for you. Everything was supposed to keep Lily Potter's son safe. Now you tell me you have been raising him like a pig for slaughter'. [*Deathly Hallows*, ch.33]

Dumbledore can't quite believe Snape's profession of outrage, here, if that's what it is. 'But this is touching, Severus', said Dumbledore seriously. 'Have you grown to care for the boy, after all?' (In the movie adaptation this line of dialogue is shifted slightly to make it even more deflating: 'don't tell me *you* have grown to care for the boy!') But Snape is quite right. These two old men are conspiring in secret to sacrifice – literally, not metaphorically, to sacrifice – a favoured son on the altar of a cruel and unresponsive Providence. It's a feature the Harry Potter universe shares with Middle Earth that none of its characters spend any time in church or temple, or devote any of their energies to worshipping God or pondering the spiritual dimension of things (though the wizarding world does, for some reason, observe Christmas holidays). In the case of Tolkien this was, as has already been noted, because he was so religious himself, the religious element absorbed into the story and the symbolism. Rowling, an Anglican, is doing something similar in these novels. The whatever-it-is that requires Dumbledore and Snape teleologically to suspend their ethics, is veiled in these novels. Rather we follow the major plot of Harry's sacrifice through Harry's eyes:

> He felt his heart pounding fiercely in his chest. How strange that, in his dread of death, it pumped all the harder, valiantly keeping him alive. But it would have to stop, and soon. Its beats were numbered. How many would there be time for, as he rose and walked through the castle for the last time, out into the grounds and into the forest? Terror washed over him as he lay on the floor, with that funeral drum pounding inside him. Would it hurt to die? All those times he had thought that it was about to happen and escaped, he had never really thought of the thing itself.
> [*Deathly Hallows*, ch 34]

It is the story of Abraham and Isaac from Isaac's perspective, and it answers the question 'but why must we die at the hands of the *nom-de-la-mort* Voldemort?' with: because there is a little piece of this mort already inside your soul. But it does so in order to twist a surprise existential short-circuit out of the encounter: death ends up destroying not us but the shard of death inside us. The conclusion is eucatastrophic. It isn't what Dumbledore thinks will happen, of course. It's clear he believed that Harry would die. When his shade meets Harry after the event, he describes himself as a 'master of Death'; we discover another secret backstory – as a young man, Dumbledore had fallen in love with a charismatic but wicked wizard called Grindelwald, and together they had sought a number of magical items called 'hallows' that would have enabled them to cheat death, although the quest had terrible consequences for the world.

> 'Was I better, ultimately, than Voldemort?' he asks, and the question is not a rhetorical one. 'I too sought a way to conquer death, Harry.'
> 'Hallows, not Horcruxes.'
> 'Hallows,' murmured Dumbledore, 'not Horcruxes. Precisely.' … 'Grindelwald was looking for them too?' Dumbledore closed his eyes for a moment and nodded. 'It was the thing, above all, that drew us together,' he said quietly. 'Two clever, arrogant boys with a shared obsession.' [*Deathly Hallows*, ch. 35]

All the twists and turns of the seven novels, all the revealed mysteries, secret identities and back-and-forth, all resolve themselves into these three fundamentally Kierkegaardian problems. Is there a Teleological Suspension of the Ethical in the Potterverse? On what grounds might it operate? Voldemort, and Grindelwald, and young Albus all suspended the ethical in search of a particular telos: overcoming death. That led to great suffering, in Kierkegaardian terms, a tragic, rather than Abrahamic, outcome. How does the specific suspension of the ethical provision not to sacrifice Harry Potter merit any more suspension than those earlier experiments? The answer is to be found in the eucatastrophic survival of Harry himself, just as, in the Genesis story, Abraham's faith is only retrospectively justified by the intervention of the angel, staying his hand. Could we say: the thing that justifies Dumbledore's secret scheme literally to send Harry Potter to his death is that he is, in a Kierkegaardian sense, a knight of faith?

The prodigious success of these novels, augmented by their movie adaptations, and other paratexts, spin-offs, theme-parks and fandoms, is ongoing, although it was at its peak in the first decade of the twenty-first century. It is, indeed, hard to overstate just how huge this series was through those years, a testimony not just to the merits of the novels themselves – the engaging characters, the effective plotting, the clever reveals and ingenious and marvellous worldbuilding – but to the appeal of the particular generic combination of fantasy and school-story, the framing of childhood and adolescence as enchanted, magical and potent. And it speaks to a continuing expansion of fantasy as a popular mode that continued through, and continued expanding, into the next century.

# PART 3
## TWENTY-FIRST-CENTURY FANTASY

# CHAPTER 17
## GLOBAL FANTASY

Across the two decades of the current century fantasy has become evermore popular, augmenting its appeal and expanding into new modes. The publication of fantasy novels proliferated, with thousands of new titles continuing to appear annually. Many of these are exercises in generic repetition, simply rehashing the heroic quasi-medievalism of Tolkien, and disposing men, elves, dwarfs and orcs (or equivalents) across a medievalized landscape, into a battle of good versus evil, quest and adventure. But there were new developments too. Most notably, writers of a variety of global heritages challenged the Eurocentric, white, trad logic of prior fantasy: significant fantasy novels were written out of African, Asian and East Asian heritages, women and people of colour centred, the implicit militaristic and imperialist logic of much earlier fantasy challenged and critiqued. One manifestation of this is a greater emphasis on violence, and cruelty: a variety of fantasy known as 'Grimdark' came to prominence.

The relative unsuccess of fantasy movies through the later twentieth century has been noted in earlier chapters, but the multibillion-dollar gross of Peter Jackson's cinematic adaptation of Tolkien's *The Lord of the Rings* (2001–3) opened the way for a multitude of commercially successful and sometimes important films in this mode. Three of the seven Narnia novels were brought to the screen: *The Lion, the Witch and the Wardrobe* (2005 directed Andrew Adamson), *Prince Caspian* (2008 directed by Andrew Adamson), and *The Voyage of the Dawn Treader* (2010 directed by Michael Apted) have collectively earned more than $1.5 billion worldwide. Netflix is developing a new series of Narnian movies, with billions of dollars budgeted.

Box office is a crude quantification of a work's significance or importance, but it does at least speak to reach and cultural penetration. Cinematic adaptation of J. K. Rowling's *Harry Potter* novels began before the series (discussed above) had completed publication in book form: *Harry Potter and the Philosopher's Stone* (1997) became a movie in 2001 (directed by Chris Columbus); its success led to a further seven films, the final instalment *Harry Potter and the Deathly Hallows* being split into two films (Part 1 released in 2010 and Part 2 in 2011, both directed by David Yates). The films are lavishly mounted and are, at present, the second most financially successful movie franchise of all time – the Marvel Comic Universe movies are number one – having earned more than $8 billion in total. They benefit by retaining their cast throughout the series, one exception being Irish actor Richard Harris, who died after playing Dumbledore in the first film, and was replaced by Michael Gambon for the remainder. But the core trio of Harry, Hermione and Ron, cast as child actors in the first movie – Daniel Radcliffe, Emma Watson and Rupert Grint – grew, as it were, in real time as their characters did, year by year, finishing the series as young adults. Rowling's increasingly bloated novels were judiciously and cleverly edited into screenplays, special effects and cinematography were high calibre, the fantastical world vividly brought to life, and the acting (once the young leads settled into their roles) excellent throughout, with supporting figures being played by a panoply of the best of British thespian aristocracy. The films' success was more than just financial: the series penetrated popular culture.

Fantasy was not a guarantee of movie success in these decades. An expensive adaptation of Philip Pullman's *The Golden Compass* (2007, directed by Chris Weitz) flopped, and a version of Le Guin's *Tales from Earthsea* (2006 directed by Gorō Miyazaki, of the Japanese Studio Ghibli) was a misfire. But box office gross is not the only index of significance. Studio Ghibli's founder Hayao Miyazaki had previously directed *Spirited Away* (2002), a gorgeously realized portal fantasy in which a young girl finds herself trapped in a hotel that services the population of Japanese deities and monsters, her parents transformed into pigs: with her resilience, courage and kindness she navigates her way to the heart of this world, saving her parents and ultimately escaping. A work of sumptuous beauty and potency, immensely enchanting and enchanted, it is one of the greatest fantasy movies.

By the twenty-teens fantasy films were a dominant presence in big-budget releases: Tim Burton's hyperbolic adaptations of *Alice in Wonderland* (2010) and *Alice through the Looking Glass* (2016) earned billions, in part by augmenting Carroll's novels with additional 'worldbuilding' and inserted action scenes and fighting. Disney remade their animated 1959 *Sleeping Beauty* as a live-action film that concentrated on, and recuperated the reputation of, the antagonist: *Maleficent* (2014 directed by Robert Stromberg) cast Angelina Jolie as the goth sorceress queen, revealed in this reboot as a wronged woman, persecuted and fighting a malevolent ex-husband. Adaptations of British author Cressida Cowell's *How to Train Your Dragon* books, aimed at younger readers, into a trio of spectacular computer animations produced major hits: *How to Train Your Dragon* (2010, directed by Chris Sanders and Dean DeBlois), *How to Train Your Dragon 2* (2014) and *How to Train Your Dragon: The Hidden World* (2019, both directed by Dean DeBlois) earned $1.7 billion at the box office. The pseudo-Viking island kingdom of Berk is under constant attack by dragons, its inhabitants huge hairy Vikings who talk broad Scottish-English, all except the son of the chieftan, young Hiccup, who for some unexplained reasons speaks with Jay Baruchel's unmediated Canadian accent. Hiccup's befriending a rare black dragon, called Toothless, and discovery that dragons are not the enemy his people believe them to be, is told with charm and panache, and the world expands into more fantastical and colourful dimensions with each film. And *Dungeons & Dragons: Honor Among Thieves* (2023 directed by Jonathan Goldstein and John Francis Daley) brilliantly transfers the vibe of the D&D game, and tie-in novels, to the big screen: a rapid-fire set of peripatetic adventures in which a varied, likeable crew of thieves combat an evil cult, passing through an inventively rendered amusing fantastical world. There had been previous attempts to capture the distinctive appeal of D&D on screen, but this film was the first to succeed in doing so.

An instance of the mismatch between box-office metrics and aesthetic merit is Peter Jackson's sprawling trilogy of 'Hobbit' movies [*The Hobbit: An Unexpected Journey* (2012) *The Hobbit: The Desolation of Smaug* (2013) *The Hobbit: The Battle of the Five Armies*

(2014)]. These were very successful (earning $3 billion against a $700 million outlay), but are bad films, and get worse as they go along. Martin Freeman delivers a persuasive performance as Bilbo, but the adaptations crack Tolkien's source novel apart and inject great quantities of cavity-foam fight-scenes and action adventure – tiresome acrobatic melée and one-on-one combat set-pieces, rendered via pasty, deflated CGI. It is like watching somebody else play a video game. Persuaded by the continuing commercial success of on-screen Tolkien, Amazon invested an eye-popping sum (reputedly more than a billion dollars, making it the most expensive TV drama yet made) in an eight-episode series *The Lord of the Rings: The Rings of Power* (2022). Set a thousand years before *The Hobbit*, the show traces the rise of Sauron to his bad eminence, but it is a mess: the visuals over-intricate and eye-wearying CGI world of fantasy citadels and landscapes, the story illogical, the dialogue atrocious. Yet, as with the adaptation of Robert Jordan's *Wheel of Time* novels undertaken by the same studio, badness proved no impediment to popularity, and further series are currently in production. This may speak merely to a new logic of dissemination, for 'streaming services' that funnel cinematic-quality content directly to people's homes (as with Amazon, Netflix and Disney+) are a wholly new thing. Fantasy, alongside science fiction, crime dramas and comedy shows, fills up the content-hungry virtual spaces of these platforms, with a view to keeping eyeballs on the screen and subscription payments flowing.

This is to return us to Jackson's original *Lord of the Rings* movie trilogy which, by and large, and despite some substantial alterations from the source text, is very good. The movies catered to die-hard fans of the original novels with a scrupulous design, costume and rendering, a distinctive and atmospheric visualization based designedly on the superb art of John Howe and Alan Lee. Howe and Lee's style, a spacious, marvellous blend of realist painterliness and imaginative inventiveness, has 'become' the look of Middle Earth, and has disseminated itself into myriad other Tolkienian forms and fandoms, as well as fantasy more broadly. We can contrast this visual logic with the illustrations Tolkien himself provided for his own writings – not untalented as an artist, Tolkien's own drawings and watercolours are quaint, stylized, sweetly mannered and flattened. Howe and Lee, and through them the movies and other realizations, expand and deepen this visual world, creating an immersive environment that actualizes the draw of enchantment.

There are, as I say, substantial alterations from the source text: Tom Bombadil is omitted, the relative absence of female characters is addressed by lifting the elvish princess Arwen from the book's appendices and giving her a major role. Scenes of melée and battle from the novel are extended and extra ones added. The novel's ending, 'the scouring of the Shire', is dropped entirely, replaced with a sluggish series of scenes of the hobbits returning home, taking up their lives again and Frodo departing for the Grey Havens. But, before that final slackening, the films build superb narrative momentum, and orchestrate a string of extraordinary, brilliant set-pieces: the company fighting their way through Moria and Gandalf confronting the Balrog; the company passing through Lothlorien; fighting orcs at Parth Galen; Gandalf resurrecting Theoden from his enchanted stupor; the extended sequence of heroic defence at Helm's Deep; the siege of

Gondor and the charge of the Rohirrim; Eowyn killing the Nazgul; Sam battling Shelob over Frodo's (as he thinks) dead body; the final struggle inside Mount Doom. Jackson is expert at exaggerating props and angles just enough for maximum visual impact but not so much that they become ludicrous and caricature. He is particularly fond of stretched verticals: the immensely high and precipitous stairways of Cirith Ungol, the soaring towers and pinnacles of Minas Tirith, Sauron's pillared fastness. The special effects, which won all the Oscars, are impeccable and render the characters different scales and sizes fluently and believably; the costume design and *mis-en-scène* are beautiful, and the performances are superb – especially Ian McKellen's Gandalf, and the motion-capture of Andy Serkis's Gollum.

Canadian composer Howard Shore wrote the score for the films, a lushly romantic, elongated orchestral suite: grand melody and counterpoint for the main theme, landscaping sonic richness, interleaved with folk-song and Celtic musical pieces (including two songs by Irish singer-songwriter Enya) and other influences. It stands as an aural correlative to the visual and verbal fantasy of the movies and films. Widely performed and replayed it is the sonic equivalent of Howe and Lee's art: an aural shorthand for fantasy as such. Chris Cummins notes how relatively old-fashioned the work is, compared to the work of such movie composers as Jóhann Jóhannsson, Hans Zimmer or Ludwig Göransson, but he thinks that a good thing.

> Howard Shore's music in the trilogy represents the last of the truly great blockbuster film scores. A bold statement to be sure … yet Shore's music for the trilogy has, like Bernard Herrman's work for *Psycho* or pretty much anything John Williams did in the 1970s or '80s, both a symbiotic relationship with its source material and the ability to be evocative on its own. When listening to key tracks like 'Concerning Hobbits' (a piece so whimsical and tranquil it has taken on a second life as a relaxation jam in spas everywhere), 'The Breaking of the Fellowship' and the rousing 'The Bridge of Khazad-dûm' – whose influence can be felt in Alan Silvestri's main theme from *The Avengers*, it's easy to be instantly transported to Middle Earth.[1]

The orchestral elements are full of Elgarian flavours and borrowings, which in turn gives it an English aural quality: Germans used to mock England as 'das Land ohne Musik', the land without music; but although there are reminiscences of Wagner, Brahms and Berlioz in Shore's score (the same is true of many movie soundtracks) the blend of Elgar symphonic touches and English and Celtic folk-tunes creates a distinctive local-British ambience. The music written to accompany the elves is written on the *maqam hijaz* scale (what used to be called 'the Phrygian'), an 'Eastern' coding. The main theme moves from the Hobbiton small scale charm of its up-down seven-note opening, to the spacious splendour of its orchestral chords, aurally embodying the movement of

---

[1]Cummins, 'Is The Fellowship of the Ring The Last Great Film Score?'

the story: travelling out of the pleasance of the Shire into the marvellous wide-open spaces of Middle Earth. It is enchanting music for a story of re-enchantment. American music critic David Hurwitz praises its melodic expressiveness and moments of grandeur, but notes its formlessness. This isn't surprising: taken together, Jackson's movies are 558 minutes long (683 minutes in the extended cut) – music composed to accompany such runtimes must dilate and slacken, will be repetitive and tend towards slackness.

> It's also important to note that 'contrast' (of which there's plenty) does not equal 'form' (of which there's none) … There are splendid episodes, such as the lighting of the watch tower fires in *The Return of the King*. But by the time we get to that point, Shore's device of stretching out time by modulating upward to increase tension has already occurred so many times that the power of this particular moment, where the technique seems justified, is weakened. You may also recall that 'death' in the film is almost always represented by a sudden switch to slow motion photography accompanied by soft, vaguely Anglican crooning by a boy soprano. I disliked it very much in the film, and it sounds especially unmotivated as a purely musical device here.[2]

Unmotivated or not, that 'Anglican' speaks again to an Englishness in the music, the sonic correlative to Tolkien's 'mythology for England'; although in fact what Hurwitz hears as 'Anglican' was actually performed by choristers from the London Oratory School, a Catholic educational establishment. The dialectic of fantasy reasserts itself, even in the smallest details.

---

[2]David Hurwitz, 'Shore: Lord of the Rings Symphony'.

# CHAPTER 18
# VIDEO GAMES

The first commercial video games appeared in the 1970s – *Pong*, an arcade game that reproduced the action of ping-pong in 2D black-and-white appeared in 1972. By the 1980s home consoles were increasingly widespread, and of the various types of game sold to be played upon these devices (the most popular were the science-fiction shooting game *Space Invaders*, the chase-round-a-maze puzzle game *Pac-Man* and the scrolling adventure *Super Mario Bros*) none were fantasy. It is to read back from the later large-scale entry of fantasy into the gaming mode to suggest that the reason for this was that the appeal of fantasy, the entrance into a whole world of enchantment and adventure, was hobbled by the limitations of early video-gaming graphics and design. Little could be simpler, visually, than the two vertically moving paddles and blipping pixel 'ball' of *Pong*; little could be less enchanting or transporting. But technology advanced rapidly. By the end of the 1980s games were visually richer, increasingly capacious, imaginatively varied and immersive. The first significant fantasy text in this mode is Nintendo's *The Legend of Zelda* (first released in Japan in 1986, released around the world in 1987). A popular success, the game is set in the Fantasyland of 'Hyrule', through which an elf-boy called Link – controlled by the player – must travel to collect the eight fragments of the 'Triforce of Wisdom' so as to rescue Princess Zelda from Ganon, a malevolent magical pig-shaped monster who plans world-domination, a scheme that begins, for reasons that aren't entirely clear, with kidnapping Zelda. The bright-coloured Fantasyland, which the game-player sees from a top-down perspective, is very spacious and varied, and the adventuring is immersive. It owes something to the *Dungeons and Dragons* board-game – Link must navigate an underworld as well as an overworld, exploring dungeons, collecting weapons, fighting enemies and uncovering secrets. The game was successful enough to lead to fully twenty sequels, from *Zelda II: The Adventure of Link* (1988) to the most recent, *The Legend of Zelda: Tears of the Kingdom* (2023), with each instalment in the series benefitting from the extraordinary advances in processing power, complexity and vividness of representation to become more visually and ludically immersive, more fluid and realizable. The gameplay in *Zelda* is not a linear progression, as it is in *Super-Mario*, and the player can explore the Fantasyland in a variety of ways, although there is something limiting about the particular through-line story: travel, fight, travel on, overcoming small obstacles until a bigger 'boss' enemy is encountered and overcome.

The idea of a Fantasyland as an environment to enter and explore is behind the notable success of *Myst* (1993; developed by Cyan, Inc. and initially released to be played upon Macintosh desk computers, although later versions were release for game consoles too). The player travels via a portal, a magical book, to a mysterious island called Myst, which she then explores both in spatial and temporal terms: pages of the magic book allow players into different ages of Myst, uncovering the mythic foundation of the magical land. The landscapes, inhabitants and history of this place are detailed, beautifully rendered, and gameplay is extraordinarily immersive. It sold six million copies, becoming the bestselling PC game of the 1990s.

The open-ended, non-confrontational nature of *Myst*'s gameplay had its influence on the development of fantasy gaming. By the twenty-first century fantasy games have become manifold, and many are very successful, but most combine exploring the Fantasyland world with more plot-driven elements, questing for specific items, encountering and fighting enemies and monsters, moving episodically through smaller adversaries to a chapter-ending 'big boss', harder to wrangle and kill. The *Elder Scrolls* games (developed by Bethesda Game Studios) allow players free-form gameplay in a fantasy world called 'Tamriel', questing, exploring, fighting – mostly fighting, in fact. In the first two games *The Elder Scrolls: Arena* (1994) and *The Elder Scrolls II: Daggerfall* (1996) players can travel where they like; magic (called 'magicka') enables players to cast spells and attack enemies, but as with all fantasy video games magic operates according to an economy: it must be accumulated before it is spent, like money; with some spells – transforming oneself into a vampire, werewolf or wereboar for instance – 'costing' more than others. The games evolved greater visual and gameplay sophistication as they went on. In *The Elder Scrolls IV: Oblivion* (2006) characters again move as they wish around an open-plan fantasy world. They can simply explore and interact, or they can engage the 'plot' of the game, in which a fanatical cult must be prevented from opening a portal to the demonic realm of 'Oblivion'. Though this game was commercially successful, and remains highly regarded by gamers, it was the follow-up *The Elder Scrolls V: Skyrim* (2011) that broke through into mainstream culture in a way not true of the earlier games. Set in a northern portion of Tamriel called 'Skyrim', a Nordic realm, the story concerns the player's character, the Dragonborn, on a quest to defeat 'Alduin the World-Eater', a gigantic dragon prophesied to destroy the world. The game is 'open world', in that players may go wherever they will, and engage their adventures in any order.

*Skyrim* was a phenomenon: in two years it sold 20 million copies, and the *Elder Scrolls* series in total has sold, to date (2024) more than 60 million games, numbers higher and reach wider than any but the very bestselling fantasy novelists. And yet there are limitations. The more detailed and spacious fantasy gaming becomes, the more intricate and over-determined its visualizations, the more hyperactive and repetitive its gameplay, the *less* actively enchanting it tends to become. Video gaming is a significant form of contemporary fantasy, but it is also, as a mode, necessarily instrumentalizing, a goal-oriented, often violent – indeed, often hyper-violent – antagonistic and flattening way of construing fantasy. Enemies must be overcome, and the overcomings totted-up; coins, jewels, power-ups or other tokens must be accumulated, success or failure being itemized, and indeed reified, in this fashion: a fundamentally monetary logic that is, in itself, bourgeois and modern. The characters in-game may move through a medievalized fantasy world, dress in medieval gear, and fight with sword and axes, but the game itself is governed by an actual and metaphorical economics that is budgetary rather than fiduciary (i.e. not to do with faith). These games are absorbing, and exciting, and they are certainly extremely popular, more so than fantasy novels or most fantasy films; but they are also, in a structural sense, modern.

In 2012 British writer Will Self, observing his teenage son endlessly playing video games, was struck by the alarming ultra-violence of many of the most popular (non-fantasy) games of the 2000s, military 'shoot-'em-ups' in which players move through battlefields killing enemies in viscerally realized manner, with much spilled blood and shattered limbs: *Call of Duty* (2003) or the game Self's son had previously been playing, to his father's alarm, *Call of Duty: Black Ops* (2010). The move into the enchanted fantasy world represented by *Skyrim* at first reassures Self:

> Compared with the violence and shattered industrial infrastructure that formed the backdrop to his *Black Ops* game play, the pinewood pixelscape of *Skyrim* seemed positively bucolic. Although when first seen, girt in his ebony Daedric armour, my son's character was beating a bogie-beast to death, there was still a refreshing lack of bloody splashback. It could be because the nomenclature of *Skyrim* – Aela the Huntress, Malacath, Yngvar and Windhelm – is triply derived (out of Norse sagas, by way of Tolkien and his film adapters) that the scenario seems so cosy. Even after my son's proxy resurrected the bogie – 'I do that a lot. I bring him back and then I punch him to death again' – I still kept faith with the game, which also involves the reading of quite large chunks of runic text. I was right to, because eventually, once we had defeated various frost trolls and sex-changing lizard men, and reached Windhelm, it transpired that my son had built a gabled house in this Arctic community, and even acquired a wife. 'My wife is a very nice lady', he told me, as a rather cowed-looking figure in a rough woollen dress shuffled about in the background. 'She runs a store and gives me money every few days.' 'Oh, really', I said, desperate to clutch at these straws of domesticity. 'And what's your wife's name?' Without pausing in the ceaseless toggling of thumb-on-lever he said: 'I don't know'.[1]

This is both funny and pointed: the copiousness of the fantastical inventiveness and visual representation of this text is not matched by any depth of characterization, the fuller engagement that a novel provides. Gaming is an instrumental textual matter, a series of over-stimulations, encounters economized according to a scarcity logic – as the player in *Skyrim* must accumulate 'coin' in order to continue the game. This detaches the possibilities of the form from the richer, deeper transports of fantasy as such. It also prioritizes violence as the idiom of the text. I, the same age as Self, and with a teenager son as much as gamer as his, share his disquiet at just how extreme and Sadean the violence of many of these works are. Nor is this just a question of gaming: violence becomes, for a major iteration of fantasy as a whole, a major consideration in the twenty-first century.

---

[1] Will Self 'Video Games', 12.

# CHAPTER 19
## GRIMDARK

The label 'Grimdark' comes from the *Warhammer* table-top miniature wargame franchise. The original game (1983) elaborated a fantasy world derivative of Tolkien, Poul Anderson and Moorcock, and a science-fictional follow-up, *Warhammer 40,000* (1987) – the number in its title is the year in which it is set – elaborates a violent, gloomy cosmos in which progress has ceased and human civilization is in a state of total war with hostile alien races and occult forces: the game's slogan being 'in the grim darkness of the far future there is only war'. The gaming origin of the term is significant. A wargame needs a war environment in which to operate. Writing novels in such a franchise means that stories become determined by war, violence and pessimism. There is nothing wholesome, idealized, beautiful, noble or pure in these worlds; life is struggle and pain, man is wolf to man. Though people may pretend to follow higher ideals, few if any actually believes them: cynicism and power-plays are the true motivations of humankind. This ethos spread by degrees through fantasy writing across the decade. David Gemmell's much-loved *Legend* (1984; discussed above) is darkling, though not entirely grim – honour, courage and duty still have some meaning in this violent, bellicose fantasy world. Glen Cook's *Black Company* books (1984–5) are grimmer, and by the 1990s the dark had fully engrimmened. Paul Kearney's *Monarchies of God* (1995) is unremitting, detailed accounts of battle, violence, rape and horror across a Europe-like fantasy continent. Martin's first Westeros novel *Game of Thrones* appeared in 1996, Stan Nicholl's *Orcs: First Blood* in 1999, and Polish author Andrzej Sapkowski published the first of his nine 'Witcher' novels in 1990 (*Wiedźmin*: 'The Witcher'), a pseudo-European early modern continent beset by monsters and riven by war between different human nations, elves and others. The title character is a kind of bounty hunter who kills the monsters, terminating with, as the phrase goes, extreme prejudice. Moderately successful, the series broke through into international success when adapted into a video game in 2007 [*The Witcher*, developed by CD Projekt Red; sequels *The Witcher 2: Assassins of Kings* (2011) and *The Witcher 3: Wild Hunt* (2015) followed] selling 60 million copies. These in turn were adapted into three series of big-budget television for Netflix (2019–23), starring *Superman* actor Henry Cavill as the title character. Even darker and more horrific – and more successful – were the three video games developed by Japanese creator Hidetaka Miyazaki: *Dark Souls* (2011), *Dark Souls II* (2014) and *Dark Souls III* (2016). Masterpieces of Gothic design, and gameplay, and notoriously difficult terrain to play through, these games pit the gamer's avatar against dark knights, demons, grotesque monsters, dragons, phantoms and other supernatural entities in a ruined and engloomed medieval landscape. The violence is very graphically rendered and the 'lore' of the world, its backstory and fantasy bona fides, is detailed and extensive: immensely successful and influential games, and a major fantasy text.

In fiction, the pre-eminent work of Grimdark fantasy is George R. R. Martin's ongoing series 'A Song of Ice and Fire', beginning in the 1990s with *A Game of Thrones* (1996) and *A Clash of Kings* (1998) and continuing with *A Storm of Swords* (2000), *A Feast for Crows* (2005) and *A Dance with Dragons* (2011). Two further volumes are promised, although Martin's delay in finishing them keeps prolonging, and has acquired an identity of its own as an item in fandom – those impatient to read the conclusion to the series, pestering Martin on social media to hurry up, were publicly rebuked by Neil Gaiman on his blog with the slogan: 'George R.R. Martin is not your bitch'. This speaks to the novels' main strength: plotting, narrative, the urge to turn the pages to find out what happens next. Baulked of this pleasure by Martin's dilatoriness fans have complained, but also have filled that gap: 85,000 fan-written stories and books had been uploaded to AO3.org by the end of 2023. Before the fifth volume was published David Benioff and D. B. Weiss began adapting the series for HBO television as *Game of Thrones*. This was a very expensive, lavishly staged piece of screen drama, at the time the most expensive TV show ever made – a gamble, especially given the prior absence of large scale successful fantasy TV drama, but a gamble that paid off. The show premiered on HBO in the United States on 17 April 2011, and concluded on 19 May 2019, with seventy-three episodes broadcast over eight seasons. A huge success, it projected Martin's fantasy to global fame, refocusing attention on the books. Production also overtook Martin's glacial pace of composition: the final series, written by Benioff and Weiss after consultation with Martin, presumably records the ending the author plans for the novels which, as of 2024, have still to emerge. It can be added that the reaction to season 8 and the show's finale was, in contrast to the dithyrambs that greeted earlier seasons, overwhelmingly negative.

*Game of Thrones* is interesting in its own right as a fantasy text, and has proved consequential: its success persuaded others that big-budget fantasy adaptation was the way forward. Across the twenty-teens and into the 2020s many of these were put into production, of varying quality and none with the degree of success or fame of *Game of Thrones*. These are discussed below, but for now it is worth saying something about the novels. The series is mostly focused on Westeros, a late medieval Europe (or more narrowly: a kind of expanded fantasy-British Isles) divided into seven realms, ruled over by a king who sits on the 'iron throne' in the southern city King's Landing. This throne, fashioned of many hundreds of swords and blades of defeated enemies, represents power as a military prize. Prior to the beginning of the first novel the throne had been occupied by the Targaryens, a dynasty who had maintained power by virtue of their war-dragons. But the dragons are all dead now, and the last Targaryen king, Aerys II, has gone mad and been assassinated. The only remaining scions of this noble house, son and daughter Viserys and Daenerys, have fled overseas. A northern nobleman, Robert Baratheon, sits on the throne, though his grip on power is uncertain. There is also an eastern continent, Essos, comprising various Orientalized realms: Mongol-like horse lords called Dothraki, decadent middle-eastern equivalents, slavers, the pseudo-sinitic location of Qarth and others.

The world of the novels experiences elongated seasons: summer might last ten years, and winter as long again. As the story opens the decade-summer is drawing to an end, and an unusually prolonged winter is anticipated. In the north of Westeros the climate is cold; a vast wall, like a hyperbolic Hadrianic construction, blocks off the arctic lands beyond, inhabited by savages and monsters. The latter include ice zombies, the reanimated corpses of dead men who are assembling in vast numbers and threatening to break through and overwhelm the rest of the continent. Ordinary weapons cannot stop these creatures.

The main focus of the series is House Stark, another northern house, the head of which, Ned Stark, serves as the king's second-in-command, the 'hand of the king'. Ned is an honourable person, as are his children: his oldest son and heir Robb, the younger son Bran who is crippled early in the story and confined to a wheeled chair, his daughters, Sansa and Arya, and especially his illegitimate son Jon Snow ('Snow' is the convention by which bastards are surnamed in this society). These characters dominate the storytelling points-of-view of the novels. There are a great many other characters: all the other noble Houses of Westeros, their rulers and heirs and people, the 'Night's Watch' that guards the northern wall, courtiers and politicians, soldiers and thieves, whores and pirates, priests and religious cultists. The main action of the first three novels is the political jockeying for power, plots and assassinations and eventually outright war, by which the seven kingdoms compete with one another for overall power. Once Robert Baratheon is killed – gored to death on a boar-hunt – war breaks between the various pretenders to the throne. The brutality and realpolitik of this are absorbing, and Martin does not stint the violence: slaughter, rape, torture. But the series gains storytelling stature by playing out against a backdrop, hinted at to begin with but increasingly coming into the fore as the books proceed, that a different, larger existential war is brewing, a conflict between the forces of death and all life, and that the jockeyings for temporal power across Westeros are petty distractions in the face of this. As the army of the dead – the 'ice' of the series overarching title – assemble, the intricate interweavings of multiple plotlines and point-of-view characters develop in unexpected ways. A distinctiveness of Martin's is to develop a character in such a way as the reader comes to view him or her as the key one, the story's hero or heroine. He plays against our expectations of the conventionalized hero's journey in order, shockingly, to upend them. In the first novel this is Ned Stark: an honourable, capable leader trying to do the right thing in a cruel, corrupt, violent world. It seems as though he will prevail; but then, entirely unexpectedly, he is arrested and executed by the psychotic child-king Joffrey Baratheon – supposedly Robert Baratheon's son, but in fact the product of an incestuous affair between Baratheon's wife, the beautiful, ruthless Cersei Lannister, and her own brother, Jamie. The narrative startlement of this at the end of the book matches the surprise at the beginning: young Bran Stark, who likes to climbing over the walls and battlements of his family house Castle Winterfell, surprises Cersei and Jamie having sex in a room at the top of a tall tower. Surprised at this, Bram almost slips and falls, but Jamie catches him.

'Take my hand', he said. 'Before you fall … How old are you, boy?'

'Seven', Bran said, shaking with relief. His fingers had dug deep gouges in the man's forearm.

The man looked over at the woman. 'The things I do for love', he said, with loathing. He gave Bran a shove. Screaming, Bran went backward out the window into empty air. [*Game of Thrones*, 81]

John Lanchester marks this, in its dramatized form, as the moment when he 'got hooked' on the series.

> That startling moment is where the first programme in the TV series ends, and it's the point at which people realise they're addicted. It has an equivalent impact in the books; even more of an impact, perhaps, because Bran has already been established as one of the characters from whose viewpoint the story is told. Plus, he's only seven. This is a world in which nobody is safe, ever. The image of a fall from a high place is relevant: in this world, everyone's position is precarious. 'This is the game of thrones', Cersei tells Eddard Stark, 'you win or you die'.[1]

Martin repeats this gimmick in later books, though calling it gimmick is perhaps unfair. It is less a trick, and more a cannily destabilizing exploitation of the way readers invest in narrative. After Ned is killed we transfer our focus to his son Robb, follow his journey, his battles, his attempt to unite Westeros. Then, suddenly and with egregious slaughter, he is gone. It's a jolt. Other likely focal characters go the same way. The exigencies of TV adaptation reduce the number of characters to make the narrative more manageable, and two soon come to the fore: Jon Snow, another honourable man, one of the few who recognizes the threat represented by the 'white walkers' beyond the wall – and, in Essos, Daenerys, the last remaining member of a lineage that had once ruled the world. Married to a Dothraki ruler she loses her husband and is reduced to near-vagrancy, with only a small band of followers. But she has something crucial: dragon eggs which she hatches in a fiery ritual, such that she is able to raise three dragons to full-size, reintroducing the species into the world. As 'mother of dragons' she is powerful, recruits an army and sets out to return to Westeros and claim 'her' throne. These dragons, the 'fire' of the series title, hang like Chekhov's gun from the story's nail: we know, even though Martin has yet to write the book, that they will be deployed against the 'ice' of the white walkers in a climactic battle.

Lev Grossman argues that 'what marks Martin as a major force for evolution in fantasy, is his refusal to embrace a vision of the world as a Manichaean struggle between Good and

---

[1] John Lanchester, 'When Did You Get Hooked?', 8. 'Most consumers of popular culture have been trained to expect happy endings, last-minute reprieves, a lucky break for the good guy in a tight spot. In *Game of Thrones*, the good guy has his head forced down on the block and then chopped off, in the presence of two of his daughters.' This deliberate violation of the 'eucatastrophe' holds until the very end of the story, when the series finally yields to that Tolkienian logic.

Evil'. For Grossman Martin adds 'moral complexity' to the simplism of Tolkien.[2] There is something in this, although it is, in its own way, simplistic. In place of enchantment and transport, Martin gives us sociopolitical and cultural detail, power politics, elements adapted from the Wars of the Roses and the clan battles of Highland Scotland. Joseph Young argues that Martin not only reworks Tolkien in terms of realpolitik and moral greyzones, he also injects Pratchettian subversions of the ordinary into the ritualized idealism of fantasy. Young picks out the scene in *A Storm of Swords* (2000) when Catelyn Stark's father, Lord Hoster Tully, dies. His body is dressed in full armour and set adrift in a boat on the Tumblestone River. The boat is to be set slight with a burning arrow fired by his son Edmure so as to burn and sink, 'uniting him bodily with the waters he ruled so nobly. Thus the Tullys observe their defining connection to their lands'. But Edmure, drunk, misses his shot three times, swears and throws the bow away (his uncle manages to hit the boat just before it passes out of range). 'How different this is from the departure of Boromir', Young notes. 'Arrayed much like Tully, Boromir is set adrift on the Anduin, a river of rich symbolic importance to his family.' But 'human error is not admitted into J. R. R. Tolkien's report of this ritual'; Aragorn and Legolas sing songs and bid farewell to their friend. 'It is exactly the sort of dignified, storied, elegiac occasion Catelyn and Edmure Tully hoped for.'

> The essential failure of the Tully funeral is indicative of Martin's story. Throughout his *Song* conceits of glamour, ritual, aristocratic pretension, and even personal dignity are frustrated or spoiled. Some of these let-downs are the result of villainy but most are due to predictable complications that these people seem nonetheless not to have foreseen – mourners drink; drunks are poor shots. Martin's characters are repeatedly denied any pretence of majesty, solemnity, or ceremonial catharsis, apparently due to sheer bad planning.[3]

It would mistake to call this 'realism', although the logic of Grimdark is a purported attention to the 'way things actually work' rather than the idealized escapism of representation in traditional fantasy. One might wonder why a writer interested in 'realism' would write fantasy in the first place, or to put it more specifically generic terms, what the relationship is in the mode between verisimilitude and idealization. One way of addressing this question would be to touch on the last series of the HBO adaptation, and the sharp downturn from energetic approbation to derisive severity amongst the show's fans. Objections were vocal, sometimes furious, widespread, that the show lost force in its final series. Zeynup Tufekci argues the problem was 'not just bad storytelling – it's because the storytelling style changed from sociological to psychological'. According

---

[2]'Martin's wars are multifaceted and ambiguous, as are the men and women who wage them and the gods who watch them and chortle, and somehow that makes them mean more. *A Feast for Crows* isn't pretty elves against gnarly ores. It's men and women slugging it out in the muck, for money and power and lust and love' [Lev Grossman, 'The American Tolkien', 139.]

[3]Young, 'The American Pratchett? Muck and Modality in George R. R. Martin's *Song of Ice and Fire*', 290.

to Tufekci, Martin's novels adopt a broadly sociological approach to their narrative, something the early series of the TV show followed; but later on, showrunners Benioff and Weiss reverted to a more Hollywood-conventional psychological understanding of what storytelling is. He argues that Martin's *Song of Ice and Fire* tells a story about society as a whole: individual characters matter, but not so much as the larger shaping forces of society and culture. Since the show ran out of novels to adapt and Benioff and Weiss took over storytelling duties they instead concentrated on a few psychologically focalized, character-based storylines.

> For Benioff and Weiss, trying to continue what *Game of Thrones* had set out to do, tell a compelling sociological story, would be like trying to eat melting ice cream with a fork. Hollywood mostly knows how to tell psychological, individualized stories. They do not have the right tools for sociological stories, nor do they even seem to understand the job.[4]

Martin is interested not just in how an army fights on the battlefield, but in how it is mustered, where the money comes from to pay it, how its discipline is maintained. 'Tolkien can say that Aragorn became king and reigned for a hundred years, and he was wise and good', Martin has said. 'But Tolkien doesn't ask the question: What was Aragorn's tax policy? Did he maintain a standing army? What did he do in times of flood and famine?'[5]

We might argue a fantasy novelist describing a dark lord marching his swarming army of orcs across green fields towards serried ranks of elven warriors in their gleaming armour without addressing the question of how it all gets paid-for is, by one metric, being naive. To say so, however, is not altogether to articulate dispraise, especially in this specific context of fantasy writing. Naïveté may be a kind of ludicrous gullibility, but it might also be a holier kind of innocence. The word comes, like nativity, from the Latin *nativitas*: which means a birth, a newness coming into the world. Here Dorothy Sayers explains her love for medieval art and culture, from the introduction to her 1957 translation of *The Song of Roland*:

> And so Roland rides out, into that new-washed world of clear sun and glittering colour which we call the Middle Age (as though it were middle-aged) but which has perhaps a better right than the blown summer of the Renaissance to be called the Age of Re-birth. It is also a world full of blood and grief and death and naked brutality, but also of frank emotions, innocent simplicities and abounding self-confidence – and world with which we have so utterly lost touch that we have fallen into using the words 'feudal' and 'medieval' as mere epithets for outer darkness. Anyone who sees gleams of brightness in that world is accused of

---

[4]Tufekci, 'The Real Reason Fans Hate the Last Season of *Game of Thrones*', 4.
[5]George R. R. Martin, 'The Rolling Stone Interview', 5.

romantic nostalgia for a Golden Age that never existed, But the figure of Roland stands there to give us the lie: he is the Young Age as that age saw itself. Compared with him, the space-adventurers and glamour-boys of our times, no less than the hardened toughs of Renaissance epic, seem to have been born middle-aged.[6]

Youth is the very currency of *nativitas*, and the life blood of fantasy. But *Game of Thrones*, like the novels upon which it is based, is not young. It's old, even its young characters, like child-soldier Arya, old before her time. Oldness does not necessarily map onto wisdom, any more than *nativitas* is necessarily naive. Real-life armies need pay, of course. They need whole logistics corps: supply lines and operations officers, organization on a huge scale, and real-life medieval or Renaissance armies also trailed long queues of camp-followers behind them. We can talk about them, if we like, in our fantasy novels, but many readers aren't going to note their lack in the fantasy blockbuster de jour, any more than we miss them in *The Song of Roland*. Omitting these details is not 'realistic', but, then, fantasy is very particularly not Realism.

A rejoinder here might be that whatever it is that fans of *Game of Thrones* go to the show for, it's not innocence. On the contrary, this text's whole point is to deconstruct notions of honour, nobility, loyalty and innocence, to reveal them for the whited sepulchres they are, or at least that the consensus nowadays believes them to be. Tolkien's vision was *Beowulf* and the *Song of Roland*; Martin's is Machiavelli and Hobbes. My point is that one consistent theme of Martin's storytelling, a point to which Benioff and Weiss as scriptwriters adhered, is the way reality keeps intruding upon our fantasies, that cold actuality is constantly shaking us out of our dreams of how things and people might be. The Danaerys storyline is just this, magnified by being moved into a narratively climactic place in the show. Life is not inclined to accommodate your fantasies. It's a core truth of social existence, and it tends to make us unhappy. That's Freud's argument, in a nutshell:

> Despite Freud's gifts of lucid expression, *Civilisation and its Discontents* is a difficult book, in some part because it undertakes to lead us beyond an idea with which we are familiar and comfortable, that society is the direct and 'sufficient' cause of man's frustration. Its central thesis is that society is no more than the 'necessary' cause of frustration. As Freud now describes the dynamics of the unconscious, the direct agent of man's unhappiness is an element of the unconscious itself. The requirements of civilization do indeed set in train an exigent disciplinary process whose locus is the ego, but this process, Freud says in effect, is escalated by the unconscious ego far beyond the rational demands of the societal situation. The informing doctrine of *Civilisation and its Discontents* is that the human mind, in the course of instituting civilization, has so contrived its own nature that it directs against itself an unremitting and largely gratuitous harshness.[7]

---

[6]Dorothy L Sayers, 'Introduction', *The Song of Roland*, 17.
[7]Trilling, *Sincerity and Authenticity*, 151.

Fantasy as a literary (and televisual) mode has a close relation to fantasy as a psychological driver, as this study has been arguing. We go to these texts because they provide something we lack in our day-to-day: some sense of enchantment, or plenitude, or some connection with a past and a land – some myth, perhaps – the pleasures of escapism to a more elegant, pre-industrial and pre-modern world. It might seem unlikely that people wish to 'escape' to Westeros, where life is so nasty, brutish and short, but it seems they do, and in large numbers. And perhaps that's not so counterintuitive, actually. There are *Game of Thrones* fans enamoured of all the Noble Houses and family trees, the city-states and legends, all the cod-chivalric trappings, and the fact that the show themselves reveals these as a mere window-dressing for a widespread Hobbesian social horrors means such fans get to have their chivalric cake and eat it too as knowing-moderns.

Grimdark's popularity has continued to grow, buoyed by the success of *Game of Thrones*. British author Joe Abercrombie – known to his fans, significantly, as 'Lord Grimdark' – is second only to Martin as a writer of fantasy in this mode. His 'First Law' trilogy [*The Blade Itself* (2006), *Before They Are Hanged* (2007) and *Last Argument of Kings* (2008)] contains much violence, torture and a Machiavellian sense of power-plays behind the façade of society and civilization: *homo homini lupus est*, the randomness of fate, 'good' characters as liable to end badly and the bad to triumph as vice versa – though there aren't really any 'good' characters in Abercrombie's books, for even the most likeable are conflicted, have darkness in their past, murder on their conscience.

Abercrombie's Fantasyland was once inhabited by demons and human beings both, until a wizard called Euz expelled all demons to a dimension on 'the other side'. Connections with this dimension exist, and it powers such magic as still operates in the human realm, but the 'first law' of the series title has been laid-down by Euz himself: 'it is forbidden to touch the Other Side direct'. This law is not scrupulously observed. The story follows three characters in particular: Logen Ninefingers is a hard-bitten northland barbarian, worn-out and wary; brattish, selfish, young aristocrat Captain Jezal dan Luthar, proud of his fencing skills but vain and inexperienced; and the crippled torturer Inquisitor Glokta. Glotka serves 'the Union', a version of Early Modern Europe. The Union is threatened by war from the barbarian North as well as, to the south, the Orientalist Gurkish Empire. During the trilogy, as war breaks out all over, a wizard called Bayaz – more powerful than his shlubby outward appearance implies – attempts to use the situation to his own purposes, to vanquish the dark mage. Ninefingers conveys Falstaff's, rather than Harry Hotspur's, view of war:

'What's a battle like?' [Jezal] asked.

'Battles are like men. No two are ever quite the same'.

'How do you mean?'

'Imagine waking up at night to hear a crashing and a shouting, scrambling out of your tent into the snow with your trousers falling down, to see men all around you killing one another. Nothing but moonlight to see by, no clue who're enemies and who're friends, no weapon to fight with'.

'Confusing', said Jezal.

'No doubt. Or imagine crawling in the mid between the stomping boots, trying to get away but not knowing where to go with an arrow in your back and a sword cut across your arse, squealing like a pig'.

'Painful', agreed Jezal.

'Very. Or imagine standing in a circle of shield no more than ten strides across, all held by men roaring their loudest ... '

'Hmm', murmured Jezal. [*Before They Are Hanged*, 211]

Abercrombie is a consummate storyteller and does not allow an overlading of worldbuilding specifics or lore get in the way of the onward narrative momentum. He is moreover a very witty writer, whose humour leavens the lumpishness of standard fantasy seriousness. There is a good deal of violence, swearing and sex in these stories, but also a winning comic panache: to appropriate Shelley's description of Byron's satires, they are a mixture of wormwood and verdigris. More, his approach to his world is as a lens on genre as much as one on socio-cultural difference, and he is not a slave to in-text worldbuilding consistency. *Best Served Cold* (2009) is set in the same imagined Fantasyland as the 'First Law' trilogy, but in a different corner that essays not medieval Europe but Renaissance Italy: elegance and cruelty, plots and (as the title suggests) revenge. *Red Country* (2012) another follow-up in the same world, is actually a kind of Western, owing much to the Clint Eastwood movie *Unforgiven*. And the most recent 'Age of Madness' trilogy [*A Little Hatred* (2019), *The Trouble with Peace* (2020) and *The Wisdom of Crowds* (2021)] moves the Union closer to modernity via an ongoing industrial revolution. Abercrombie, here, is knocking on the door of the divide between our modern world and the pre-modern past that is the structuring logic of fantasy as such. The 'Madness' books pick up the next generation, the children of the characters from 'First Law', though the pace of technological change seems improbably concertinaed (the societies in the original trilogy don't even possess cannons; yet here are manufactories and ironworks, steam engines, chimneys everywhere). When an equivalent to the French Revolution sweeps the continent, it seems strange that the immensely powerful wizard Bayaz does not use his magic to avert it. But magic and demons, still notionally part of the storyworld, are diminishments in these later books, and that may be the point. The logic of Grimdark is that of re*dis*enchantment, something all these books follow through.

There's no question that Abercombie is a major figure in contemporary fantasy, which in turn restages the question. We might recall the story Vladimir Nabokov tells about the inspiration for his novel *Lolita* (1955): a newspaper story he read 'about an ape in the Jardin des Plantes, who, after months of coaxing by a scientist, produced the first drawing ever charcoaled by an animal: this sketch showed the bars of the poor creature's cage'. Grimdark is that literature that draws the cage-bars: a strange kind of escapism, we might think. It sometimes adopts the posture of satire, but that only deepens the conundrum. What, after all, is being satirized? Life in some general sense? To say so only muddles the picture, since the world of the novel is, by virtue of the estrangement of fantasy as a mode, not life. Expressions of cynicism and worldliness impair rather than distil the thrust of the whole. 'When one man knowingly kills another, they call it

murder! When society causes the deaths of thousands, they shrug and call it a fact of life'
[*A Little Hatred*, 202]. Abercrombie's novels are at their weakest when they rehearse such
bromides. They are stronger when they reflect back upon the mode that construes them.
Here two characters admire a heroic statue.

> 'Stolicus was the inspiration, I understand, ordering the famous charge at the
> Battle of Darmium'.
> Monza raised an eyebrow. 'Leading a charge, eh? You'd have thought he'd have
> put some trousers on for work like that'.
> 'It's called artistic licence', snapped Salier. 'It's a fantasy, one can do as one
> pleases'.
> Cosca frowned. 'Really? I always felt a man makes more points worth making if
> he steers always close to the truth'. [*Best Served Cold*, 252]

This is funny, and to the point. But the truth mentioned at the end is jesting-Pilate
nomenclature. Whose truth? The cynical adult, cathecting his (to gender it) sadism into
a worldview that justifies his own bitterness? The Wordsworthian child, who can still
apprehend the sublime glory in the world?

Through the first decades of the century Grimdark fantasy novels assumed a greater
share of fantasy publishing as such. Mark Lawrence's 'Broken Empire' trilogy – *Prince
of Thorns* (2011), *King of Thorns* (2012) and *Emperor of Thorns* (2013) – is as barbed as
its thorny titles suggest: anti-hero Jorg, only thirteen when the story starts, rapes and
slaughters his way across a collapsing Fantasyland empire, eventually seizing the throne.
In Peter McLean's *Priest of Bones* (2018) a gang return from a Fantasyland war and settle
into the mafia life in the big city, using violence and murder to jockey for their position:
a sort of magicland *Peaky Blinders*, or perhaps a fantasy *Boardwalk Empire*, with much
swearing and savagery. Reference to those two non-fantasy TV serials suggests that this
focus on darkness, violence and exploitation was part of a wider cultural storytelling
phenomenon, as it was. Adam Kotsko identifies a cultural fascination with sociopaths in
twenty-first-century popular entertainment, either interactional sociopaths (Cartman
in *South Park*, Don Draper in *Mad Men*) or sociopaths given to the kinds of explicit,
torturous violence we associate with Grimdark (in shows like *The Sopranos*, *The Wire*,
*Dexter* and, indeed, *Game of Thrones*).[8]

Rather better written than many examples of the mode, Richard Morgan's 'A Land
Fit For Heroes' trilogy [*The Steel Remains* (2008), *The Cold Commands* (2011) *The Dark
Defiles* (2014)] centres on an elvish character, Ringil Eskiath: a war veteran from a conflict
between the Yhelteth Empire and the saurian Scaled Folk, shunned by his aristocratic
family due to his homosexuality. The series inhabits its familiar throughline story with
determined, unforgiving focus on hardship, struggle and violence. There is honour and
hope in the story, but it is consistently betrayed: what Morgan himself identifies as the

---

[8]Adam Kotsko, *Why We Love Sociopaths*.

'central conceit' to which his writing keeps returning: 'a sense of something grand and worthwhile being abandoned by vicious and stupid men in favour of short-term profit and tribal hegemony'.[9] M. D. Lachlan's lupine fantasy series [*Wolfsangel* (2010), *Fenrir* (2011), *Lord of Slaughter* (2012), *Valkyrie's Song* (2015) and *The Night Lies Bleeding* (2018)] ranges across many centuries, opening in a vividly rendered Viking world and carrying a Vikingr logic through the whole. It is a werewolf story, but situated in an exceptionally well-rendered milieu: King Authun believes a prophecy that, if he retrieves a child stolen by Saxons, the returnee will grow into a king to lead his people to glory, but on a raid in England he discovers not one child but twins. Killing his own raiders to keep this secret, Authun carries the babies back to Scandinavia, to be raised by the witches who live on the troll wall. This world is one where the brutality of Grimdark is matched by a potent sense of the enthrallment of the pre-modern world, its terrors and sublimities. The laborious, uncomfortable and costly methods by which the witches accrue their powers and the transporting, shattering manner of the werewolfian transformation, speak to a world in which violence *is* enchantment, cold and brutal but enthralling, magical. This is a world defined by war. Here a Viking warrior converses with a merchant on the topic of love.

'It does not do to love women too much, don't all your people say that? An Umayyad merchant told me one story of a caliph, a king of many lands, who fell in love with a slave girl. He could demand from her anything he wanted but that wasn't enough for the idiot. She had to give it freely. He saw the wrong sort of look in her eye one night when they were in bed together and threw himself off a tower'.

'What is a tower?' said Vali.

'A high building, too high to jump off, big as a cliff. They have them in the east, like a fort, but not for war'.

'What's a fort not for war?' said Vali. [Lachlan *Wolfsangel* (2011), 212]

But love is the story, for all that. The following three novels happen centuries later across medieval Europe and Constantinople, and *The Night Lies Bleeding* is set in London during the Blitz, but through all the novels the werewolf character mediates past and present. Better again are two novels Lachlan wrote under the pseudonym Mark Alder (though 'M D Lachlan' is itself a pseudonym): *Son of the Morning* (2014) and *Son of the Night* (2017). These books construe a version of the Hundred Years War in which angels can be recruited to the battlefield, and Hell is a real location, one in which several of the characters must sojourn. The story is superbly rendered, and the novels – as modern novels – get inside a medieval mindset and world in a way rare in fantasy writing. The novels match a deeply researched medievalized Gnostic theology with the lineaments of fantasy as a mode, to brilliant effect.

---

[9]Quoted in Sara Martín Alegre, 'Martian Politics and the Hard-Boiled Anti-Hero: Richard Morgan's *Thin Air*', 85.

Herbert Tucker, discussing William Blake's idiosyncratic fantastika, rendered into a word-and-image fantasy mythography that its creator called 'prophesies', argues that 'Blake had a redemptive vision of wrathful prophesy' which he 'expressed in forms of an unsurpassed meditative depth and polemical impact'.[10] Grimdark, though it cannot apprehend the spiritual correlative of Blake's vision, and over-literalizes and coarsens his dialecticism, does at least take to heart his gnome from *The Marriage of Heaven and Hell* (1793), that 'the tygers of wrath are wiser than the horses of instruction'. One of Blake's most famous 'proverbs of hell', this glosses at least the ambition of Grimdark. And a few lines earlier in Blake's great poem, we read

The wrath of the lion is the wisdom of God.
The nakedness of woman is the work of God.

And so we move on, from wrath to eroticism.

---

[10]Tucker, *Epic: England's Heroic Muse*, 63.

# CHAPTER 20
## ROMANTASY

A significant, continuingly popular idiom of twenty-first-century fantasy is denominated by this rather ungainly portmanteau combining 'romance' and 'fantasy'. Here the intensities – the enchantments of the fantasy reversion, the magic and wonder – refract love-story and sexual connections. We could say the intensities that Grimdark cathects via violence are, often in this mode, addressed with sexual explicitness, although the violence of the former often crosses over into the latter, with a predominance of sado-masochistic sexual play.

We can take Jacqueline Carey's *Kushiel's Dart* (2001), a major bestseller and influential work, as an adjunct of the 1990s vogue for 'angel fantasy' fiction, discussed above. The setting of this novel is a medieval Europe in which Christianity was never proselytized (it remains a small Jewish sect) but where angelic beings have established a kingdom in France called 'Terre D'Ange', and have interbred with human women (as per Genesis 6:2, 'that the sons of God saw the daughters of men that they were fair; and they took them wives of all which they chose'). The direction Carey develops this familiar magical fantasyland emphasizes the BDSM erotic-fantastic. The main character, beautiful young Phèdre nó Delaunay, is born with a red mote in her eye – the 'dart' of the title – that is actually a magical signifier, indicating that she is an *anguissette*, an individual who experiences pain as pleasure. This enables her to take part in a series of elaborately choreographed BDSM sex-scenes with a succession of handsome, haughty aristocratic men. The novel is more than a thousand pages long, and more happens in it than just sex: there is courtly intrigue, the uncovering of a plot to destroy Terre d'Ange, elaboration of the hierarchical social system, rituals and culture of the world. But the core of the book is sex. Phèdre is purchased as a bondsmaiden by the nobleman Anafiel Delaunay and trained in the connected arts of sexual engagement and spycraft, which gives the reader plenty of the following, here with a nobleman called D'Essoms, who has purchased Phèdre from Delauney:

> 'Prove it then, little *anguissette*; as you are on your knees, please me'. ... The muscles of his thighs twitched beneath my gliding hands ... 'On your back!' With one smooth thrust D'Essoms pierced me to the core, even as I cried out at the pain of it I gasped with pleasure ... He was Delauney's enemy and I should have hated him [*Kushiel's Dart*, 168]

This is followed by a beating ('I stood spread-eagled against the X-shape cross, his whipping post ... and then the lash began to fall') intimately described, and more punishingly described sex. Carey extended the work into a trilogy of trilogies, all markedly erotic in focus, following *Kushiel's Dart* with *Kushiel's Chosen* (2002) and *Kushiel's Avatar* (2003); plus a pendant volume, *Cassiel's Servant* (2023), all of which revisits exactly the same story from a different character's perspective, and then the 'Imriel Trilogy' (*Kushiel's Scion* (2006), *Kushiel's Justice* (2007) and *Kushiel's Mercy* (2008)) and the 'Moirin Trilogy' (*Naamah's Kiss* (2009), *Naamah's Curse* (2010), *Naamah's Blessing* (2011)). There is a good deal of repetition in this, but that is apropos, for there is a great deal of repetition in sex itself, not just in the actuality of the physical act, but in the way our sexual fantasies are fixations to which we return over and again. Something similar can be seen in the prodigious success of British author E. L. James's *Fifty Shades of Grey* (2011), not in itself fantasy, although James began the project as fanfiction written in the vampire fantasy world of the *Twilight* novels by Stephenie Meyers [*Twilight* (2005), *New Moon* (2006), *Eclipse* (2007) and *Breaking Dawn* (2008)]. *Fifty Shades of Grey* sold furiously for half a decade, clocking up 150 million copies by 2017, before fading away to nothing in popularity: indicative of a significant cultural moment in the twenty teens, a widespread fascination with female sexual exploration, with eros, power, domination and submission. James is also an intensely repetitive writer, extending her big success into a trilogy that provides readers with small variation on essentially the same sexually charged encounters [*Fifty Shades Darker* and *Fifty Shades Freed*, both published 2012] and then writing exactly the same story again as another trilogy, this time from the perspective of the man rather than the woman [*Grey: Fifty Shades of Grey as Told by Christian* (2015); *Darker: Fifty Shades Darker as Told by Christian* (2017); *Freed: Fifty Shades Freed as Told by Christian* (2021)]. Carey's commercial success was not on the same scale as James, but her achievement is significant, not least in that it presages a development in fantasy towards sexualized and romantic books. Carey's books were important for a female demographic, their open attitude to its subject matter, bisexual characters, and a female-gaze approach to sex a salutary contrast to earlier masculine pulp fantasy such as John Norman's exploitative, objectifying *Gor* novels. In the trend towards more morally grey protagonists and antagonists in fantasy the book is also a touchstone.

There is a confluence of terminology here: 'Fantasy' as a cultural mode, and fantasy in the sense of imaginative speculation about, here, sex. The two can be distinguished, but Carey's success suggests ways in which the two usages productively overlap. For Freud, fantasy refers to a psychological domain that is not only no less important but no less *real* than the 'actual' world in which we live. What distinguishes it from our world is the fertility of its transformative capacity. Carey's novels engage with this excession beyond the just, the only and the merely – that pain be experienced as bliss, that suffering be transmuted into joy – as well as the elimination of the kinds of material consequences verisimilitude might insist upon (Phèdre suffers no infections or scars from this rough usage, her wounds heal magically, she does not become pregnant). Sexual masochism might not be everyone's taste, but in these novels Carey is doing more than simply notating a personal kink. She is making the nature and meaning of fantasy the subject rather than the substance of the book, linking this to 'Fantasy' in a generic sense: articulating a religious, or angelic, transcendence as a re-enchantment in which the conflict of Eros and Thanatos is sublimated and resolved. This relates to her repetitiveness as a writer, and, more broadly (if not always sexually) by fantasy as a mode.

We have already looked at the way, through the 1990s and 2000s, fantasy novels proliferate, an efflorescence of sequels and prequels and retellings, trilogies piled upon trilogies: the same characters in the same worlds having more-or-less the same adventures over and over again, re-enchantment, glamour, peril not merely iterated but endlessly reiterated. A Freudian might point to a compulsion to repeat as symptomatic of psychic distress – we have already mentioned Lady Macbeth washing her hands over and over – though we might also consider it symptomatic of something less pathological, something pleasurable and sustaining and even transcendent, as in sex, there is a dialectical involution linking it back to the compulsive. Repetition is the fort-da game of infancy, staging a denial of the future, a constant return. This perhaps relates to the backward-looking nostalgia of fantasy as a mode, its repeating returns to an idealized medieval or older past world. Call it not nostalgia, pain at the past, but nostohedonia, the pleasure at returning to what has been: key for fantasy as a mode. For Nietzsche repetition is the logic of the eternal cosmos as such, and true freedom, and joy, is to be found in embracing that destiny. This grandiose theory is, we could say, a sort of 'worldbuilding', of the kind fantasy necessitates from its authors. The root, though, is in the fetish-compulsiveness to go over and over the same sexual stages, the retreat from the future into a hedonism of the enchanted past, that Carey's work reveals as libidinous.

What cannot be denied is that 'Romantasy' has become a major, perhaps the major, version of fantasy in the twenty-first century. Sarah J. Maas's *A Court of Thorns and Roses* (2015) and its sequels [*A Court of Mist and Fury* (2016); *A Court of Wings and Ruin* (2017); *A Court of Frost and Starlight* (2018); *A Court of Silver Flames* (2021)] retell the 'Beauty and the Beast' story in an elaborated fantasy kingdom, with a great deal of intensely vigorous coition: beautiful nineteen-year-old Feyre, from our world, is transported to the elvish realm of Prythian by a masked 'High Lord of the Fae' called Tamlin, where she must navigate courtly intrigue and magical peril and eventually war, but above all must work through her erotic connection with her handsome, green-eyed abductor, becoming eventually herself a Queen of the Fae: 'I tore at his shirt, needing to feel the skin beneath one last time, and I had to stifle the moan that rose up in me as he grasped my breast. I didn't want him to be gentle – because what I felt for him wasn't at all like that. What I felt was wild and hard and burning, and so he was with me' [*Court of Thorns and Roses*, 256].

The titles of Jennifer L. Armentrout's various fantasy novels tell their own story: *Obsession* (2013), *White Hot Kiss* (2014), *Moonlight Seduction* (2018), *A Kingdom of Flesh and Fire* (2020), *A Fire in the Flesh* (2023). In her most successful work, *From Blood to Ash* (2020) beautiful young virgin Princess Penellaphe Balfour, fated to ascend to the throne of her fantasyland, is forbidden by magic lore from speaking to or touching any man, but when her handsome young bodyguard Hawke defends her from attack by supernatural creatures the two are thrown together, with predictable fornicatory consequences ('he was staring down at me with eyes so bright, they looked like the gods had polished the amber themselves and placed them there ... he kissed me, and my skin heated at his flavor, the taste of me and those strangely sharp teeth of his', etc.). Danielle L. Jensen's *The Bridge Kingdom* (2018) puts Lara, warrior princess of Ithicana in the company of her notional enemy, King Aren of the titular Bridge kingdom – named for its pontic architecture, rather than its love of card games: the bridge links various islands in a tempestuous sea, for the use of which Aren charges a lucrative toll making him wealthy and powerful. The novel traces the path of the deuteragonists from enemies to lovers, via many lubricious sex-scenes, and a quantity of courtly plotting, spying, fighting and enchantment. Native-American author Scarlett St Clair turns the Greek myth of Hades and Persephone into a sexed-up romance in *A Touch of Darkness* (2019). In Holly Black's *The Cruel King* (2018) two human sisters are transported into the world of Fae by their parents' killer: one pursues power, and the other love. The sex is not as explicitly rendered as some other examples of this mode, Black being governed by the protocols of 'Young Adult' marketing, but sexual fantasy is the underpinning logic. And in Rebecca Yarros *Fourth Wing* (2023), Violet Sorrengail, a bookish female cadet in the 'dragon-riding academy', cops off with the handsome Xaden Riorson, the son of a traitor. Once again, the two start as enemies, and the story, with its various fantastical garnishes, traces their coming-together. There are a great many other examples amongst fantasy writing over the last decade and more, some better than others.

Very successful was Leigh Bardugo's 'Grishaverse' series, beginning with the 'Shadow and Bone' trilogy [*Shadow and Bone* (2012), *Siege and Storm* (2013), *Ruin and Rising* (2014)], and presently comprising a dozen volumes. The story takes place in Ravka, a Russia-flavoured Fantasyland, that is divided by a magical rift called the 'Shadow Fold' (a stretch of perpetually dark desert land filled with supernatural monsters) created by an evil wizard called 'The Darkling'. Since it cuts Ravka off from the European-flavoured west and the sea, this must be crossed to carry and return goods and imports: a perilous business. The main story manifests the influence of Harry Potter: the protagonist Alina is an orphan who belatedly discovers that she possesses light-summoning magical powers, making her one of the 'Grisha', a cast of elemental magicians. Alina and her friends must battle the Darkling by accumulating various plot-coupons – magical artefacts called 'amplifiers' that augment the powers of the Grisha – and there is much to-ing and fro-ing, questing and battling. But the books also trace the romantic complications of what we might call a 'love rectangle': a triplet of love-interest possibilities for the feisty heroine: a childhood friend called Mai (who loves her, but is willing to set aside his feelings so that Alina not be distracted as she leads the revolution against the Darkling); handsome, witty and cunning Nikolai, heir to Ravka's throne, who offers Alina the chance to become queen; and finally The Darkling himself, who variously pursues, enslaves and flees from Alina as a romantic bond between them grows. The series success speaks for itself, and has been augmented by screen adaptation (Netflix and David Heyman, the producer of the *Harry Potter* films, have so far made two eight-episode series based on the novels, broadcast April 2021 and March 2023). At the same time, these books are also representative of the deadening facility with which commercially successful franchises can be mashed together: the publisher promotes the books with a line from *The Stylist* magazine's praising review of *Shadow and Bone*: 'it's like *The Hunger Games* meets *Potter* meets *Twilight* meets *Lord of the Rings*': as if this is a good thing rehashment. The deadening literalism by which moral darkness manifests literally *as darkness* informs through the whole, and the reader whose heart is not captured by Alina's romantic choice – will it be the hot boy-next-door, the hot high-status boy and the hot bad-boy? – may find the over-familiar iterations of the story tending to pall.

Like Bardugo, Robin Bridges's 'Katarina' trilogy [*The Gathering Storm* (2012), *The Unfailing Light* (2012), *The Morning Star* (2013)] concerns a young woman in an alt-Russian Fantasyland who discovers she has magic powers (in this case, the ability to raise the dead) and undertakes romantic adventures. Catherynne M. Valente's *Deathless* (2011) mixes the Russian fairy tale 'The Death of Koschei the Deathless' with the events of the 1917 Russian Revolution, and J Nelle Patrick's *Tsarina* (2014) also reconfigures the Russian Revolution, though less skilfully than Valente: this novel concerns a quest to obtain possession of a magical Fabergé egg, as well as on the love-story of the aristocratic heroine Natalya. None of these works are fully interested in history. Katherine Magyarody, discussing the way 'the fall of the Soviet Union led to a flood of new fantasy books', also notes that 'a great deal of them are of the Tolkien-influenced swords-and-sorcery variety … drawing on Slavic mythology but keep the trope of imagining alternative premodern worlds'. Russia in this case works as a way by which anglophone writers can '"provincialize" the Euro-American canon by exploring a context that is at once European but also politically and culturally Other'. Mentioning Bardugo, Bridges and Patrick – and praising Valente's more folk-tale focussed novel – Magyarody notes how

> the treatment of Slavic culture in many of the texts written in English shows a mix of careful study and exoticization, with a bias toward the latter. Authors seem dazzled by Russian imperial culture, with its grand duchesses, Fabergé eggs, and the ballet. The fantasy narratives that do engage with history end their narratives at the turn of the twentieth century, insulating their privileged characters from historical upheaval.[1]

## Jonathan Strange and Mr Norrell

Arguably the major fantasy novel of the 2000s was *Jonathan Strange and Mr Norrell* (2004), the debut novel of British writer Susanna Clarke. It is significant that this is not a fantasy novel in the imitative or Grimdark-reactive Tolkienian mode. It is, rather, an expert pastiche of a Regency or Victorian novel, disposed into three volumes (though sold as one 1,000-page book), telling in leisurely, detailed and superbly involving fashion the story of two English gentleman-magicians: bookish, pedantic, middle-aged introvert Norrell and more adventurous, outgoing, younger and more dashing Strange. Both

---

[1]Magyarody, 'Translating Russian Folklore into Soviet Fantasy in Arkadi and Boris Strugatski's *Monday Begins on Saturday* and Catherynne M. Valente's *Deathless*', 338, 360.

aim to 'restore' English magic – for in the world of the novel, what was once a major part of English life has fallen into desuetude, a matter of merely antiquarian interest. Bibliophile stay-at-home Norrell comes from that book-learning tradition, although he also possesses a large natural innate magical ability. Strange is more intuitive, more self-taught, and though he does consult (and by the end of the story, has written) books, the contrast in characters between the two titular deuteragonists is a large part of the charm of the novel. Once, long ago, John Uskglass, 'the Raven King', ruled three kingdoms, one of which stretched across northern England (the other two were in Fairyland and in Hell). Back then, magic was common, and fairy interventions (mischievous, destructive, rarely helpful) in human affairs widespread. Now Uskglass has abandoned this world – or so it seems – and a disenchanted bourgeois materialist Church-of-England modernity is the logic of the novel's world. Norrell, by dint of intensive study amongst books of lost magical lore (combined with his innate talent), has restarted magic as a practical, rather than merely theoretical, business. He comes to London to offer his services to the realm during the darkest days of the Napoleonic war. Strange comes later (it's characteristic of Clarke's approach as a writer that she holds off introducing this title character until we're more than 200 pages in) his gift more spontaneous, although he does become Norrell's apprentice, or assistant, for a while to learn what he can. More adventurous and outgoing than his friend, Strange accepts the governmental commission to travel to Ibera and assist the Duke of Wellington with his campaign against Bonaparte. Various recurring characters and subplots thread the larger story of Strange and Norrell's coming together and falling out. In one strand, Sir Walter Pole begs Norrell to use his magic to bring his fiancé – young, beautiful, untimely dead – back to life. Norrell does this by striking a deal with a powerful fairy, known only as 'the Gentleman with the Thistle-Down Hair'. Lady Pole will be reanimated if Norrell agrees that she live half her life as a human and the remaining half in the fairy realm. Thinking this would at least give Lady Pole several decades of human living – and judging this to be better than death – Norrell agrees. But the Gentleman with the Thistle-Down Hair has tricked him. The half-and-half deal runs concurrently, not consecutively. Lady Pole lives her days in London, but every night she is compelled to journey to fairyland, where she must dance at endless balls in the Gentleman's fairy-mansion of Lost Hope. During waking hours she grows listless, despairing, half-dead, unable (because of enchantment) to tell her living companions what she goes through. In another plot-strand, the Gentleman with the Thistle-Down Hair takes a liking to Sir Walter's butler, Stephen Black. He compliments Black on his physical beauty and demeanour and promises to make him King of England. Black, though always courteous, is increasingly ill-at-ease in the Gentleman's company. He declines the offer, but must accept the many extravagant gifts the Gentleman bestows upon him, which clutter his servant's quarters.

The overall story is very leisurely in its development and is hospitable to many digressions and inset-tales, often in footnotes: a textual strategy that takes us back to Walter Scott's novels. Some foot-of-the-page notes are brief, but others run on for many thousands of words, leaving the main text a thin dribble of larger font across the top of the page. And the larger structure of the whole is episodic: a series of magic spells and their consequences. Although there's much magic in the novel, a book in large part *about* magic, there is no single magic 'system' that applies. Some spells are simply executed: for example, a book is placed in front of a mirror and the physical object is swapped with its reflection. Other spells require convoluted and bizarre performances. Late in the novel the Gentleman with the Thistle-Down Hair desires to find out Stephen Black's real name – for Stephen, a man of African heritage, was sold into slavery at an early age before ending up in England (as a servant, not a slave, though the Gentleman can't understand the distinction). To that end the Gentleman needs to enact a complex spell: he must locate certain planks from a ship, now sunken, plus a particular pearl necklace, a certain garment and finally he must find the magical essence of a particular kiss. None of this is easy: the planks have been salvaged and are now part of a poor man's house (the Gentleman burns this down, killing the occupant, and takes the ashes). To get the necklace he strangles a French Revolutionary official who happens to be trying it on. The garment has been repurposed as the counterpane for an old woman's bed, which the Gentleman takes, leaving her to freeze to death. The kiss is the most troublesome of all: it had been taken by a man hanged several years earlier, but it had been transferred from him to all the women he kissed before dying, requiring the Gentleman to kill each of them to draw enough of the kiss's essence together. Not all the magic is as ruthless in its operation as this. Indeed, a major moral theme of the novel is the question of using magic to harm. The Duke of Wellington, at war in Iberia, asks Strange how deadly his powers are:

'Can a magician kill a man by magic?' Lord Wellington asked Strange.
    Strange frowned. He seemed to dislike the question. 'I suppose a magician might', he admitted, 'but a gentleman never could' [*Strange and Norrell*, 389]

Norrell and Strange fall out over the nature of magic itself. Strange believes, as he says in the article he publishes, that 'it is John Uskglass's magic that we do' [532] and that the future of magic in England depends upon allying with fairyland and recuperating Uskglass. To Norrell this idea is obnoxious. He concedes that Uskglass may have originated magic, but Norrell's vision is of a reformed, clarified, fairy-purged magical future. As Strange puts it, in the book (within the book) that he writes, *The History and Practice of English Magic* (John Murray, London, 1816): 'It is the contention of Mr Norrell of Hanover-square that everything belonging to John Uskglass must be shaken out of modern magic, as one would shake moths and dust out of an old coat. What does he imagine he will have left? If you get rid of John Uskglass you will be left holding the empty air.' 'Hanover Square' points to the modern, whiggish, Protestant, Hanoverian side of this Scottian dynamic, in opposition to the old, Tory, 'Catholic' magical side. This dialectic powers the novel.

The opposition is a matching as well as a tension: a mirroring. Who, what, is Uskglass? His name combines Usk + Glass: the first portion of deriving from the Old Norse *œskja*, 'to wish'. The name, then, means: 'John Mirror-wish'. *Jonathan Strange and Mr Norrell* is replete with looking-glasses and mirrors. Lady Pole is oppressed by the mirror in her room. Strange vistas are sometimes glimpsed in mundane looking-glasses. Strange uses magic to travel from place to place via mirrors, which is to say, mirrors are portals. Wishing-glasses. Clarke's apparently expansive and episodic text actually does a series of tightly controlled and interesting things with doubling, mirroring, reflection (and self-reflection). It's a book with two similar but dissimilar characters named on its title page. Various characters have their paired antagonists, animas, shadows. England is at war with France. Our world is mirrored by fairyland and, perhaps most importantly, modernity – which is where we live – is mirrored by and shadowed by elder times. Broadly the dynamic here is: magic is the pre-modern logic that has, largely, been superseded and has passed away into history, a matter of dryasdust antiquarian researching (until Norrell resurrects it).

The Regency world of *Strange and Norrell* is a disenchanted space into which enchantment is, marginally, variously, sometimes disruptively, reinserting itself. In this sense *Strange and Norrell* is, as it were, 'about' the relationship between the pre-modern and the modern – about fantasy as such. What the respectable, bourgeois, reformed English Protestantism of Clarke's Regency world sees when it looks in the mirror is: the glamorous, romantic, dangerous antique Catholicism it once was. That's what 'magic' is in this book: a kind of Catholicism – which Norrell wishes to reform, to rid of supernatural and priestly and enchanted aspects (a thumbnail definition of the Protestant Reformation as such) and which Strange wishes to restore in something like its original form. Both men are gentlemen, but Norrell is a bourgeois gentleman – which is to say, a Protestant – and Strange, though also notionally Church of England, is rather more aristocratic, a touch more cavalier (or Cavalier), more sympathetic to the old ways. *Strange and Norrell* has Jane Austen qualities, but it is also a very Walter-Scott-ish piece of writing, and as fantasy – that is, as fantasy as an engagement with history – it is best glossed via Lukács's reading of Scott as the paradigmatic historical novelist, dramatizing the dynamic of history as such as a dialectical process by which older socio-cultural theses come into conflict with antithetical present-day forces and are sublated into a synthetic future. By its nature fantasy looks back to an enchanted past of one kind or another, and navigates the gap between that ancient glamour and modern Weberian disenchantment as history. As such this novel is absolutely characteristic fantasy.

Often, in other works, the structural violence of this state of affairs is parleyed, with a kind of dead-eyed literalism, into in-story violence, sometimes egregiously so. Tolkien is not violent in this manner; and Clarke is very much not writing in the grisly, Grimdark idiom of so much other fantasy from this period. But she is writing a war-story. It's just that this is a war story of a very particular kind. We could compare Naomi Novik's popular series of Napoleonic fantasy novels: starting with *Temeraire* (2006; titled *His Majesty's Dragon* in the United States) and followed by *Throne of Jade* (2006), *Black Powder War* (2006), *Empire of Ivory* (2007), *Victory of Eagles* (2008), *Tongues of Serpents* (2010), *Crucible of Gold* (2012), *Blood of Tyrants* (2013) and *League of Dragons* (2016). The early nineteenth century of Novik's novels is very like the actual early nineteenth century, rather oddly so, considering the fact that in this world dragons are real. They come from various parts of the world: the titular Temeraire is a Chinese dragon although born in Britain and raised by a British officer. This premise enables Novik to write Napoleonic battle scenes that include air forces, crewed dragons swooping through the sky, steered by pilots whilst sharp-shooters hang from leather straps and try to aim their rifles. The dragons can also, being dragons, spit fire from their mouths.

> The other officers shuddered all around and nodded; few things were as deadly to a ship as uncontrolled fire upon her deck. 'I was on the Goliath myself,' Laurence went on. 'We were not half a mile distant from the Orient when she went up, like a torch; we had shot out her deck-guns and mostly cleared her sharpshooters from the tops, so the dragon could strafe her at will.' He fell silent, remembering; the sails all ablaze and trailing thick plumes of black smoke; the great orange-and-black beast diving down and pouring still more fire from its jaws upon them, its wings fanning the flames; the terrible roaring that was only drowned out at last by the explosion. He had been in Rome once as a boy, and there seen in the Vatican a painting of Hell by Michelangelo, with dragons roasting the damned souls with fire; it had been very like. [*Temeraire*, 40–1]

The premise of the series is that both the British and the French have dragons, since, if one side had dragons and the other didn't, the side with dragons would win. (Indeed one of the points of the later novels is that a dragon plague from North America puts many of the British dragons out of commission, which enables Napoleon to press his advantage and invade Britain, forcing the English army to retreat to Scotland). This is not the set-up in *Strange and Norrell*. There is a revival of magic in England but not in France. 'Napoleon Bonaparte, it was said, was scouring France to find a magician of his own – but with no success' [*Strange & Norrell*, 135]. Doesn't the fact that the British Army can draw upon a powerful magician tip the scales comprehensively on their side, and abbreviate the war? It seems not. The first act of what we can call 'military magic' is performed by Norrell. He conjures a magical armada that blockades the French fleet at Brest, 'arriving in a single instant out of an empty sea. The ships were all ships of the line, heavily armed, two- and three-decked warships.' [128] The French fleet is immobilized for a week and a half until some enterprising French officers row out and discover the truth:

> They could see how the sunlight shone through [the ships] and made them colourless until they were just a faint sparkle upon the water. 'Glass', said the Admiral. It was clever Perroquet who hit upon the truth. 'No my Admiral, it is the rain. They are made of rain.' As the rain fell from the heavens it the drops were made to flow together to form solid masses – pillars and beams and sheets, which someone had shaped to the likeness of a hundred ships ... Being ships of rain they made no sound at all – no creaking of timber, no slap of sail in the wind, no call of sailor to his mate. Several times groups of smooth-faced men of rain came to the ship's rail to gaze out at the wooden ship and its crew of flesh-and-blood men, but what the rain-sailors were thinking no one could tell. [133]

These rain-sailors are marvellous creations, but the fact remains: what material benefit, in terms of Britain's war-aims, does this magic trick do? Clarke tells us that Norrell was widely celebrated in England, but eleven days is nothing in a war lasting many years, especially for ships that might manage four knots on a good day. It's a cool trick. So what can an English magician actually do? Strange, in Portugal and Spain with Wellington, performs various things: he renders rough and difficult roads smooth and passable; he terrifies enemy troops with conjured apparitions of dragons and angels in the sky; he brings dead French soldiers and Italian mercenaries back to life to interrogate them for useful military intelligence, and various other things. In Iberia he shifts the course of an entire river, to put Wellington's army on the advantageous bank. And before Waterloo, informed that Napoleon is threatening Brussels, he waves his hand and moves the entire city to the wilds of North America. He later returns Brussels to its rightful situation, but this is a gesture to give one pause. If Strange can do so prodigious a thing, then why is there a war at all? This is greater potency than whole flocks of Novikian dragons. Why doesn't Strange simply move the entire French army to Siberia, or Australia, or the moon? Why not put the whole army to sleep, as in 'Sleeping Beauty'? Make it so that Napoleon can only speak gibberish and so not communicate his orders? Turn all the French cannons to nougat and cannonballs to candy-floss? Why not simply cast a wish 'the war ends now in English victory'?

It is as if magic, in this novel, is a marvellous phantom, there to provide display, simulacra of things, rain-ships crewed by blank-faced rain sailors – an empty, mirror image. Did Strange *actually* move the city of Brussels, physically transport it lock, stock and Belgian barrel to Indiana? Or did he only provide the appearance of doing so – a vacancy instead of a city and, for the inhabitants, a desert beyond the city limits through which Native American warriors rode? The archetype of magic, by this reading, would be the moment when Strange, in Norrell's library, puts a book on a table in front of a mirror and then swaps physical object and reflection about. It is a novel of wishing-glasses, that ends, fittingly, with Strange and Norrell both trapped in some kind of mirror dimension, dark, and trying to magic their way to freedom.

Late in the novel, Norrell conjures an invisible wall at the Kent coast 'to protect the cliffs from erosion, people's houses from storm, livestock from being swept away'. Lascelles, one of Norris's associates, objects that, being invisible, nobody will know about it.

'Could you not have placed beacons at regular intervals to remind people that the magic wall is there? Burning flames hovering mysteriously over the face of the waters? Pillars shaped out of sea-water? Something of that sort?' 'Oh!' said Mr Norrell. 'To be sure! I could create the magic illusions you mention. They are not at all difficult to do, but you must understand that they would be purely ornamental. They would not strengthen the magic in any particular way whatsoever. They would have no practical effect'. 'Their effects', said Lascelles, severely, 'would be to stand as a constant reminder to every onlooker of the works of the great Mr

Norrell … ' 'Indeed?' said Mr Norrell. He promised that in future he would always bear in mind the necessity of doing magic to excite the public imagination. [S&N, 885]

*Strange and Norrell* is a novel about the way social norms, the fronts we all put on, conventions and expectations, get disturbed, put out of true, vexed and miracled by the impossible. Strange's wife, visiting Lady Pole, often sees the Gentleman with the Thistle-Down Hair at Sir Walter Pole's house, and assumes he is merely a cohabitant, perhaps a servant. She realizes only belatedly that nobody else (Lady Pole aside) can see him. The sense that there is somebody else about, one person more than you can count, has always struck me as an acme of uncanny. The Gentleman with the Thistle-Down Hair is there but not there, glimpsed in mirrors or out of the corner of the eye, and he is a performer, someone who lives for courtly show, for dancing and balls and dressing up and generally acting his role.

# CHAPTER 21
## FANTASY IN THE 2010s AND 2020s

The continuing and growing popularity of fantasy through the twenty-first century has been global in reach, and increasingly global in provenance. The most significant development in the mode across these decades has been the way writers of various heritages have challenged the euro-centric, white, trad logic of prior fantasy: fantasy novels written out of African, Asian and East Asian heritages, women and people of colour centred, the implicit militaristic and imperialist logic of much earlier fantasy challenged and critiqued. One manifestation of this is a greater emphasis on violence, sometimes very extreme and torturously represented.

This is not to say that the older Tolkien-influenced style of fantasy-writing has dried up. On the contrary, it is still being produced in great amounts, and sometimes it is well done. Brandon Sanderson, a consistently bestselling author, writes entirely within the older tradition. His 'Mistborn' trilogy [*The Final Empire* (2006), *The Well of Ascension* (2007), and *The Hero of Ages* (2008); subsequent volumes have been added to this series, and more are to come] concerns a secret group of magicians, called 'allomancers', who are attempting to overthrow a dark lord's tyrannical rule across an ashen Fantasyland: the series was conceived after Sanderson read the *Harry Potter* series and wondered how the story might go if the dark lord triumphed and the prophesied hero failed.[1] Sanderson's many sequels to this series, and his various other fantasy trilogies and series, are all lengthy, involved, construing intricately complex magical systems across derivatively Fantasyland locations, characters and by-the-numbers plotting. The speed with which Sanderson produces these immensely lengthy books gives them an extruded polystyrene quality: his prose is flavourless, repetitive, clumsy, and his characterization extraordinarily flat and dull. Nevertheless he enjoys enormous popularity, and all his titles have been bestsellers: 'The Stormlight Archive' [ten volumes are promised, beginning with *The Way of Kings* (2010), *Words of Radiance* (2014) and *Oathbringer* (2017)] is set in a Fantasyland across which gigantic storms periodically rage, and concerns the aftermath of an ongoing magic war. Centuries before, the 'Knights Radiant', a consecrated order of chivalric warriors, had been destroyed, but their magical weaponry and armour remain, 'Shardblades' and 'Shardplate', and are in use across the realm. As with Sanderson's first published novel *Elantris* (2005) the structural logic of fantasy as such, in which an ancient magical world and an emergent modernity come to terms with one another, provides the armature: the *Mistborn* novels will, their author has revealed, eventually take their Fantasyland into the world of computing and space-travel.

---

[1]Sanderson, 'Where Does a Book Begin for You? How I Came up with *Mistborn*'.

But the myopic detail-attentiveness with which he constructs his elaborated magical systems does not liberate any actual enchantment, and the puppet characters trudging around the pasteboard sets are the antithesis of the sublime. Neither he nor his very many fans consider this a problem, though. To quote Matthew Sangster, 'the pleasures of calculation' underpin his success: 'Sanderson writes that "he likes mystery more than mysticism" and his approach aligns with that of detective fiction, where readers often feel cheated if the knowledge necessary to solve the mystery is withheld.'[2] Magic as system rather than magic as enchantment, as reassuring as a smoothly functioning repetitive machine.

The influence of Peake continues to shape contemporary fantasy. Alex Pheby's 'Cities of the Weft' trilogy [*Mordew* (2020), *Malarkoi* (2022), *Waterblack* (2025)] is Peake-rich, strange, often surreal, sometimes Lovecraftian but also distinctively Phebyan. The story opens in a fantastical tiered city ruled over by a lofty 'Master' who lives at the top, swarming with slum-kids, magicians, citizenry, thieves and monsters. The city has been built over the dead body of God Himself, and His corpse is having a strange effect upon the urban mud, breeding strange creatures and effecting a 'weft' of magical potential into which some, like protagonist Nathan Treeves, can tap, a process called 'sparking'. Nathan starts the story as an outcast kid who, via perseverance and innate magical ability, breaks through the inertia of a stratified fantasy society to achieve remarkable things. All the baroque curlicues of this neo-Gothic realm are laid before the reader: urchins, mages, whores, suspicious gentlemen, supercilious servants, talking dogs and talking books, resurrected megafauna and a retrospective odeum. But the work folds itself together in complex patterns, a phantasmagoria both revolting – at one point Nathan encounters a woman's corpse floating down a sewer with a rats'-nest living in its groin – and sublime. Nathan, coming into his powers, walks the beach and the sand fuses to glass beneath his feet. Firebirds flap through the sky. God's corpse stirs uneasily. It is an outré work, often mannered and sometimes arch, but it is also immensely vital – is indeed, *about* vitality, in both its creative and its cancerous form.

Some writers work within the conventions and traditions of fantasy; others strive to make something new, imaginatively to escape the crushing force of the 'back-list' of prior books in this mode, to create something new. Chris Wooding's *The Ember Blade* (2019) and its sequel *The Shadow Casket* (2023) follow the farm-boy-who-discovers-he-is-the-chosen-one trope across a familiar Fantasyland, with much incident and adventure, questing for the titular magical objects in each volume: the Excalibur-type magic sword of the first book's title, and the umbrous casket of the second: lengthy books, expertly worked and satisfyingly familiar. On the other hand is Will Wiles's *The Last Blade Priest* (2022) and its sequel *The Dead Man's Empire* (2024) are exceptionally well-written Fantasies, set in a world in which a giant mountain is worshipped, huge birds, called 'the Custodians', are offered human corpses by way of religious sacrifice, and the books' elves are psychotically deranged. Two main characters, Inar a skilled

---

[2]Sangster, *Introduction to Fantasy*, 157.

builder, and Anton, a priest of the Mountain cult (though not necessarily the titular cleric). These books touch on the familiarities of fantasy in order, deftly, to reconfigure them.

But much of the most significant fantasy writing of the last two decades draws not on European models, but comes from around the world. Saladin Ahmed's *Throne of the Crescent* (2012) is set in the Middle-Eastern-styled 'Crescent Moon Kingdoms': Abassan and Rughal-ba, with a large peninsular, 'the Soo Republic', a kind of fantasy Africa. The land is troubled by zombie-like 'ghuls' and fire-monster 'djenn'. In the city of Dhamsawaat, elderly ghul-hunter Adoulla Makhslood and his swordsman, young holy warrior Raseed bas Raseed, investigate a series of gruesome murders against a backdrop of political intrigue and upheaval, as the mysterious Falcon Prince foments revolution against the ruling powers. A dark sorcerer seems to be behind the killings, and Adoulla, Raseed and Zamia, a young woman with the ability to shape-shift into a lion, quest after him, embarking on a series of familiar sword-and-sorcery adventures: it is fast moving, engaging, violent storytelling ('Rat-face, who was still on the ground nursing his broken nose, tried to stab Raseed's leg. Raseed snaked back and stomped on the man's wrist, which broke with a satisfying crunch' [116]) enlivened by its recentring Fantasyland away from Europe. American writer Shannon A. Chakraborty's 'Daevabad Trilogy' [*The City of Brass* (2017), *The Kingdom of Copper* (2019), *The Empire of Gold* (2020)] covers a similar fantasy territory, although at a later notional epoch. Nahri, a young orphan scraping a living as a con-artist in a version of eighteenth-century Cairo, discovers she has magical healing powers and is, despite her humble present situation, a descendent of a noble family. She and a djinn warrior called Darayavahoush e-Afshin whom she has accidentally summoned, journey to the great, brass-walled city of Daevabad in the heart of the Indian subcontinent, which Nahri's ancestors had built long before. Magical war follows, and Nahri's ascent to royalty, and the ins-and-outs of the storytelling, is well handled.

P. Djèlí Clark, the pen-name of American academic and author Dexter Gabriel, has assembled his steampunk fantasia 'Dead Djinn Universe' out of varied elements: the novelette 'A Dead Djinn in Cairo' (2016), the short story 'The Angel of Khan el-Khalili' (2017), the novella *The Haunting of Tram Car 015* (2019) and finally the multiple-award-winning novel *A Master of Djinn* (2021). In this last, set in a version of 1912 Cairo, Agent Fatma, of the 'Ministry of Alchemy, Enchantments and Supernatural Entities', investigates the murders of a group of Englishmen called the 'Hermetic Brotherhood of Al-Jahiz', acolytes of the ninth-century Sudanese mystic – a real person in our world, although in the world of Clark's story he reappeared, in the late nineteenth century, and restored magic to the world. The recency of this return and the balance of the mundane with the possibilities of the djinn-powered magic thread-through an account of imperialism and the colonial mindset. Egypt has recruited the djinn, and other magical entities, to rebel against foreign control, and magic signals the imminent collapse of the British Empire and the coming of the First World War – in passing we learn that in India djinn and 'an even older magic that was said to flow with the Ganges' have forced British occupiers from most of the country.

Kacen Callender's *Queen of the Conquered* (2019) is set in Hans Lollik, a fantasyland version of the Caribbean. Her protagonist, Sigourney Rose, is fighting the colonial occupation of the pale-skinned Fjern, who have enslaved her people and massacred her family – a Scandinavian or Viking-like people from 'the farthest north, smallest of the empire nations [who] have spread themselves across the world, starting wars and claiming more land for Koninkrijk on behalf of their gods'. Rose has magic-telepathic abilities, able to both read and control the minds of others, although these powers are not always reliable. She makes her way to the royal island hoping to influence to the king, and there becomes caught up in court politics, murder and vengeance. It's a novel that uses its magic as a way of thinking-through the logics of oppression and slavery, issues of control and empathy, in the context of the postcolonial moment, although the Black-skinned inhabitants of Hans Lollik are, it seems, aboriginal: the imagined history of this place does not see them displacing any prior peoples.

Ken Liu's 'Dandelion Dynasty' quartet [*The Grace of Kings* (2015); *The Wall of Storms* (2016); *The Veiled Throne* (2021) and *Speaking Bones* (2022)] is a vast, five-thousand-page saga of power, war and the technology set in an Eastern-ized Fantasyland. Through his two main characters, the bandit Kuni Garu (based on Liu Bang, the founder and first emperor of the Han dynasty), and Mata Zyndu (based on Xiang Yu, a noble from the state of Chu), Liu rewrites the Chu-Han contention as fantastical fiction: the civilized Ano people come under attack by the light-skinned Viking-like Lyucu, savage invaders who ride fire-breathing antlered dragons called garinafins – Kuni develops silken airships and war-kites to fight this threat. The sheer size of this series, its vast cast and intricate plotting-out of its various worlds, presents something of an impediment to reading, but the detail and richness of rendering here are immense.

Somali-American Sofia Samatar's *A Stranger in Olondria* (2013) is set in the titular Olondria and the Tea Islands, a fantasy version of South Asian, Malaysian and Indonesian worlds. Jevick, the son of a pepper merchant from the tiny island of Tyom, dreams of visiting the great city of Bain, at the heart of the Olondrian Empire: but when he does he finds himself caught up in the machinations of empire. Jevick connects with the ghost of a girl, trapped between the worlds of the living and the dead. She dictates her life story and he writes it out in an ancient, magical language, for magic in this novel construes itself as a *grimoire*, the grammar of writing as enchantment. The amanuensis falls in love with the girl, hopelessly, for she is dead, and the dead are not receptive to being loved.

> Come angel, I said. I called her Visible, the Ninth wonder, Empress of Sighs. Come, I said, and I will show you magic from the north, your own words conjured into a vallon. A book, angel, a garden of spears. I will hold the pen for you, and I will weave a net to catch your voice. I will do what no one has done, I will write in Kideti, a language like you and me, a ghost hesitating between worlds. Between the rainstorms, angel, and the white light of the north. Between the river dolphins and the wolves. Between the far south, the lands of elephants and amber, and this: the land of cypresses and snow. So come. Sing to me of Kiem, speak to me of rivers. Pour your memories into my pen. [*Stranger in Olondria*, 280]

The beauty and re-enchantment of the book are in its hesitation between worlds, the disjoined magical and material. Andrea Stewart's 'Bone Shard' trilogy [*The Bone Shard Daughter* (2020), *The Bone Shard Emperor* (2021), *The Bone Shard War* (2023)] is set in another East Asian-coded world, an archipelago of migrating (and sometimes sinking) islands on 'the Endless Sea'. The Emperor of this realm wields absolute power that is maintained by his mastery of 'bone magic': shards of people's bones are harvested and used to divert their life energy to other magical purposes: the Emperor benefits but the costs of his magic are borne by others ('I knew that hollow look. Shard-sick. Somewhere, her bone shard was in use, and it had nearly drained her life'). This painful secret speaks to violence. Fonda Lee's 'Green Bone' trilogy [*Jade City* (2017), *Jade War* (2019), *Jade Legacy* (2021)] is a Sinofantasia set on the island of Kekon. This is the only place in the world where the titular jade can be found, a gemstone that activates potent magical powers of strength and speed in those Kekonese who have the potential to use it, making it extremely valuable. This series blends traditional fantasy elements with tropes from Hong Kong martial-arts cinema, and the gang war of rival crime syndicates and mafia-style jockeying for control of Kekon's capital city. It's a lively, fast-moving piece of storytelling that works its melange of pastiche elements well, if a touch decumbently. Violence, again, is the idiom of the story.

M. L. Wang's *The Sword of Kaigen* (2018) is military fantasy set in a Japanese-coded world. The Kaigenese Empire is invaded by the (Chinese-coded) Ranganese: there is a great deal of fighting, and many magical duels deploying ice magic, wind magic and blood manipulation. The perspective is reversed in R. F. Kuang's 'Poppy War' trilogy [*The Poppy War* (2018), *The Dragon Republic* (2019), *The Burning God* (2020)] where the pseudo-Chinese Nikara Empire is invaded by the Federation of Mugen (in effect, the Japanese). Styling this story as fantasy allows Kuang to introduce elements of magic into her story, and to reorient historical actuality to underline her main points in the service of her larger story. Fang Runin, known as Rin, is a scrawny orphan and outcast from the provinces who manages, by sheer determination, to win a spot in the elite Imperial college in Sinegard, where her abilities with magical 'Lore' single her out for future greatness. The first half the novel is Rin's training, and the rest a series of crunchy, gruesome accounts of battlefield ultra-violence. Rin kills a shape-shifting monster called a chimei, 'she smashed the blunt of the torch into his face … his face lost shape altogether. She beat out those eyes, beat them bloody … when he struggled she turned the torch around and burned him in the wounds' – and afterwards 'Rin climbed off the corpse and sucked in a great, heaving breath. Then she vomited' [*The Poppy War*, 366]. But the cause is just, the enemy are monsters both figuratively and in some cases literally, so (as it might be) torturing prisoners is a justified and effective strategy and so on and so forth ('the jammed boats began to burn in earnest … the soldiers on the boats began to scream in earnest. It was utter carnage. It was beautiful' [*Poppy War*, 313]).

This is to return to the question of Grimdark's prominence in twenty-first-century fantasy writing. There's a whole mode of gore-lit, ultra-violent horror shows, especially dominant in culture over the last quarter century: in cinema with a genre of movie known as 'torture porn', and everything from Quentin Tarantino to Omaha Beach at the beginning of *Saving Private Ryan*; in literature too, as we have seen, in which Kuang's account (for instance) of the invader's atrocities can be situated:

> I saw women disembowelled. I saw the soldiers slice off their breasts. I saw them nail women alive to walls. There was a pregnant woman in the house with us … the general howled and grabbed at her stomach. Not with his knife. With his fingers. His nails. He knocked her down and he tore and tore. And he pulled out her stomach and her intestines and finally the baby, and the baby was still moving … the general ripped her baby in half the way you'd split an orange. [*The Poppy War*, 425]

As a fantasy set in an African-coded world, Evan Winter's *The Rage of Dragons* (2019) is even more consistently ultra-violent than Kuang. The Omehi people have been engaged in a centuries-long war. Some few Omehi people have magical powers: some women can command dragons, some men can transform themselves into super-strong warriors able to survive what would be for others fatal wounds. But most are ordinary mortals, fodder for the battlefield. The story follows Tau, a humble farmboy, who works to acquire the magical warrior skills to avenge himself on those who killed his loved ones. The tenor of the book is repeated, extreme violence, both inflicted by Tau on others ('Tau launched himself into the fray, swords whirling, and the closest man took a dulled blade to the face, shattering his eye socket' [417]) and inflicted upon him. (The creature closed its jaws on the back of his neck, cracking his spine and dragging him to the ground. With his spine severed Tau could not feel the leg or his rib cage being torn open by the two demons. He could hear them though, as they slopped up his innards and shook his body with their jostling … He was dying. It hurt. It hurt so much [315]; 'The pain coursed through Tau like a tsunami … he looked down at his wound. The demon had him open from belly to groin' [509].)

Most violent of all is Marlon James's 'Dark Star' trilogy [*Black Leopard, Red Wolf* (2019), *Moon Witch, Spider King* (2022), *White Wing, Dark Star* (2025)]. Set in a Fantasyland that draws on East African culture and mythology, the story concerns Tracker, a man with 'a nose' who can find people – among the living, or the dead. He is lupine, as per the title, and travels often in the company of the titular Black Leopard. The story develops at length, an occasionally confusingly involuted set of adventures that start with a search for a lost boy, encompassing a series of mortal and magical horrors across the 'thirteen kingdoms' of the tale. There is a great deal of rape of boys and girls, of gang-rape and bestiality, of murder and decapitation and cannibalism. Much of this is referenced in a throwaway fashion: brothel keeper Miss Wadada refuses entry to 'people who are not themselves … she let a shape-shifter fuck one of her girls once, until he swatted her in a fit of ecstasy and snapped her neck' [256]. The narrator observes a slaver contemplating two new captives, a man and a woman:

'Kill this bitch now', the slaver said. 'Only one thing the northern masters love
even more than unblemished woman. Unblemished eunuch. Take him away
and make it so'. …
They took the woman away to drown her and the man to cut all manhood off.
'This is what you took me here to see?' I said to the Leopard.
'The world isn't always night and day, Tracker. Still haven't learned' [*Black Leopard,
Red Wolf*, 125]

As they come closer to the object of their search they discover another boy in a torture
room: he has been tied up and serially abused, 'every limb – legs, feet, toes, arms, hands,
neck and fingers – was tied to and pulled a rope', unable to scream 'because of something
like the innards of an animal pushed through his mouth and down his throat'.

He looked blind but he could see us, so terrified at us moving closer that he pulled
and yelped and grabbed and tried to shield his face from a blow. It made the room
go mad, with the table pushing out and in, the door swinging open and shut, the
shit bucket emptying. [434–5]

Is this a correlative of the ways colonial violence the central and west African countries
and cultures from which James has reworked his magical, monster-haunted fantastical
realms? We might say: yes, although if we do, we could also note that the specific story of
James's African-esque 'North Kingdom' and 'South Kingdom' does not entail, as it might
be, pale-skinned invaders encroaching from over the seas. The rape and violence in which
the novels trade are entirely a function of the aboriginal societies and masculinities they
portray.

American author N. K. Jemisin achieved something unprecedented with her
'Broken Earth' trilogy [*The Fifth Season* (2015) *The Obelisk Gate* (2016), *The Stone
Sky* (2017)]: becoming the first person to win three consecutive Hugo awards – the
Hugo being the blue-riband prize for SF/Fantasy – for three consecutive books. The
Fantasyland of this trilogy is 'the Stillness', a continent of exceptional geological activity:
constant volcanic activity, earthquakes and tremors, scalding geysers and acid rain. The
world includes a despised caste, the orogenes, who have the magic ability to affect the
energy in the ground and to syphon off heat: they can lessen or control earthquakes,
or cause them, and the other populations in the Stillness fear and hate them. When
orogenes manifest their powers, growing up, they are often killed, or shunned. Some
are recruited by an organization called 'the Fulcrum', trained, with much punishment
and brutality, to devote their powers in the service of the Empire. The story follows
three main characters, all orogenes: Damaya, an ambitious young girl newly recruited
to the Fulcrum; Syenite, an angry woman who is forced to bear a child to her mentor,
and a middle-aged woman named Essun, whose son is murdered by her husband, for
being an orgone. These are eventually revealed to be the same woman at different stages
of her life, their narratives posed simultaneously through the book: a powerful work of
Deleuzian narrative folding.

The empire is collapsing, and a huge rift has opened in the land, pouring quantities of ash to darken the sky for many years. Essun travels through the environmental collapse attendant on this event: sunless, dirty water, failing crops and war coming. The suffering is powerfully rendered, as the churn of the land breaks settlements and societies. New settlements are sometimes built on the ruins of the old, and sometimes the past is forgotten. These are novels that use fantasy to engage with racism, and the legacy of slavery. Kim Wickham reads the trilogy as 'a contemporary novel of slavery' one 'concerned with the legacy of slavery and marginalization … resonating with the project of Black identity formation'. The use of a second-person narrative means that the novels address Essun directly, a strategy that Wickham argues 'highlights the fracturing and tenuous construction of Essun's identity while involving the reader in the reconstruction that takes place as her disparate selves are united – Essun, as the internal audience of the "you" address, learns the story of her own life at the same time that the reader does'.[3] The splintering of Essun's identity actualizes the traumatic wrenching of the slave experience. The larger environmental catastrophes that dominate the Stillness externalize the pressures of racism. Accepting her third Hugo, Jemisin said:

> This has been a hard year, hasn't it? A hard few years. A hard century. For some of us, things have always been hard. I wrote the *Broken Earth* trilogy to speak to that struggle, and what it takes just to live, let alone thrive, in a world that seems determined to break you.[4]

The orogenes, oppressed, enslaved, murdered, yet with the power to reshape or even destroy the world, are the apprehension via magic of the dilemma of racist oppression. 'I'm trying to depict a story', Jemisin has said, 'about people who have reasons to destroy the world, people who view the state of existence they've been forced to live in as literally worse than death. And a lot of what I was feeling about being an African American living in this country – that has over the centuries done so wrong by us, and continues to do so – came through'.[5]

Matthew Oliver notes how rarely epic fantasy is written in the first-person, and how striking is Jemisin's deployment of that form, 'used to disrupt epic "objectivity"' which most fantasy novels assume. He goes on: 'but where a first-person narration might usually revert the novel back upon the unified individual subjectivity of the narrator, the particular first-person identity *The Broken Earth* books entail not just a "disruption of subjectivity" but a disruption of the temporal dimension: not just "who is the self?" but "when is the self?" How is the self related to history?'[6] Traditional fantasy concerns

---

[3] Kim Wickham, 'Identity, Memory, Slavery: Second-Person Narration in N. K. Jemisin's *The Broken Earth* Trilogy', 392–3.

[4] Joel Cunningham, 'Read N.K. Jemisin's Historic Hugo Speech' [20 August 2018] https://www.barnesandnoble.com/blog/read-n-k-jemisins-historic-hugo-speech/

[5] 'WIRED Book Club: Fantasy Writer N.K. Jemisin' [June 2016] https://www.wired.com/2016/06/wired-book-club-nk-jemisin/

[6] Matthew Oliver, *Magic Words, Magic Worlds: Form and Style in Epic Fantasy*, 140.

history, revisits and reenchants history, with a pretence to neutrality of perspective. Jemisin articulates how history striates the individual consciousness, how personal and intimate it is, how disruptive.

Nobel Laureate Kazuo Ishiguro is also interested in the way history intersects individuality, the workings and opacities of memory. *The Buried Giant* (2015) is an Arthurian story, although one written at an oblique angle to traditional Arthuriana. Two very elderly Britons, Axl and Beatrice, leave their village in search of their son, with whom they hope to live. The landscape they move through is often literally foggy, and the storytelling is fogged by amnesia, the blurred half-memories of things done and forgotten. Slowly the book reveals itself to be, in Robert Eaglestone's words, both 'the personal story of an elderly couple of, and a national and genocidal story: the mass-murder of Saxons, and their subsequent subdual by Britons led by Arthur'.[7] The two main characters suffer personal memory impairment, as elderly people often do, and much of the novel is concerned with their quest to recover their son, though they can remember little about him. But the various people they meet have, as it were, cataracts in their memory-vision. It transpires that the mists that drape the landscape are enchanted, and issue from a great dragon called Querig, overseen by the aging Sir Gawain, who hopes that this magical fog will 'allow old wounds to heal for ever and an eternal peace to hold among us' [*The Buried Giant*, 311]. Yet the general forgetfulness has manifold malign and insidious effects. On their quest, Axl and Beatrice fall in with a Saxon orphan, Edwin and a Saxon warrior called Winstan, who hopes to find and kill the dragon and restore memory, even the memory of hatred and revenge, to the land. Ishiguro's telling is slow, oblique, nebulous – fittingly, we might say – but also pointed: fantasy, as history, is a mode of forgetting as much as it is one of remembering. More, the novel often appears to be half-remembering, or attempting to forget, fantasy as a mode. Axl and Beatrice's home village is a congeries of underground spaces, like hobbit holes, and from it the two set off eastward, a diminished fellowship, past ogres and goblin-like pixies, through ruins and danger, all misted by the breath of the gigantic dragon Querig that obscures, as if seen via genre-eyes afflicted by cataracts, the template to which the story relates. It is one kind of dialogue with the history of fantasy. Another type of dialogue, more common in twenty-first-century writing, is instaurational, but Ishiguro, by defocusing and slowing the material with which he works, achieves something unique and important.

---

[7]Robert Eaglestone, 'The Past', *The Routledge Companion to Twenty-First Literary Fiction*, 312.

# CHAPTER 22
## INSTAURATION FANTASY

Dhonielle Clayton's *The Marvellers* (2022), first in a projected 'Conjureverse' sequence, concerns a diverse cast of characters who attend a global school of magic, located in the clouds. Clayton has said that 'publishing *The Marvellers* could be seen as an act of aggression and critical commentary on the Harry Potter universe, because it includes all the children J.K. Rowling marginalized, stereotyped, and frankly, forgot'. She insists she is 'not writing to be in conversation with her or her world, though it may seem like it and I can't seem to escape the comparisons. I'm writing for the children that are not seen by her, and that are not seen in general'.[1] The fantasy conceit, the school for magic, is valuable; but Rowling, by centring her story on white, straight characters and including only a few, marginalized characters of colour, has told this story badly. *The Marvellers* addresses and corrects the anomaly.

Samantha Shannon's recent bestseller *The Priory of the Orange Tree* (2019) gives us both a quasi-European 'Queendom of Inys' and a far-eastern, quasi-Japanese 'Empire of the Twelve Lakes'. Chapters alternate 'West' or 'East', to enable us to locate ourselves on the novel's axis. In the West the House of Berethnet has ruled Inys for a thousand years, but the present Queen Sabran IX is under pressure to marry and provide an heir. There is political turmoil, there are threats of war, assassins are lurking to terminate Sabran's rein. The queen's low-born lady-in-waiting Ead Duryan is, secretly, an adept in an occult organization and is protecting Sabran with forbidden magic. In the novel's east ('across the dark sea') Tané is training to be a dragonrider, but an encounter with a shipwrecked westerner alters her destiny. The west have 'western' style dragons, and the east have 'eastern' style ones. There are plots and machinations, battles, voyages, pirates, quests, dragon attacks:

> Tané stumbled after them. Beneath the bridge was a fatal drop to the Path of the Elder. Treetops rose from a bowl of fog. Another shadow fell from above … a fireball slammed into the roof of bridge. Seconds later a spiked tail turned it to an explosion of splinters. A third fire-breather smashed one of the pillars that had anchored it. Faceless silhouettes cried out as they slid off the edge and plummeted. [*Priory of the Orange Tree*, 484]

The novel is also Romantasy, the events and conspiracy backdrops to a story of forbidden love between queen and servant girl: 'Ead leaned in to kiss her brow, but before she

[1]Darren Chetty, 'An interview with Dhonielle Clayton', *Books for Keeps* [January 2023]: https://booksforkeeps.co.uk/article/an-interview-with-dhonielle-clayton/

could Sabran caught her face between her hands and pressed her parted lips to hers. Ead returned to her duties. But the nights were for Sabran. Their secret was like wine in her. When they were behind the drapes of the bed all else was forgotten' [387]. It is a remedial engagement with Tolkienian fantasy, amending the sexism of the traditional model. In Shannon's fantasy world women are not marginalized or oppressed; 'queendom' is as regular a term as 'kingdom'; there are no gendered property laws, and we are as likely to encounter a female as a male knight. Same-sex marriage is widespread and accepted. The ahistoricality of this – in the sense that it mismatches the 'actual' medieval status of women and gay people – is in a sense the point: the novel is an instauration of the prototype.

In the *Game of Thrones* TV show (2011–19), as in the books upon which it is based, Westerosian characters are all white, played by white actors. Characters of colour, as played by actors of colour, are limited to those scenes set in the eastern and southern continents of Essos and Sothoryos. This reflects the sense, implicit in the original works, that the Europe of the Middle Ages, the prototype of Westeros, was racially monotypical. In fact it was not – indeed, it was medieval Europe that generated, through religious as well as ethnic discrimination, the concept of 'race' as such.[2] But it is the myth, rather than the reality, that obtains in classic fantasy.

The myth has, latterly, changed emphasis. The success of the show led to a new show: *House of the Dragon*, based on George R R Martin's *Fire & Blood* (2018), which has so far entailed two series (2022, 2024). Though set a hundred years *before* the all-white Westeros of *Game of Thrones*, the world of *House of the Dragon* is considerably more racially diverse. For instance, the powerful House Velaryon is Black – its patriarch, Lord Corlys Velaryon, is played by British-Barbadian actor Steve Toussaint. Other Westeros individuals are from non-white demographics: for instance, Mysaria, the paramour of the series antagonist, Prince Daemon Targaryen, played by British-Japanese actor Sonoya Mizuno. This speaks to the shift in the cultural norms regarding diversity of representation even across the less than a decade from one show to the others: in the 2020s a TV programme in which all the characters are white would look odd, anomalous, unreflective of the reality of the demographic variety of life in the UK upon which, howsoever abstractedly, the worldbuilding of Westeros is based. Accordingly the representational logic of the franchise has been amended to include characters from a range of ethnic backgrounds. How this is rationalized in terms of the in-world worldbuilding logic of Westeros is unclear: for surely if Westeros *used to be* a place of racial diversity and *later became* a place of singular whiteness, some alarming interlude of genocidal ethnic cleansing must have intervened. Nothing so dreadful is in the minds of the show-runners, though. They are, rather, producing *instauration fantasy*, remedying what now looks like deplorable limitations in racial representation in the earlier work.

A parallel case: the elves, dwarfs and hobbits in Peter Jackson's *Lord of the Rings* and *Hobbit* movie-trilogies (2001–3, 2012–14) are all played by white actors, but the

---

[2]See Geraldine Heng, *The Invention of Race in the European Middle Ages*.

later-made if earlier-set *Rings of Power* TV series (Amazon Prime Video 2022–ongoing) includes ethnically diverse elves, dwarfs and hobbits (or proto-hobbits). Since this later-made series happens earlier in the imaginary chronology of Middle Earth, we may again find ourselves wondering how these rainbow nations, in which no racial tension is manifest, became the world of the later-set movies, in which people of colour had been purged, and expunged into the social abjection of evil orcs, as in Tolkien's original. But to say so is, in one sense, to miss the point: this revisionary approach to casting reflects a commendable embrace of the fact that society today is a matter of racial diversity, and that reflecting that fact is not only a matter of accuracy but of health, fairness and equality.

Critic John Clute talks of 'instauration fantasy' in a review of Robert Holdstock's third *Mythago Wood* novel, *The Hollowing*, in 1993:

> *The Hollowing* makes up part of a new *instauration* of fantasy … Instauration fantasy: a term we might use to describe a late twentieth century tale in which the contemporary world is transfigured and/or restored through the metamorphic intersection of normal reality and some reality or conjoined realities out of deep fantasy; characterized by an acute attention to the invasive and sometimes death-involving potency of the metamorphosis-bearing fantasy world by genre-crossing plots which tend to evoke a plethora of themes and icons, by a powerful tendency to mix time future, time present and time past, by plot structures which serve as conscious enactments of a deep Story which absolutely must be told, by an obsession with Portals, and by the almost constant presence of Visitors from Other Tales.[3]

In fact this mode goes back much earlier than Holdstock. Lewis's *The Magician's Nephew* (1955) is an instauration fantasy in Clute's sense; Kingsley's *Water-Babies* (1863) is another – a story that starts in our world, loops into its fairyland of riverine and marine metamorphosis only in order to return to a version of our world recuperated by Tom's redemption in that place. Indeed, and to return to the discussion in the first portion of this work, Spenser's *Faerie Queene* is about the 'instauration' of the virtues and tenor of the 'faerie-land' splendours of its narrative into the actual functioning of Queen Elizabeth's England. The term itself comes from Francis Bacon:

> From about 1603 until his death in 1626 Francis Bacon referred to his plan for the reform of learning as the *Great Instauration* or, since he usually wrote about it in Latin, the *Instauratio Magna*. The phrase became his trademark. He apparently first used it in a work he never completed or published called *Temporis Partus Masculus, sive Instaur Magna Imperil Humani in Universum*, 'Time's Masculine Birth, or the Great Instauration of Human Dominion over the Universe' (1603).

---

[3]Clute, *Scores: Reviews 1993–2003*, 62y.

Bacon never explained or discussed the notion of instauration even in his most important work on the new science, the *Instauratio Magna* of 1620, which includes the *Novum Organum*. Since the English cognate, coined in the late 1500s, never caught on and has remained inkhorn, Bacon's illuminating uses of the word *instauratio* in a variety of contexts as part of his working Latin vocabulary are themselves obscured in translation.[4]

Whitney, here, notates 'restore', 'reconstruct' and 'establish' as common English versions of Bacon's 'hard term'. The Latin *instauratio* meant 'the act of renewing, renewal, repetition' and more specifically referred to an Ancient Roman practice of redoing of a ceremony or ritual that has gone awry in some fashion, no matter how minor. The word derives from the first conjugation verb *instauro*: 'I repeat, start, or perform anew or afresh; renew (after a period of disuse); I repair, restore, renew (from wear, age, or damage)', itself deriving from *in* + *sto*, 'I stand'. This is at root what an instauration is: a standing, or re-standing of something; a recuperative setting-up of something in good standing. It seems likely that Bacon himself took the term out of the Vulgate, where *instauratio* is the term used for the proposed restoration of Solomon's Temple, and thereby more broadly to spiritual edification and repurification. The temple stood; then it was demolished; it will stand up again, brick built on brick. The word is also used in non-biblical literature: Livy describes an 'instauratio templorum' at the Great Games in Rome, following what might look to us like a fairly trivial infraction of the religious protocol:

> It so happened that at Rome preparations were making for the repeat [*instauratio*] of the Great Games. The reason of the *instauratio* was as follows: at an early hour of the day appointed for the games, before the show had begun, a certain householder had driven his slave, bearing a yoke, through the midst of the circus, scourging the culprit as he went. The games had then been begun, as though this circumstance had in no way affected their sanctity. Not long after, Titus Latinius, a plebeian, had a dream. He dreamt that Jupiter said that the leading dancer at the games had not been to his liking; that unless there were a sumptuous repetition of the festival the City would be in danger.[5]

A properly 'instauration fantasy' would do one of two things: it would rerun the ritual properly, correcting some prior ritualistic delinquency; or, more ambitiously, it would rebuild the temple. The 'rerun' angle is particularly interesting, since fantasy is, or has become, such a repetitive, reiterative mode – there are so many, so very many new fantasy novels that in essence retread the same Tolkienian, Lewisian, Robert Howardian, Peakeian or Grimdark formats, adjusting one or other small element (say: a slightly different magical system, or a more ethnically diverse cast of characters) in an attempt

---

[4]Charles Whitney, 'Francis Bacon's Instauratio: Dominion of and over Humanity', 371.
[5]Livy, *History of Rome*, 2:36; transl. Benjamin Oliver Foster.

to, this time, get the ritual right. Tolkien (let's say) is taken as the Ludi Magni, and seen as still worth performing: it's just that he doesn't quite exercise the ritual correctly, doesn't attend to the needful hieratic exigences: – he doesn't have enough female characters, his racial politics is offensive, his morality is too black-and-white, he doesn't include the realpolitik or the supply-side practicalities of military campaigns. And so in ten thousand new fantasy novels Tolkien is rewritten with these elements tweaked, instaurated.

These 'instaurations', in their myriads, don't actually improve or correct or resacralize Tolkien. But, by speaking to a belief that there is an as-it-were Platonic form of the ritual that is fantasy literature that has fallen into desuetude but which can be restored, these reworkings and reimaginings say something very interesting about the mode itself. This original Solominic fantasy novel, this temple which has been knocked down but which Brandon Sanderson or Marlon James or N K Jemisin can stand back up, is not a prior historical construction. William Morris's fantasy novels, or Tolkien's, or Lord Dunsany's, reflect commonplace attitudes of their time with respect to gender and race and so on; and these things can now be amended in the fantasy literature being published in the 2020s. But such amendment does not construe an actually historicized narrative: as it might be 'Tolkien didn't know any better back then, but we have evolved into a more virtuous and better-behaved society now'. Rather it says 'this is how Fantasy ought to be' and, in a sense, how it always was before sexism, racism, neoliberalism, etc. poisoned it. Something that 'fell into' time and which needs to be rescued from it – as with the tidal overcoming of time-bound Erl by timeless, glamorous, beautiful Elfland. This is, in other words, to speak to the fundamental appeal of fantasy as such – its backward-looking nostalgic logic, so different to the fundamentally forward-looking, futurist, restless logic change and extrapolation and strange new worlds that informs SF. There was a temple: a old world of magic and wonder, a transcendent place. But it was demolished. The world fell into Modernity: life grew disenchanted (as per Weber), secularized and 'buffered' (as per Charles Taylor). This change happened because of capitalism and industrialization – Tolkien's bugbear – or because of the 'Orbis Spike', the coming of colonization, slavery and genocide, neoliberalism. Fantasy is that mode that seeks to instaurate the old ritual, rebuild the temple, to reactivate the wonder and glamour, as also the terror. It's a myth, but that's fitting for a mythographic mode like fantasy. It urgently and continually renews itself, and urgently and continually strives to be the same, to repeat the ritual precisely and accurately. It restores, renews, reenchants and makes fresh again.

# BIBLIOGRAPHY OF SECONDARY SOURCES

Ackroyd, Peter, *English Music* (London: Hamish Hamilton 1993).

Adorno, Theodor, *In Search of Wagner* (trans. Rodney Livingstone, London: NLB 1981).

Alegre, Sara Martín, 'Martian Politics and the Hard-Boiled Anti-Hero: Richard Morgan's *Thin Air*', *Revista Hélice*, 4:11 (2018), 84–7.

Armitt, Lucie, *Fantasy Fiction: An Introduction* (London: Routledge 2005).

Ashley, Mike, *Transformations: The History of Science Fiction Magazine, 1950–1970* (Liverpool: Liverpool University Press 2005).

Attebery, Brian, *Strategies of Fantasy* (Bloomington Indiana: Indiana University Press 1992).

Bachelder, Linda, 'Young Adult Literature: Looking Backward', *The English Journal*, 69:6 (1980), 87–8.

Batchelor, David, *The Luminous and the Grey* (London: Reaktion 2014).

Beer, Gillian, *The Romance* (London: Routledge 1970).

Benjamin, Walter, *The Origin of German Tragic Drama* [1928] (trans. John Osborne, London: Verso 2003).

Benjamin, Walter, *One Way Street and Other Writings* (trans. James Alan Underwood, Harmondsworth: Penguin 2008).

Boletsi, Maria, *Barbarism and Its Discontents* (Redwood City California: Stanford University Press 2013).

Bono, Barbara J., 'The Prose Fictions of William Morris: A Study in the Literary Aesthetic of a Victorian Social Reformer', *Victorian Poetry*, 13:3/4 (1975), 52.

Bould, Mark, and Michelle Reid (eds), *Parietal Games: Critical Writings by and on M. John Harrison* (London: SF Foundation 2005).

Boyce, Frank Cottrell, 'Five Things to Learn from the Moomins', *The Guardian* (25 December 2015).

Bryan, Jennifer, 'Memories, Dreams, Shadows: Fantasy and the Reader in Susan Cooper's *The Grey King*', *Arthuriana*, 27:2 (2017), 29–54.

Bryson, James, '"It's All in Plato": Platonism, Cambridge Platonism, and C.S. Lewis', *Journal of Inklings Studies*, 11:1 (2021), 1–34.

Butler, Marilyn, *Romantics, Rebels and Reactionaries: English Literature and Its Background 1760–1830* (Oxford: Oxford University Press 1981).

Byatt, Antonia, 'Harry Potter and the Childish Adult', *The New York Times* (7 July 2003).

Carlyle, Thomas, *Past and Present* (London: Chapman and Hall 1843).

Chandler, Alice, *A Dream of Order: The Medieval Ideal in Nineteen Century English Literature* (Lincoln: University of Nebraska Press 1970).

Cheyne, Ria, *Disability, Literature, Genre: Representation and Affect in Contemporary Fiction* (Liverpool: Liverpool University Press 2019).

Claessens, Mieke, 'The Presence and Role of Female Characters in Raymond E. Feist's *The Riftwar Cycle*' (BA thesis, University of Utrecht, Netherlands, July 2018).

Clute, John and John Grant (eds), *The Encyclopedia of Fantasy* (London: Palgrave 1997).

Coates, Donna, 'Bear (Novel)', *Canadian Encyclopedia. Historica Canada* (2 June 2006).

Cobb, Richard, *Something to Hold onto: Autobiographical Sketches* (London: J. Murray 1988).

Cohn, Norman, *The Pursuit of the Millennium: Revolutionary Millenarians and Mystical Anarchists of the Middle Ages* (2nd ed., London: Pimlico 1993).

Commire, Anne, *Something about the Author: volume 2* (Detroit, MI: Gale Research 1971).

Como, James, *C. S. Lewis at the Breakfast Table, and Other Reminiscences* (New York: Macmillan 1972).

Coveney, Peter, *The Image of Childhood: the Individual and Society: A Study of the Theme in English Literature* (1957, 2nd ed., Harmondsworth: 1967).

Cowan, Bainard, 'Walter Benjamin's Theory of Allegory', *New German Critique*, 22 (1981), 109–22.

Craig, Patricia, 'Narnia Revisited', *Irish Pages*, 3:2 (2006), 161–2.

Crane, Mary Thomas, *Losing Touch with Nature: Literature and the New Science in 16th-Century England* (Baltimore, Maryland: Johns Hopkins University Press 2015).

Cummins, Chris, 'Is The Fellowship of the Ring the Last Great Film Score?' *Den of Geek* (6 Aug 2018) https://www.denofgeek.com/culture/is-the-fellowship-of-the-ring-the-last-great-film-score/

Dagbovie, Sika Alaine, 'Long Live King Babar! Long Live Bourgeois Imperialism! Racist Elitism in *The Travels of Babar*', *CLA Journal*, 49:4 (2006), 446–61.

Davidson, Jenny, *Reading Jane Austen* (Cambridge: Cambridge University Press 2017).

Davies, Michael and William Robert Owens, *Oxford Handbook of John Bunyan* (Oxford: Oxford University Press 2018).

DeLaura, David, *Hebrew and Hellene in Victorian England: Newman, Arnold, and Pater* (Austin, Texas: University of Texas Press 1969).

Deleuze, Gilles, *The Fold* [1988] (trans. Tom Conley, Minneapolis, Minnesota: University of Minnesota Press 1993).

Dunan-Page, Anne (ed), *The Cambridge Companion to Bunyan* (Cambridge: Cambridge University Press 2010).

Duriez, Colin, *C.S. Lewis: A Biography of Friendship* (Oxford: Lion 2013).

Dusinberre, Juliet, *Alice to the Lighthouse: Children's Books and Radical Experiments in Art* (New York: St. Martin's Press 1987).

Eaglestone, Robert (ed), *Reading The Lord of the Rings: New Writings on Tolkien's Classic* (London: Bloomsbury 2005).

Eaglestone, Robert, 'The Past', in Daniel O'Gorman and Robert Eaglestone (eds) *The Routledge Companion to Twenty-First Literary Fiction* (London: Routledge 2019), 311–20.

Empson, William, *Some Types of Pastoral* (London: Chatto & Windus 1935).

Erizi, Andrea, 'Different Origin, (Almost the) Same Function: The Concept of Subrogation in Max Weber's Work', *Max Weber Studies*, 11:2 (2011), 231–48.

Evans, Timothy H., 'A Last Defense against the Dark: Folklore, Horror, and the Uses of Tradition in the Works of H. P. Lovecraft', *Journal of Folklore Research*, 42:1 (2005), 99–135.

Filmer, Kath, 'Religion and Romanticism in Michael Ende's The Neverending Story', *Mythlore*, 18:1 (1991), 59–64.

Fimi, Dimitra, *Tolkien, Race and Cultural History: From Fairies to Hobbits* (Palgrave Macmillan 2008).

Finley, C. Stephen, 'Bunyan among the Victorians: Macaulay, Froude, Ruskin', *Literature and Theology*, 3:1 (March 1989), 77–94.

Forrest, James and Richard Greaves, *John Bunyan: A Reference Guide* (Boston: GK Hall & Co 1982).

Gallagher, Joel, 'Nothing according to Anselm and Michael Ende's The Neverending Story', *Literature and Theology*, 34:2 (2020), 131–49.

Gifford, James, *A Modernist Fantasy: Modernism, Anarchism and the Radical Fantastic* (Victoria BC: ELS Editions 2018).

Gifford, James, 'On Reading Monsters' (3 February 2020) https://gifford.mla.hcommons.org/2020/02/03/on-reading-monsters/

Graves, Robert, *The White Goddess: A Historical Grammar of Poetic Myth* (London: Faber 1949).

Gray, William, *Fantasy, Myth and the Measure of Truth: Tales of Pullman, Lewis, Tolkien, MacDonald and Hoffman* (London: Palgrave 2009).

Grossman, Lev, 'The American Tolkien', *Time*, 166:21 (2005), 13–15.

Habermas, Jürgen, *The New Conservatism: Cultural Criticism and the Historian's Debate* (trans. Shierry Weber Nicholsen, Cambridge: Polity 1990).

Harbison, Robert, *Deliberate Regression* (New York: Knopf 1980).

Heinecken, Dawn, 'Haunting Masculinity and Frightening Femininity: The Novels of John Bellairs', *Children's Literature in Education*, 42 (2011), 118–31.

Heng, Geraldine, *The Invention of Race in the European Middle Ages* (Cambridge: Cambridge University Press 2018).

Herron, Don, 'Three Sought Adventure', *The Pulp Net* (Accessed March 2023) https://thepulp.net/pulp-articles/three-sought-adventure/

Hirtle, Kala B., 'Rhetorically (De)constructing AIDS', *African American Review*, 48:3 (2015), 319–32.

Hodgson, Amanda, *The Romances of William Morris* (Cambridge: Cambridge University Press 2011).

Hofmeyr, Isabel, 'How Bunyan Became English: Missionaries, Translation, and the Discipline of English', *Journal of British Studies*, 41:1 (2002), 84–119.

Hofmeyr, Isabel, *The Portable Bunyan: A Transnational History of the Pilgrim's Progress* (Princeton, New Jersey: Princeton University Press 2004).

Hogan, Emma, 'I Dream of Islands Every Night', *London Review of Books*, 42:18 (24 September 2020), 8–10.

Holbo, John, 'Titus Awakes', *Crooked Timber* (18 June 2011) https://crookedtimber.org/2011/06/18/titus-awakes/

Holbo, John, 'Conan', *Crooked Timber* (31 August 2015) https://crookedtimber.org/2015/08/31/conan/

Honig, Edwin, *Dark Conceit: The Making of Allegory* (London: Faber 1959).

Hurwitz, David, 'Shore: Lord of the Rings Symphony', *Classics Today* (August 2013) https://www.classicstoday.com/review/review-16281/

Jacobs, Alan, 'The Devil's Party', *First Things* (12 December 2007) https://www.firstthings.com/web-exclusives/2007/12/the-devils-party

Jacobs, Alan, 'Fantasy and the Buffered Self', *The New Atlantis*, 41 (2014), 3–18.

James, Edward and Farah Mendlesohn (eds), *The Cambridge Companion to Fantasy Literature* (Cambridge: Cambridge University Press 2012).

Jenkins, Richard, 'Disenchantment, Enchantment and Re-Enchantment: Max Weber at the Millennium', *Max Weber Studies*, 1:1 (2000), 11–32.

John, Juliet, *Dickens and Mass Culture* (Oxford: Oxford University Press 2013).

Joshi, Sunand Tryambak, *A Subtler Magick: The Writings and Philosophy of H. P. Lovecraft* (Cabin John, Maryland: Wildside Press 1999).

Josipovici, Gabriel, 'A Human Kafka', *London Review of Books*, 3:4 (5 March 1981), 9–11.

Kelso, Sylvia, '"Across Never": Postmodern Theory and Narrative Praxis in Samuel R. Delany's *Nevèrÿon* Cycle', *Science Fiction Studies*, 72:24 (1997), 289–301.

Kermode, Frank, *Shakespeare, Spenser, Donne: Renaissance Essays* (London: Routledge 1971).

Kern, Stephen, *The Culture of Time and Space 1880–1918* (London: Weidenfeld 1983).

Kincaid, Paul, *Robert Holdstock's Mythago Wood: A Critical Companion* (London: Palgrave 2022).

Kohl, Herbert R., *Should We Burn Babar?: Essays on Children's Literature and the Power of Stories* (New York, New York: The New Press 1995).

Kotsko, Adam, *Why We Love Sociopaths; A Guide to Late Capitalist Television* (London: Zer0 Books 2012).

Lancelyn Green, Roger, *C. S. Lewis* (San Diego, California: Harcourt Brace 1974).

Landes, David, *Revolution in Time: Clocks and the Making of the Modern World* (Cambridge, Massachusetts: Harvard University Press 1984).

Le Guin, Ursula, *The Language of the Night: Essays on Fantasy and Science Fiction* (London: Women's Press 1989).

Lévi-Strauss, Claude, *The Raw and the Cooked* [1964] (trans. John and Doreen Weightman, New York, New York: Harper & Row 1969).

Lewis, Clive Staples, *Rehabilitations and Other Essays* (Oxford: Oxford University Press 1939).

Lewis, Clive Staples (ed), *George Macdonald: An Anthology* (London: Centenary Press 1946).

Lewis, Clive Staples, *Surprised by Joy* (San Diego, California: Harcourt Brace 1955).

Lewis, Clive Staples, *The Discarded Image: An Introduction to Medieval and Renaissance Literature* (Cambridge: Cambridge University Press 1964).

Lewis, Clive Staples, *On Stories: And Other Essays on Literature* (London: Gregory Bles 1966).

Lewis, Clive Staples, *Of Other Worlds: Essays and Stories* (San Diego, California: Harcourt, Brace & World 1967).

Lowe, Nick, 'The Well-Tempered Plot Device', *Ansible*, 46 (July 1986), n.p.

Lukács, György, *The Historical Novel* [1937] (trans. Hannah and Stanley Mitchell, London: Merlin Press 1965).

Maas, Jeremy, *Victorian Fairy Painting* (London: Merrell Holberton/Royal Academy 1997).

Magyarody, Katherine, 'Translating Russian Folklore into Soviet Fantasy in Arkadi and Boris Strugatski's *Monday Begins on Saturday* and Catherynne M. Valente's *Deathless*', *Marvels & Tales*, 31:2 (2017), 338–60.

Malcolm, Noel, *The Origins of English Nonsense* (London: HarperCollins 1997).

Manlove, Colin N., *Modern Fantasy: Five Studies* (Cambridge: Cambridge University Press 1975).

Martin, George, 'The Rolling Stone Interview', *Rolling Stone* (23 April 2014) https://www.rollingstone.com/movies/news/george-r-r-martin-the-rolling-stone-interview-20140423

Matthews, Richard, *Fantasy: The Liberation of Imagination* (London: Routledge 2001).

McCaffery, Larry, 'On Encompassing the Entire Universe', *Science Fiction Studies*, 15:3 (1988), 334–55.

McGregor, Jamie, 'Two Rings to Rule Them All: A Comparative study of Tolkien and Wagner', *Mythlore*, 29 (2011), 133–53.

Mendlesohn, Farah, *Rhetorics of Fantasy* (Middletown, Connecticut: Wesleyan University Press 2008).

Mendlesohn, Farah, *A Short History of Fantasy* (London: Middlesex University Press 2009).

Miesel, Sandra, *Against Time's Arrow: The High Crusade of Poul Anderson* (San Bernardino, CA: Borgo Press 1978).

Milbank, John, *Beyond Secular Order* (Oxford: Wiley Blackwell 2014).

Miller, Laura, *The Magician's Book: A Skeptic's Adventure in Narnia* (New York: Back Bay Books 2008).

Miltner, Robert, '*Watership Down*: A Genre Study', *Journal of the Fantastic in the Arts*, 6:1 (1993), 63–70.

Moorcock, Michael, *Wizardry and Wild Romance* (London: Victor Gollancz 1988).

Moretti, Franco, *The Modern Epic: The World-system from Goethe to García Márquez* (London: Verso 1996).

Morris, May (ed), *William Morris: Artist, Writer, Socialist* (Oxford: Blackwell 1936).

Morris, William, *Collected Letters* (ed. Norman Kelvin, Princeton, New Jersey: Princeton University Press 1984).

Morton, Timothy, *Ecology without Nature: Rethinking Environmental Aesthetics* (Cambridge, Massachusetts: Harvard University Press 2007).

Norberg, Jakob, *The Brothers Grimm and the Making of German Nationalism* (Cambridge: Cambridge University Press 2022).

Oliver, Matthew, *Magic Words, Magic Worlds: Form and Style in Epic Fantasy* (Jefferson, North Carolina: McFarland 2022).

Parker, Joanne and Corinna Wagner (eds), *The Oxford Handbook of Victorian Medievalism* (Oxford: Oxford University Press 2020).

Philip, Neil, *A Fine Anger: A Critical Introduction to the Work of Alan Garner* (London: Collins 1981).

Phillips, Adam, *Houdini's Box* (London: Faber and Faber 2001).

Phillips, Leah, *Female Heroes in Young Adult Fantasy Fiction: Reframing Myths of Adolescent Girlhood* (London: Bloomsbury 2023).

Prickett, Stephen, *Victorian Fantasy: Imagination and Belief in Nineteenth-Century England* (2nd revised ed., Waco, TX: Baylor University Press 2005).

Pringle, David, *Modern Fantasy: The Hundred Best Novels* (London: Grafton 1988).

Pullman, Philip, *Dæmon Voices: Essays on Storytelling* (Oxford: David Fickling Books 2017).

Reeves, Marjorie and Warwick Gould, *Joachim of Fiore and the Myth of the Eternal Evangel in the Nineteenth Century* (Oxford: Oxford University Press 1987).

Reynolds, Kimberley, *Children's Literature: A Very Short Introduction* (Oxford: Oxford University Press 2011).

Ripp, Joseph, 'Middle America Meets Middle-Earth: American Discussion and Readership of J. R. R. Tolkien's *The Lord of the Rings*, 1965–1969', *Book History*, 8 (2005), 245–86.

Roberts, Adam, *Silk and Potatoes: Contemporary Arthurian Fantasy* (Leiden, the Netherlands: Rodopi 1994).

Roberts, Adam, *Sibilant Fricative: Essays and Reviews* (London: Steel Quill Books 2014).

Roberts, Adam, *The History of Science Fiction* (2nd ed., London: Palgrave 2016).

Roberts, Adam, 'Crossing Caradhras: A Second Note on Tolkien and Scott', *Adam's Notebook* (1 September 2022) https://medium.com/adams-notebook/crossing-caradhras-a-second-note-on-tolkien-and-scott-d3238cf65c3a

Rowland, Ann Wierda, *Romanticism and Childhood* (Cambridge: Cambridge University Press 2012).

Rushdie, Salman, *The Wizard of Oz* (London: British Film Institute 1992).

Ryan, Derek, *Bloomsbury, Beasts and British Modernist Literature* (Cambridge: Cambridge University Press 2023).

Sacks, Oliver, *The Man Who Mistook His Wife for a Hat and Other Clinical Cases* (London: Duckworth 1985).

Sangster, Matthew, *An Introduction to Fantasy* (Cambridge: Cambridge University Press 2023).

Sayers, Dorothy, *The Song of Roland* (Harmondsworth: Penguin 1957).

Schmitt, Carl, *Political Theology: Four Chapters on the Concept of Sovereignty* [1922] (trans. George Schwab, Chicago: University of Chicago Press 2006).

Schwartz, Hillel, *The Culture of the Copy: Striking Likenesses, Unreasonable Facsimiles* (2nd ed., Princeton, New Jersey: Princeton University Press/Zone books 2014).

Schweitzer, Darrell, 'The Novels of Lord Dunsany', *Mythlore*, 7:3 (1980), 39–41.

Self, Will, 'Video Games', *London Review of Books*, 34:21 (8 November 2012), 38–9.

Shippey, Tom, *The Road to Middle Earth* (2nd ed., London: HarperCollins 1992).

Shippey, Tom, *J. R. R. Tolkien: Author of the Century* (London: HarperCollins 2001).

Shurin, Jared, 'Underground Reading: *Dragonlance Chronicles*', *Pornokitsch* (8 April 2013).

Spencer, Kathleen L., 'Deconstructing *Tales of Nevèrÿon*: Delany, Derrida, and the "Modular Calculus, Parts I-IV"', *Essays in Arts and Sciences*, 14 (1985), 59–89.

Sperring, Kari, 'Matrilines: The Woman Who Made Fantasy: Katherine Kurtz', *Strange Horizons* (30 March 2015) https://web.archive.org/web/20150405043602/http://www.strangehorizons.com/2015/20150330/sperring-c.shtml

Spotts, Frederic, *Bayreuth: A History of the Wagner Festival* (New Haven, Connecticut, U. S: Yale University Press 1994).

Spufford, Francis, *The Child That Books Built* (London: Faber & Faber 2003).

Strom, Kirsten, *The Animal Surreal: The Role of Darwin, Animals, and Evolution in Surrealism* (London: Routledge 2017).

Taylor, Charles, *A Secular Age* (Cambridge, Massachusetts: Harvard University Press 2009).

Teehan, John, *Complete Guide to Writing Fantasy* (Calgary, Alberta: Dragon Moon 2002).

Thompson, Edward Palmer, *William Morris: Romantic to Revolutionary* (2nd ed., London: Merlin Press 2011).

Thompson, Joseph T., *A Dictionary in Oordoo and English: Compiled from the Best Authorities* (1838), Serampore: India, 199.

Tolkien, John Ronald Reuel, *Tree and Leaf* (London: Allen & Unwin 1964).

Tolkien, John Ronald Reuel, *The Letters of J R R Tolkien* (ed. Humphrey Carpenter, 2nd ed., London: HarperCollins 2023).

Trilling, Lionel, *Sincerity and Authenticity* (Cambridge, Massachusetts: Harvard University Press 1972).

Tucker, Herbert F., *Epic: Britain's Heroic Muse 1790–1910* (Oxford: Oxford University Press 2008).

Tufekci, Zeynup, 'The Real Reason Fans Hate the Last Season of *Game of Thrones*', *Scientific American* (17 May 2019) https://blogs.scientificamerican.com/observations/the-real-reason-fans-hate-the-last-season-of-game-of-thrones

Tunnell, Michael, 'Eilonwy of the Red-gold Hair', *Language Arts*, 66:5 (1989), 558–60.

Turner, Jenny, 'Reasons for Liking Tolkien', *London Review of Books*, 23:22 (15 November 2001).

Unwin, Stanley, *The Truth about a Publisher* (London: George Allen & Unwin 1960).

Veliki, Martina Domines and Cian Duffy (eds), *Romanticism and the Cultures of Infancy* (London: Palgrave 2020).

Vidal, Gore, *Reflections upon a Sinking Ship* (New York: Little Brown 1969).

Vidal, Gore, *Pink Triangle and Yellow Star, and Other Essays* (London: Heinemann 1982).

Vidal, Gore, *Pink Triangle and Yellow Star* (London: Granada 1983).

Vila-Matas, Enrique, *Dublinesque* (trans. Anne McLean and Rosalind Harvey, Harmondsworth: Penguin 2012).

Vögelin, Erich, *The New Science of Politics: An Introduction* [1951] (Chicago, Illinois: University of Chicago Press 1987).

Ward, Michael, *Planet Narnia: The Seven Heavens in the Imagination of C. S. Lewis* (Oxford: Oxford University Press 2010).

Warner, Michael, Jonathan VanAntwerpen and Craig Calhoun (eds), *Varieties of Secularism in a Secular Age* (Cambridge, Massachusetts: Harvard University Press 2010).

Watkins, Tony, *Dark Matter: Shedding Light on Philip Pullman's Trilogy, His Dark Materials* (Lisle, Illinois: Intervarsity Press 2006).

Watson, Peter, *The German Genius: Europe's Third Renaissance, the Second Scientific Revolution and the Twentieth Century* (New York, New York: Simon and Schuster 2011).

Weber, Max, *The Protestant Ethic and the Spirit of Capitalism* [1905] (trans. Talcott Parsons, ed. Richard Swedberg, New York, New York: Norton Critical Editions 2009).

Weingrad, Michael, 'The Best Unicorn', *Jewish Review of Books* (15 April 2019) https://jewishreviewofbooks.com/uncategorized/5276/the-best-unicorn/

Weis, Margaret and Tracy Hickman, *Realm of Dragons: The Worlds of Weis and Hickman* (New York: HarperPrism 1999).

Westfahl, Gary, *The Greenwood Encyclopaedia of Science Fiction and Fantasy Themes* (Westport, Connecticut: Greenwood Press 2005).

Westin, Boel, *Tove Jansson: Life, Art, Work* (London: Profile Books 2014).

Wheeler, Jill, *Lloyd Alexander* (Edina, Minnesota: Abdo & Daughters 1997).

Whitney, Charles, 'Francis Bacon's Instauratio: Dominion of and over Humanity', *Journal of the History of Ideas*, 50:3 (1989), 371–90.

Wickham, Kim, 'Identity, Memory, Slavery: Second-Person Narration in N. K. Jemisin's *The Broken Earth* Trilogy', *Journal of the Fantastic in the Arts*, 30:3 (2019), 392–411.

Williamson, Jamie, *The Evolution of Modern Fantasy: From Antiquarianism to the Ballantine Adult Fantasy Series* (London: Palgrave 2015).

Wolf, Shelby, *Handbook of Research in Children's and Young Adult Literature* (London: Routledge 2010).

Wood, Michael, 'Eaten by Owls', *London Review of Books* (26 January 2012), 11–14.

Young, Joseph, 'The American Pratchett? Muck and Modality in George R. R. Martin's *Song of Ice and Fire*', *Journal of the Fantastic in the Arts*, 27:2 (2016), 290–308.

Zaleski, Philip and Carol Zaleski, *The Fellowship: The Literary Lives of the Inklings* (New York, New York: Farrar, Strauss and Giroux 2016).

Zipes, Jack, *The Oxford Encyclopedia of Children's Literature* (Oxford: Oxford University Press 2006).

# INDEX

# Index